THE CPPER SMITH FARM HOUSE

A Jamison Valley Series Novel

DEVNEY PERRY

THE COPPERSMITH FARMHOUSE

Copyright © 2017 by Devney Perry LLC

All rights reserved.

ISBN: 978-1-950692-38-5

This is a work of fiction. Names, characters, places and incidents are the product of the author's imagination or are used fictitiously. Any resemblance to actual events, locales or persons, living or dead, is coincidental.

Editor: Elizabeth Nover, Razor Sharp Editing

www.razorsharpediting.com

Cover Artwork © Sarah Hansen, Okay Creations

www.okaycreations.com

Proofreader: Julie Deaton

www.facebook.com/jdproofs

OTHER TITLES

Stone Princess

Noble Prince

Fallen Jester

Runaway Series

Runaway Road

Wild Highway

Quarter Miles

Forsaken Trail

Dotted Lines

Calamity Montana Series

Writing as Willa Nash

The Bribe

The Bluff

CONTENTS

To Kaitlyn
For the countless hours you've spent giving me constant support and encouragement, thank you.
This book would not exist without you.

PROLOGUE

Gigi,

The lawyer should have told you by now that you'll be getting my estate. It includes a farmhouse in Prescott, Montana, that I lived in years ago. I loved that house and never could let it go. I was happy there.

I want you to move there. Be happy there too. I know it's a big ask but it's time for you to start a new life. For you and Roe. Spokane has nothing left for you but memories and tombstones.

A man named Brick has been watching over the farmhouse for me since I moved. Nineteen years, he's taken care of it. I'd like you to give him $50,000 from the estate proceeds. He's always taken good care of the place. My guess, it's in better condition today than it was when I left. If it wasn't for him, I would have had to sell that house and then my girls wouldn't have a place to start their new life. So, Georgia, you get him to *take the money. It will give me peace to know I've made it right by him.*

Love you, my Gigi girl. Love my Roe too. With all my heart. Thank God every day you came into my hospital room.

See you on the other side,
Ben

CHAPTER ONE

GIGI

New town. New house. New car. New job. New life.

That's what Ben had asked me to do. To start a new life for my four-year-old daughter, Rowen, and a new life for me.

And as much as I would have liked to explain that a major life change was completely unnecessary, it was tough to argue with a dead man.

So here we were in Prescott, Montana. Starting a new life.

Rowen and I had made the trip from Spokane to Prescott today, pulling into town late in the hot summer evening.

I had no clue what to expect, having just uprooted our life to move to a town where I had never been and knew not one person. As we passed a sign reading, "Welcome to Prescott! Population 823," my anxiety peaked.

Prescott wasn't a town, it was a *small* town.

Correction. It was a *very* small town.

Prescott was close to Yellowstone National Park and located in the southwestern corner of Montana. Bordered by mountain ranges, the town sat at the base of the Jamison River Valley.

Buildings started popping up along the highway as I drove toward Prescott. At the farthest edge was the hospital where I'd be working, followed by an auto parts store, a taxidermist and a police station. I doubted I'd ever set foot in one of the latter buildings. I did make a mental note when I spotted the grocery store though. Past the motel, the road veered to the left and the speed limit dropped.

I crept down Main Street to take in as much as I could. Shops and offices filled the downtown street from one end to the other. Interspersed between them were two bars, a bank, a handful of restaurants and the hardware store. Overflowing flower baskets hung from old-fashioned lampposts. Clean and tidy windows featured Western apparel and paraphernalia.

I was looking forward to spending a day wandering the street and exploring the shops. I dreamed of how it would feel to walk into a store and have the owner greet me by name. I longed to be a part of this small community. To feel like I was a part of something, not just on my own and left behind.

"Mommy, look! Ice cream!" Rowen screeched from the back seat, kicking her legs wildly.

"Uh-huh," I muttered automatically.

After we passed the ice cream store and a community fishing pond, I stopped looking around and focused on the directions in my hand, trying to navigate to our new house that was so country I couldn't use GPS to find it.

"Can we stop? Please?" she begged.

I glanced quickly over my shoulder. "Sorry, Roe. Not today. But we'll stop a different day. Sometime soon, I promise. I really just want to get to Ben's farmhouse and get settled for the night. The moving truck gets here in the morning and we need to be ready."

She let out a frustrated "humph," the first grumble she'd given me all day. She'd been a trooper on the seven-hour trip, keeping me company while I drove and quietly watching a couple of movies. But I knew she was totally over this long drive. Way over it. So was I.

"When we get to the farmhouse, you get to pick out your new room," I said into the rearview mirror. "Won't that be fun? And if you want, we can set the air mattress up in there tonight. Okay?"

"Okay," she muttered. She wasn't overly excited but it was better than another grunt.

I drove my new gray Ford Explorer down two roughly paved county roads before turning onto a long gravel drive. The farmhouse itself was situated in the foothills outside of Prescott. The land to the front of the house, toward town, was covered in golden prairie grasses. Behind the farmhouse was an evergreen forest.

I double-checked the address with the number by the front door. Wow, this was really it. My heart fluttered.

Paradise. My new house was in the middle of a mountain paradise.

After parking in the circular gravel driveway, I hopped out of the car and jogged around to unbuckle Rowen from her booster seat.

"Well, what do you think?" I asked.

"It looks cool!" Her big smile beamed brightly.

"It sure does," I agreed, touching her freckled-covered nose with mine.

The farmhouse had a simple square footprint. Windows on both levels were framed with black shutters and faced the open land across the driveway. The exterior was painted a clean, classic off-white. Perpendicular to the house was an old wooden barn. Between it and the house, two enormous trees shaded the yard.

I grabbed the bare essentials from the car, anxious to get settled for the night. I was exhausted from the long drive and late nights spent packing.

"Let's go in!" I said, swinging Roe's hand in mine.

We climbed the five front steps and walked across the wide wraparound porch with its chocolate wood posts. I unlocked the heavy wooden door so Rowen could push her way inside.

The front door opened to a tiled entryway and a long staircase that split the house in half. To the left was the living room and dining room. On the right was the office and kitchen. A short hallway connected the dining room and the kitchen at the back of the house.

My dark leather furniture and cozy toss pillows would go perfectly with the main floor's honey-colored hardwood. And I couldn't wait to put my old reading chair in front of the brick fireplace in the office.

With the exception of a small powder room underneath the stairs, the bedrooms and bathrooms were all upstairs. I let out a loud "Woo-hoo!" at the walk-in closet in the master bedroom.

Rowen picked out her room, and after blowing up an air mattress, we settled in for our first night in the farmhouse.

I cuddled my girl closer and stared up at the ceiling. *We're here.* I actually did this.

I just effing moved to Montana!

Though it was terrifying to be in a whole new place, it felt amazing to be starting over. Starting an adventure. Replacing the loneliness I had felt in Spokane with excitement. Leaving all of the bad memories from the past behind.

Settling deeper into the mattress, I gave my girl a long hug. "Do you like Ben's farmhouse, sweetie?"

"I love it," she sighed.

"Me too."

During the drive over today, I had guessed at what shape the house would be in, how well the caretaker had done his job over the last two decades. I had mentally prepared myself to find the house infested with mice and bugs, but the house was like a dream. Clean and varmint-free.

Like the rest of Prescott, the farmhouse had a quaint and unique character you couldn't find in a large, commercialized city. I would get to enjoy my morning coffee while staring at the beautiful Rocky Mountain range instead of the shopping center that had been across from my house in Spokane. There weren't neighbors to block my driveway or glare at me when my grass was overdue for mowing. When I walked down the street, people would actually say hello, not just look at their feet and avoid eye contact.

I had space. I had privacy.

It was perfect.

"I love you, Roe," I said into her hair.

She yawned her "Love you too, Mommy."

And with that, we both promptly passed out, getting as much sleep as we could before a busy day of officially moving into our new life.

———

AFTER A WEEK of unpacking boxes and painting Roe's room (because she'd declared that she "simply couldn't imagine trying to sleep in a room without pink walls"), I had our home put together. Even so, we were heading into our first "regular" Monday morning a bit frayed and slightly nervous.

Rowen was at her preschool, Quail Hollow, and I was rushing into Jamison Valley Hospital.

The long, two-story building was much smaller than the towering Spokane hospitals I was used to. The ER was situated at one end and the main entrance at the other. I would be forgoing some of the luxuries of a big hospital, but I would gladly trade efficiency for the chance to get to know all of my coworkers, to feel that I was part of the small-town hospital team with its three doctors and ten nurses.

After meeting my nursing manager and doing the standard HR orientation, I set off to start my training.

"Hi!" I called to the nurse sitting at the ER desk. "I'm Gigi. You're Maisy, right? I think you're going to be hanging with me the rest of the week and showing me the ropes."

"Hey!" she said, shaking my hand and flashing me a million-megawatt smile. "Yep, I'm Maisy Holt. I'm super, *super* excited you're here! Usually we have to work the ER by ourselves because Prescott doesn't have many emergencies and it is so, *so* boring," she said. "This is the first time I've actually looked forward to being down here. And we have the whole week to gab. Oh . . . and I've never gotten to train anyone before so I am, like, stoked I get to."

Maisy was adorable, with white-blond hair cut into a short bob. Her big, doe eyes were a light grayish blue.

I couldn't help smiling back. "Well, I'm excited to be the first to experience your amazing training skills."

"Thanks! So how long have you been a nurse?"

"Almost ten years," I said, taking a seat. "I worked at a big hospital in Spokane before coming here."

"Well, I've only been a nurse for three years and only ever worked here. I came right back home after college. Ida— she's the senior nurse here. She's taught me so much. But now I can learn from you too!"

We spent the next two hours going over the computer system and getting to know each other, though I learned much more about her than she did about me. For the first hour, she switched between showing me the patient chart procedure and telling me about the town. I didn't utter more than ten words in that hour, mostly just variations of "Yep," "Okay," or "Gotcha" when I could sneak them in.

She must have finally realized she'd been dominating the conversation (or she'd gotten light-headed from her nonstop chatter) and started asking me about myself. When I told her where I was living, she got so excited she shot out of her chair and flailed her arms above her head.

"You live at the Coppersmith Farmhouse? Sweet! That place is, like, amazing! Total shame it's been empty for so long but how cool that you get to live there. If you need any help getting moved in or decorating, I'll totally come help. I'll volunteer my brothers to pitch in too if you need some muscle. We'll bribe them with beer and pizza."

This girl was a total sweetheart. She had energy. She was spunky. She didn't say anything without a smile. She used the word "like" *way* too much. And I loved her immediately.

A few hours later, almost lunchtime, Maisy and I had our heads together gossiping. She was telling me about the "hotter than Hades" new doctor. She had yet to learn much about Dr. Everett Carlson other than he'd started at the hospital about four months ago, he wore no wedding ring, he drove a sporty black BMW, and he'd bought a house in town where he kept mostly to himself.

A man clearing his throat scared us both out of our huddle. Heads and hair went flying up to see none other than the hot doctor smirking at us. At least I assumed he was the hot doctor.

He had brown eyes and chocolate-brown hair trimmed and styled neatly. He was good-looking, likely in his mid to late thirties, though not really my type. His look was a bit too put together for my tastes, but I could see why Maisy was interested.

And he definitely knew we were talking about him.

Maisy's face turned a brilliant shade of red. Luckily, she was saved from the impending awkward conversation when the phone rang and she ducked away.

"Uh . . . hi. I'm Gigi Ellars." My own cheeks were turning pink. This was how I made my first impression on one of Prescott's few doctors?

One corner of his mouth twitched as he shook my hand. "Everett Carlson. Nice to meet you."

Before I had to think of something else to say, Maisy called out to us in a loud, panicked voice.

"The EMT crew is on their way. They'll be here in about three minutes. A man was nearly beaten to death last night! They've revived him twice on the way here but he's got a very weak pulse and has lost a lot of blood." Her face started to pale.

Dr. Carlson started issuing orders. "I'll meet the ambulance outside and get the report from the EMTs. If he needs surgery, I'll be the doctor in the operating room. You two will need to get him prepped while I get scrubbed."

"Okay," I said.

Maisy didn't move or say a word.

"Maisy, get ahold of Dr. Peterson and tell him to come in and cover my other patients. Ida is here today. Make sure she's the one in the OR with me if we need to do surgery," he said before jogging to the ER doors.

Maisy was standing still, frozen in her spot. Normally I would let her take the lead because she had tenure at the hospital, but we didn't have time for her to freak out and from the looks of it, she wasn't going to be taking that lead anytime soon. We needed to get going.

"Maisy, do you want to meet the ambulance with Dr. Carlson?"

She shook her head as her eyes widened.

"Okay, how about you get the cart ready? Then get ahold of Dr. Peterson and Ida."

After she nodded, I turned and followed Dr. Carlson outside to wait for the ambulance.

The next hour went by in a hurried blur.

After doing a quick scan of the patient's internal injuries, Dr. Carlson decided he would indeed need surgery. Maisy managed to pull herself together and we worked side by side to prep the patient for surgery.

The man had been so badly beaten I could barely make out his facial features. His swollen body was covered in cuts and bruises, and there were glass shards in one leg from what appeared to be a broken beer bottle. Maisy and I cut off his bloody clothes and removed the dried blood caked on his body. When the bulk of the blood was cleaned away, we rushed him to the operating room.

I said a silent prayer that my first patient in Prescott would make it through.

Standing in the ER bay, I was in the middle of bagging what was left of the patient's bloody clothes when I glanced over at Maisy. She was supposed to be disposing of the bloody bedding before the cleaning crew came in to sanitize the room, but instead, she was just standing by the bed, clutching a white pillow streaked with dark red stains.

"Maisy, are you okay?" I asked softly.

When she didn't answer, I walked to her side.

"Maisy? I asked if you were okay." I touched her shoulder.

She flinched and then turned to me, her beautiful eyes flooded with tears. The next thing I knew, she was sobbing into my shoulder while I hugged her.

My heart went out to her. She'd probably never seen such a violent case before. It had taken me years of working in the ER to build up a strong enough stomach to handle seeing such things on a regular basis.

"You okay?"

"Yeah." She sniffled.

"Do you want to talk about it?"

"I've just never seen anything like that. Someone did that to him, tried to kill him. Who would do something like that?"

"I don't know, sweetie, but unfortunately, not everyone has a good heart."

She wiped her eyes and sniffled again. "I'm really glad you were here."

"Me too," I said, gently rubbing her arm.

"Excuse me?"

A newcomer poked his head around the bay's curtain. He was wearing a long sleeve, tan button-up shirt with dark jeans and cowboy boots. A badge shone brightly on one side of his belt, a gun on the other.

"Hi . . . ah, Officer?"

"Deputy," he corrected. A blood-soaked wrap was wound around his right hand, and blood smeared the front of his clothes.

"Deputy. Are you—" I started.

"Milo!" Maisy shrieked from behind me, then ran to his side. "Oh my god! What happened to you?"

"Maisy, calm down," he said. "I'm okay. Got a cut on my hand that's small but pretty deep, so I need to get a couple of stitches."

"How'd you get that cut?" she asked.

"I cut it on some glass."

"Where? How? Weren't you in your patrol car all morning? What were you doing today where you had to be touching broken glass?" she asked, examining his wounded arm.

He opened his mouth to respond but she cut him off.

"Oh my god! You found the beaten man, didn't you? He had glass in one of his legs!" She was shrieking again.

"You know I can't answer that question or talk about work," he said.

"Well, today you will. Tell me what happened."

"I. Cut. It. On. Glass. End of story, Maisy."

"Where. Was. The. Glass. Milo?"

Since Milo was bleeding and neither one of them gave any indication of backing down, I decided to interrupt their standoff.

"How about we get Milo admitted before he wrecks the floor? Then you two can continue your conversation." I pointed to the blood spots at our feet.

They both immediately dropped their eyes, then nodded. The ER bay where we put Milo was surrounded by a long curved curtain. Closing it behind her, Maisy left me with Milo to go and call Dr. Peterson for the stitches. I pulled up a stool and snapped on some latex gloves, preparing to remove the bloody wrap from Milo's hand and clean his wound.

"You're new here," Milo said.

"Yep, just started today. My name is Gigi."

"Sorry about that scene with Maisy. Our moms are best friends so we grew up spending a lot of time together. She's like my little sister." Milo sighed.

I smiled. "Ah . . . hence the squabble."

"Milo Phillips. Glad to meet you." He smiled back.

We sat quietly for a few moments while I worked.

"Sure has been a crazy day, huh?" he said into the silence. His lean shoulders slumped and his head drooped, giving me a close-up view of his buzz cut.

"You could say that. It sure wasn't the quiet and relaxed work environment I was promised," I joked.

"Ha. Yeah, I bet. I'm sure that in two weeks, you'll get quiet and relaxed. Today has been . . . different. This is the craziest thing to happen to me in my two years as a deputy here."

Milo was attempting to mask it with a brave face, but his shaking hands betrayed his shock.

Just as I was about to ask Milo more about himself, a deep, rumbling voice from outside the curtains interrupted.

Milo's hand jerked in mine and I turned as the curtains surrounding the bed flew to the side.

I opened my mouth to ask what was going on but the words got stuck in the back of my throat. My brain short-circuited. All of my attention was focused on the man standing right in front of me.

Seated on my stool, I had to tip my head way back to examine his face. I blinked a few times because this man was so ruggedly handsome I had to be imagining him.

He had light brown hair, long and messy at the top. It was styled in the I-just-showered-and-ran-my-hands-through-it look. What would it feel like if my hands were the ones to give it that style?

He had defined cheekbones and a strong jaw dusted with a bit of stubble. Along with the matching gun and badge, he wore the same tan shirt as Milo. But instead of the draping and boxy shape it had on my patient, the tight fit hinted at strong muscle and broad shoulders.

My mind wandered from the lines of the starched cotton shirt tucked into the jeans at his narrow hips to his rippled abs and how hard they would feel underneath my fingertips.

From his large thighs to his square-toed boots, his faded jeans fit his long legs so well they looked custom-made for him and only him.

I couldn't be sure, but based on the rest of his physique, he probably had a great ass. There was no way a man could have those powerful thighs, that flat stomach and those strong arms without an ass sculpted perfectly with rounded muscle.

And I loved a man with a great ass. An ass that just begged to be squeezed while he was on top of you.

But what catapulted him beyond any good-looking man I'd ever seen before were his eyes, light blue eyes flecked with white. Bright, like the color of ice. I had never seen such a hue before. Did they melt when he kissed someone, or did the ice become even brighter?

Shaking my head a little, I blinked rapidly. I was sitting here, fantasizing and ogling this guy. I needed to stop staring and turn back into a professional. Maybe try and breathe again?

Thankfully, the perfect man wasn't paying me the slightest bit of attention. His focus was solely on Milo. Had he even registered my presence? No, but at the moment, that was probably a good thing because he was *not* happy.

He firmly planted his hands on his hips and leaned into Milo's face, firing question after question.

"Milo, you want to tell me why it's taken nearly two hours after you arrived at the Silver Dollar this morning for me learn about the situation?"

He didn't wait for Milo's response.

"Why it wasn't called into the station? Why you chose to call Sam from your cell? So while I've been doing paperwork at my desk, Sam's been standing around the crime scene wondering where the fuck I was. Or while you've been sitting in the hospital, waiting to get stitched up, I've been doing *fucking paperwork*?"

Milo's face paled at the verbal assault and he looked to his boots, muttering, "I'm sorry, Sheriff. I'm wigging out. That scene was fucked. I don't even remember calling Sam or driving up here. I swear I thought I was in the waiting room for just a few minutes."

The sheriff calmed down marginally, in that he was no longer yelling, and let out an audible breath. Then he reached out and placed a large hand on Milo's shoulder.

"You wig out, Milo, you call me. I'll help you sort it."

Milo nodded.

Scowling, the sheriff turned to me and looked me over

from head to toe. He actually appeared to be angrier at me than he had been at Milo.

What was that about?

"Are you about done drooling over me so you can finish patching him up?" he snapped.

My cheeks instantly flushed. My tongue swelled to about three times its normal size and I couldn't find the right words to respond.

Damn. He *had* noticed me staring.

Which made sense. He was a cop. Being observant was probably in the job description. Regardless, he didn't need to be so rude. Or to call me on it. He could have just ignored it and been nice.

When I didn't respond, he cocked his eyebrows, waiting for me to answer his question.

"Can you speak?" he grumbled.

Jackass!

All previous thoughts of his perfection were pushed way, way back in my mind. You could be seriously hot on the outside but if you were nasty on the inside, all the exterior goodness disappeared.

I'd known a man like that once. Nate Fletcher. He'd been hot, cocky and confident. He'd taught me that lesson. And the way he'd taught it made sure I never forgot. Never.

I inhaled a deep breath and clamped my mouth shut. Because the words that wanted to come spewing out of my mouth were not good ones. I really wanted to call him an asshole and tell him to go to hell. But verbally accosting the town sheriff wasn't on my list of things to do today so I mustered all of the mental fortitude I had and swallowed my insults.

"The doctor hasn't been to see him yet," I said, my smile

saccharine. "I'm almost finished cleaning him up but Dr. Peterson will want to do the stitches."

The sheriff stared at me for a moment, his jaw clenched.

"Fine. Make it fast," he muttered, giving me one last glare. "When you're done here, head to the station," he told Milo. "I'll meet you there after I talk to Sam."

Turning on his boot heel, he stormed out of the room, grabbing the curtains and jerking them closed. They flew in the air and fell quickly but not before I caught a glimpse of him from behind.

I was right. He had a *great* ass.

Damn.

CHAPTER TWO

GIGI

One day later, the hospital was still abuzz. After Sheriff Jess Cleary had stormed out of the hospital, both Maisy and Milo had made it a point to apologize for his behavior. And since he hadn't bothered to introduce himself before being a jackass, they'd also told me who in the hell he was.

Both Maisy and Milo seemed relieved I wasn't holding the ordeal against Jess. I'd nonchalantly brushed it aside, blaming Jess's behavior on the intensity of the situation. As far as *they* were concerned, Jess was on my "Good" list.

But as far as *I* was concerned? Jess was in the number two spot on my "Go to hell" list.

Remarkably, the John Doe brought into the ER yesterday had made it through surgery and was currently in an induced coma. Dr. Carlson, who had insisted I start calling him Everett, had decided the coma would last for four full days, until Friday, to let the man's severe swelling subside and give his broken body a chance to heal.

Even in a coma, John Doe had attracted a lot of attention from the sheriff's office. Three times a day, a deputy checked in on his recovery. Thankfully, the great Sheriff Jess Cleary was above these personal visits and had sent others in his stead. Sometimes it was Milo, other times it was Sam or Bryant, both of whom were very friendly and nice.

Apparently, the only asshole in the Jamison County Sheriff's Office was the sheriff himself.

John Doe had also attracted attention from the local newspaper. The weekly Tuesday bulletin had come out this morning with the entire front page dedicated to John Doe's story, or lack thereof, seeing as no one knew who he actually was.

John Doe had been discovered behind the Silver Dollar Saloon's large Dumpster by the gentleman who cleaned the bar before it opened each day. John Doe hadn't had a wallet in his possession and none had been found in the surrounding area.

None of the other bar patrons had known his real identity either. Everyone had just assumed he was one of the many tourists passing through Prescott. Unfortunately for the investigation, he had also paid in cash, leaving no credit card trail.

Maisy and I learned all this from Milo, who had stopped by this afternoon to have his stitches examined. Maisy had been relentlessly pecking at him since the minute he had walked through the door, and after realizing there was no need to keep it a secret and that she was absolutely not going to stop pestering him, he told us how he had gotten hurt.

"When the call came in from the bar, I was covering the

dispatch desk. Our dispatcher, he was, ah, indisposed. So I took the call and panicked. I wrote a note for the dispatcher and then hightailed it out of there. Got to the Silver Dollar and found the guy was still alive. Freaked out and called the ambulance and Sam from my cell, since they hadn't gotten there yet. Asked them where in the fuck they were. Guess that should have been my first clue that no one saw my note."

"You think?"

"Shut up, Maze," Milo said.

"Then what happened?" I asked before the two of them could start bickering again.

"The guy's body was pushed way behind the Dumpster, so I snapped a few pictures of the scene and then started moving the Dumpster, thinking that would help the EMTs get him out of there. Between the phone to my ear and trying to push a heavy Dumpster, I lost my footing and fell. Landed on a big shard of glass. Dug right into my hand."

"Now, don't you feel better for telling us?" Maisy asked smugly.

"Not really," Milo said.

"Well, I feel better." She grinned and gave him a quick peck on the cheek.

As Milo and Maisy chatted a bit more, I started packing up my purse. I was planning to squeeze in a quick run before I picked up Rowen at Quail Hollow.

"I'm outta here!" I waved good-bye and headed to my car.

Running was something I didn't do much of anymore but years ago, I had been a running addict. But then my mother had been diagnosed with breast cancer and all the free time I'd had was spent with her, taking care of her household chores. Her body had been so weak while it battled the cancer that she'd needed the help. And with all the extra work, I hadn't had time to run anymore.

Then in the middle of it all, I'd gotten pregnant from a one-night stand at a wedding. Being a single parent to an infant while taking care of my own had put a long-term hiatus on my running.

But today I was making time for it. It was so beautiful outside and I wanted to spend some time enjoying the fresh air.

Ben had loved fresh air. He'd always told me how much good it did for your body. Anytime I had felt sick or blue, he'd push me outside.

I missed him so much. I wished that he were waiting at the farmhouse for me. That instead of a run, we could go on a walk together and visit. I missed his presence. Talking to him. Laughing with him. Our banter.

Ever since we had first met, he and I had teased one another. Our relationship had been easy. Natural. Ever since the day I had walked into his hospital room.

———

THREE YEARS EARLIER . . .

My foot was killing me. Any minute now, the blister on the back of my left heel was going to start gushing blood and I'd bleed out right here on the linoleum floor. Death by heel blister.

The twelve Band-Aids I had used to try and cover the damn thing were not helping.

I limped toward the last room of the rehab unit on the sixth floor of Spokane Deaconess Hospital.

I was an ER nurse normally and loved its fast pace.

Unfortunately, today had been a slow one, and rather than organize supply cabinets and clean the nurses' station, I had volunteered to head upstairs to rehab.

Knocking with two quick knuckle taps, I pushed the door open and walked into room 612 while looking down at the iPad in my hands displaying the patient's chart.

"Hi, ah . . . Mr. Coppersmith?" I called.

"Ben," he muttered.

I looked up to see Mr. Coppersmith sitting on his hospital bed in near darkness. Just a faint glow coming from the bathroom lit his room. About six pillows were propped up behind his back, and he wasn't sleeping or watching TV. He was just sitting there on his bed, staring at the wall, seemingly lost in thought.

It was too dark to get a good look at Ben so I walked to the windows. Rather than turn on the intense and unfriendly florescent overhead lighting, which made skin look gray and sick people look sicker, I'd let the warm afternoon sunshine light the room.

"Hi, Ben," I said after the curtains were open. "My name's Gigi. How are you today?"

"Ready to get out of here and head home." His voice held no conviction and his eyes remained focused on the wall. His fingers played nervously in his lap.

Ben was an older man, seventy-eight according to his chart, but I would have guessed much younger, judging by the shape of his body. His frame only carried a small amount of extra weight at the middle, and his shoulders and chest were broad. Straight, not slumped like most of the elderly patients I saw. His legs extended nearly off the end of the bed. He had to be at least seven or eight inches taller than my five foot seven. Ben had a full head of dark gray hair, neatly combed and not too long. His skin was tan and leathery, likely from spending years outdoors.

I glanced down at his chart again and did a quick scan to familiarize myself more with his stay in rehab.

"Is your hip feeling better?" I asked.

He had come in with severe bruising on the entire right side of his body from a fall. His hip had been so swollen he couldn't walk for a week. Where the hell had he fallen from to cause such damage?

Ben didn't answer my question. He nodded once while keeping his eyes locked on the wall.

"Is there anything I can tell the physical therapist before you meet with her one last time today? She shouldn't have much to do with you today now that your hip is back to normal but I could leave her a note if you'd like."

Silence. His eyes didn't even shift.

I waited a few uncomfortable moments to see if he'd eventually respond, but he remained quiet.

"Okay. So that means I'm here to do a last check of your vitals and, if you'd like to get out of bed, take you for one last walk. Would you like to go for a stroll?"

I prayed his answer was no. The thought of extra steps made me feel nauseous now that the pain in my heel was radiating through my entire foot and ankle.

He grunted. Not a yes or a no. Just a grunt to his wall.

I wasn't sure if his mind was on other things or if it was just plain rudeness, but Ben was absolutely not interested in engaging in conversation with me. Not that I was feeling particularly chatty myself.

"All right, Ben, here's the deal. The last thing in the world I want to do right now is take any more steps than absolutely necessary. I've got a huge blister on my heel that

I've been walking around with all day. A lap around this floor will probably bring me to tears. How about I check your vitals, then we skip your walk?"

He didn't answer.

"I'll just sit here with you and stare at that wall for thirty minutes. Then I'll move along to your neighbor's room. Okay?"

I didn't wait for a response, not that I had planned on getting one.

"Or if you feel like it, you can tell me more about how you landed yourself in the hospital. If you don't, well, I'll just be quiet. All right?"

Again, no answer.

"What a surprise? He's speechless," I deadpanned. "Really, Ben. You've got to learn to let me get a word in. It's rude to do all the talking. Now if you'll please just be quiet for a minute. All that talking is giving me a headache to go along with my hurting foot."

Ben was silent for a moment, then turned his head toward me, smirking. "How about we take that walk after all? I'm feeling the need to stretch my legs. Think today I could do an extra lap."

The defeated and pained look on my face must have been hilarious because his smirk turned into a full-blown smile, exposing straight but yellowed teeth.

"Kidding, girl." He chuckled.

Relief washed through my whole body.

"You're a funny man, Ben." I sagged down into his visitor's chair. "Do you feel like telling me the story of how you fell and landed yourself in the hospital?" I asked, using his joke as my opening to learn more about Ben Coppersmith.

Ben shifted on his bed of pillows to look my way.

"Was up on my roof, fixing a leak by the chimney. Trying to balance myself, the bucket of tar and my putty knife at the same time. Don't know how but as I shifted to get down, lost my footing and slid down and over the side. Was able to grab hold of the gutter on my way down and slow my pace. But still fell about ten feet and hit cement sidewalk at the bottom," he said. "Gettin' old, girl. Years ago, probably would have landed on my feet. Now, well . . . my body's starting to fall apart."

My eyes bugged out. What in the hell was he doing up on a roof at seventy-eight years old? Yes, he appeared to be in good shape. I probably would have pegged him mid-sixties if I'd run into him on the street. But despite his physique, old men should not be on rooftops.

"Ah . . . okay," I said. "You sure don't look like most seventy-eight-year-old men I see in the hospital, Ben. But regardless, no one over the age of, well, I don't know . . . forty-five should be traipsing over rooftops. Don't you have family or friends who could have done that work for you?"

"Got lots of friends. Never had much family. None of them were gonna be able to do this job though. And I'm too old and stubborn to pay some roofing company to come out and fix something I know how to do and could do myself in an hour."

"Well, just to point out, you might know how to fix a leaky roof but your current location indicates you maybe couldn't do it by yourself after all," I returned. "Why couldn't your friends do it for you?"

"They're all out at Highland."

"Highland? Is that where you're from?" I didn't know any towns near Spokane called Highland but maybe it was out of state.

26

Ben turned his brown eyes back to the wall. "Highland Cemetery. Only friend left to help lives in Montana."

If Ben didn't have anyone to help him with the leaky roof, who was going to help him after he got home from the hospital? Or help him even *get* home from the hospital?

"How were you planning on getting home, Ben?"

"My car's at home. Ambulance brought me here when I called 9-1-1. Figure I'll just call a cab in the morning once you people set me free," he said.

"What about clothes? Do you have something to wear home?" He couldn't leave in a hospital gown.

"Just wear the ones I came in with," he said.

My eyebrows came together as I frowned. I went to his closet and inspected his clothes.

"Ben, you can't wear these clothes. They are filthy and covered in dried blood!"

"They're fine," he said.

"What about neighbors? Could one of them swing by your house and get something fresh for you to wear? Bring you home?"

"Live out in the country. Closest neighbor is a mile away. Never met them," he said.

No family, friends or neighbors.

Eff.

I dropped the clothes and faced the window. Even though I had just met the man, Ben's situation was really getting to me. I should leave it be and get on with my rounds. Ben's clothing and transportation dilemmas were not my problems to solve. He had a plan, albeit a poor one, but it was a plan that would get him home. The man had managed to stay alive for seventy-eight years; surely he could manage a trip home from the hospital. I had enough of my own problems to worry about. I didn't need to take on Ben's too.

But something about him called to me and I had to do more. He didn't have anyone close that he could count on and I knew that feeling all too well. I couldn't count on anyone else to be there for me either.

So when I turned around from the windows toward Ben, I knew that on top of my own problems, I was going to pile on Ben Coppersmith's.

"Are those your keys?" I asked Ben, nodding to the set on his bedside table.

"Yeah."

"Good. Hand them over and then write down your address," I said, holding out my hand.

He blinked twice and shook his head. "Huh?"

"I need your address and those keys to get into your house. That way, I can go there tomorrow morning and get you some clean clothes to wear home. Then I'll be back here to deliver said clothes and take you home."

With his mouth hanging open, he stayed quiet.

"Now other than your keys, address and directions to your place if it's hard to find, is there anything I need to know before I head out there tomorrow? Pets? Alarm system? Gate code?" I asked, shaking my outstretched hand.

We stared at each other for a few moments until the shock on his face was replaced by a warm softening around his eyes.

"Appreciate you offering to do such a nice thing for me, girl. But we just met fifteen minutes ago. You've got better things to do than cart around an old man. You don't even know me," he said.

"Are you a serial killer?" I asked.

"Uh . . . no," he replied.

"Criminal of any sort?"

"No."

"An asshole?"

"Probably been called that once or twice in my day." He grinned.

"Well, okay. You were on your own if you'd have said yes to being a serial killer or a criminal. But an asshole I can deal with. Just try and keep a lid on it and we'll be fine. Now how about those keys?"

———

BEN and I had become fast friends.

From the day I took him home from the hospital to the day he died, he had been my surrogate grandparent.

My mother had finally lost her battle with breast cancer about six months before I had met Ben. Growing up, it had always just been Mom and me. Until the day I'd found out I was pregnant, Mom had been my whole world. Rowen had just turned one and I had been struggling to care for her while dealing with the loss of my mother. Ben had come into my life when I needed him most. When I'd never felt so alone.

Now Ben was gone. That loneliness was back. And though I was a fiercely independent person, I missed having another adult around to talk to.

I steered the Explorer into the drive and parked. I sucked in a jagged breath and blinked away the tears.

Fresh air.

That's what I needed to make the ache in my heart go

away. So away I went, running along a county road with the mountains as my backdrop.

Not so much enjoying the fresh air as desperately trying to suck it in. Surely this was not what Ben had meant.

I hate altitude. I can't breathe.

Turn around now. Just quit. Be a quitter. No one needs to know.

I can do it. I'm almost there. I can make it.

No you can't.

Those thoughts were looping on repeat as I hit the halfway point on my run.

This jog was nothing like those from my past in Spokane. I was miserable. My head was pounding, my heart was beating out of my chest, my lungs were on fire, my legs felt like Jell-O, and I was drenched with sweat. Any minute now, I was going to puke.

But I had to get back to the farmhouse. Otherwise I was going to be late to pick up Roe, and for every minute you were late past six o'clock, Quail Hollow charged you ten dollars.

Ten dollars a minute!

Robbery.

So I inhaled a deep breath and swallowed, tasting blood, while I pushed my feet forward.

You can make it.

You can make it.

You can make it.

I chanted with every step, hoping my positive mental affirmations would get me through the next mile and a half.

I stared at the rough pavement and decided if I kept my head up, maybe it would make the run go easier. My chin lifted just as a huge truck headed down the road, coming my way. I inched to the far side of the road but kept running, expecting the driver to give me a wide berth and pass me by.

But the truck was not just a truck, it was a behemoth police truck. The bronzy-brown monster had a rack of lights on top of the cab, plus one of those menacing grill guards. The sheriff's emblem was proudly displayed on the driver's side door. And so was the sheriff in the driver's seat.

As I came to a stop, Jess stopped right next to me. He started speaking but the loud roar of the diesel engine drowned out his words.

"What?" I shouted just as Jess cut the engine on his truck.

He leaned out his open driver's side window. His eyes were covered with aviator-style sunglasses.

"I said you shouldn't be running out here. It's a dumb fucking thing to do."

Did this guy just keep getting nicer and nicer, or what?

My heart rate was already well past the elevated range. At the sheriff's harassment, it was now thundering. There was a good chance it would sprint back to the farmhouse without me.

"How is it that running in broad daylight in warm weather is a 'dumb fucking thing to do'?" I panted, throwing my hands up in air quotes.

"These old county roads don't get a lot of traffic. People don't pay attention to where they're driving. You could get hit and no one would have a fucking clue where to start looking," he said.

"Well, thanks for the warning, Sheriff. I'll be sure to take that under advisement."

"Don't have to be snappy about it. Christ, I'm sorry I stopped."

"Not as sorry as I am. So please, don't let me keep you. Feel free to leave me here on the road and share that sunny attitude of yours with other citizens in Jamison County. I wouldn't want you to waste it all on me."

He clenched his jaw and even though I couldn't see his eyes behind his glasses, I knew he was glaring at me.

"Mouthing off to a cop. Not smart," he said.

"What are you going to do, write me a ticket for speaking? Does Montana not abide by that whole freedom of speech thing?"

"How about I write you a ticket for being on the wrong side of the road? You should be running over here on the right."

"Fine. Write me a ticket. What's the fine? Fifty cents? I'll drop it by the station on my way to work tomorrow. I should be able to find some spare change in my couch cushions."

"Stay put," he ordered, pointing to my feet. Then he turned back into the cab of his truck and pulled out a pad of paper.

Was this jackass seriously going to write me a ticket for running on the wrong side of a basically deserted road?

Yes. Yes, he was.

Two minutes later, I had a yellow ticket in my hand with my name scribbled on top. Obviously he'd learned my name sometime in the last day, which made me nervous. Either he'd been asking about me or someone in town had been talking about me.

Below my name was the fine amount and it wasn't fifty cents. It was one hundred dollars. Daycare late fees weren't robbery. This was.

"You've got to be effing kidding me."

"Payment is due in ten days. Appeals must be filed

before the ten-day limit." He was all business now that he'd served me with the ticket.

Before I could dismiss him, he leaned out his truck a little farther. "Oh, and the word is fucking. Not effing."

"I have a four-year-old. In my world, the word is effing. Am I free to go?"

He didn't answer. He just leaned back into his truck, brought it back to life and roared down the road.

I didn't need chanting or positive mental affirmations for the remainder of my run. Fueled by adrenaline and anger, I sprinted the return mile and a half in record time, arriving at Quail Hollow fifteen minutes before closing.

———

"I NEED TO PAY A TICKET," I told a deputy at the sheriff's station.

"Gigi?"

I turned around to see Milo and Sam walking my way.

I waved. "Hi, Milo. Sam."

"What are you doing here?" Sam asked.

I took my yellow "running" ticket and held it out for them to read.

Milo just muttered, "Wow," while Sam started laughing.

"What? What's funny?"

"Bogus ticket, Gigi. There's no law stating which side of the road you have to run on. Sheriff is messing with you."

"You're kidding."

He shook his head. "Wasted a trip to the station. But at least you can save yourself a hundred bucks."

"Ha!" Milo laughed. "You had a run-in while getting a

run in. Get it. A run-in with the law? While you were running?" He kept laughing.

Sam thought Milo's pun was hilarious and he, too, burst out laughing.

I, however, did not find it funny. Not in the slightest.

CHAPTER THREE

GIGI

The wraparound porch was one of my favorite features of the farmhouse. Like I had the last few nights, I'd gotten Rowen into bed and come outside to the wooden porch swing to drink a couple glasses of wine while watching the sun set behind the hills.

I'd been keeping a consistent routine for Roe's evening and bedtime activities since our move, hoping to ease her transition into Ben's old home.

Though Roe loved her mother absolutely, I'd always come in second place behind Ben. It had never bothered me because I had been more than willing to take a backseat to their relationship so he could feel the full force of Rowen's unconditional love. She was missing him, but if we had a nice nightly routine, she might not get too sad thinking about how we were living in his house because he was dead.

The nights were still warm but I had on a soft, light gray cardigan that hung loosely over my white tank top and frayed denim shorts. I loved this sweater with its huge pockets and long sleeves that draped nearly to my fingertips. It was cozy and soft. But mostly I loved it because it had been my mom's.

As I swayed in the swing, I thought about what tomorrow had in store for me.

It had been a long week at the hospital. Not only had it been my first week, which meant my brain had been working overtime to learn the hospital's protocols, but John Doe's presence had kept a steady flow of visitors at the ER desk. People were constantly stopping by to check on his status and speculate with Maisy about who could have delivered the beating.

Most of our visitors were from the sheriff's office and I tensed any time I saw a tan shirt. I hadn't seen Jess since the ticket incident but the chances of him coming into the hospital tomorrow were pretty high.

Tonight, the evening nurses were stopping the meds keeping John Doe in his coma and he'd likely come awake sometime in the morning. Everett would give him a thorough examination and then an officer would take his statement.

I expected to be dragging my feet home tomorrow, more than ready for a quiet weekend at the farmhouse with my daughter.

Pushing thoughts of work aside, I took a long, deep breath and sank further into the swing. It was time to do something I'd been procrastinating since arriving in Prescott. I needed to contact the farmhouse's caretaker.

From my cardigan pocket, I pulled out two letters. Both were from Ben, one addressed to me and another to "Brick."

Taking a deep, fortifying breath, I eased my wrinkled letter out of its battered envelope to read it again. Ben's letter always left me feeling empty. Why I kept reading it was a bit of a mystery. It made me sad. It made me cry. It made me miss him so much my bones ached. Reading it was self-inflicted torture to my heart, but I'd done it countless times these last six weeks.

But tonight was it.

I would read it one last time and then put it away in a box of Ben's keepsakes stored in the attic, holding onto it in case Rowen wanted to read it someday.

Ben's attorney had given me both letters after the reading of his will and asked that I deliver Brick's letter upon my arrival in Montana. But I'd been postponing. Mostly because I'd been so busy with the move and first week at work, but partly because it was one of the last things Ben had asked me to do. The longer I stalled, the longer I could pretend that he wasn't truly gone.

My eyes traveled over Ben's rough scrawl, blurring as I read the last line.

Drying my teary eyes, I reached for my phone. It was time to text Brick. No more delaying the inevitable. Ben was gone and he wasn't coming back. I needed to see to his final wishes.

This Brick guy had cared for the farmhouse for almost two decades. He'd certainly have heard by now that I was settled into the farmhouse. One thing I'd learned this past week, news in Prescott traveled fast.

Me: Hi. My name is Georgia Ellars. Ben Coppersmith's attorney asked me to get ahold of you. I've got a few things from Ben he wanted you to have. Would you be available to meet me at the farmhouse this weekend or next week?

His response was almost immediate.

Brick: Be there in 5.

Tonight? It was a little late, almost nine o'clock, and he hadn't asked if it was okay for him to come over. But I might as well get it over with. It shouldn't take too long and Roe was asleep. I didn't really want her around for this conversation.

She'd been dutifully pretending Ben's passing hadn't happened, acting like we were on a fun vacation and when it was over, life would go back to the way it had been.

She'd had a total breakdown the day I told her that he'd died, but ever since, she had shut that part of her world away. She needed time to process it in her head. I got that, so I hadn't pushed. But we were coming up on two months and I was getting worried that we were on the edge of an impending meltdown when it finally settled in her heart that he was gone.

Maybe I should try and talk to her this weekend.

I stood up and walked inside. Five minutes gave me just enough time to throw on some lip gloss, re-knot the hair on my head and refill my wineglass.

I was stepping through the front door, wine in hand, when the sheriff's truck drove up with none other than the sheriff himself.

Just what I didn't need right now. A confrontation with Jackass Jess right before I needed to meet with Brick.

My breath hitched as he took long strides toward me. His jeans accentuated his long, muscled legs and that white T-shirt was just a tad too tight across his chest. His face had a little stubble on his jaw from the day.

He looked good, of course.

Damn.

Why did he have to be so perfect? Couldn't he have gotten uglier these last few days?

But I wasn't going to let him fluster me. He was just a hot guy and I needed to keep my cool and get him the hell out of here. Because even though he was hot, he was a complete jerk.

I didn't want to be verbally sparring with him when Brick came by. I needed to make a good impression so he would agree to take Ben's fifty thousand dollars.

Jess stopped at the bottom of the stairs and crossed his arms over his chest, pulling his T-shirt tightly at the biceps. My breath hitched again at the sight of his bulky arms and I forced my eyes away from his bulging muscles. His signature scowl was aimed my way.

Would a smile kill him?

It was his glare that brought out my inner smart-ass. That, and the two point five glasses of wine I'd already had.

"Good evening, Sheriff. Is there something I can help you with? Here to write me another ticket? I was at the grocery store earlier. Maybe I was pushing my cart down the wrong side of the aisle?"

"I'm here, Ms. Ellars, because you asked to meet me."

What was he talking about? "I'm certain I would have remembered asking to meet with *you*. You see, Mr. Cleary, I'm not your biggest fan. And I'm not in the habit of inviting people I don't like to my home. Ever."

He narrowed his eyes and opened his mouth to speak but I lifted a hand, palm out, and talked right over him.

"It's not lost on me that for some reason you do not like me. Fine. Whatever. I'll happily avoid you for the rest of my life. So how about you kindly state your purpose for wrecking my evening and get on your way? I'm expecting someone any minute now and I'd like to get this over with before he arrives," I said.

He started up the stairs, coming right into my space when he reached the landing. As he tilted his glare down at me, I craned my neck to watch his face.

Heat radiated off his chest and he towered over me in my bare feet. He had to be at least six three. Maybe six four. And even bigger than I had originally noticed.

His body was like a magnet to mine. His tight chest, just a couple inches away from my face, tempted me to lean in, just a little, and run my fingers over his T-shirt. To feel each muscle's rise and fall as he breathed.

I was completely attracted to him and it was making me dizzy. I didn't even know how that was possible given his personality. He was a jerk. But unfortunately, he was a jerk that made my hands itch to touch.

"*You* texted *me*, Ms. Ellars," he said, forcing my thoughts away from touching him. "Got something for me from Ben?" He waved his phone in my face. "I don't know how much of that wine you've had, but if you can't remember sending me a text not ten minutes ago, maybe you should call it quits for the night. Get some professional help."

Did he just say that *I* texted *him*? Was he Brick?

Yes. Yes, he was.

I had expected someone older, someone closer to Ben's age. Someone who was actually nice. I was speechless, so astonished that I didn't reply to his question. I just stood there blinking, my mouth open.

Finally, my brain reengaged.

"*You* are Brick? I thought your name was Jess Cleary."

He didn't mask the annoyance on his face and rolled his eyes.

"It is. And yeah, I'm Brick. Nickname from high school football. Hitting me was like hitting a brick wall. Get it?"

"Well . . . no. I don't watch football," I said, taking a step back. "You're the man who's been taking care of the farmhouse for Ben? For nineteen years?"

"Yep. Now how about you hand over whatever it is Ben left for me and I can get the fuck on my way? Then we'll move along to you avoiding me. Liked the sound of that."

Jackass!

"Right," I said.

How could Ben say this guy was a good man? Obviously he'd misjudged Jess, which was strange because Ben had been an extremely good judge of character. And he'd thought I should trust Jess? This guy that had been nothing but rude and abrasive to me since the moment I laid eyes on him? Uh . . . no.

Unfortunately, I needed to give him Ben's letter and money, so I had to suck it up and be nice for a few minutes.

"Would you like to sit down? Can I get you something to drink?" I asked, gesturing toward the swing.

"No." He leaned on the porch railing and again crossed his arms. As I sat on the swing, his eyes narrowed in a disapproving glare. Like he absolutely did not want my ass on his swing.

Be nice.

Be nice.

Be nice.

I silently chanted while taking a deep breath.

"Sorry for the confusion when you got here. Ben only ever referred to you as Brick. He actually never mentioned

41

you to me personally. Only in a letter. I didn't know Prescott, this house or you existed until after he died six weeks ago," I rambled.

Jess's posture didn't change and he didn't acknowledge my apology. He didn't even ease up on the glare.

Being nice to a jerk was really, really, *really* hard.

"Whatever. Moving on," I said, shaking my head.

I gathered the letters and my checkbook from the swing's seat.

"Ben left you fifty thousand dollars as payment for your upkeep of the farmhouse all these years. I've got the proceeds from his estate in my account, and if it's okay with you, I'll write you a personal check? Or if you'd prefer a cashier's check, I can go to the bank tomorrow and get one."

Jess straightened off the railing. "Told the old man over and over again. Didn't keep an eye on his house for money. Did it because it was his and he was good to me. Keep the money."

He started stomping his way down the porch but after two long strides, he glanced over his shoulder and said, "Love this house. Worked hard to make it something great. Do me a favor? Don't fuck it up."

Ouch.

That wasn't just rude or abrasive. That was just plain mean.

Sure, I had been a smart-ass to him during our previous interactions, but I didn't think that gave him the right to be so hurtful. He didn't even know me, and suggesting I would destroy Ben's farmhouse, something I was growing to love, was hurtful.

It hurt enough that I instantly decided I would do whatever

it took to get Jess "Brick" Cleary off my property once and for all. If I had to beg him to take Ben's money, so be it. Because once that check was cashed, I was never going to speak to him again.

"Please wait!" I jumped off the porch swing. "Giving you that money was important to Ben. Just . . . before you take off, he wrote each of us a letter. Please read them before you say no. Please?"

I extended the letters toward his back.

Jess turned and yanked the letters from my grip, walking to the swing before opening his letter.

"I'll just . . . give you some time to yourself," I said. "Just come on in whenever you're done."

"Stay," he ordered, not glancing up.

I didn't argue. I just picked up my wineglass and stood by the porch railing, aiming my eyes back to the sunset.

This was progress. At least he was reading the letters. Maybe I wouldn't have to persuade him to take the money. Maybe whatever Ben had put in his letter would do the convincing.

I drained my wineglass and set it on the railing, focusing on the brilliant colors of the horizon until Jess cleared his throat behind me.

"I'll take the check."

"Okay. Great," I breathed, my frame relaxing.

I wrote the check, which he shoved in his back jeans pocket along with his letter, and turned back to the sunset. He left without another word.

I didn't watch him go. I didn't want to give Jess Cleary any more of my time. I'd done what Ben needed me to do and now Jess had his money. And I wouldn't ever have to deal with the sheriff again.

Relieved to have the encounter behind me, I watched the sun set, wondering if Ben had ever done the same.

I smiled. He'd probably spent many nights in this very spot. It made me feel good to have that connection to Ben. A bond we would always have through his farmhouse.

———

JESS

As I drove home, all I could think about was the letter in my back pocket.

Take the money, Brick. Don't make Gigi fight you on it. She'll do it and won't stop because I asked her not to. She's a damn stubborn woman.

Proud to have known you, kid. Grew into a good man.

Look after my girls. Let them look after you. You won't regret it.

Ben

Over the years, Ben had made it a point to call me about once a month. We wouldn't talk for long and the conversations were never serious. Mostly just checking in and Ben asking if I needed money for any of the work I was doing on the farmhouse. Something I'd always refused.

I would have done just about anything for Ben Coppersmith. Keeping up the farmhouse was the least I could do to repay the kindness he had shown me when I was a kid. And after nineteen years, that farmhouse felt more like my home than the house where I actually lived.

If I needed to unwind or get some perspective, that's where I went.

Three years ago, I'd noticed a change in Ben's monthly phone calls. He'd started to share things about his life rather than just asking me about mine. And all that Ben had to share was about Georgia Ellars and her daughter. I didn't know much about her. Ben didn't share her past. But he'd tell me little things. What Gigi had made for dinner the night before. What Rowen had said that made him bust a gut laughing.

I was happy for Ben. That he wasn't alone all the way out there in Washington.

I liked it up until the day Ben called me six months ago and asked me to make sure the farmhouse was in good enough shape for Gigi to live there.

Gigi had just been out for Ben's money. His property. She was tricking an old man out of his possessions.

I kept my opinions to myself though, hoping that Ben would never see her true colors. That he could live his final years thinking she was the daughter he'd never had. Ben had endured enough sadness. He'd deserved a few years of happiness in his old age.

Even if it had all been a show from a greedy, gold-digging woman.

Ben had been getting up there in years, and every day I had checked the Spokane obituaries. The day I found out he died, I drank an entire bottle of Crown and passed out in the swing at the farmhouse.

Then I'd watched and waited.

With Ben gone, I had known that woman would soon come to claim what wasn't hers.

And like usual, I'd been right.

It had only taken her two weeks to start making phone calls throughout Prescott, arranging for her upcoming move. Two weeks after that, she'd pulled into town.

I knew she had spent last week moving into the farmhouse. I knew this was her first week at the hospital. There wasn't much that happened in Prescott that the sheriff wasn't aware of.

But what I hadn't known was that sitting on a stool in the ER, cleaning Milo's hand, she was the most beautiful woman I'd ever lay eyes on.

She had true beauty, like nothing I'd ever seen before. Something that brought men like me to their knees. Something that went straight to my dick and shut off my brain.

There was nothing artificial about her. No fake tan or fake tits. She was perfect without all the heavy makeup and teased-out hair. And she clearly ate more than lettuce and diet pills. Not that she was fat. She had a fit body with toned muscle on her arms and legs but soft curves around her breasts and hips.

One look at Georgia and I wasn't sure what I'd ever seen in the Hollywood-styled tourists I normally took to my bed. All the money in the world couldn't make them as stunning as the woman dressed in plain navy scrubs.

She had deep blue eyes the color of Yogo sapphires and chocolate-brown hair that fell in long, loose waves to her waist. But it was her freckles that made her beauty stand apart. They were scattered all across the bridge of her nose and upper cheekbones.

True beauty.

And dangerous as fuck.

I didn't need to get swept up in her beauty and let her lead me around by my balls. I could never forgive the fact that she had snaked her way into Ben's life to manipulate a payday and steal the farmhouse out from under me.

So I'd done the only thing I could think of to get her to stay far the hell away from me. I'd treated her like shit.

And now, driving home with that letter and check in my pocket, I realized what a complete and total prick I'd been.

I prided myself on my ability to read people. It made me one hell of a good cop. But never in my life had I read someone so incredibly wrong.

Georgia hadn't manipulated Ben. Christ, she hadn't even known Ben had owned a house in Prescott. Plus, she could have easily ignored Ben's request to pay me the fifty thousand dollars and just kept it herself. It's not like I would have ever known.

"You're a fuckin' asshole, Cleary," I muttered to the windshield.

I needed to fix this. I owed it to her and to Ben to right this wrong.

I'd show her that I was indeed the good man Ben professed me to be.

CHAPTER FOUR

GIGI

Sitting behind the ER counter, I studied the patient chart layout on an iPad. Jamison Valley had managed to make the transition to electronic charting, which was impressive for such a small hospital. The file layout was fairly straightforward but I wanted to make sure I was well prepared to input vitals, med intake and other notes without Maisy at my side over the next week.

My manager had stopped by first thing this morning and asked if I was ready to start my rotation to other units. Seeing as John Doe and Milo had been my only patients in the ER, I was more than ready. With Maisy's constant chatter and the excitement surrounding John Doe, I hadn't been bored these last few days, but I was ready to see more patients.

Georgia Rae Ellars was not made for desk work.

I was so focused on my studies, the sound of something hitting the counter made me gasp and jump.

I looked up into ice blue.

Jess.

Not yet nine o'clock in the morning, and I was only on my second cup of coffee. I didn't have the energy or sufficient caffeine levels in my body to deal with him.

"Sorry. Thought you heard me walk up," he rumbled.

I shrugged.

"Here." He slid a paper coffee cup over the counter.

It was a tall, white cup with a cardboard coffee collar, black lid and two red straws. On the side, written in green, swirly handwriting, was *Double Irish Cream Latte*.

My favorite.

I'd only splurged once this week, but I knew that green, swirly scribble was from the coffee place downtown, Maple's.

Jess had brought me my favorite coffee.

Had hell frozen over last night while I'd been sleeping?

Because that's what I figured it would take for Jess Cleary to willingly talk to me, let alone buy me a frou-frou coffee. Before I could ask, Maisy came bounding around the corner.

"Hey, Jess!"

"Maze," he said before taking a drink from his own cup.

His was labeled *Black*. Not surprising that Jess was the type of man who went to a coffee hut where you could get any number of delicious, complicated caffeinated concoctions and left with a plain, black coffee.

"Are you here to question John Doe?" Maisy asked.

"Yep. Meeting Sam here in a little bit. Thought I'd come early, bring Georgia some coffee. Visit with her before we get the okay from Carlson to head upstairs."

"Sweet," she said before disappearing behind the corner. Where she was going, I had no clue. She was supposed to be

49

sitting with me, reviewing the patient chart layout. But now that she'd abandoned me, I was stuck here with a Jess that wanted to "visit."

"Coffee's getting cold, Georgia." He leaned on the counter with his forearms.

Forearms that were tanned and sinuous. Forearms that I really wanted to touch, with veins I really wanted to trace as they snaked their way across the muscle.

Forearms I should not be thinking about.

I needed to focus. My mission? Get Jess away from my ER counter.

"Did you poison it, Sheriff?" I asked, grabbing my cup.

He chuckled but didn't answer.

The sheriff probably wouldn't poison me and more caffeine was a necessity, so I took a healthy pull.

Bliss.

"Thank you," I muttered.

I had no desire to feel indebted to Jess but also didn't want to be rude. I wasn't a rude person, normally. Something about him brought it out in me.

"So why the coffee, Sheriff? And how did you know what I liked?" My curiosity was piqued.

He smirked and took a drink from his own cup. What he didn't do was answer me.

"You do realize a smirk is not an answer."

Still no response.

"Seriously, what's going on?"

He sighed. For once, his beautiful eyes weren't glaring at me. They were kind and gentle. He could melt me with those eyes.

Damn.

"I made some wrong assumptions about your relationship with Ben. Been an asshole this week. Sorry."

Yep. Hell *had* frozen over. Why wasn't it on the news?

In less than twenty-four hours, Jess had changed personalities. He'd been utterly mean to me last night, and now here he was being nice, buying me coffee and making apologies.

I appreciated his admission but I wasn't going to let down my guard. One apology wasn't enough to erase the way he'd treated me. To make me think he was as wonderful as everyone professed him to be.

"Would you mind expanding a bit on these assumptions? I'm interested to know what type of relationship you thought I had with an eighty-one-year-old man."

His answer was a wide smile filled with perfect, straight white teeth.

During our previous and rather unpleasant encounters, I hadn't seen Jess smile. So far, I'd only gotten scowls, glares and smirks.

But damn if his smile wasn't perfect.

Shivers erupted across my skin. My cheeks flushed and there was a throbbing sensation between my thighs. My core temperature skyrocketed a couple hundred degrees.

I was hot for the town sheriff. I was hot for a man who I absolutely did not like one bit.

He didn't miss my reaction and his smile faltered. But instead of assuming the standard scowl as per usual when he caught me ogling, his gaze heated. Was he hot for me too?

He held my eyes with his intense stare, his ice-blue eyes firing. So they *did* darken when he was turned on.

The air around us was charged, hot and stuffy. I could practically see the sparks crackling between us. And the rest of the world disappeared. All I could feel was that magnetic pull.

My heart was pounding so loudly I was certain he could hear it. I held the air in my lungs so he wouldn't see me breathing hard.

This was bad.

I tore my eyes away from his and focused all of my attention on my coffee cup.

I needed to get far away from Jess Cleary. Never in my life had I felt such an intense attraction to a man. His hotness did things to me. It made my brain misfire and my body want things it hadn't craved in years. And I needed my brain fully engaged when he was around. I didn't like him, but more importantly, I didn't trust him. I couldn't be stupid enough to fall for his perfectly handsome face and amazingly sculpted body.

Nate had dazzled me with his looks. And other than giving me Rowen, I regretted everything else about my decision to be with him.

As I struggled to get control of my hormones, I felt Jess's eyes on me. Thankfully, I was saved from having to meet them again when the sound of footsteps rang in my ears. Sam was making his way toward us.

"Morning, Gigi," he said.

I smiled and wiggled my fingers in a small wave before taking another long drink of my coffee.

Sam smiled back and looked at Jess. "Carlson called me a few minutes ago and wants us to go ahead and question John Doe now. He's awake and lucid but in about an hour, Carlson's going to give him more pain meds that could knock him out for the rest of the day."

Jess nodded and Sam took it as his cue to get a move on.

But before Jess left the desk, he grinned, saying, "Back in a few, Freckles. Enjoy your coffee."

Freckles? He'd christened me with a pet name?

Oh, no. This was really, really, *really* bad.

I had no idea how long it took for the police to question the victim of an intense act of violence. Probably not long, maybe only an hour. I needed to reengage my brain, fast, and come up with an action plan to deal with this new, confusing Jess. If he was messing with me, trying to toy with me using his extreme hotness, I needed to be prepared.

I was well practiced at building walls around my heart. Leaving it raw and unsheltered was not an option with as much loss and heartbreak as I had experienced in my life. I couldn't risk letting someone come in and obliterate me. Rowen depended on me. She needed those walls just as much as I did.

So I had an hour. One hour to throw up some new brick and mortar.

———

AN HOUR AND A HALF LATER, Jess and Sam walked downstairs from the second floor where John Doe was being treated. Both men looked perplexed. Sam was speaking quietly to Jess as they rounded the corner of the stairs and headed toward Maisy and me.

Maisy had returned from her random wanderings not long after Jess had left. When I'd asked her where she had gone, she'd shrugged and smiled.

Montana people often answered questions without actually speaking.

"So what did he say? Does he know who attacked him?"

Maisy pounced on Jess and Sam as soon as they were within ten feet of the counter.

Maisy had to ask because she couldn't *not* be in everyone's business, it was just who she was. I assumed they'd give her a polite brush-off. Surely, any details regarding a crime would be kept very hush-hush.

"His name is Alex Benson," Sam said.

Then again, this was Prescott. No wonder news traveled so fast here.

"He's been traveling through Montana for the last couple of weeks to hike the national parks. Spent his first week in Glacier and was on his way to Yellowstone. Been camping out of his car by the river."

Poor John Doe. He was on vacation and had gotten beaten within an inch of his life.

"Monday night after dinner at the Dollar, he figures it was around eight or eight-thirty, a guy jumped him on the way to the bathroom. Dragged him out to the alley. The attacker started beating him, then found a broken bottle and stabbed him in the leg. He blacked out after that. Can't remember much about his attacker. Just that he was wearing a hat, sunglasses and a gray hoodie. He figured it was all for the eighty bucks in his pocket."

Maisy muttered, "Huh." I remained quiet.

"He's got holes in his story," Jess said. "We both think he knows more than he's letting on. Maybe he's lying altogether. A beating of that severity would have taken at least five minutes. Maybe ten. And it's still light out at eight o'clock. Seems strange there were no witnesses when downtown Prescott is crawling with people during the summer."

"Yeah. And the Silver Dollar isn't that big of a bar," Maisy said. "If he was jumped by the bathroom and dragged out back, he probably would have yelled or screamed for help. In a place that small, someone would have heard him. Right?"

"Right," Jess said. "My guess is he was doing something illegal and didn't want to tell us. We didn't push too hard because he's got a week or so left here before he can leave the hospital. We'll let him get some rest for a day or two. Then Sam's gonna come back and start pushing harder."

Jess turned to Sam. "When you get back to the station, get this written up. Then pull the files for the three unsolved cases we've had this summer and put them on my desk. I'd like to go over them again this afternoon."

"Sure thing, boss. You think they're related?" Sam asked, flicking his head toward the stairs.

"Don't know, but my gut's unsettled. Never had this many cases in such a short time period. And I hate that we're struggling to close them up. Feels like we're missing something bigger at play here."

"What other cases?" I asked. "Is there anything I should be concerned about?"

Both men turned to me and shook their heads but Maisy spoke up before they could.

"Oh, it's nothing to worry about, Gigi," she said. "Last month, someone broke into one of Jack Drummond's barns and stole a bunch of fertilizer. Then there was a theft at the jewelry store downtown. Someone smashed through the back window and stole, like, a bunch of silver. Most of the expensive stuff was locked up, thank goodness, but their silver was left out in the open. Oh . . . and a couple of weeks ago, Silas Grant reported trespassers on his ranch. So totally sad. Whoever it was drove through one of his pastures and hit one of his baby calves and killed it."

Before I could absorb it all, she kept going.

"I'm guessing the Drummond break-in was someone cooking meth up in the mountains and needed the chemicals. It would be pretty hard to resell stolen fertilizer. The jewelry has totally been pawned for cash. And the trespassing could have just been stupid kids driving around but I seriously doubt it. Local kids would *never* mess with Silas Grant. He's ex-military and, like, terrifying."

When she was finished, I swallowed a laugh at the look on Jess's and Sam's faces. Sam was wide-eyed, whereas Jess looked pissed.

Maisy had either missed her calling as a police detective or one of the deputies, probably Milo, had been a bit too forthcoming with information that should have stayed within the walls of the sheriff's department

I was thinking Deputy Milo Phillips was about to have a not-so-fun conversation with his boss about what was and was not appropriate to share with Maisy Holt.

"All right, I'm heading out. Gonna drive up and take a look at Mr. Benson's car. Make sure it's still at the campground. Might be able to spot something from a window to give us a lead. Meet you back at the station, Sheriff." Sam left with a two-finger wave.

Before I could excuse myself and run away from Jess—I mean, get back to work, Maisy asked, "Jess, you still eat at the café every Friday night, don't you?"

He opened his mouth but she talked right over him.

"Because Gigi was telling me earlier that she's planning on going there for dinner tonight. You know, as a celebration for making it through her first week. And, like, a break from cooking. Oh, and I told her she definitely needed to check out the homemade desserts. You guys should eat together."

My mouth fell open and I stared at her, unblinking.

Was she trying to set me up with Jackass Jess?

Yes. Yes, she was.

Maisy and I had developed a fast friendship this week, and despite our age difference, we had a lot in common. But we hadn't gotten around to discussing past relationships. She didn't know enough about me or the previous men in my life to start playing matchmaker.

Plus, she knew how I felt about Jess. The day after he wrote me that ticket, I ranted to her for a good twenty minutes about how much of an asshole I thought he was.

I shook my head. "I'm not eating with him. I'm eating with my daughter."

"I can babysit Rowen," she said. "It would give you a chance to eat with another adult. And I've been dying to meet her anyway and check out the farmhouse."

"I appreciate the offer, but Rowen doesn't know you. I don't feel comfortable with you watching her."

The second the words left my mouth, I knew they'd come out wrong.

"You don't trust me?" she whispered.

"Of course I trust you." I sighed. "It's not that you can't watch her. It's just—"

"Six-thirty," Jess announced.

At the same time I asked, "Huh?" Maisy shouted, "Great!"

"Six-thirty. I'll be at the farmhouse to pick you up. Maze is good with kids."

"I'm not going to dinner with you."

"Be ready," he said.

I opened my mouth to tell him, again, that I would not be

eating with him but he didn't give me the chance. He turned and started walking to the door.

"I'm not going!"

He kept walking but lifted a hand to wave. "Six-thirty."

I crossed my arms as he strode through the door. He was too far out of earshot for me to keep yelling. Who did he think he was? Who did he think I was? I wasn't a woman who liked to be ordered around and I certainly wasn't desperate enough for a dinner date to go out with him.

When I turned back to Maisy, she had a huge smile on her face.

"Would you mind telling me why you're playing Yente today?" I asked.

"Yente?" She tilted her head as her eyebrows came together.

"Yeah, Yente. You know, from *Fiddler on the Roof*."

Nope. Nothing.

"Yente was the matchmaker in *Fiddler on the Roof*," I said. "It's a popular musical. I'm surprised the Prescott High School drama club hasn't done a rendition. My high school did it every two years."

"Prescott High doesn't have a drama club."

"They don't?" I asked. "Never mind. Whatever. That's beside the point. Why are you pushing me to eat dinner with Jess?"

She shrugged. "He's a good guy, Gigi. Even though he was a jerk to you this week. But he called me this morning and asked what kind of coffee you liked. He told me it was going to be a peace offering."

"I appreciated the coffee and his apology, Maisy, but that doesn't mean I want to have a meal with the man."

58

Maisy's mouth turned down and she peeked at me with doe eyes from underneath her lashes.

I was not going to be able to stay mad at that face.

"I really like you, Gigi. I guess . . . I just already think of you as a friend. You guys might hit it off and that would be super cool. I mean, he's taken care of that farmhouse almost his whole life. How awesome would it be if he hooked up with you and then he could finally live there? Plus, he's way hot and a real gentleman. He could be so totally good to you. If you just give him a chance, you'll see he's not the jackass he's been pretending to be this week. I promise. He is a nice guy."

"I am really not a Jess Cleary fan. But I appreciate where you're coming from." I hoped she would drop this ludicrous idea.

"Please?" she begged. "Just consider going? I know! Don't decide yet. Like, see how your day goes and then decide tonight when he comes to pick you up. I'll still come by to hang with Rowen, just in case."

"It's not going to happen, Maisy, but you're welcome to come by," I said.

"You won't even consider dinner?"

Letting out a deep breath, I dropped my eyes to my feet to think.

I was curious why Jess had switched personalities today, and maybe over a quick meal I could figure out what his angle was. Was he trying to hook up with the new girl in town? Brag about his conquest? Could this nice-guy façade last for more than thirty minutes? I was betting it couldn't.

"We'll see," I said.

"I'll take it." A huge smile instantly replaced her sad, pathetic look.

I shook my head and changed the subject. "If you want to avoid a tirade tonight, I highly recommend not telling Rowen that Prescott doesn't have drama clubs. In Spokane, she was part of a kiddie club called Glamour Girls where a group of little girls would get together once a week and pretend to be famous actresses and singers. She has a flair for the dramatic."

Maisy smiled and pretended to zip her lips shut, then popped them back open to toss in the key and swallow it.

I giggled at the gesture and left her to finish my study of the patient charts.

An hour later, I was reading the same line for the hundredth time. With all that had happened this morning, I was having a hard time concentrating.

The crime spree in Prescott was concerning. Leaving Spokane meant leaving behind a city with a high crime rate, but now it seemed like some of the security I had been feeling just because Prescott was small and in Montana was naïve. Prescott certainly would never be as bad as Spokane, I hoped, but I would need to take more care than I had been so far with my safety and Rowen's. I hadn't even been locking the front door at night. Just because we were in rural America didn't automatically make it safe. Look at what had happened to John Doe.

The rest of the free space in my mind was swirling around Jess. If I did decide to go to dinner, what could I expect? And could I control myself around his hotness?

I had no idea why he wanted to take me to dinner. I wasn't anything special, just a single mother, trying to set up a new life for herself and her daughter. Maybe make some new friends along the way.

And Jess was in a whole different league. One where the plain and average girls, like me, didn't belong.

So why me?

Did he think a dinner was necessary to go along with the coffee he had brought me so I would forgive him?

Maisy's comment about Jess and the farmhouse got me thinking. Perhaps Jess's interest in me had more to do with my house than my panties. Maybe he was working an angle to keep the farmhouse. After all, what woman wouldn't want the dreamy sheriff to take interest in her? And he'd told me himself he loved that house.

Dinner or not, I was going to find out what Jess Cleary was up to.

CHAPTER FIVE

GIGI

Fidgeting in front of my bedroom mirror, I assessed my outfit. I had chosen one of my favorite go-to ensembles for a boost of self-confidence. I was going to need it for the inevitable face-off with Jess about dinner.

I'd chosen to wear heels with my skinny jeans and sleeveless black top. The shoes were a risk in Montana but they were me.

My hair had been pinned up in a bun today so when I took it out, it had an awesome wave.

Rowen and I had gotten our hair from my mother. In the end, Mom had lost all of her hair from chemotherapy, and after she died, I made the decision to let my hair grow long, at least past my waist. I never wanted to take for granted how lucky I was to have it, and how lucky I was that every day I could look in the mirror and get a glimpse of something Mom had given me.

And tonight, it looked a lot like hers when it had been long.

I straightened my shoulders and held my chin high, inhaling and exhaling a deep breath.

But my shoulders slumped. The nerves pooling in my stomach indicated that I'd chosen the wrong outfit.

Who cared what I was wearing for a five-minute conversation with Jess to tell him I wasn't going to the café with him?

Me. I always cared about what I was wearing.

My clothes helped me deal with my insecurities. I wasn't super-model gorgeous and I could stand to lose ten pounds—or more as Rowen's father had been certain to inform me. But the one thing he'd never done was ridicule my clothes. And when I stepped out in a killer outfit, I felt good. More sure of myself.

"Stop overreacting, Gigi," I told my reflection. "Step away from the mirror."

Giving myself a sure nod, I followed my own orders.

At six o'clock on the dot, Maisy arrived with a huge plastic tub in her arms. She informed me it was her "babysitting kit" that she had used all through high school.

"You look hot!" she said. "All ready for dinner?"

"I'm not going."

She smirked. "Right. That's why you're all dressed up. Sweet necklace, by the way."

"Maybe I want to look cute when I tell Jess to take a hike?"

"We'll see how that works out for you," she said.

Roe came skipping into the entryway. "Hi! Are you Maisy?"

"Yep. And you must be the beautiful Rowen I've heard so much about."

Rowen smiled as her eyes landed on the tub. "Did you bring me a present?"

"Well . . . it's not a present. But it's totally full of fun stuff we can do together. As soon as your mom leaves, we'll dig into it, okay?"

"I'm not leaving."

Maisy's mouth formed a mischievous one-sided grin.

"Mommy, can I show Maisy my room?" Rowen asked.

"Sure, baby girl. How about we give Maisy a tour of the whole house?"

"Yay! I'll give the tour," she shouted and led us around for the next twenty minutes.

———

"I DON'T THINK dinner is such a good idea," I said from the top step of the porch.

Jess's foot had just landed on the bottom step.

Maisy was keeping Rowen inside. I didn't see any reason to introduce her to Jess since I was getting rid of him and he'd never be here again.

Not responding to my declaration, Jess assessed my body from top to toe. As his eyes lingered on my curves, my temperature started to rise. I shifted my weight back and forth between my feet, and my fingers pulled at the hem of my shirt.

I could feel the burn of his gaze on my legs. When he met my stare, his eyes were heated. My outfit was definitely a success.

My belly fluttered as we stared at each other and I fought to pull my eyes away from his.

He was still wearing his sheriff garb and was no less breathtaking. Who would have known a tan, colorless shirt could look so good?

What would he look like without the shirt? The mental image made me shiver.

"You're going," Jess finally said, breaking the heated moment. "Even if that means I have to pick you up and carry you to the truck."

"You wouldn't dare," I hissed.

"Try me."

My hands fisted on my hips. "I'm not going."

Jess jumped up the steps and came right into my space, forcing me backward. Then he bent down so his nose was centimeters from my own.

I was expecting him to order me again or actually pick me up and carry me away. So his voice, gentle and soft, caught me off guard.

"Georgia, give me a chance to show you that I'm not the asshole I've been this week. Please?"

It was the "please" that did it. I had a feeling Jess didn't say that word much.

"Fine," I whispered, taking another step back.

I couldn't think when he was that close to me. The intoxicating, clean, fresh scent from his skin made me woozy.

Rushing inside, I said a quick good-bye to Rowen and a smugly smiling Maisy. Then I hurried back outside, dipping my chin so I could watch my feet as I walked to the truck. In the three minutes he'd been here, I was already fumbling to keep my cool.

My fingers brushed the truck's door handle but were

held back when Jess gripped my elbow, gently pulling my arm away so he could open the door for me.

When his fingers touched my skin, a current jolted through me from my elbow through my arm and down to my feet.

He must have felt something too because he pulled in a sharp, short breath and didn't make another move to open the door. Instead, he moved his body closer to mine until just an inch separated us. All I had to do was turn slightly and my chest would be pressed against his.

Before I did something stupid, like wrap my arms around his neck and crush my lips to his, I murmured a quiet thank-you and stepped back. He opened the door and I hopped inside, taking a few long breaths while he jogged around the hood.

We drove to town in silence. Usually I would have tried to make idle conversation but I had no idea what to say. My elbow was still tingling and the sexual tension between us was stifling in the confines of the truck.

Thankfully, the drive was short and soon we were at the café.

"I'll have the special, please," I said to the waitress at the café, handing her my menu.

"Same. Side of ranch too. Thanks, Tina." Jess didn't have a menu. Tina hadn't even brought one over for him.

We were seated in a booth at the front window of the Prescott Café, looking out over Main Street, having both just ordered the chicken fajita wrap with shoestring fries.

Booths hugged three walls of the Prescott Café while square tables filled in the middle. At the back, stools lined the counter that separated the kitchen from the restaurant floor. About three-quarters of the café was full of patrons.

From my seat in the booth, I could see the cook working away in the kitchen behind the counter and the five-tiered display case of pies and cakes next to the register. My eyes had zeroed in on the chocolate cake on tier two when Jess mumbled, "Jesus."

"What?"

He tipped his head toward the window. An older couple was standing right outside, staring down at us. When I faced them, they both smiled and the man winked. I wasn't sure what to do but they seemed friendly, so I smiled back and gave them a tiny wave with my fingers.

"You're not helping, Georgia."

"What? They seem nice. Do you know them?" I asked.

"Seth Balan and his wife. Seth's part of the Coffee Club. You and your little wave there are gonna be the only topic at Club tomorrow morning."

"Ah . . . what's the Coffee Club?"

"Local group of old men who meet here every day for coffee. When they're not talking about grain prices or the cattle market, they gossip worse than a bunch of teenage girls. Any time I need to know what's going around town about something, I come to Club to get the scoop. You sitting here with me, looking like that, it's all they'll talk about tomorrow."

"So what? They'll talk about how I ate dinner with you once? That doesn't seem so bad," I said.

He sighed and leaned forward. "I don't eat with anyone on Friday nights, Freckles. Anyone. I prefer to sit alone and been doing it that way for years. You're new in town. You're beautiful, especially in those jeans and shoes. And you're in my booth. By nine-thirty tomorrow morning, everyone in town will know about you and me."

"Oh." I blushed and looked at the table.

There was a lot in that statement for me to process. Me being the hot topic at tomorrow's old-crony gossip group. Jess eating alone every Friday night. Jess thinking I was beautiful. Him noticing my jeans and shoes.

It was sweet and it made me feel good. So good my belly fluttered.

Not once since he'd arrived at the farmhouse tonight had I gotten the impression he was faking anything, putting on a show or hiding ulterior motives. In fact, Jess didn't seem the type of man who would be fake about anything. And if that was true, maybe I was reading him all wrong. Maybe his apology this morning had been sincere.

But I wasn't ready to stop being cautious. We hadn't spent enough time together for me to get a good sense of his intentions or to forgive him for how he had acted toward me earlier in the week.

My best course of action would be a subject change. "How long have you been sheriff?"

"Going on five years."

"So you were pretty young when you got elected. That's impressive. You're, what, thirty-three, thirty-four?"

"Thirty-four. You?"

"Thirty-one."

"What's your family think about you moving to the middle of Montana?" he asked.

"Well . . . ah . . . I don't really have any family. My mom passed away a few years ago. My dad died when I was young."

"Sorry," he said.

"It's okay. My mom was amazing. I rarely felt like I was missing out by not having a big family."

"How'd she pass, if you don't mind me asking?"

"Breast cancer."

"Sorry," he repeated.

I just shrugged. Talking about my mother and her battle with cancer was not a topic I wanted to get into during dinner.

He didn't say anything for a few moments but then he reached out with his hand and covered mine on the table. The gesture was so kind a lump formed in my throat.

"It's okay," I said. "How about we change the subject to something lighter? We don't want the old-crony gossip group to see the first dinner companion you've had on a Friday night in years start sobbing at the table because she was talking about her dead mother."

"Old-crony gossip group?" He chuckled.

"By far a better name than the Coffee Club."

That earned me a smile. A smile that I couldn't help but return. A smile that sent a warm wave of happy through my body, from the top of my head to the tips of my toes.

The rest of our dinner conversation was casual and easy. Never once did I get the feeling Jess was playing an angle or that he was just putting in his time until he could get me into bed. He was genuine. And being together felt comfortable. Relaxed. Natural.

Jess told me about growing up in Prescott. He had lived here his whole life except for his time at the police academy. The previous sheriff had retired, leaving behind a team of deputies whose average tenure was twenty-five years. As most of them were looking forward to their own retirement, Sam and Jess were the only viable local candidates. Sam had no desire to go for the position so Jess had entered the election, racing against a man from Idaho.

Another thing I was learning about Prescott: There was a clear divide between the locals and everyone else. Though the community was welcoming, outsiders were treated with a bit of apprehension. It came as no surprise that the people of Jamison County had chosen to elect the hometown high school football hero even though his out-of-state rival had possessed more experience in law enforcement.

We both smiled and laughed a lot through dinner. Jess had a dry sense of humor and a sharp wit. We teased each other with harmless jests, and by the end of our meal, he'd almost made me forget about the jackass he'd been earlier in the week. Almost.

Jess insisted on paying and I didn't argue after I made an initial reach for my purse. After years of eating out with Ben, I'd learned that manly men paid. The end. And Jess, much like Ben, was a manly man.

Stepping outside the café, Jess asked, "You been downtown yet?"

"Not really. I'd love to wander around a bit. Do you have time?"

He nodded and we set off to stroll up and down Main Street.

"Are you going to make it in those shoes?" he asked after we'd been walking for five minutes.

"Absolutely. I love my heels and they love me back. I could walk for miles."

His eyebrows lifted in disbelief but he didn't comment. He just swung out a hand so I could keep walking by.

Even though most of the shops were closed, it was nice to peer into their windows and get a better sense of what Prescott had to offer. There were a few clothing stores.

Another with kitchen gadgets and fancy oils. A fly-fishing shop. An old-fashioned drugstore.

We walked mostly in comfortable silence along the sidewalk. I liked that we didn't need to fill every second with conversation.

The farther we strolled, the more I had to remind myself not to reach out and hold his hand, something I wanted to do so badly that I finally tucked my hand into my pocket so it wouldn't get a mind of its own.

Strolling back to his truck on the opposite side of the street, we passed the door to the Claim Jumper, Prescott's second bar. Two men pushed their way outside and bumped right into me, sending me stumbling backward into Jess's arms. He caught me at the hips, both hands steadying me.

"I've got you." He held me until I regained my footing.

"Shit. Sorry," one of the men said.

I was about to say it was okay when Jess rumbled, "Wes."

He didn't sound at all happy to be seeing this Wes guy.

"Well, well, well. If it isn't the sheriff," Wes said.

"Been trying to get ahold of you for a few weeks. Need to talk, Wes."

"Mom told me you left a couple messages at the house. Kinda busy right now," Wes said, dismissing Jess and turning to me.

"Hey there, darlin'. Wes Drummond." He gave me a crooked smile before sliding a bit too close into my personal space.

Wes was good-looking. Blond with light brown eyes. Not as tall or broad as Jess. Not as hot as Jess, but good-looking. I was betting most women would swoon if not currently being held up by the town sheriff.

But Wes's eyes were glassy and he had a menacing presence. Arrogant. Maybe even a bit dangerous. His movements were too confident and cocky.

I hated cocky. Rowen's father was cocky.

"Gigi," I said, hesitantly shaking Wes's hand. Jess radiated tension behind me, and his fingers dug into my hips the second Wes touched my hand.

"Nice to meet you, Gigi. You must be passing through if you're with Brick. He always gets the pretty tourists. But since Prescott's Good Prince here will probably be done with you after the night, you come find me. We'll have some real fun before you leave town," he said with a smug grin.

At this point, Jess lost all calm and pushed me behind him to step in Wes's face. I backed away, intimidated by Jess's aggressive movements. At any moment, he was going to pummel Wes Drummond.

Jess spoke to Wes in a low and menacing tone. "Off-limits, Wes."

Wes retreated a few steps, raising both his hands in surrender, but the smirk stayed on his face. "Take it easy, Brick. Didn't mean to offend her. She's a sweet piece, man. Can see why you'd stake your claim."

A sweet piece? *Asshole.*

Jess fisted his hands twice and advanced on Wes. I braced, sure that at any moment one of Jess's fists was going to fly up into Wes's face.

Thankfully, Wes's friend grabbed one of his arms and pulled him back a foot.

"Let's go, Wes," his friend said, still jerking him away.

Wes grinned at me one last time, then raised his eyebrows to Jess before finally leaving.

Before he was out of earshot, Jess called his name.

"We're gonna talk. Soon. Be best if you came in for that discussion. You won't like it if I have to come find you."

Wes didn't respond to Jess's threat. Instead, he glared at him and then turned his eyes to me. "See you around, Gigi."

My feet were frozen in place on the sidewalk. That scene had been intense. I stayed back from Jess, hoping a little space would help him cool off. The rage still poured off his body in waves.

After a few moments, I unlocked my feet and gently placed a hand on Jess's back.

"Are you okay?"

"Yep," he clipped. "Let's go."

He grabbed my hand and towed me back to his truck, pulling me at such a rapid pace I had to jog to keep up with his long strides. When we reached the truck, he hoisted me into the passenger seat and slammed my door shut.

I stayed quiet as we headed out of town, unsure what to say. But once we started down the county roads, Jess broke the silence.

"You see him again, you head the other direction. He's into some bad shit. I don't want you around him."

"Uh . . . okay."

What the hell had I just stumbled into?

Jess sensed my unease. "Don't stress about it. Just want you to be careful, okay? Word gets around town that we're dating, he'll know folks will be looking out for you and he'll back off. It's not about you. He's just trying to get to me."

I was more than a little nervous that someone into "bad shit" was interested in using me to piss off Jess. But on top of that, I was now freaked that Jess thought we were dating. Even though we'd had a nice dinner, I hadn't decided if I even liked him yet.

"Okay. I'll avoid Wes. No problem. But one thing . . . I'd appreciate it if you wouldn't tell people we're an item. It was nice of you to take me to dinner and I had a good time, but I don't think we'll be dating."

"Do you find me attractive?"

"Uh . . ."

"I thought so," he said. "Already told you tonight you were beautiful. So since we've got some major fucking chemistry and we get along, how about we cut the bullshit and see where this goes?"

I took a moment to collect my thoughts and formulate a response. "Physical attraction is not a great foundation for a relationship. Again, thank you for dinner. But with the exception of tonight, so far you have spent more time insulting me than treating me nicely. Surely you can understand why I don't think we'd be a good pair. Let's call it quits after you drop me off."

"I apologized and I meant it. I was an asshole this week. Now fucking get over it."

"Are you trying to piss me off, Sheriff?" I said. "I don't like your tone. You don't get to order me around and make the decision we're dating without my agreement. That's absurd. It doesn't work like that."

"It does. And we are. Exclusively, Georgia," he said, glancing over at me as he stressed his last point.

"Wait a minute. Let me get this straight," I said, the hold on my temper loosening. "Not only did you just ignore me but you also felt the need to emphasize that our nonexistent relationship is exclusive. Something that if you knew me at all, you would never have had to emphasize because, in any relationship, I have never been nor will ever be a cheater."

Jess pulled in a deep breath and let it out slowly. "Not

saying you're a cheater. Jesus, Georgia, relax. Just saying we're exclusively together. Don't want people around town thinking we're just friends or we're just fooling around. We're gonna see where this goes."

"We've had one kind-of date, Jess. And I wouldn't call us friends."

"Because we're not just friends."

"I'm not dating you. I don't even like you. Find someone else to keep you company at the café."

"You like me. Can see it in your eyes when you look at me."

"Physically, yes. But personally, you're a jackass."

He yanked the truck to the side of the road.

"What are you—" I started but Jess reached across the cab, grabbed me at the back of the neck and slammed his mouth down on mine.

I wanted to protest, I really did. To push him away and assert myself so he knew that he couldn't just dazzle me with his looks and muddle me with his kisses.

But he totally could.

And the jackass knew it too.

At first, his lips were hard as he unloaded his frustration into the kiss. Because I was mid-sentence, my mouth was open, so he took the opportunity to push his tongue inside. Frozen for a moment, I sat there as he ravaged my mouth with his tongue.

But once the initial shock passed, I melted into him, my fingers trailing across his forearms, feeling the muscles I had been longing to touch.

We kissed for a while, me leaning across the console, until the space was too much and he reached over and unbuckled my seat belt. Then he pulled me across the cab, never once breaking his mouth away from mine.

Settling onto his lap, my legs straddled his muscled thighs. The air in the truck was scorching. Our tongues dueled and our teeth nipped at each other's lips. His hands framed my face to pull me closer and I slanted my head so he could have full access to my mouth.

I framed his neck with my hands as we went at each other with abandon for what felt like hours. His hands traveled from my face to my shoulders, down to my ribs, barely grazing my breasts before settling on my hips. He pulled me even tighter into him and as his hardness pressed against my core, wave after wave of heat pulsed through my body.

We broke away at the sound of a passing vehicle, our heads flying up to watch the car streak by. I was struggling to catch my breath and my heart was still pounding when I turned back to look down at Jess.

"Damn, baby. You can kiss," he said.

I let my head fall forward so my forehead was resting on his. I could not believe that just happened. I just kissed the most perfectly handsome man I had ever seen in my life and it was effing incredible, like nothing I had ever felt before.

"We're gonna see where this goes between us." A smile tugged at the corners of his mouth.

"Okay." I mean, what else was there to say? That kiss was life changing. From now until the end of my life, I would compare all first kisses with his. And I doubted any man in my future would ever measure up.

He lifted me at the waist and I climbed back into my seat, still dizzy.

I wasn't sure exactly what to make of Jess. He was a lot all rolled into one confusing hot guy. He'd been a gentleman. He'd been playful at dinner, teasing me and making me laugh. When confronted with Wes, he'd acted as my protector.

But then as soon as I had disagreed with him, he'd turned into a jackass. Ordering me around. Not listening to what I was telling him. And instead of talking it all out, he'd manhandled me onto his lap and kissed the living daylights out of me.

Not that I was complaining about the kiss. I'd be okay with one of those every day for the rest of my life.

Damn.

Why had I let him kiss me? I shouldn't have let him win the argument. I should have pushed away. I was effing confused.

I had hoped that by going to dinner with Jess, I would have a better idea of what he was up to. Learn more about his ever-changing moods. Unfortunately, I hadn't learned a thing except what I had already suspected. Jess and I had some major chemistry.

As we turned onto the gravel drive, he said, "Need to come out and do the mowing tomorrow."

"No, that's okay. I've got a mower and can take care of it. There's no need for you to continue taking care of the farmhouse."

"Be there some time in the afternoon to take care of it. Around three or four. It'll make me mad if you do it before I get there."

"Really, I can do it."

He grabbed my hand off my lap and laced his fingers between mine. "I am doing the lawn. Just let me take care of it, okay? Cook me dinner as a thank-you."

"Fine. If you want to get all sweaty and gross mowing my lawn, be my guest," I said.

Wait. What?

I'd given in again! Not that I wanted to mow the lawn. But two disagreements in a row, and he'd gotten his way.

Usually I had much more willpower. What was wrong with me? It had to be the kiss. My head was still fuzzy. I needed to make sure I didn't let him kiss me again. But I really wanted him to. Quickly, I thought of an excuse. If I gave into the mowing, I couldn't give in to dinner.

"I don't want to have a sitter two nights in a row, so we'll have to do dinner another time," I said.

"You got a problem with me meeting your kid?" he asked.

"It's a bit early. We've only gone out once."

"Right. Dinner tomorrow after I mow. You can decide between now and then how to introduce me to your kid. Either as the town sheriff or something more. Your kid, your call. But as far as the rest of the town is concerned, we're more."

I was definitely still messed up from our kiss because once again, even though I had just told myself to stay strong, I didn't put up any kind of a fight. I just whispered, "Okay."

CHAPTER SIX

GIGI

The next morning, I was consumed with worry, wondering if Jess coming over was a mistake. Never once had I brought a man home to meet Rowen.

I hadn't really dated since she was born. When she was a toddler, I'd been set up on two blind dates that had gone so badly, I'd vowed never to be set up again. Since then, I hadn't met anyone worth seeing. Until Jess.

He showed up around four that afternoon in his non-work uniform of a white T-shirt, jeans, tennis shoes and a faded green baseball hat. Rowen sprinted out the front door and practically attacked him the second he stepped foot outside his truck.

"Are you a police officer?" she asked, bouncing around his legs.

He chuckled. "Yep. I'm the sheriff."

"That is *so* cool! Do you catch bad guys and put them in jail?"

"Sometimes."

Before she could ask her next question, I interrupted, "Rowen, what do we do when we meet new people?"

She looked at me for a second before sticking her little hand out to Jess and reciting, "Hi. My name is Rowen. Nice to meet you."

Jess took her hand in his. "I'm Jess. Nice to meet you too, Rowen."

"How does jail work?" she asked, cocking her head to the side.

He smiled at her without answering and then gave me a quick peck on the cheek. Just that little kiss and I was woozy again, swaying a little as I shifted weight from one foot to the other.

Damn.

Jess turned back to Rowen and gave her his undivided attention, answering all her questions regarding jail, bad guys, speeding tickets, badges and police cars. I finally had to pull her away so he could get to work on mowing and we could go inside to start on dinner.

Roe selected the dinner menu of hot dogs wrapped in Grands biscuits, Velveeta shells and cheese, green beans (my requirement) and watermelon.

Dinner conversation was light and easy. Rowen peppered Jess with her "why" questions and when I could finally get a word in edgewise, I asked, "Roe, did you know that Papa Ben was friends with Jess?"

She gave me a long stare but didn't respond.

Turning back to Jess, she said, "I go to Quail Hollow and my teacher's name is Miss Billie."

Jess and I shared a look. It wasn't lost on him that her reaction to Ben's mention was odd.

I shrugged and let her change the subject. I wasn't going to press. Not tonight.

After dinner, Roe showed Jess all around the farmhouse.

I remembered the look he had given me the night I handed him Ben's letter. The disapproving glare he'd had when I sat on the swing. So all through the tour, I watched him closely, seeing if I could catch a glimpse of the same behavior. I was eyeing him so intently that I tripped twice.

But not once did he let on that he knew the house better than she or I did. And I never got the impression that he felt like we were intruding on his space. That he should have been living here instead of us.

Was I reading too much into Maisy's comment about Jess living at the farmhouse? Regardless, I wasn't ready to trust Jess. His actions earlier in the week had left a mark.

I had given Nate my trust after one night. A colossal mistake. Until I could say with confidence that Jess was not a jackass, I was on high alert.

Around eight o'clock, Jess announced it was time for him to be heading home. Roe and I walked him to his truck, where he knelt to say good-bye to my girl. He caught her chin between his thumb and the side of his index finger.

"I had fun getting to know you tonight, Rowen."

She gave him a wide, beaming smile and turned to me. "He's like a prince from my movies. Can Jess be your boyfriend, Mommy?"

"Ah . . . we'll see."

It should have made me happy that he was so good with her. That she liked him. And deep down, it did. My heart swelled with warm and fuzzy feelings because he was so sweet to her.

But on the surface I was annoyed. My own daughter had just foiled my plans.

I'd been planning to keep some distance between Jess and Roe, using her as an excuse to control the speed of our relationship. I'd be unavailable for dinner dates because Roe had this or that going on. I'd be busy on the weekend taking Roe out and about. But now that she'd declared her wish for Jess to be my boyfriend, he'd see through all of my excuses.

Jess stood and gave me a knowing grin. "Yeah. We'll see."

Unlike my response, it was not a deflection of her question. His was a challenge. He was daring me to try and keep up my walls, block him out. The defiant and determined look in his eyes told me that no matter how many barriers I put in his path, he'd crash them all down.

Roe and I stood watching his truck as he drove it down the lane. She waved like a crazy person at his taillights until he was no longer in sight.

She was completely smitten.

And if I was being honest with myself, so was I.

But I wasn't going to be honest with myself. I was going to keep up my guard, just in case.

Over the next two weeks, Jess and I fell into a comfortable routine.

Phone calls to say hello. Texts to check in. Quick lunches if we both had the time. Dinners at the farmhouse one or two nights a week. Rowen, Jess and I at the café on Friday nights.

Everything I learned about him made me like him more. What Ben, Maisy and Milo had said about him was true. He was a good man.

But I still had reservations about our relationship.

I was just waiting for the inevitable. For him to realize that he could do so much better. He had a good job, was loved by his community and was the most perfectly handsome man I'd ever laid eyes on. I was just . . . me.

I had to be missing something. Maybe if I'd had more dating experience, I would have been able to see past his charming demeanor and beautiful face. But as it was, I hadn't a clue.

I'd slept with Rowen's father because of his charisma. That, and I'd been lonely. At the time, my mother's treatments hadn't been working and when I wasn't at work, I was taking care of her. It had been extremely stressful and emotionally draining. So when a hot guy dressed in an expensive tux had started showering me with affection, I had believed he was sincere. It wasn't until after we'd had sex that Nate showed his true colors.

At least with Jess, I had maintained some sexual distance. The most we'd been doing was kissing.

Every day I reminded myself to proceed carefully. To put some distance between us. To take a step back so I could more objectively judge Jess's character.

But the trouble was, I couldn't stay away.

Maybe once I got to know him a little bit more, I'd be able to make sense of Jess Cleary.

And I told myself that when he did dump me, it wouldn't hurt that much.

———

THE FARMHOUSE PROPERTY included twenty acres in total. Since I didn't know what type of creatures roamed the wild areas of Montana, Rowen and I had limited our outdoor explorations to the areas where the grass was short. And I had only spent a few minutes in the barn.

Today I was cleaning it out so I could park the Explorer in there this winter. Eventually I wanted a garage but this year, it wasn't in the budget.

The barn was an old building. The wood siding had long since lost its original color and was now a battered shade of gray with small patches of brown too stubborn to fade. Rust splotches from old nails dotted the boards.

I heaved open a large paneled door and assessed the room. The main area was spacious and empty. Filthy, but otherwise bare. My sandaled feet were dusty from the inch of dirt covering the floor and my nose was scrunched from the musty smell.

At the back of the barn was an old stall I presumed was built to keep a horse.

I decided that was where I'd start my cleaning. The small stack of moldy, rotting hay bales in the corner was likely the cause of the smell.

Along the stall's walls were rows of leather straps and ropes. I knew nothing about horses so they were either for riding or bondage. The image of Ben practicing bondage jumped into my head involuntarily and I gagged.

I struggled to picture happy thoughts. Anything to replace the icky image in my mind's eye.

I was so focused on lollipops, unicorns, butterflies and rainbows, I wasn't paying too much attention to anything else. When I bent to pull a moldy bale away from the wall, I heard a quick hiss, which was followed by a sharp, blinding pain in my right forearm.

What the hell? That effing hurt!

I gasped and pulled my arm to my chest as a rattlesnake darted out in front of me. I stumbled backward and nearly fell on my ass.

Oh my god, there is a rattlesnake in the barn!
Holy shit! You just got bit by a rattlesnake!

It was probably about three feet long and as wide as a baseball bat. In the second it took me to realize what had happened to my arm, it had slithered into the corner and coiled in on itself. Its head was poised a foot off the ground, hissing through hideous fangs dripping venom. Its tail was sticking straight in the air, rattling with abandoned fury.

It was warning me that it was ready to strike again.

And it didn't need to warn me twice.

I regained my footing and backed out of the stall, then whipped around and ran toward the barn doors as fast as my flip-flopped feet could go.

Did snakes chase people? Running as fast as I could, I cursed myself for choosing flip-flops instead of tennis shoes. Because of my poor footwear selection, I was going to be eaten by the biggest rattlesnake on the planet.

I hit the barn door and glanced over my shoulder.

I relaxed marginally when I saw it wasn't chasing me.

My arm was really starting to throb and blood was running toward my fingers. It was either the poison or the adrenaline coursing through my veins, but my vision started to blur and my head was swimming.

I needed to get it together. I needed to get to the hospital. I needed to slow down my heart rate so the poison wouldn't spread too fast.

I needed to *breathe*.

So I forced myself to take two extremely long and slow breaths before moving away from the barn and walking straight to the house.

By some miracle, I'd had the foresight to keep Rowen out of the barn while I was cleaning. She was currently reenacting *Sleeping Beauty* with a couple of dolls in the front yard.

"Rowen!" I screamed, rushing toward the house.

She looked at me and knew instantly something was very, very wrong. A look of sheer terror came over her face and she went ghostly white.

I was clutching my arm to cover the bite mark but my face was pale and my eyes were wide. I wasn't hiding my fears from her.

"Get in the car, baby girl," I said as calmly as I could, which meant it came out shaky and a little too loud.

"Mommy?" Her lower lip started to quiver and tears started pooling in her eyes.

"I'm okay, sweetie. Just do as I say, okay? Quick, get in the car and buckle yourself into your seat."

She nodded and I passed her running to the car as I jogged into the house. I took two seconds in the entryway to stop and think through what I needed.

Keys. Purse. Phone.

I grabbed them all and hightailed it back to the car. After glancing over my shoulder to confirm Roe was strapped in, I threw the car in drive and flew down the driveway to the hospital.

I didn't freak out. I didn't cry.

I just drove. Fast.

———

"ALL SET, GIGI. TRY AND RELAX."

"Thanks, Everett."

He had just finished putting an IV into my arm that would administer an anti-venom plus some morphine for the pain. The puncture marks on my arm were covered with gauze and I was praying they wouldn't leave much of a scar.

Because every time I thought about that snake, I shivered. To say I was terrified of snakes was an understatement. Bugs, rodents, heights. Totally fine by me.

Snakes?

No thank you.

I didn't want to be reminded of this incident for years because of two circular scars.

I'd been in the ER for about ten minutes and was going to need to sit there and let the medications do their work for an hour.

Ida was working in the ER today, and since it was slow, she'd taken Roe to get a snack and walk around a bit while Everett tended to me. He was the weekend's on-call doctor and luckily, he was already in the building when I arrived so I hadn't waited long to be treated.

This was a very good thing. Because I had firmly held it together on the drive into town and when explaining my situation to Ida, but as I was getting set up in the ER bed, the adrenaline was leaving my system and pain was taking the spotlight.

My fraying ends were going to unravel soon and I didn't want to scare Rowen more than I already had.

She was a trooper, my girl. I was absolutely getting that karaoke machine she'd been begging me for. The least I could do to reward her for such a stoic show was listen to her sing *Frozen* songs on loop for endless hours each night. Torture for me, yes, but today she'd earned it.

Since Rowen still wasn't back, I decided to close my eyes for a minute. No sooner had my top lid hit the bottom than a pounding noise rang in my ears.

Not a headache.

I opened my eyes to see an extremely unhappy Jess storming down the hallway.

Destination? Me.

He stopped a few feet into the ER bay, gave me a once-over and planted his hands on his hips. Today, he had traded his white T-shirt for a navy one. It made his eyes appear even bluer than normal. Blue, but very pissed off.

"She okay?" he asked Everett.

"She'll be fine. I'll get out of your way and she can give you the details," Everett answered, then scurried out of the room.

Coward.

Jess turned back to me and removed his hands from his hips to cross them over his chest.

"Where's Rowen?" he asked.

"She's at home, cleaning the house and baking a cake."

Jess's eyes narrowed and I swear steam started to roll from the top of his head.

"Kidding. She's right behind you."

I made a mental note not to joke with Jess when he was angry.

He swung around to see Roe walking up to us with Ida.

When she saw him, Roe ran the last few feet toward him and jumped into his arms.

Neither Jess nor Rowen said anything for a few moments. He just held her as she burrowed her face into his shoulder and wrapped her little legs as far around his waist as they could stretch.

To my knowledge, Roe hadn't ever hugged Jess, so a running leap into a full-body embrace meant my baby girl was one hundred percent freaked way the hell out.

"You okay, little bit?" he asked softly in her ear.

She nodded and unwrapped her arms from his neck, leaning toward me.

Jess deposited her onto my lap and I cradled her with my good arm.

"Everything is going to be okay. I'll be good as new, really soon. Promise," I whispered. "You were my brave girl. I'm proud of you."

"That was scary, Mommy."

"I know, sweetie. I'm sorry."

"Can we go home?" she asked.

"Soon. I need to sit here for a while so the medicine can do its job and make me feel better. Then we'll go home. Maybe we should get some pizza for dinner? And ice cream?"

She gave me a small smile and nodded. "Chocolate ice cream."

"You got it."

"Time to explain, Georgia," Jess said.

I sighed and squeezed Roe a bit closer. "I was in the barn cleaning out the back stall. There was a rattlesnake behind one of those old hay bales. I wasn't paying attention, so when I grabbed the hay bale to throw it out, it bit me."

Thinking about it sent a new wave of shudders through my body. Rowen tensed on my lap as she got chills of her own.

"I'm never going in the barn again." Tears filled my eyes.

"Me either," Rowen said.

Jess's anger vanished at the sight of my tears and he moved into us, putting a hand around the back of my neck.

"I'll take care of the barn. And the snake. Make sure it's safe," he said.

I sniffled and blinked a couple of times before the tears could fall.

"That's sweet, Jess. But I really don't think I can ever go in there again. Snakes scare the crap out of me. That place is tainted forever. Can you board the doors closed?" I asked. "Oh, wait! Let's burn it down instead. We can roast marshmallows and make s'mores in the fire."

He grinned and squeezed his hand at my neck. "Fire season, baby. Think Nick at the fire department would frown upon the sheriff lighting up a barn and causing a prairie fire."

"Oh . . . dang. Then let's lock up the doors, and this winter, I'll be sure to leave a burning cigarette or twelve out there. I don't smoke but that gives me five or six months to start."

"Not a big fan of kissing an ashtray, Freckles. How about you don't worry about the barn right now?" he asked.

"Fine."

Not thinking about the barn was a very good idea. But he was dreaming if he thought I'd ever go back in there. That barn was as good as gone. As soon as I could afford it, I was hiring someone to tear it down. Then I was going to build a garage and stock it full of mongoose babies. Because anyone who'd ever read *Rikki-Tikki-Tavi* as a child knew a mongoose would take care of snakes. So I was buying a lot of mongooses for my new garage, assuming that a mongoose could live in Montana, of course.

He dropped his hand from my neck. "How much longer do you need to stay here?"

"Forty-five minutes, give or take a few," I said after looking at the wall clock.

"Right," he said. "C'mon, Roe. We've got a few things to do while your mom finishes here."

"What things?" Rowen and I asked in unison.

"Gotta get my truck to the farmhouse so I can drive you home in your car. Pick up pizza and chocolate ice cream. Those things. Where are your keys?"

"Jess—" I started but he interrupted me.

"Got narcotics in that drip?" He tipped his head to my IV tower.

"Uh . . . yeah."

"Then you're not driving. And Roe can't ride in my truck without her booster seat."

He had a point.

"Keys are in my purse. And some cash in my wallet for dinner," I said.

He just gave me a look.

"Roe, go grab the keys," he told her.

He shook his head at me and lifted both hands to frame the sides of my face.

"Worried about you, baby," he murmured before leaning in and giving me a soft, gentle kiss on the lips.

I raised the hand on my unbitten arm and placed it on his at my cheek.

"I'm okay."

He nodded and kissed me lightly on the nose, then took Rowen's hand.

His gesture was so sweet, so perfect, it overwhelmed me with emotion. So far I hadn't let myself cry, but now I had a lump in my throat and I knew it was a matter of seconds before I couldn't contain the tears.

With the sight of Jess and my daughter walking away from me, hand in hand to do their "things," I let go.

CHAPTER SEVEN

GIGI

J ess and Rowen arrived to pick me up from the hospital while I was signing my discharge papers. We rode home with a pepperoni pizza, a mixed green salad and a pint of chocolate ice cream in the back. While Rowen gave me a play-by-play of the last forty-five minutes, Jess held my hand on the center console the whole trip home.

Bryant, one of his deputies, had helped Jess transfer his truck to the farmhouse. Roe had learned that Bryant had two kids. His daughter was six, close to Rowen's age, and Bryant had invited her to come over for a weekend sleepover (as long as it was okay with me, of course).

I gave her the go-ahead and promised to get ahold of Bryant's wife and set it up soon. This had evoked a wailing scream of glee from the back seat as we drove home.

The terror from earlier was nearly forgotten. My girl was happy in the back and Jess was holding my hand. Things had started to right themselves in my world and my fraying ends were twisting back together.

"Do you know who that is?" I asked Jess after dinner.

I was standing in the living room watching a large black truck pull up to the house.

"Yep," he said with no further explanation as we all made our way outside.

Our visitor was tall and attractive. His blond hair was sticking out from beneath a dirty brown baseball hat. He was leaner than Jess but about the same height.

"Georgia, this is Silas Grant. Silas, my girls Gigi and Rowen," he said.

"Nice to meet you, Silas," I said while trying to remember where I'd heard his name before.

I'd met and heard about so many people since we moved to Prescott, I couldn't place it immediately. Finally it dawned on me. He was the rancher whose calf had been killed mysteriously and the man Maisy described as "ex-military and, like, terrifying."

She obviously knew more about him than I did because at first glance, terrifying was hardly the word that came to mind. In fact, his dark brown eyes, pointed at my Roe, might have been some of the kindest I'd ever seen.

Silas opened the tailgate to his truck, revealing a large box.

"What's in there?" Rowen asked.

From the box, Silas lifted out a huge black and white cat, setting it quickly on the ground. It darted under his truck as he set the box on the ground. In the bottom were three teeny, tiny adorable black kittens about the size of my hand. They couldn't have been more than two weeks old.

"Kitties!" Rowen shrieked, jumping up and down. She

went straight for the box and immediately began playing with the little bundles of fur. Nothing existed in her world at that moment except those kittens.

"The mother here is gentle with a calm demeanor," Silas said. "She's not afraid of people and will come around the house, especially if you get in the habit of feeding them on the porch."

"Okay." I nodded.

"Kittens are two girls and a boy. Boy is the one with white paws. They're barn cats so they've never had shots or been to a vet. But they'll keep the rodents away."

"Sorry, I'm new to country life. Rodents are bad because . . . ?"

"Mice attract snakes, Freckles," Jess said.

I shuddered. Too many rodents in my barn. Hence the snake.

And if there were mice in the barn, there could be some scurrying close to the house, leading snakes from the confines of the barn to my yard where my four-year-old little girl loved to play.

"She loves to play outside, Jess. You don't think snakes would come out here, do you? Is it safe by the house?"

"Most critters, including snakes, stay away from people. They're more scared of you than you are of them," he said.

"I seriously doubt that, honey." The "honey" just slipped out but I liked it.

"Baby, you were too close, and you scared that snake in the barn today. It didn't seek you out and viciously attack you. It just reacted on instinct. Nine out of ten times, it would have left before you ever got close. Could be you were being quiet and it didn't hear you. Could have a nest in there and didn't want to leave it," he said.

"Okay, now I'm totally freaked again!" I threw a hand out in the direction of the barn. "A nest? Meaning miniature evil creatures are on my property?"

"It'll be fine. I said I'd take care of the barn and I will. Promise. Just stay out of there," he said, wrapping an arm around my shoulders.

"Soon?" I asked.

"Tomorrow."

"Okay. And for the record, that snake absolutely did seek me out and attack me viciously. Don't you dare defend it," I said, pointing my index finger up to his face.

Silas chuckled before hauling an enormous bag of cat food out of his truck. The bag was twice as big as Rowen.

"How about we take a look in the barn?" Silas asked Jess.

"Sounds good. Let me grab a shovel," he said and walked toward the side of the house.

"For the record, Gigi, cats will help keep snakes away. Haven't seen a snake by my house or barns in years. Not even a garter snake."

"Thanks. That helps," I said.

He nodded once and left to catch up with Jess.

I crouched down to examine the kittens. My kittens. I'd never had a pet before. Not even a goldfish.

"What should we name them?" I asked Rowen.

"Mommy, I need to think about it. I can't just *give* them names. I just met them. I have to get to know them first."

"Oh . . . sorry. Silly of me to assume otherwise. How about we take them up to the porch and you can get to know them up there while Mommy drinks a little glass of wine?" I asked.

As we walked, she said to my back, "I could get to know them even better if they stayed in my room."

"Not happening, Roe. These are outside cats."

I carried the box up the porch steps and went inside to get my glass of wine. A big glass.

It was almost gone by the time Jess and Silas stalked out of the barn with something hanging over the end of Jess's shovel.

Correction. A dead rattlesnake hanging over the end of Jess's shovel.

I got chills at the sight of the now dead reptile.

If Jess put that thing in my garbage can, he'd buy himself garbage duty for life. I'd never go near that trash can again. Ever. Even after it had been emptied a hundred times.

Thankfully, they deposited the corpse into the back of Silas's truck.

I waited until it was out of sight, not wanting Rowen to look over and see it, then I called out to Jess, "Might as well send that shovel with Silas too. I'll never touch it again."

They both grinned while Jess handed Silas the shovel.

"Nice to meet you, Gigi," Silas called, raising his hand to me. I waved back before he shook Jess's hand and drove away.

"Captain Lewis," Rowen said to Jess. He had just stepped onto the porch and she immediately lifted the boy kitten in the air.

"What?" Jess asked.

"His name. It's Captain Lewis."

Jess bent at the waist and grabbed the kitten. It looked even smaller in his large hands. "Captain Lewis."

"It's getting late, sweetie. Time to get ready for bed. Say good night to Jess," I said.

"What about the kitties?" she asked.

"I've got them. Their mother is around the side of the

house. I'll move them there and put out some food. They'll be ready for you to play with in the morning," he said.

"Thanks, Jess," we said in unison before I shuffled Rowen inside to get into her pajamas.

Rowen fell asleep quickly and when I came downstairs, Jess was sitting on the living room couch, checking something on his phone. His eyes followed me as I sat next to him.

"Would you like something to drink?" I asked.

"Water."

"Okay," I said, unwinding my legs to stand.

"Just bring it to bed, Georgia."

"Uh . . . what?"

I sank back into the couch, now panicked at the prospect of him spending the night.

"I'm staying here tonight, Freckles. You had a traumatic day and were in the hospital. I'm not leaving you alone to have a nightmare."

"Jess, I appreciate that but Roe's room is right across the hall from mine. And I don't have a guest bed yet. I'll be fine. You made everything better tonight so I won't have a nightmare. Go home."

"I'm staying," he said and stood, grabbing me under the arms and hauling me up.

The second my feet hit the floor, his mouth came down on mine and his arms circled my back, pulling me close. The kiss was long, hot and wet with lots of tongue. When he finally broke away, my lips were puffy and I was dizzy.

"Water," he said. "Meet you upstairs."

He walked around me, and then his footsteps echoed up the stairs.

Damn.

If he kissed me during every debate, I was never going to win.

I unfroze and walked to the kitchen, getting us both a glass of water and taking them upstairs. He had turned off my bedroom light and switched on both end table lamps.

He'd also taken off his shirt, shoes and socks.

My knees nearly buckled at the sight of him in only a pair of jeans. Jeans that hung perfectly from his hipbones. I fumbled my next step and nearly dropped the water glasses.

His body was, as expected, perfect. Better than I had been picturing over the past two weeks. Strong shoulders. Cut, muscled arms. A well-defined chest dusted lightly with dark hair. He had a six-pack of chiseled abs and a happy trail of hair on his lower stomach that disappeared beneath the waistband of his jeans.

Standing there shirtless, he instantly heated my blood. I wanted him so badly that I almost forgot Roe was across the hallway. Almost.

Jess must have read my mind because he stalked toward me and removed a water glass from my hand. My gaze was glued to his chest so he hooked his finger under my chin, forcing my head back.

"Not tonight, baby. We're not going there until we have all night to ourselves. Okay?"

I nodded, dropping my eyes.

"You get ahold of Bryant's wife and get that sleepover scheduled. Soon."

I nodded again.

He grinned. "Get ready for bed, Freckles."

I stayed still. I was working to find the courage to make my next move.

Leaning in, I placed a kiss against his bare chest, something I had wanted to do since the night he came over and got his letter from Ben. Before he could see my cheeks flush, I walked around him and into the bathroom.

Had I just done that? It was so unlike me to be forward with a man.

With brushed teeth, I came back into the bedroom. Jess was sitting at the foot of the bed, his jeans stripped off and now wearing only a pair of black boxer briefs.

I swayed a little on my feet. Certainly he had a flaw somewhere. Right?

His legs were powerful and strong, just like the rest of his body. His calves had a sexy ball of muscle at the top that tapered down to his ankles.

He stood, then walked past me, lightly brushing my arm. That little touch ran through my entire body, sending tingles to all the right places.

I jumped into bed and sank down into my pillow-top mattress. My mind was racing and I was on the verge of a full-on panic attack at the idea of a man sleeping in my bed.

And it wasn't just any man. It was Jess.

Trying to relax, I took a deep breath and swiveled my head around, assessing my bedroom.

I loved my room. It was like my own personal sanctuary. My rich, charcoal duvet had all of these randomly placed pin tucks and gathers so it billowed on my bed. My king-sized frame matched my dresser and two end tables. All of them were a dark, dark brown. My end table lamps were made of a bronze metal that had been fired with swirls of red, blue and copper.

Besides the kitchen, it was my favorite room in the house.

Jess emerged from the bathroom and came to the bed. All of the calm I had found moments ago evaporated.

He climbed in, lying on his back, and immediately pulled me into his side with one arm wrapped around my shoulders, the other propped behind his head.

At first, I wasn't sure what to do. Every muscle in my body was tense. Jess felt it too because he shook me lightly. "Relax, Georgia. Sleep."

"I can't relax, Jess. You're in my bed."

"I'm aware."

"Well, at least let me slide over to my side," I said.

"No. Just relax. You're sleeping here."

"Seriously, Jess. I've never slept next to anyone other than Rowen before. I won't be able to like this."

"Really?" he asked.

"Really what?"

"Never slept next to a man before?"

"Uh . . . no."

Damn.

I had just opened the door for us to talk about my past relationships, something I was not ready to do. Obviously I wasn't a virgin, having a four-year-old kid across the hall, but I didn't think we were at that point yet where we shared the intimate details of our pasts.

And I really didn't feel like talking about mine. The words "Nate Fletcher" tasted sour and made me sick.

"Good," he muttered.

Well, that was surprising. I figured the sheriff would jump all over the chance to interrogate me. I was so relieved that he didn't, I inhaled a deep breath and settled into his side.

It took me a few minutes, but the tension finally left my

body. And when it did, I was shocked to find that sleeping on Jess was comfortable. Really comfortable.

I'd read about it in romance novels and seen it in movies but it had always seemed fake. I doubted that any woman could be comfortable squished into a man's hard body. Sleeping like that wasn't real, it was just a romantic notion.

I was glad to be proved wrong. This was nice.

Enjoying his warmth, I curled into Jess's side and relaxed my head in the crook of his neck. One of my arms was underneath me while the other rested on his torso.

Jess's scent filled my nose. I had gotten hints of it before, but now that I was lying on him, I could really breathe it in. It was amazing. Clean and fresh.

"What kind of soap do you use?" I asked.

"Not sure. Cheapest one they have at the store. Green apple, I think."

"Hmm . . . I like it."

Tomorrow I was adding green apple soap to my grocery list.

We lay there in the quiet darkness for a few minutes and I replayed the events from the day, managing to keep my body relaxed when I thought about being bitten.

"How did you know I was in the ER?" I asked.

I hadn't called him on my way into town, and even though we'd spent a lot of time together these last two weeks, I didn't think the general populace knew we were a new couple.

"Bryant was sitting in his cruiser outside town. Saw you come racing by. Decided to follow you instead of pull you over. When you hit the ER, he called me."

"Oh," I said.

If our relationship progressed to the point where we

were together for major gift-giving holidays and birthdays, I needed to shop online or out of town. Jess had spies everywhere.

"Thanks for coming to the hospital and for being there for Rowen," I said. "She was freaked. It was nice of you to take her so she didn't have to sit in the ER with me. And thanks for being there for me too."

"Not a hardship taking care of my girls," he said into my hair.

That was the second time tonight he'd called us "my girls" and I liked it even more this time than I had the first. It was possessive, but sweet and caring. Like we were his treasures.

"I like it when you call us your girls," I whispered, smiling against his chest.

"You are."

My smile got bigger and I wrapped my arm firmly around his torso.

I wasn't sure how, but Jess had turned a bad afternoon into a wonderful night. Not once since he had arrived at the hospital had I tried to put some distance between us. I'd just let things happen naturally, and it had felt great letting him care for us without worrying about what it meant or doubting his intentions. All of the worry and doubt I'd been keeping up these last few weeks was tiring.

Today, I just hadn't had the energy to sustain it.

Jess hadn't seemed burdened at all by today's drama. Not for a minute. Maybe he really did like us and wanted to be with me, just because of, well . . . me. No ulterior motives.

Here he was in my bed and not once had he made a move for sex. And nothing about today's events suggested he was trying to get the farmhouse from me. Hell, if he wanted it, all he had to do was put a rattlesnake on the front porch and I'd never walk through the door again.

I was starting to second-guess myself. Maybe it was time to start trusting Jess and just let this relationship between us take its course.

But I wasn't there yet. I needed more time.

Shutting off my mind, I snuggled deeper into Jess's broad chest, soaking up the strength from his body. I breathed easy. Clean and fresh.

"And thank you for getting us mongoose babies."

———

JESS

"Mongoose babies?" I asked.

When she didn't respond, I tipped my eyes down and saw that she was out. I'd known she'd fall asleep next to me if she just got the hell out of her head.

But I still had thoughts running through my own, so I lay there, unsleeping, with Georgia curled into my side.

Not a bad place to be.

Bryant had called me earlier and said Georgia was dashing into the ER with blood dripping down her arm. My chest had constricted so badly in that moment I'd thought I was having a heart attack. The drive to the hospital was tense. Never in my life had I been so worried. And that was saying something, considering my home life growing up.

Georgia and her daughter, living in Ben's farmhouse, were taking over my life.

I was a man who had diligently avoided tying himself to

anything but his job for the last decade. But I just couldn't push them away. Instead, I kept trying to pull them closer.

And every time she tried to put up a wall or distance herself, I just kept pulling. She was scared, but she'd get over it. And the less room she had to run, the better.

Christ, we hadn't even had sex yet. Something I was going to remedy soon.

Part of me wanted to say fuck it and take her right here, tonight. But for our first time, I wanted her full, undivided attention. I wanted to get her so worked up she screamed my name. And with Rowen across the hall, loud sex was not an option.

I needed to stop thinking about fucking Georgia. My hard-on was just inches away from her leg. So I switched my mind to the barn.

A rattlesnake bite.

What. The. Fuck.

In all my years at the farmhouse, I'd never seen a snake out here.

But sure enough, when Silas and I had gone into the barn, there it was. Right where she said it had been. It had likely been trying to build a nest behind that bale but hadn't had the chance to lay its eggs yet. And it never would. I'd been more than happy to cut that fucker's head off.

On Monday, I was talking to Ryan at Jamison Valley Construction about tearing down that barn. I'd pay extra to have it done within a week and then I was going to have him build a heated garage in its place. Georgia could keep her car inside during the winter and I'd make sure it was big enough for my rigs too.

Because in the not-so-distant future, I was going to be living at the farmhouse with my girls.

CHAPTER EIGHT

GIGI

"Mommy?"

I jolted awake and shot out of bed. I had slept unmoving on Jess's side and he, too, was jumping up to pull on some jeans. As I raced to the door, I glanced at the clock.

Five a.m.

I flipped the lock, threw open the door and knelt in front of Rowen.

"What's up, baby girl? Are you okay?" Certainly there must be something wrong if she was up this early.

"The sun is coming up, Mommy. That means I can get out of bed."

When she was three, I'd instituted a rule that she couldn't get out of bed until the sun was up. She had developed a bad habit of getting up in the middle of the night and coming into my room to sleep with me. Well, *she* slept. I got kicked in the face, stomach and ribs.

I twisted my neck to the windows. The sun was definitely *not* up.

"Uh, sweetie, the sun isn't up yet. It's still dark out. You need to get back into bed," I said.

She ignored me completely because when I turned to look at the windows, her eyes caught a glimpse of Jess.

"Did Jess have a sleepover?"

It was way too early to have this conversation.

"Yeah, Roe, I had a sleepover. You okay with that?" he asked, picking her up.

"Yep," she said, giving him a once-over.

Her eyebrows came together in the middle. "Are those your jammies? Why do you sleep in jeans? Mommy won't let me sleep in anything except my jammies. She says if I sleep in my dresses, they will get wrecked."

I couldn't help but laugh.

"Roe, sweetie, how about we save the questions until after Mommy and Jess get some coffee. Okay?"

"But, Mommy—"

"No 'buts,' Rowen. Let me get a sweater and we'll go down and start on breakfast, okay? And then you can ask all the questions you want."

"Ohhh-kaaay," she pouted.

"We're all up early and it's a Sunday. Only a few weeks left to enjoy the summer. How about we head to Wade Lake and go fishing?" Jess asked.

I grumbled, "Fishing?" at the same time Roe shrieked, "Fishing!"

Both of them looked at me with big smiles on their faces.

I guess we were going fishing.

———

I MET Jess outside when he returned to the farmhouse with his boat. Behind an older blue truck was a shiny silver aluminum boat with rods and oars sticking out the sides.

The boat wasn't a surprise since obviously we had to have one to go fishing. The truck was a bit of a shock but only because I'd had no idea he drove anything other than the bronze behemoth. But I was totally taken aback by the big black dog he'd brought too.

"Oakley," Jess called. The dog took a flying leap out of the truck and walked to Jess's side.

"You have a dog?" I asked.

He didn't get a chance to answer. Roe walked through the door, carrying her little pink backpack, and froze at the sight of Oakley. She immediately darted behind my legs, clutching them for dear life.

"Mommy, is that a nice doggie or a mean doggie?"

There were a lot of dog owners in Spokane and I'd seen my fair share of bites in the ER, so I had taught Roe early on that some dogs were nice and others were not. She needed to ask me before approaching a strange one.

"This is Oakley," Jess told her. "He's nice. You want to come say hello?"

She nodded hesitantly and slowly walked to him.

Jess came up the steps and snapped his fingers for Oakley to follow.

"Come here, little bit," Jess said, kneeling down by the dog and reaching out his hand.

When he called Roe "little bit," it warmed my heart. No one except for me, not even Ben, had called her by a pet name. I loved that she had that kind of special affection from Jess.

"See? Nice," he said, helping her pet the dog's head.

She gave him a little smile but was still apprehensive.

"Let's get going, okay? You and Oakley can get to know each other a little while later," I said.

An hour later, we were driving on a bumpy gravel road that wound up the side of the mountains through the thick, green forest. The trees cleared and we pulled into a wide, gravel parking lot on the shore of Wade Lake.

I sucked in a short breath as my eyes traveled over the scenery. We had just driven to heaven.

The lake stretched out in front of us. The water was flawless, like glass, and not a breath of wind in the air disturbed its peaceful surface. The forest sloped down steeply to meet the water's edge, its pristine, mirrored surface reflecting the green trees and blue sky.

Magnificent.

"Pretty, huh," Jess asked.

"You could say that." I was in total awe of the beauty before me.

With the boat in the water, a life jacket on Roe and Oakley dancing from side to side, we set out into the lake.

The wind breezed through my hair as we sliced through the still waters, the only sounds the buzz of the engine and the whir of the air rushing past us.

Jess took us through the main part of the lake and then down a channel hidden behind a large hill. He slowed, then cut the engine so we were drifting and bobbing in the middle of the lake. Beautiful blue water beneath us gently slapped against the aluminum boat. Green forest walled us in at a distance. The mountain air was cool and refreshing but the sun shone brightly, keeping us warm.

I was loving fishing and we hadn't even put a pole in the water.

Jess taught us to fish while he showed us around the lake. There were five different channels in Wade Lake. When Roe would get restless in one spot, he'd buzz us around to a new one.

Jess caught three fish. Roe caught two. I was content to watch and pet Oakley.

Rowen was so excited the first time her pole jerked that she jumped up and let go of the rod. If Jess hadn't had secured it to the boat, it would have gone overboard. Then while she was reeling in her line, she started bouncing up and down so much Jess worried she'd lose the fish. He let her abandon the reeling and took over so she could grip the edge of the boat and peer over the edge, waiting to see her catch.

She didn't even try reeling with the second fish. She just leaped up in her seat and thrust the pole at Jess so she could assume her perch and watch him bring up the fish, Oakley right at her side, both staring intently down at the water.

After about ten minutes in the boat, Roe had warmed up to Oakley and they had become fast friends. He was a sweet dog with a mild temperament and he obeyed orders better than any dog I'd ever seen before.

Jess told me that Oakley wasn't actually his dog, but instead belonged to the station. He spent most of his time with Jess or a deputy during the day but his bed was at the station and he'd stay the nights there with whoever was on shift to take dispatch calls.

Along with fishing, we spent a lot of time looking for wildlife. Jess would usually spot the animals and birds and show us where to look. In total, we saw five deer, a turtle near one of the shores, a mama duck and her six ducklings and a flying bald eagle.

But no other people. Today, the lake was ours. Just

Rowen, Jess and me surrounded by beauty only God could create.

Bliss.

As we were driving back to the farmhouse, Roe asleep in the back seat, I reached over and grabbed Jess's hand.

"Thanks, honey," I said, giving it a squeeze.

He laced his fingers with mine. "Great day."

Yes. It absolutely was. "The best."

———

JESS

"The best," she'd said in that sweet, soft voice she used for me often. Right after calling me "honey," something I liked a whole lot.

I'd never taken anyone to Wade Lake before.

Fishing gave me a chance to free my mind, to ignore the burdens from my job, my mother and whatever else was weighing me down. Just a couple hours on crystal-clear water to find some peace. Let it all go. I usually drove the boat to a quiet, deserted corner and stayed there all day, unmoving.

Today had certainly not been quiet. Roe had clamored the entire time, taking turns talking to me, her mother or the dog. Georgia would call attention to animals, birds or whatever else she thought Roe would want to see. And I'd spent most of the day driving them around the entire lake. Christ, I used more gas today than I had in all of last year combined.

But just like Friday night dinners at the café, I'd never go fishing alone again. Because what I'd thought was peace was just an illusion. Today, with Georgia and Roe, I learned what peace truly felt like.

———

GIGI

"Hey, baby."

I was at the kitchen island chopping vegetables for stir-fry. Roe didn't like it so I was glad she was outside playing with the kittens and not in the kitchen complaining about my dinner choice.

It was Tuesday night, two days since our fishing trip and his first sleepover, and Jess was just getting off work, coming to the farmhouse for dinner.

"Hi," I said, lifting my cheek so he could give it a quick kiss. "How was crime fighting today, Sheriff?"

He leaned back against the counter opposite me. His arms crossed over his chest and his legs were planted wide, making his jeans pull just right at his thighs. He had rolled up his sleeves, revealing his strong forearms. His stance was hot. But my favorite part of Jess coming over was the way he'd walk around in bare feet. Now that was sexy.

I needed to fan my now-flushed face but didn't want Jess to see.

He hadn't shaved this morning so he had stubble on his handsome face. I couldn't wait to feel that stubble against my skin later tonight. We'd been having some pretty hot make-out sessions. Jess always stopped us before we could get too carried away, usually leaving for his own house shortly after we stopped kissing.

At first it was fun. Like when you started kissing as a teenager. But, after weeks, I was over it. Way over it.

Both of us desperately wanted relief from the sexual tension that kept building tighter and tighter. But he was adamant about waiting until Rowen wasn't at the house.

"Had to close the case on Alex Benson today," Jess said, pulling my thoughts away from sex.

"Who?"

"Alex Benson. Guy who got that beating last month."

"Oh, right. John Doe. Why did you have to close the case? Did you find out who beat him up?"

"Nope. He never did give Sam anything else to go on. Kept tight-lipped and then left town the day he got released from the hospital. I kept the file open a week in case someone came forward but decided today it was dead. Marked it unsolved and pulled Sam from digging. Not that he was finding much anyway."

"Sorry," I said.

He shrugged. "Nothing else to do. Need Sam working on other shit. It just sucks. I fucking hate not solving a case. It gnaws at me. Up until this summer, I was on a streak. Two years of a hundred percent closed cases."

"Mommy?" Rowen called, interrupting our conversation.

"Kitchen!"

She came rushing through the door, carrying Captain Lewis in her arms.

"Mommy—"

"Rowen, you get that kitten outside. They don't come in the house. We've talked about this."

"But—"

"No. Outside now."

"Fine," she pouted and stormed her little feet down the hallway.

Shaking my head, I told Jess, "She has been a terror since I picked her up from Quail Hollow this afternoon. We're doing an early bedtime."

He pushed away from the counter and fitted his big body to my back, wrapping his arms around me and leaning in to whisper in my ear.

"That means we get extra time tonight. Maybe try something other than kissing on the couch."

My whole body shivered as he lightly kissed my neck in that hidden spot just behind my ear. I was never going to leave my hair down again. I wanted him to have full access to that spot at any time.

"I can think of a few things we could do," I whispered.

Rowen's footsteps sounded in the hall as she headed toward the kitchen once again.

"Mommy. Can I—" She stared at Jess holding me for a second and then her eyes darted to the countertop. "What are we eating?"

"Stir-fry."

"No! I don't like stir-fry!" she shouted. "Can I have chicken nuggets? Please?"

I shifted out of Jess's hold. "No, Roe. I'm making dinner for us and we're all going to eat the same thing. You can have chicken nuggets for lunch tomorrow at school."

"No! I want them now! I don't want to eat stir-fry!"

"Rowen Grace Ellars! Stop that yelling," I said, using my mom voice. "That is enough attitude, young lady. You can either go straight to bed without dinner or stop yelling at me and eat stir-fry with us. Now what's it going to be?"

She screwed her lips together in a scowl and looked

down at her feet. Her arms crossed over her chest as she let out an angry "humph."

"Well? What's your choice?"

"Dinner," she muttered.

"Good choice," I said. "Now why don't you help Jess set the table. He can carry the plates and you can put out the silverware."

We ate dinner in near silence because Rowen was pouting and didn't pepper us with her typical myriad of questions. Jess and I didn't have much to say either so we focused on eating. Rowen's bad mood had infected the atmosphere.

After clearing the dishes, I ordered Rowen to say good night to her kittens but then come back inside.

My jaw was clenched as she stomped down the hall. Tonight my sweet, chatty, curious daughter was nowhere to be found. In her place was a little brat.

"Sorry about Roe."

"No big deal, Freckles. She's a kid. They're allowed to be grumpy now and again."

"Thanks." I was grateful he was so patient with my girl.

An hour later, bath time was done and I was walking down the hall to Roe's room.

"Rowen, time for bed, baby girl. Did you lay out your clothes for the recital tomorrow?"

I came to an abrupt halt the second I stepped inside her door. The floor was covered with a mountain of clothes. Sweaters, dresses, pants, skirts and shirts covered the floor. Clothes that I had once painstakingly hung up in her closet or folded nicely in her dresser.

"What is going—"

I stopped my question when a frustrated scream came

from the closet and its last remaining article came flying through the air.

"Rowen. Get your bum out here."

She emerged from the closet and stomped over clothes to the center of the room.

"This mess is not okay. What is going on?" I asked.

"I can't find my pink fluffy skirt anywhere! I wanted to wear it to the recital!" Her eyes flooded and her chin quivered.

"What pink fluffy skirt?" I asked, even though I was certain I knew which one she was talking about. And if I was right, we were on the verge of a meltdown.

"The pink one with the shiny silver dots and the poufy skirt."

My little super volcano was about to blow.

"The one that Papa Ben gave you?" I asked.

"Yes!" she cried. "I want to wear it for my recital." Her chest heaved with a spastic breath.

I stepped further into the room, walking over strewn clothes, to kneel down in front of her. What I was about to tell her wasn't going to be fun.

"Baby girl, that skirt was really small. Ben got it for you when you were three. Now you're four and a big girl. It didn't fit you anymore so I had to give it away to the Salvation Army with all of your other three-year-old clothes."

"Nooooo!" she screamed before collapsing in a fit of sobs.

I wrapped my arms around her in a tight hug, gently stroking her back as she cried.

This wasn't about the skirt, this was about Ben.

She broke away to yell at me. "Ben gave that skirt to me, Mommy. Why did you throw it away? I need it back! He gave it to me! Get it back!"

I tried to pull her close again but she wasn't having it. She started squirming and pushing away with her little arms.

"I'm so sorry, Roe. I gave it away last year. It's all gone and I can't get it back," I said.

"I want my Papa Ben!" she shrieked. Then her little body collapsed again into mine as she wailed uncontrollably.

I held onto her tightly, sitting on the floor and cradling her in my lap. She sobbed and sobbed and it broke my heart. But all I could do was hold her close and rock her back and forth. I couldn't bear to see my girl so devastated and heart-broken. The sounds coming from her little body were so full of pain that I started crying too.

We sat there bawling together until two big arms circled us both, lifting us off the floor.

Jess carried us to my bed, setting me and Rowen down gently before sliding in behind us. Then he wrapped us up again in his arms, giving us his strength and his warmth. I burrowed into his side while Roe clung to my chest, still sobbing.

After a while, I managed to get my own tears under control and started whispering to the top of Roe's head, encouraging her to try and stop her own.

When she was finally cried out, she stayed tight in my lap. Her cheek was resting against my heart and she was looking over my shoulder to Jess.

"You okay, little bit?"

She nodded and sniffled.

"How about you, Freckles?"

"I'm okay."

He lifted a hand to the side of Roe's face. His big hand engulfed her tiny jaw as he gently stroked his thumb across her cheek, drying her tears.

"Don't cry, Roe," he told her.

"I miss my Papa Ben," she said, crying again. "Mommy said he was in heaven with Gramma and the angels."

"I'm sure he is," Jess said, catching the new tears.

I didn't know how to ease her pain. To explain death in a better way. And I didn't know how to get her through this tough period. She was so young and innocent, and Ben had been such a big part of her life. All I could do was hold her close and remind her how much I loved her.

"Want to know how I knew Ben?" Jess asked.

"Yeah," Roe nodded.

"When I was a kid, I didn't have a dad around the house."

"Kind of like me?" Roe asked.

"Yep. But my mom isn't like your mom. Your mom is strong. Takes great care of you. My mom, well, she was sick a lot so I had to take care of her. Big job for a little kid. One day I was walking home from the store with my arms full of grocery bags. It started snowing and I had a long way to go. A truck pulled up beside me, and Ben got out. He made me put the bags in the back and he drove me home."

"He did?" she asked.

"Yep."

"How old were you?" I asked.

He thought about it for a couple of seconds. "Nine."

I winced. We hadn't talked about his family yet but I couldn't believe he'd had to take on such responsibilities. Nine-year-old kids shouldn't be shopping for groceries. Sooner rather than later I needed to ask about his parents.

"Ben never let me walk to the store again. Picked me up from school every Wednesday and took me to the store. Then drove me home," Jess said.

"Mommy always went to the grocery store for Ben," Rowen told him.

Jess smiled. "Glad she could help him out."

"What else did you guys do?" Roe asked.

"Well . . . he let me come over here after school a lot. Let me help him mow the grass or work on projects. Taught me a lot of stuff. How to use tools. How to fix his truck. He came to my football games. Sometimes practices too."

"What else?" Roe asked.

"He took me fishing."

"He did?"

"Yep. Same place we went. It was his favorite spot. Said it was where he caught his biggest fish."

"Really?"

"Yep," he said. "What kind of stuff did you do with Ben?"

"He read me books. And we'd color crowns. He built my dolls block houses so they had a place to sleep," she said.

"Sounds like fun," Jess said.

We stayed quiet for a little while longer, enjoying the comfort of being wrapped tightly together in my soft bed. Then we all went downstairs to play with the kitties before bed.

"Those girl kittens need names," I said.

While Rowen was toying with her pets, I was reclined on the porch swing, enjoying the view of the beautiful sunset.

Jess was sitting on the floor, the kittens between his long legs stretched wide. Rowen was perched by his feet, their makeshift blockade keeping the kittens from escaping.

"How about flower names?" Roe asked.

"I like it. Which flowers?"

"Can you tell me some flower names?"

"Well . . . there's Rose, Iris, Lily, Peony."

"Rhododendron," Jess added.

"Row-da-nen-drum?" Roe giggled. "That's funny. What else?"

"Delphinium," he said.

She giggled again. Music to my ears, making my smile bigger.

"Del-if-ni-um? What else?"

"Chrysanthemum."

Roe belly-laughed and collapsed against the floor. "Chris-thee-mum?"

My eyes met Jess's. The huge smile on my face matched his, while Roe's laughter filled the air.

Bliss.

"Thank you," I mouthed.

He didn't respond. My heart skipped when his smile just got bigger.

"Okay, little bit. Which ones are you gonna pick?"

"Hmm . . ." she said, taking a moment to get her laughter under control. "I think Rose and Peony."

"Excellent choices," I said. "What about the mom cat?"

"Jess, can you pick a name?" Rowen asked.

He stared for a moment, then rumbled, "Mrs. Fieldman."

I laughed at the same time Rowen asked, "Mrs. Fieldman?"

"Yeah. After my fifth grade teacher," he said.

"Was she your favorite teacher?" I asked.

"Nope. But she looked just like that cat."

"You're funny, Jess," Rowen said through her giggles.

She went back to playing with the kittens and I resumed my appreciation of the evening's sunset.

"Jess?" Roe called.

"Yeah?"

"Can you come to my recital tomorrow?"

"Sure."

She turned her eyes to me and smiled huge.

We were going to be okay. Soaking up her smile, I was certain it was true. Someday the sting of losing Ben wouldn't hurt so much. I would always be sad Mom and Ben couldn't be with us to watch Rowen grow up, but the hurt would subside.

"Georgia, you want to pick me up at the station?" Jess asked.

"Sure. The recital starts at six. I'll get Roe at five, buzz back here to get changed and then come get you around five-thirty. Is that okay?"

"Sounds good."

"Why do you always call Mommy 'Georgia' instead of 'Gigi' like everybody else?" Rowen asked.

I'd noticed his preference for my full name but hadn't asked him why.

His eyes sparkled as they traveled from her to me. "Because behind Rowen, Georgia is the most beautiful name I've ever heard."

Never in my life had a man said something so kind and wonderful to me and my daughter.

Another warm wave of happy coursed through my body and settled in my heart.

CHAPTER NINE

GIGI

"You've reached Jess Cleary. If this is an emergency, call 9-1-1. You can also try me at the sheriff's office. Otherwise, leave a message."

"Jess," I clipped. "I just got off the phone with Ryan. He said you've already paid him to tear down the barn, and that since they've started, they can't stop. It would be too dangerous leaving it partially up. Then he informed me that he's got the plans drafted for the new garage his crew will be starting next week. Of course, I told him that under no circumstances is he allowed to start that project, seeing as I had no idea what he was talking about. But too late. You've already signed the contract and paid the deposit."

I sucked in some air. "When I told him I was the property owner, not you, he said something about precedence and you being the long-term caretaker and having done projects there in the past, blah, blah, blah. He's basically being a coward and doesn't want to back out on the contract and piss you off. Oh, and then he informed me that if I was having a conflict with the caretaker, I should file an official complaint with the sheriff's office."

Another breath and I continued with my ranting message. "This is not okay, Jess. You can't make these decisions without discussing them with me first. So, Sheriff, you can take this as my official complaint. You can also find new plans for the evening because I'm telling Maisy she doesn't need to bother coming over to babysit Roe."

I hung up the phone and let out a frustrated growl.

It was the Friday following Roe's recital, and I was sitting in the staff lounge at the hospital.

Correction. I was *seething* in the staff lounge.

"Ah, Gigi? Are you okay?" Maisy asked from behind me.

"No. I'm not. But good news for you, you're off the hook to have a sleepover with Rowen tonight."

She took the chair across from me.

The staff lounge was a small, square, colorless room with no windows.

I hadn't spent much time in the lounge. I think most of the hospital staff felt the room was as depressing as I did, because it was almost always empty. People would swing in to grab some coffee or stow a packed meal in the fridge, but then they tended to find somewhere else to spend their time.

I didn't want an audience for my phone call so I had come into the lounge, thinking it was my safest bet. But with the way my day was going, I wasn't entirely surprised that alone time wasn't in the cards. I should have gone to my car.

"Sorry," I said. "I didn't mean to snap at you. I'm just so . . . so . . . pissed off!" My hands were fisted and shaking.

"I take it you and Jess are fighting?"

"Oh yeah, we're fighting."

"What happened?" she asked.

I huffed out a breath. "Well, you know about the incident last Saturday with the devil creature."

She nodded.

"On Saturday, he and Silas killed said devil creature, so I was thinking we were all good, right?"

She nodded again.

"Wrong. This morning, right before I was leaving, three trucks and a semi-truck carrying a huge Dumpster arrived at my house. Apparently, Jess hired this Ryan guy to come tear down my barn."

"Ryan Edwards. Like, the nicest guy ever," she said.

"Yes, he did seem nice. Whatever. That's beside the point. Jess didn't even discuss this with me. He just made a decision. No communication. To hell with what I wanted," I said, flicking my wrist in the air.

"That sucks. Did you like the barn?" she asked.

"Of course not. I was going to have that thing torn down myself. But the point here is he didn't communicate anything with me. I hate having someone make decisions for me. I'm not a child. It is my house and it should have been my choice. I could have arranged to have that thing taken down without his effing help!"

"So what did Jess say when you told him all that?"

"Well, when I called to give him a piece of my mind, he didn't answer. So I've now left two rather irate voicemails on his phone. The first one telling him I was pissed and why. The second, well . . ."

"Sorry, Gigi," she said.

"It's okay. Thanks for letting me vent. Rant over."

"Anytime," she said.

"Distract me. Tell me what's new with you. Take my mind off this whole barn business."

"Well . . . I was actually coming to find you because I've got the best news ever!" She squirmed in her chair. "So you know how I took that extra evening shift last night?"

I nodded.

"Well, Dr. Carlson was working late too. It was so slow. Like, the slowest night ever. I only had two patients on the second floor and the rest of the units were empty. So after the patients fell asleep, I didn't have anything to do. I was sitting at the nurses' station upstairs, bored out of my mind, and he came over to talk to me for hours! Until the end of my shift."

"Nice!" I said.

"I thought he might ask me out because there was *a lot* of flirting going on. He didn't so I was way bummed out. But I just bumped into him in the hall and he asked me out for drinks tomorrow night. Isn't that the most amazing thing ever?"

"Yeah it is! I really like him. He seems like a nice guy and not too hard to look at." I winked.

She did a girly clap in front of her chest and bounced up and down in her chair. The smile on her face was infectious.

Over the last few weeks, she'd been trying to get Everett to notice her. Nothing too in his face or obnoxious. She just always made sure to include him in conversations and ask him how he was doing. It was sweet how she'd made her approach.

"So what are you going to wear for drinks?" I asked.

"Gosh, I don't know." Before she could continue, her phone chimed in her pocket. Taking it out, she looked at the screen and then her eyes shot straight to mine.

"Hello?" she said, dropping her eyes to her feet.

The other person was doing all the talking because Maisy didn't say anything else.

"Uh . . . okay," she muttered before hanging up. She glanced up at me and scrunched her nose.

"What?" I asked.

"Well, that was, um, Jess," she said.

My blood boiled and I closed my eyes to listen to what she had to say next.

"He said, um, I'm still on for spending the night with Rowen."

"What! He is dreaming!" My head was going to explode. "You know what? Fine. He wants a sleepover, he'll get a sleepover. I don't know what I'm going to do yet. But, oh boy . . . he is messing with the wrong girl!"

"Sorry," Maisy said.

"Oh, sweetie, don't apologize. I'm not at all mad at you. But I am absolutely livid with Sheriff Cleary."

Taking a deep breath, I fisted and un-fisted my hands a couple of times. With one final deep breath in through my nose, I said, "If you're still okay with it, come on over at six?"

She nodded.

"Okay, perfect. If you want to come over at five-thirty, you can raid my closet for a date outfit on Saturday."

"Sweet! I'll be there."

"I'm going to do a couple of laps around the parking lot to cool down before I head back to the clinic. Come find me if anything else awesome happens with Everett today, okay?"

"You got it," she said.

I blew her a quick kiss, then headed outside, contemplating all the ways I could legally torture the Jamison County sheriff.

I managed to get my anger under control in one parking lot lap instead of two and walked back to the clinic.

It was located at the opposite side of the building from the ER. The clinic's primary doctor, Dr. Seavers, specialized in family medicine. She held traditional business hours, Monday through Friday, and only worked outside the clinic if she was the on-call weekend doctor. Everett and Dr. Peterson rarely worked in the clinic. Instead, they were typically covering the rest of the hospital.

The nurses rotated on a weekly basis through four different hospital units and the clinic was by far my favorite. I secretly wished I could work here full-time like Dr. Seavers.

We didn't have a lot of traffic through the clinic but it was far more active than any other rotations I'd completed. Today, I had seen a pregnant women coming in for a routine check-up, two different high schoolers getting their summer physicals for fall school sports and one toddler with a bad cold.

I was wrapping up my charting for the day, having only thirty minutes left, when an older woman walked in the door.

She was about my height and probably half my size. Her frame was skeletal and she had light brown hair with streaks of gray framing her face. Her eyes were a bright, ice blue.

I knew those eyes. I'd spent a lot of time over the last three weeks staring into eyes just like hers. They belonged to the man who was currently at the top of my shit list.

"Hi. Can I help you?" I asked.

"I was wondering if I could see Dr. Seavers today," she said in a voice so weak I had to strain to hear it.

"Sure. She's got some time open now. Let me get you all checked in. What's your name?"

"Noelle Cleary."

Yep, I was right. She was somehow related to Jess.

"Okay, Noelle. Have a seat and I'll call you back in a minute."

I walked back to the desk and checked her into the hospital's system. Could she be Jess's aunt, maybe? Certainly, she wasn't his mother. She was far too frail to have such a big, strong son.

"Noelle? Come on back," I called into the waiting room.

She followed me back to the exam room and climbed up on the table while I sat opposite her in a rolling black stool.

"All right, Noelle. My name's Gigi. Can you tell me what brings you in?" I asked.

"This afternoon I went into the bathroom and I tripped and fell into the shower. I think I've sprained my wrist," she said.

"Oh, no. I'm so sorry to hear that. Let's take your blood pressure and then I'll get Dr. Seavers to come in."

Dr. Seavers was quick to attend to Noelle and while she finished her examination, I perused Noelle's hospital chart.

I scrolled through injury after injury. She appeared to be Jamison Valley Hospital's most frequent visitor.

So far just this year, she'd been in to see Dr. Seavers three times, all for different ailments. One visit was to treat a bad burn on her hand. Another, a sprained ankle. The most recent, a bruised tailbone.

What the hell was happening in this woman's home? And how was she related to Jess?

"Gigi, will you call in a prescription for Mrs. Cleary?" the doctor asked. "I want her to take a painkiller while her wrist recovers. I've wrapped it but it's likely to hurt for a while."

"Sure thing, Dr. Seavers. Anything else?"

"A neighbor brought her here and dropped her off. Can you help make arrangements to get her home?"

"Yes, no problem," I said before walking back to Noelle's exam room.

"I'm sorry you hurt your wrist but that wrap and the painkillers should help," I told Noelle.

She gave me a small smile but didn't speak.

"Dr. Seavers said a neighbor dropped you off. Is there someone I can call to come and take you home?"

"Well . . . I've been trying to get ahold of my son all day but he's not answering his phone."

"Would you like me to try him again for you?"

"If you don't mind," she whispered.

"Not at all. What's his name?" I asked, even though I was ninety-nine point nine percent sure I knew the answer.

"Jess Cleary," she said and then rattled off his cell number.

Should I tell her Jess and I were together? No. I wanted to talk to him first. There was absolutely a story here, one he hadn't been comfortable sharing with me yet.

Never in a million years would I have pictured Noelle as Jess's mother. Everything about him was sturdy. Solid. His personality, his voice, his body. Everything about her was the exact opposite. He had said she was sick a lot but I had not expected her to be so fragile.

I left her to collect her things while I headed to the back hallway of the clinic, pulling up Jess's name on my phone as I walked. His phone rang three times, and I was starting to get worried I'd hit his voicemail again when he answered.

"What, Georgia?" he snapped. I knew he'd gotten my messages but now I knew he didn't like them very much.

"Jess," I said gently.

He was obviously expecting me to be pissed, so my quiet tone took him by surprise. "You okay?"

"Yeah, I'm fine. But I'm in the clinic and your mother just came in."

"Fuck. Did she hurt herself? She okay?"

"She sprained her wrist but she'll be fine. The thing is, a neighbor dropped her off but she needs a ride home. I guess she's been calling but couldn't get ahold of you."

"Damn it," he said. "Just drove out to the Drummond place. I'll be at least a half an hour. Probably more like an hour. She's gonna have to wait at the hospital for me. Or walk over to the station. That means by the time I get her home and settled, cook her some dinner, it's gonna be late." He let out an audible breath. "Fuck. I guess Maisy didn't need to babysit after all."

"It's almost five," I said, checking my watch. "I'm leaving here in a few minutes to get Rowen. Maisy's coming over at five-thirty. Why don't I take your mom to the farmhouse with me? She can wait with us until you get back. We can all eat together, then we'll go from there."

"Don't want you to have to take care of her. Especially if she's hurt," he said.

"Ah, Jess, you do realize what I do for a living, right?"

"Georgia, she's . . . she's not right."

"It's a couple of hours. It's no big deal."

He took another deep breath. "I hate that you have to deal with this shit."

"And I hate that you are dealing with my barn. How about we get my daughter and your mother settled for the

129

night and then we can discuss all the things we'd rather not have the other person in this relationship deal with."

Another deep breath. "Okay, Freckles."

"Can you call your mom and let her know the plan? I didn't tell her about us. I wasn't sure if you'd want that or . . . well, I just wasn't sure," I said.

"Georgia, I didn't intentionally *not* tell her about you. Just haven't had the chance to talk to her in person. As soon as I hang up with you, I'm calling her. Give me five minutes and she'll know what you mean to me."

"What I mean to you?" I whispered.

"Yeah, baby. What you mean to me."

I stayed in the hallway for a minute, thinking about Jess's words and their hidden meaning.

Jess meant something to me too. More and more every day, and it had only been three weeks. Not even a month since our first Friday dinner together at the café.

He'd proven not to be the jackass I had originally expected.

But I was learning that Jess wanted things done in his way. And so far, all of our arguments had ended with him winning. Was I letting him walk all over me? I wondered what would happen when he pushed me too far.

When he crossed the line and I didn't let him get his way.

———

"HELLO?"

We all looked to the hall as Jess's deep voice called into the house.

"Jess!" Rowen screeched and ran out of the kitchen.

Two seconds later she was back, this time perched on Jess's hip.

He looked tired and worn out. His eyes were bloodshot and his shoulders were hunched. He was still utterly handsome, but I could tell he'd had a long day.

I was at the stove, stirring the sauce for dinner. We were having spaghetti and meatballs, garlic bread and a tossed green salad.

After ending my call with Jess at the clinic, I had rushed to close everything down for the weekend. Noelle had just hung up her phone when I walked out to the waiting room. She'd kept her eyes to the floor as she apologized for being a nuisance. I had assured her it was no problem and that I was looking forward to spending time with her. She had relaxed a bit but not entirely. But by the time we had picked up Rowen and made it back to the farmhouse, she had seemed much more at ease.

While Rowen had entertained Noelle in the living room, I had changed and started working on dinner.

Maisy had arrived right on time and thoroughly raided my closet. She had a stack of five different outfits as options for her date with Everett the next night.

Then we'd all congregated in the kitchen. I had buzzed around, preparing dinner, while Maisy and Noelle stood at the island, watching Rowen run in and out with different books, toys or stuffed animals to show our guests.

When Jess hit the island, he set Rowen down on her bum and kissed the top of her head before moving over to me at the stove.

"Hi." In bare feet, I had to tip my head way back to look into Jess's eyes.

"Hey, baby." He bent down and gave me a soft, short kiss on the lips.

Next, he went to his mother, throwing his big arms around her small frame in a long embrace. "Hi, Ma. Are you feeling better?"

"Yes. Much better. I've been in good hands here."

He released the hug but kept her tucked under an arm. "Hey, Maze."

"Hi, Jess. Looks like you've had a rough day."

"You could say that."

"Did you catch any bad guys today, Jess?" Rowen asked.

"No," he said, shaking his head. "Not today, little bit."

"I had lunch with Milo today. He told me you were going out to the Drummond place?" Maisy asked. "Are you still looking for the guy that stole Jack's fertilizer?"

"Yeah," he said but didn't expand. Instead, he turned his attention to Rowen. "Have you showed my mom your room yet, Roe?"

When it dawned on her that she hadn't, her face broke out into a big smile. "Mommy, can I show Noelle my room?"

"Of course. And while you're up there, how about putting away some of those toys you took out?"

"Ohhh-kaaay," she said, her excitement fading a little.

"Come along, Rowen. Show me this room," Noelle said, grabbing her hand after Jess lifted her off the island.

After they left the kitchen, Jess said, "I went to the Drummond place to see if Jack would finally talk to me about his missing fertilizer. He knows more than he's telling."

"Why would he keep it from you? Wouldn't he want to get it back? Or at least find out who did it?" I asked.

"Wes," Maisy said.

Jess nodded. "That much chemical could make a fuck load of meth. And if Wes took it, Jack wouldn't turn him in."

"I'm confused," I said.

"Wes is Jack's son," Jess said. "Wes has been into drugs for years. Mostly just hanging with that crowd. Getting high. But recently he's started dealing meth. Started taking over production too. For the last year, I've been trying to pin something on him but he's been careful. I was hoping Jack might finally be willing to give me a lead so I could bring Wes in."

"Did he?" Maisy asked.

"No." Jess sighed. "He's just as tight-lipped now as when I went out to investigate the theft the first time. Which tells me it was Wes."

"Why did you go out there again? Did something else happen?" I asked.

"Yeah. Last night, Sam busted up another meth deal. The dealer he picked up hinted that the valley's about to get flooded with product. So I went back out to the Drummond place to see if I could reason with Jack. It was a long shot that Jack would talk but I had to try."

Jess raked his hands through his hair.

"Word from a couple of sources is Wes built a cookhouse tucked away in the mountains. Never been able to find it and I've had guys looking all summer. If Wes is planning a big cooking bender, that's where the flood will come from."

"Oh my god," I whispered.

Spokane had a lot of meth addicts and I'd seen some come into the ER. Their bodies were so wrecked with the chemicals they were inhaling it was a wonder they could even walk. I did not want that for Prescott.

"Don't worry. We'll stop it before that happens. I just

have to find Wes's cookhouse or catch him in a mistake." Jess turned to Maisy, his look stern. "You keep all this under wraps. Last thing I need is Wes getting jumpy because he thinks I'm getting close. Got it?"

"Of course, Jess. I won't say a thing," she promised.

"Not even to Milo."

She nodded in agreement and did her zip-the-lip-and-swallow-the-key gesture.

"Don't want Ma knowing about this either. Once they come back down, we don't talk about it again," he ordered.

Maisy and I nodded simultaneously

As I set the table, I said a silent prayer that Jess would stop Wes before he could inundate Prescott with meth. Drugs were horrifying and with them came desperation. Addicts were willing to cross any line necessary for their next fix. I just hoped that when lines were crossed, Rowen and I would be safe.

CHAPTER TEN

GIGI

"Time to talk, honey. Before we get back to the farmhouse."

Jess and I had just left his mother's place, an old rundown trailer on the edge of town.

Maisy was hanging with Rowen until we got back to the farmhouse and then she was taking off, likely to start prepping for her date with Everett. While raiding my closet, she had gone on and on about exfoliation, hair removal, nail painting and such. With all she had planned to do, I figured she'd need every minute of the next twenty-four hours to get ready for her date.

Jess and I had originally planned for an evening alone. We were going to eat at the café and then I'd have my first sleepover at his house while Maisy stayed with Rowen.

And I really wanted that. All of the making out and groping we'd been doing for the last three weeks had me so hot and bothered I was about to combust.

But this day had not gone as planned. Not even close. Starting with Ryan and his construction crew and ending with my first trip tonight to Jess's childhood home. And now we would be delaying a night alone together again.

"I know you're mad about the barn, Georgia. Wasn't a big fan of you telling me over voicemail."

"Sorry. I should have waited to talk to you but I couldn't keep it in. I was too angry and your voicemail was all I had," I said.

"Maybe next time try and contain it until I answer the damn phone, huh? At least yell at me when I can fucking respond."

"I'll try but can't make any promises."

"Good enough," he muttered.

"Jess, I am not okay with you tearing down the barn."

"Don't know if you noticed, Freckles, but it's almost done. Ryan's crew probably has half a day left, tops. Next week, it'll be gone. Besides, isn't that what you wanted? You're the one that was willing to risk lung cancer to burn it down."

"You're right. Let me rephrase my protest. I'm not okay with the *manner* in which you went about having the barn torn down," I said.

"Yeah? And what manner was that? Making it so you never had to go in there again? Never had to think about it again?"

"I understand you were trying to do something to help me, Jess. And I appreciate that. But you can't just make those types of big decisions without talking to me first." I was trying to keep calm but his tone was making my blood pressure rise.

"Georgia, you were the one that said you wanted the

barn gone. That you couldn't go in there again. Now you don't have to. How is that a problem?"

"Fine. It's gone. You win." I threw my hands in the air. "But you're not paying for it. That is my responsibility."

"I'm getting sick of reminding you that I pay, Georgia. Jesus, seems like I have to remind you every fucking day."

"This isn't a dinner, Jess. Or coffee. This is a barn. And, apparently, a garage too."

"I. Pay."

"No. You. Don't!" I yelled. "Not with something this big. It's my property and, I'll repeat, my responsibility."

Rather than respond, Jess yanked the car to the side of the road and threw it in park.

"You saw where I grew up tonight, Georgia. Saw the mess. Saw the filth. I never had a home worth keeping up. Worth making into something nice. Because why would I bother fixing up a shit hole? I could spend thousands on that place and it'd still be a shit hole. So when Ben asked me to keep up his place, I jumped at the chance to have something good. Something clean. Something she wouldn't neglect and ruin. And I've been working at that for almost twenty years. Imagine my fucking disappointment when I thought I had to give that all up."

The farmhouse. That was why he was with me. Why he pushed so hard to date me. Why he went from a jackass to a boyfriend overnight. Why all of a sudden he was bringing me coffee and taking me to dinner. Why he was calling Rowen "little bit" and bringing us kittens. He didn't want me. Why would he? He could have someone much better.

Tears started to fill my eyes because it finally all made sense.

"I knew it. You're with me because of the farmhouse," I said.

"What?" he clipped, "Fuck. You're not even listening to me."

"Oh, I'm listening, Jess. And it sounded like you just said that the house I'm living in has been your sanctuary for the last twenty years, and your only shot at keeping it is to hook up with me."

He scrubbed his face roughly and groaned into his palms. Lifting his hands to the sides of my face, he said, "Please, baby. Please listen to me."

Tears escaped from both my eyes but I managed a small nod.

"Do I seem like the type of man who would get with you for your house?" he asked.

"Well . . . no."

"No. I'm not. If I wanted a house like that, I've got the money in the bank to have them start construction tomorrow. Build a place twice as big, twice as nice on twice the land. I'm with you because you are you. Not because of your fucking house."

"It doesn't make sense, Jess. Why you'd be with me. I'm just me. And you're you. The whole town knows you and loves you. You're perfect. So handsome it takes my breath away. And I'm just plain old me. Of course you'd be with me for the house. That makes sense."

A few more tears started to fall. He stared at me for a minute with a blank face, but then his eyes softened. Gently he swiped my tears with his thumbs.

"I love the farmhouse, Georgia," he said. "Ben giving me that place to look after gave me a purpose. Kept me from getting into trouble. And I've been looking after it for a long-ass time. Turning that responsibility over to someone new was always gonna be difficult for me. But not so difficult that I'd choose to be with a woman just to try and keep it. How could you think I was that type of man?"

"I'm sorry, Jess. I just . . . I didn't mean to insult you. But the house—" I started but he stopped me, gently shaking me still in his hands.

"Listen. To. Me," he said. "I'm with you because you're who I want to be with. Because to me, it makes perfect fucking sense. Even if you don't see it yet. You've got beauty like I've never laid eyes on before. It was the first thought that crossed my mind when I saw you in the ER room with Milo. You're not plain. Get that shit outta your head. You're my girl because I want you to be my girl."

"But—"

"No. We're not going over this again. You gotta get it right in your head. I choose to be with you. Just because of you. Can you please try and process that?" he asked.

I sniffled and blinked fast to stop my tears. I wanted to believe him. Down to my bones, I wanted to believe every one of his words and to trust what he was telling me was the truth. But I needed more time.

My brain just could not comprehend why he'd want me.

He sighed and lifted his palms off my face to hold my hands. "Three weeks ago, I was feeling pretty fucking lucky that the person who took over the responsibility of the farmhouse turned out to be my girl. So not only did I get her, but in a way, I get to keep the farmhouse too. And my girl, she's my responsibility. She gets bit by a fucking rattlesnake, she gets a garage where that shit will never happen again."

"It's too much money, Jess. I'm the one who should pay for it," I said.

"Baby, this is something I need to do. Let me."

"Jess—"

"I've got fifty thousand dollars sitting in my checking account I have no intention of keeping. I always planned on getting it back to you somehow. Paying for a new garage will make that happen a hell of a lot quicker than buying you coffees and dinners. Even when those coffees cost a fortune."

My shoulders sagged. "Ben wanted you to have that money."

"And Ben asked me to take care of his girls. I think he'd be okay with that money going to a new garage. Don't you?"

Ben would absolutely want me to have a garage. And he would have done the exact same thing as Jess. Made arrangements for the barn that terrified me to disappear.

Damn.

"I feel like I'm always losing our arguments," I said.

He chuckled. "Don't worry, baby. Someday, you'll probably win one."

I shrugged and looked down at our linked hands. His joke didn't make me feel better.

Fighting with Jess was not how I'd planned to spend my evening. This was miserable. Sure, we were getting to know each other and an argument here or there was bound to happen. But tonight was supposed to be about us taking our relationship to the next stage. Instead of being together and happy, here we were in my car, wrapping up a fight.

We needed to move forward. To connect. Literally.

And I didn't want to delay any longer. Jess would never push to have sex with Roe at home but at some point that was going to happen. We couldn't limit our sexual activities to only the nights when she was gone, so we might as well start tonight.

"I really want you to stay the night tonight. No more waiting," I blurted.

His hands jerked in mine. Clearly, he had not been expecting me to say that. Honestly, I was a bit surprised myself.

His eyes were staring at me intensely, like he was holding back from ripping me out of my seat and having his way with me in the back of my car. In a flash he was back at the wheel and peeling away from the side of the road, driving to the farmhouse at warp speed.

He didn't say a word but I knew exactly what he was thinking.

We'd be locking my bedroom door tonight.

———

"DON'T FREAK OUT, Georgia. Don't freak out. It's just sex. Sure, sex with the most beautiful man you've ever seen in your life. But still. It's just sex. It will be fine. No reason to panic."

I was giving myself a pep talk in the bathroom mirror.

It wasn't helping.

Jess and I hadn't spoken the rest of the way back to the farmhouse. I had been too busy planning how I could get Maisy out of there and Rowen to bed in record time.

Jess had given me a sexy smirk after parking the car and I'd winked at him before jumping out and moving quickly into the house.

After giving Maisy a quick hug and saying good-bye, I had ushered Roe upstairs for a bath. I'd breezed through bath and bedtime, so focused on my tasks that I hadn't had time to start freaking out. But after Roe had fallen asleep during story time, I'd snuck out of her room and gone to my bathroom to get ready for bed.

Correction. Get ready for sex. Something I hadn't had in a little over five years. And the last time, I'd gotten pregnant.

So here I was, staring at myself in the bathroom mirror. Telling Jess I wanted him to stay the night had been a huge mistake. All of the confidence I'd had in the car earlier had evaporated.

My hair was down and I was wearing a spaghetti-strap white tank top and a pair of light blue shorts. It was the raciest sleepwear I had.

I didn't own sexy nightgowns, because I didn't need them. Why would I? Besides Sunday when Jess stayed over, the only person to stay in my bed was Roe. And though she loved pretty things, I doubted she would truly appreciate an expensive silky lace chemise.

I'd heard him come into my bedroom earlier. Him and his perfectly sculpted muscles and strong, amazing body.

My body was not amazing. My breasts weren't small but they weren't big either. Just average. And those ten extra pounds were evenly distributed across my belly, hips, thighs and ass. I wasn't fat but I wasn't skinny either. Just average.

That was me. Average Gigi. And now I was moments away from being naked in front of not-so-average Jess.

Body issues aside, I was also freaking out because I hadn't had sex in five years. Even though I'd wound up pregnant from a one-night stand at a friend's wedding, I wasn't promiscuous. Damn tuxedos and tequila.

Before Roe's father, I'd had three lovers, none of whom had professed I was a sexual dynamo. In fact, Nate had told me repeatedly that I was horrible in bed. That his one night with me was the worst he'd ever had in his life.

I was sure Jess had more than four sexual partners in his past and certainly those women knew what they were doing. What if Jess dumped me after tonight because I was lousy at sex?

"Don't freak out. Don't freak out. Don't freak out," I chanted quietly.

"Georgia, you've been in there for thirty minutes talking to yourself. I'm coming in."

I guess I hadn't been so quiet after all.

Before I could protest, the door opened and Jess walked directly to me, fitting himself at my back. He leaned down to talk softly in my ear, resting his chin on my shoulder.

"What's going on in that head of yours?"

"Nothing," I lied.

"Georgia."

"I'm fine," I lied again.

We stared at each other through the mirror for a few moments until I was no longer looking at our reflection. Jess spun me around and I was now looking at his naked chest. I didn't get to look at it for long because seconds later, he bent down, hoisted me at the back of my thighs and carried me out of the bathroom. I wrapped my legs around his waist and my arms around his shoulders so I wouldn't fall as he hauled me straight to bed.

He dropped me on my back and followed me down as we both sank into the soft mattress. I was about to warn him that this was likely going to be the worst sex of his life when his mouth came down hard on top of mine.

Jess took control of my mouth with his, and even if I could have remembered what I was going to say, speech would have eluded me. All of my nervous energy was

143

suddenly replaced with heated desire. Right now, my body was in control and it needed Jess.

My brain could process all of that other stuff later.

We kissed with no hesitation. We didn't need to rein ourselves in tonight because finally, we weren't going to stop.

Jess left my mouth and started kissing my neck. He sucked and kissed down my jaw to my collarbone. I was already hot from the kiss, but the farther he progressed down my neck, the more I ignited. My sex was throbbing like never before and I was taking deep, labored breaths, trying to suck in enough oxygen so that I wouldn't pass out.

"Did you lock the door?" I asked breathlessly.

Jess murmured, "Uh-huh," against my neck, dragging his tongue over my earlobe. His teeth bit it lightly before he sucked it into his mouth, sending a shiver straight to my core.

I moaned quietly and sank into the bed, stretching out my neck to give him better access.

His kisses trailed lower on my chest and down my sternum until he leaned back away from me. I instantly missed the heat and weight of his body on top of mine.

He grabbed the hem of my tank, and with a whoosh, my top was gone.

I fell back into the bed and he splayed his hands at my sides. Those bright blue eyes of his were heated, taking me in. With another whoosh, my shorts and gray lace panties were gone too.

I lay there bare for him, my legs wide, bracketing his thighs.

Again his beautiful eyes roamed my body, but this time, he whispered, "True beauty."

My breath hitched, and my heart beat so hard in my chest it hurt. I hoped and wished with all I had that he was sincere. That he thought I was beautiful. That it wasn't just a line.

Because those powerful words were like a balm to my heart, healing what had been broken in the past. I desperately wanted them to be real.

He came back down on top of me and took my mouth in another deep, wet kiss. My hands lifted to the sides of his face and my fingers pulled at his hair.

He broke apart from me once more to take off his black boxer briefs. I caught a glimpse of his cock as he moved back on top of me. Jess was beautiful. Every inch. And there were a lot of inches to admire.

My eyes met his as he settled his hips between my thighs. His arms at my sides, his weight on his elbows, his hands touching my face. He gently caressed both sides of my jaw with his thumbs while looking deeply into my eyes.

Jess communicated a lot with his eyes. Anger. Humor. Affection.

And in that moment, his eyes told me I was the most beautiful woman in the world. A woman desired and cherished.

"You ready, baby?" he whispered.

"Yes." I nodded.

He studied me for a moment to make sure I wasn't lying. Then his mouth came down on mine again. There would be no more talking or gentle caresses.

I battled his tongue with my own as our kiss became a frenzied mashing of lips and teeth.

His hands left my face and traveled to my breasts, stroking both thumbs across my nipples and sending a shock wave between my legs. The feel of his hard cock pushed up against my sex made me soaking wet and ready for him. His mouth broke from mine as he sucked a nipple into his mouth. Trailing wet kisses across my chest, he turned his attention to the other one and gave it a strong suck and a tug with his teeth. One of his hands traveled down my stomach to my sex. He stroked me gently, rubbing my wetness around as he kept at my nipples with his mouth. I turned my head so I could moan into the pillow as I savored the feel of him playing with me.

When he slipped a finger inside me, I went from being hot to on fire. I was so primed and ready I ached with the need for him to be inside me.

"Jess," I moaned as my fingers tugged his hair.

He abandoned my nipples to grab the foil packet from the nightstand. He sat back on his calves, straddling me, and pulled on the condom. Coming back down on top of me, he put one elbow in the bed beside my head while his hand guided the tip of his cock to my entrance. He flicked it over my clit once and then again, each time making me tremble.

Slowly, he pushed inside. He'd move in an inch and then back out. Again and again. It was torture. Amazing torture. The ache in my core was so strong I grabbed and clawed at the sheets under my hands.

I groaned as he pulled out again. His mouth formed a sexy grin before he pushed himself in to the root with one powerful thrust.

My back arched off the bed while my eyes squeezed shut. Jess was big and I needed a second to adjust to his size.

"Fuck, baby," he groaned. "So tight."

"Move, Jess." I caught my breath just enough to issue the order.

He pushed his hips hard against me, sending his cock so far back it bottomed out. Then he was moving in and out in a steady rhythm. Over and over. With each inward thrust, he hit a spot inside me that made my legs tremble. My body was shaking, building toward a blinding release.

And then I was there.

He reached down and found my clit with his middle finger. The second he touched me, a rush of heat traveled through my body and I exploded with the hardest orgasm of my life. White spots erupted behind my eyes and my body clenched around him, pulsing intensely while my hands held tight to the sheets beside me. I clamped my mouth shut, biting my bottom lip to hold in a scream.

Jess kept thrusting through my orgasm until he dropped his chest to mine and buried his face in my neck and came.

We stayed connected, my legs wrapped around his hips, while we both worked to catch our breath.

He gave me a tight squeeze with his arms as he pulled out, then went to the bathroom to get rid of the condom.

I stared at the ceiling for a minute before searching for my clothes. I'd managed to shut off my brain while we were having sex, mostly because Jess's mouth, hands and cock had shut it off for me. But now it was working again. And all I could think about was how effing incredible that had been. Like nothing I'd ever felt before.

I was really hoping that Jess thought so too. That I wasn't a disappointment.

All of my nervous energy and anxiety was back in full force.

With my clothes back on, I burrowed under the covers. My back was to his side of the bed as I lay there, freaking the hell out.

I heard Jess come out of the bathroom but I didn't turn to watch him grab his briefs and pull them on. I didn't turn when he climbed into bed. And I didn't turn when he shut off the light on the end table.

I did, however, turn when one of his arms went under me at the same time the other went across my waist and he forced my body to his side.

"What's wrong, Georgia? I left here two minutes ago and you were good. Come back and you're huddled so far on your side of the bed it's a wonder you didn't fall on the fucking floor."

"I'm fine," I lied, whispering against his bare chest.

"Stop lying to me, Georgia," he said. "Especially not after what we just had."

"What did we have?" I asked, nervous for his response.

Every muscle in my body snapped tight.

I replayed my words in my mind and realized that they hadn't come out right. Not at all.

Damn.

"I was hoping you thought it was the best sex of your life, seeing as that's how I feel. Maybe that you felt as lucky as I do right now knowing that not only do we click outside the bedroom but we're pretty fucking great in it too. That we don't have to have one without the other. That's what I thought we just had. But what the fuck do I know," he clipped.

A thousand-pound weight disappeared from my chest. He'd just said that I was the best sex of his life!

I couldn't stop the smile that spread wide on my face.

"Okay, now I'm fine. And I'm not lying this time. I was freaking out that you might have thought it was bad and then you would have dumped me. I thought that was pretty, ah, effing great too," I said.

He didn't respond and his body didn't relax. I started

panicking again until I felt his chest and shoulders start to shake.

I lifted my head up to look down at his gorgeous, laughing face. Then I laughed too, feeling relieved but mostly just feeling happy.

After he stopped laughing, he caught me in a deep, hot kiss that led to us having sex again. We took our time exploring each other's bodies the second go, building each other up in a slow burn. He made me come with his fingers and then again with his cock.

Three amazing orgasms later and my body was as relaxed as it had been in years. I was totally content and pliable. But my mind was still active, unable to shut down and find sleep, thinking about all that had happened today.

Jess wasn't asleep either. His arm underneath me was wrapped around my back and his hand was lightly rubbing my hip.

"What's going on with your mom?" I was tucked tightly to Jess's side, my arm across his torso, fingers drumming lightly on his chest.

"She's just not always there. Like she gets lost in her own head. Spaces out completely. Doesn't even realize she's doing it."

"Is that why she's been in the hospital so much?"

"Yeah. She forgets the oven is hot and reaches in without a pad. Goes outside, doesn't pay attention to where she's walking and trips. Shit like that. Once when I was in high school, she walked outside to get the mail when it was snowing. Must have gone out sometime in the middle of the morning. Spaced out and stood by the mailbox all damn day. Found her there mostly frozen when I got home. Wasn't wearing a coat or shoes. Took her to the hospital and she had frostbite on her fingers, ears and toes. Lucky she didn't lose any."

I didn't know what to say. My mom could have won consecutive mother of the year awards. I couldn't imagine growing up knowing you couldn't depend on your mother. But it was starting to make sense to me why Jess was the way he was. Always in charge. Always taking care of everyone. He had started doing it early and probably didn't know any other way.

"Has it always been like this?"

"My whole life. Felicity and I learned early on not to rely on her," he said. "It wasn't that she was neglecting us on purpose. She just can't help it. She loves us. Has a good heart. Just . . . has a broken mind."

"Felicity?" I asked.

"My sister. Moved to Seattle the day after she graduated high school. Haven't seen her since. She's two years younger than me so that was, what, fourteen years ago?"

"Do you talk to her at all?"

"Couple times a year. Try and call each other on our birthdays and Christmas."

"What about your dad?"

"Stuck around until I was eight, then left. Moved to Billings to work for the refinery. Came back to visit off and on for a couple years. But then he met a woman over there and stopped coming back altogether."

"That's terrible," I said.

"Just the way it was. Think he just got tired of taking care of Ma."

"So he left an eight- and a six-year-old to do it instead? That's not right, Jess."

"Nope," he agreed and gave my hip a firm squeeze with

his hand. He could tell I was getting worked up. "But it doesn't matter anymore, Freckles. I got what I needed from him as a kid, that being the checks he sent us twice a month. Once I got hired at the station, I wrote him a letter telling him he didn't need to send them to Ma anymore. We were done with him. He doesn't have a place in my life and hasn't in ages."

"I'm sorry, honey," I whispered.

"It's okay."

We lay there in silence, me slowly starting to drift to sleep. It was getting late and though there were thoughts still racing in my head, my body was exhausted and needed to shut down.

Just before I nodded off, Jess squeezed my hip. "Georgia?"

"Yeah?" I yawned.

"Ma latched onto Roe tonight. Talked about her the whole ride home."

"I know. Is that a bad thing?"

"She'll want to babysit. Under no circumstances are you to let that happen."

"Okay." I nodded.

Jess's mother couldn't be trusted with her own children. He didn't need to tell me twice not to leave her with mine.

CHAPTER ELEVEN

GIGI

A week later, Jess and I were spending our nights learning more about each other's bodies.

Tonight, I was on my back in bed, legs spread wide, with my knees angled up. His mouth was on me and I was almost there. My legs were shaking and I writhed on the sheets.

Jess so knew how to use his mouth. I'd never had a partner go down on me before so I didn't have anything to compare him to. Regardless, I sent a silent prayer of gratitude to the heavens. It was bliss.

His tongue was working my clit while he moved two fingers in and out.

"Oh my god," I moaned. My hips bucked when he gave my bud a hard suck.

He eased up and with one last flick, I came undone. Turning my head into my pillow to keep from shouting, I let my body shudder and explode.

My back collapsed back into the bed as I came down, panting for air.

Jess kissed his way up my stomach and lined himself up with my entrance. With one powerful thrust, his bare cock was buried deep.

I loved it when he did that.

He started to move in and out with slow, deep strokes. To reach a second orgasm, it usually took him a while to work me back up, but tonight I knew it wouldn't take much for him to get me there again.

And it didn't.

He kept his unhurried pace until I was on the edge.

"I'm there, Jess," I breathed.

"Yeah, baby," he said. "Fuck, you feel so good. So tight and wet. Love fucking my Georgia."

His dirty words in my ear sent me over the edge and my orgasm ripped through me. I covered my mouth with a hand to muffle my moans as I clenched tightly around Jess's cock.

He gave up his slow pace and started thrusting faster and harder until he moaned into my neck and let himself come.

Our hearts pounded in sync as he released his weight on top of me, crushing me into the bed. I loved the feel of him lying heavily on me. I couldn't take it for long, but while I could, I savored it. My legs wound around his thighs and I trailed my hands over his muscled back, down to his ass.

Jess had such a great ass. I gave it one good squeeze and felt his cock jerk to life inside me.

He chuckled into my neck. "So glad we're done with condoms, baby."

"Hmm," I hummed. "Me too."

We had run out of condoms tonight and decided to sally forth without. After having Rowen, I'd gone on birth control pills to help regulate my periods, and before Jess, I hadn't had sex in half a decade. Jess assured me he'd only ever used condoms. Ever. And since he was the poster boy for responsibility, I knew we were safe.

Jess kissed my neck and slowly pulled out so we could hit the bathroom.

We each did our cleanup, and while I pulled on my pajama pants and tank, he crawled back into bed with his black boxer briefs.

"Do you own any other color boxers?" I asked.

He chuckled.

I guess that meant no.

Smiling, I tucked myself into Jess's side.

Tonight, we'd spent a quiet evening together. The three of us had gone on a short hike to enjoy the September weather. The mountains were bright with color. Winter wasn't far away and soon the leaves would fall, so we'd taken advantage of the short autumn season.

"I loved that hike, honey. And the sunset." After our hike, we'd driven to a lookout and watched the sun set while drinking hot cocoa.

"Yeah. Proud of Roe for hiking the whole thing," he said.

"She's getting so big. Feels like yesterday she was just starting to walk." Before I could get all weepy thinking about my baby girl growing up, I changed the subject. "Are you doing okay? It's been a tough week, Sheriff."

On Tuesday night, someone had come to the station and slashed the tires on all of the cruisers. Granted, most of the deputies took their cars home with them, but the three extras left in the back parking lot had been hit. Twelve shredded tires.

Jess had been furious. He'd watched the security camera

footage a hundred times and still couldn't make out the bastard that did it. Whoever it was had known exactly where the cameras were. After slashing the last tire, he'd walked up to the camera, given it a mock salute, flipped it the middle finger and bowed.

Someone was taunting Jess. He assumed it was Wes, and I was sure he was right. But his hands were tied without proof.

"I needed tonight, baby. Some time away from the station to clear my head. To see my girls. It helped out. It's been a shit couple of weeks. Feels like I'm getting nowhere and losing control of my town."

Resting my chin on his chest, I stared into his blue eyes. "You'll get to the bottom of it. I know you will. It just might take some time."

"Yeah," he responded, not sounding like he believed me.

"And we'll be here whenever you need another getaway. Okay?"

"Okay," he said, stroking the side of my hair.

I dropped my head back onto his shoulder and twisted my legs so they were entwined with his.

"Night, honey," I whispered.

"Night, Freckles."

Jess was so exhausted he fell asleep before me.

Before I drifted off, I decided to start a new Friday rotation until it snowed. One week at the café. The next on a hike, enjoying the beauty of Montana and the comfort of our little unit.

———

JESS

"Sheriff Cleary," I answered my desk phone.

"Jess. Frank down here at Pawn One. Think you'd better come down here right now. I got a kid in my shop trying to sell me some jewelry that I recognize from Big Sky Jewelry."

"Be right there," I said and raced to Prescott's one and only pawnshop.

The kid in the shop was probably sixteen or seventeen. He stood at the counter, looking over a gold coin collection locked in a display case. Next to him was a small stack of silver. At an initial glance, I recognized one of the bracelets that the jewelry store owner had described in her list of stolen articles.

I walked up behind the kid and slapped one hand on his shoulder, causing him to spin around with wide eyes.

"Oh, shit," he muttered.

"Yeah. I think you'd better start explaining what you're doing with that jewelry, kid."

"I, ah, was just . . ." he stammered.

"You were just trying to sell a handful of stolen silver. Time to take a trip to the station. We'll call your parents when we get there," I said, reaching for my cuffs.

Hours later, the kid had confessed and been released to his parents. I had just sent the preliminary report to the county attorney and tomorrow, the court would decide his punishment.

"Hey, boss. You got a minute?" Sam asked from my office doorway.

"Anytime, old man. Come on in." I was packing up for the day but stopped to sit so Sam would take a load off too.

He slumped in a chair across from my desk.

"Appreciate you sitting in there with me today. Know long hours in those damn metal chairs are hard on your back," I said.

"Ah, it's no problem. I just can't believe we're looking for another dealer," Sam said.

"Shit keeps getting deeper."

After bringing Zander Baker and his parents into the station's interrogation room, I'd learned why he had stolen the jewelry.

To buy illegal prescription pills.

Zander would take a couple of pills himself, usually oxycodone, and then resell the rest at a markup to his friends.

So not only was I trying to track down Wes's meth operation, now I was looking for a pill mill.

Fuck. Me.

After hearing Zander's confession, I had more questions than answers.

Zander didn't know who he was buying the pills from. The exchanges were done using texts and remote drop locations, and every day was in a new place. Underneath a rock by a light pole. Behind a garbage can of a shop downtown. In an envelope taped underneath a mailbox.

The phone numbers had all been linked to disposable phones, which made tracking the dealer using texts impossible. And the pills were always picked up outside of town. Also at different locations during each deal.

"You believe him that he didn't hit Silas's calf?" Sam asked.

"He confessed to everything else. Even told us he went out there for a pill pickup. Don't know why he'd lie about it. Could have been the seller that killed the animal."

"Or worse. Could be a whole other bunch of kids picking up pills," Sam said, shaking his head.

"Fuck, Sam. I don't want Prescott's kids on drugs. We gotta get to these fucking dealers."

"What are the chances Wes is behind the pills?"

"Doubt it," I said. "Doesn't make sense that he'd branch out. He controls all aspects of his crystal meth operation. He does production so he isn't reliant on a supplier. Probably keeps eighty to ninety percent of his profits. Pills would mean an outside source. Big cuts into his profit margin. I just don't think he'd do it."

"Yeah," Sam said. "You're probably right. You'll get them, boss."

I sure as fuck hoped he was right.

By the weekend, nothing had changed. I was putting in some extra hours doing paperwork so come tomorrow, I could hit the streets. I needed to be more present in town. See what was happening with my own eyes.

"Working on a Sunday, Brick? No rest for Prescott's Good Prince, I guess."

Wes waltzed into my office.

I grumbled but didn't respond. Instead, I contemplated firing my dispatcher for letting a suspected criminal approach me without warning.

"What do you want, Wes? Here to turn yourself in? Draw me a map to your meth house? Go to rehab?" I asked.

"Whatever are you talking about?" Wes said. "I just came to talk to my old friend Jess."

"Spit it out, Drummond. What do you want?"

"I heard you went out to talk to Dad last week," he said.

"Your point?"

"They just love you. Mom and Dad. So disappointed that I didn't turn out more like you."

"You know how they feel about drugs. No surprise they're disappointed. Maybe get some help and make them proud. Take over the farm like your dad always wanted."

Wes scoffed. "I'm not running that farm. And I don't need help."

I shook my head. We'd had this conversation too many times to count. No one could get through to Wes. Not his parents. Not his friends. Maybe we were all stupid for holding out hope that he'd turn his life around.

"What do you want, Wes?"

"You know, I'm just so happy for you, Brick. Finding Gigi. She's stunning. And that little girl? So cute."

My frame locked tight. What the fuck was he doing bringing up Georgia and Rowen?

"It just so happens I've been in the area lately when Gigi picks up the kid from school. It's nice. To watch them together. So nice, I think I'll do it every day," he said.

I shot out of my chair and leaned over my desk.

"Stay the fuck away from them. If I hear you're bothering her, you're dead. Cop or not, I'll end you."

He sneered and started backing away.

Then he gave me a mock salute, flipped me the middle finger and bowed. Just like the man had done on camera the night he slashed the cruisers' tires.

It had been Wes. I knew it.

And I couldn't do a fucking thing about it.

I stood and watched him leave the station. Then I picked up a cup on my desk and sent it flying into the wall, the glass shattering on impact.

"Fuck!"

I gave myself a few moments to calm down. Then I grabbed a dustpan to clean up the glass before Oakley could cut his paws. When I was done, I hit the vending machine for a soda before sitting back down in front of my paperwork.

I was stressed to the max. Wes kept pushing me into a corner and all I wanted to do was push back. But I fucking couldn't. My badge bound me to follow the rules. Most of the time, I liked those rules. The structure. Not today.

My fuse was short and I knew it wouldn't take much for me to blow. I pitied the person who pushed me over the edge.

———

GIGI

The weekend was going by quickly. While Jess was at work, Rowen and I had spent time doing fall yard work. We had also cleaned the entire house and done the laundry.

It was nice to have a quiet weekend with my girl. We were settled from the move and getting into a good routine. Our lives were officially here in Prescott and it was starting to feel like home.

Rowen had made princess crowns this morning and instead of one for me, she'd made a "boy princess crown" for Jess. His was decorated with green and blue glitter pens, hers with yellow and pink.

She hadn't seen him since our hike Friday and she'd been asking about him all day. It was Sunday afternoon heading into another busy week. Even though he was working, it would be nice to surprise him with a quick visit. Rowen could deliver her present and he could take a little break from the madness.

Roe fidgeted in her seat as we drove into town, barely able to contain her excitement. Her little legs kicked back and forth wildly the whole trip.

The station was dead quiet. The dispatcher up front was the only one in the building except for Jess.

I had a hold of Rowen's hand as we walked through the bull pen, but when we got close to Jess's office at the back corner, she pulled away and sprinted toward his door, waving his crown and shouting his name.

The front of his office had two big windows on either side of the door. It gave him an open view of the bull pen and deputies a view into his office.

Rowen's shouting startled Jess. The second before she'd started yelling, he'd lifted a can of soda to his mouth. When she shouted, he flinched and fumbled the can, dropping it on his messy desk, spilling soda all over his sea of papers.

Shit.

He stood up from his desk so quickly, his chair went flying back, crashing into the wall.

Oakley got startled and started barking the second Rowen entered the office.

I hurried behind Rowen so I could help Jess clean up the mess but before I could make it to the office, he bellowed, "Damn it, Rowen! Shut up!"

Between Jess's yelling and Oakley's barking, Rowen dissolved into tears. I reached the doorway just as she collapsed to her knees, Jess's crown falling to the floor.

"What the hell is your problem, Jess?" I bent and picked Rowen up.

"Me? What the fuck are you two doing here? Look at

this fucking mess, Georgia! Would a phone call to warn me have been too fucking much to ask?" he shouted.

Jackass Jess was back.

It was one thing to yell at me. But to be an asshole to my child? Uh . . . no.

I shoved my hand, palm out, in his direction.

"She was bringing you that crown she made you today," I said. "She was excited to give it to you and we wanted it to be a surprise. Well, I guess the surprise was on us because I'm standing here, shocked that you could be such a jerk to a four-year-old kid. I knew you could be a jackass to me. But to Rowen?"

"Georgia—" he started but since my hand was still out, I waved, stopping his words.

"No. Not okay, Jess. Stay at your house for a while. I'll call you when I'm ready to talk. Maybe." I turned and walked out.

He followed, Oakley right on his heels.

"Georgia, wait."

But with Rowen burrowed into my chest, still sobbing, there was no way I was stopping.

"Let's talk about this," he pleaded.

"Nope. No talking. Think of me like NASA. I need space." I kept moving, Rowen's legs swinging wildly at my sides as I stormed out to the parking lot.

Jess didn't follow.

As Rowen continued to cry, I scolded myself on the drive home. How could I have been so stupid? Hadn't I done this once before?

Nate had said horrible and nasty things to me. When I'd told him that I was pregnant, he'd thrown a glass of water in my face. I'd been humiliated, sitting in a restaurant crying and soaked.

After he signed away his parental rights, I had vowed not to let assholes into my life. Or Roe's.

I had thought Jess was an asshole at first, but he had been proving me wrong. I guess it had been too good to be true. If he couldn't keep a hold of his temper, I couldn't trust him with Rowen. Or with my heart.

I had let down my guard again.

Stupid.

CHAPTER TWELVE

GIGI

"Mommy?" Rowen called.

"Kitchen!"

We'd already had bath time and both of us were dressed for bed. I had come to the kitchen for a glass of wine and gotten lost in thought.

"What are you doing?" Rowen asked when she walked in.

"Just thinking, baby girl. I'm tired."

"Thinking about Jess?" she asked.

"Yeah. About Jess."

She frowned.

We'd left the station on Sunday and come straight home. After I'd calmed Rowen down, we'd sat together on the couch and I'd apologized for Jess's behavior. Her feelings had been raw. He had hurt them. Mine too.

I'd had a fitful night's sleep, tossing and turning, the faintest noise sending me back and forth to the windows so I could look outside and make sure no one was there. That Jess wasn't there.

The next day had been brutal. I'd checked my phone at least a hundred times, expecting to see some sort of communication from Jess. But there had been nothing.

That had been four days ago and I still hadn't heard from him.

I was confused and angry. Jess's silence was making me nauseous. Just because I'd asked for space didn't mean he couldn't apologize.

I hated that I didn't know what was going to happen with us. I was mad at him but that didn't mean my feelings for him had disappeared. This separation between us had made me realize how much it would hurt if we ended our relationship.

Even though I'd said I would call him, I couldn't find the courage to pick up the phone. I didn't know if I wanted to break up with him or try and work it out.

I was scared. Scared we'd be here again.

"Do you want to have a dance party, Mommy?" Rowen asked, pulling me from my thoughts.

"Do you?"

She smiled huge and nodded, bouncing from one foot to the other.

When she was two, I had invented dance parties as a way to cheer her up or distract her from a tantrum. And we'd been having them ever since.

I would crank the music and we'd dance around the house like crazy people. We'd shake our booties and laugh until our cheeks hurt. The last dance party we'd had was before Ben died and we were overdue.

"Okay." I smiled. "Go get the speaker from the office."

She scampered as fast as her feet could carry her, squealing with joy, and met me in the living room, shoving the Bluetooth speaker into my hands.

"Ready?" I asked.

"Yeah!"

"The Middle" by Jimmy Eat World started blaring through the house.

As we danced and laughed, I raised my arms above my head and let loose, jumping around my beautiful daughter as she giggled and danced her heart out. The lyrics reminded me of what I needed to hear.

Everything was going to be all right.

When it was over, I was laughing and dancing so hard I was out of breath.

"That was fun!" Rowen shouted, beaming with happiness.

"Yes it was." The smile on my face was real and wide.

"I liked it."

At the sound of Jess's voice, I jumped back and clutched my hands to my pounding heart.

He was leaning against the wall, his long legs crossed at his ankles, his arms resting lightly on his chest. And he had a huge smile on his face.

"Jess!" Rowen screamed and launched her little body at his. Either she had forgotten about the incident at the station Sunday or she had already forgiven him.

He picked her up and threw her up in the air a couple feet. She giggled hysterically as she flew. He caught her on the way down and planted her firmly on his hip.

"We were having a dance party," she said.

"Is that what that was?"

Jess set Rowen down and knelt in front of her. "Little bit, I wasn't very nice on Sunday, was I?"

She tipped her head to the floor and shook it. "You hurt my feelings."

"I'm sorry, Rowen. I promise I won't do it again. I overreacted and just snapped. Can you forgive me?" he pleaded, tipping up her chin so she would see his apologetic face.

"Yeah." She smiled and then threw her arms around his neck.

I was glad he'd made amends with Roe. But we had a lot to talk about, so I interrupted their hug. "Okay, baby girl. Time for bed. Let's go up and read a story."

"Georgia—" Jess started, but I cut him off.

"We can talk after she's in bed."

He closed his eyes and dropped his chin. He gave me a small nod before I led Rowen upstairs.

I did my best but it was hard concentrating on Rowen's bedtime stories. My mind was on the man downstairs and what our upcoming conversation would bring.

Jess and I sat on the porch swing and watched the sunset. Soon it would be winter and my evenings outside would be over until spring.

He had on his coat while I was bundled up under a big blanket.

We sat in silence, neither one of us wanting to start the conversation.

"I'm sorry, Freckles. I fucked up," Jess finally said.

"I don't know what to do," I said softly.

"About what?" he asked.

"About us. She's my life, Jess. What you did to her? I can't risk that ever happening again. Because what happens next time? What will you say? Something worse? Something that will destroy her? She doesn't have a father in her life because he is an asshole and I won't allow him to treat her the way he treated me."

He took in a long, deep breath while letting my words sink in. "You've been looking for a chance to push me away. First, thinking I was with you to get the farmhouse. Now this. Doesn't it make sense to you yet?" he asked.

"What do you mean 'make sense'?"

"Those were your words, not mine. You said that we didn't make sense together. So you keep pushing me. Which means you still don't think we make sense. If you did, you'd be fighting a lot harder to get over your fears."

"Don't turn this on me, Jess. You weren't here on Sunday with her."

"No, I wasn't. Because you needed space. I gave you almost a week to cool off when what I wanted to do was follow your ass here from the station Sunday and work it out. Wanted to apologize to Rowen the minute you walked out the station's door and make it right. But I didn't get that. So I've been waiting for you to be done with your space. Praying she'd forgive me for being a dumbass. And she did. Right away. Because I meant it and she knows it. So why can't you forgive me?"

"It hurt, Jess." Tears started to fill my eyes. "Not just Sunday. How you treated me when we first moved here? It hurt. And then seeing you yell at Rowen made it worse. The fact that you went days without reaching out to me and apologizing hurt too."

Up until this point, we hadn't touched. But he'd had enough of the distance and shifted me across the swing and into his lap.

"I'm sorry, baby," he said into my hair. "I don't know

what else to say. I didn't know you wanted me to call you. If I had, I'd have been here on Sunday night. Thought you'd want me to stay away. I'll try, I swear. I'll try to not let it happen again. I had a lot on my mind and I snapped. Just like you let it blow when you're pissed, I do the same. I just need to find a way to let it out without hurting my girls. And I will. Promise. Just don't give up."

I sat in his arms and contemplated my options. Let *him* go or let *it* go.

"You're right. I am scared," I admitted. "I don't trust that you won't hurt me. That you can keep a hold of your temper and won't break our hearts. But this fight, it hurts too. I didn't like that you weren't here this last week. I've been sick to my stomach, wondering if you'd come back or if you were done with us. I don't want to be done, but at the same time, I don't want to get hurt. I feel like I'm torn in half and neither side knows what to do."

He pulled me tighter into his chest so I had to turn my face and rest my cheek against his heart.

"I've got you, baby. I swear you're safe with me. It hurt me being away too. I don't much feel like ever doing that again. You can trust me and I'll prove it to you. But you can't give up and push me away. You have to give me time to earn your trust and prove we make perfect sense. Forgive me for being an asshole? One last time?"

Maybe sharing my fears with him would make overcoming them easier. I wasn't sure but it was worth a shot. He was worth a shot.

So I whispered, "Okay."

After we finished our talk, Jess carried me inside from the porch swing and took me straight to bed. Then he showed me what the hype about make-up sex was all about.

Now we were ready for sleep, talking quietly and catching up from our week apart. I wasn't in my usual position, tucked to Jess's side. Instead, his arms were banded around me, pulling my back tightly to his front. When he talked, I felt his breath at the top of my head.

"Uh . . . how much of the dance party did you see?" I asked.

"A lot." His chest was shaking as he tried to muffle his laughter.

I was completely embarrassed he had seen me shaking my ass off, dancing like a fool in the living room.

Correction. I was completely mortified. My cheeks were so hot I was sure they were as red as an apple, so I turned my face into the pillow.

"Don't be embarrassed," he said. "I had a shit week without you. Coming here to see you laughing and dancing made it all go away. Besides, now I know you've got some moves, Freckles. You've been holding out on me." He squeezed his arms a little tighter around my body.

"What?" I asked, confused.

He unlaced his fingers from mine and one hand traveled under the covers to my bum.

"You can shake this ass, baby."

"Oh my god," I muttered into the pillow, now even more embarrassed. Jess lost his hold and started howling. His laughter filled the room. And mortified as I was, it felt great to have him back.

———

THE SHRILL RING of Jess's phone woke us from a dead sleep.

He reached quickly for his phone while I turned to look at my alarm clock.

2:23 a.m.

In all the nights that Jess had slept in my bed, not once had his phone gone off at odd hours. The latest I'd ever seen him get a call was nine o'clock. A call to the sheriff after two in the morning could not mean good things.

"Yeah," he answered. Ten seconds later, he rumbled, "Be right there."

He threw the covers back and leaped out of bed.

"Emergency in town, Georgia. There's a house on fire. I gotta get down there."

"Okay," I said to his back.

I sat up and waited for him to emerge from the closet.

I wasn't surprised when he came out wearing different clothes than he'd come over with tonight. Jess had been building a collection of clothes in my closet. A few pairs of jeans, a sweater and an extra work shirt. I'd even started putting his T-shirts, boxer briefs and socks in my top drawer. I hadn't asked but I assumed he stopped by his house a few times a week to reload the backpack he brought with him to the farmhouse.

"Don't know when I'll be back. I'll lock up when I go." He had pulled on jeans and a brown wool sweater.

"Be safe."

He planted one hand on the bed to lean in and give me a quick kiss. Then he took three long strides and was out the door. Twenty seconds later, I heard his truck roar to life and speed down the gravel drive. To make it to his truck so quickly, he must have been running by the time he hit the front door. And the sound of spraying gravel from his spinning truck wheels meant he wasn't slowing down.

Things were not good in Prescott tonight.

———

"BABY, WAKE UP."

I jolted awake and it took me a second to realize where I was. The office, in my chair.

Jess was on one knee, crouched down in front of me. One of his hands was gently shaking me awake.

After he'd left, I'd tried to get back to sleep. But an hour later, I'd still been tossing and turning. I'd finally given up and come to the office to read. I must have fallen asleep not long ago because the last thing I remembered was the early light of dawn coming through the front windows.

"What time is it?" I asked.

"Almost six."

I was curled into my reading chair in front of the fireplace. My feet were tucked into one side and my knees were drawn up to my chest. Unfolding myself, I turned to inspect him.

He was a mess. His hair was sticking up in all different directions and his face and clothes were streaked with soot. The only thing that would get all of those black streaks out was a shower. His frame was hunched and his eyes were bloodshot and puffy.

And he reeked of smoke. I scrunched my nose after taking a breath.

"Sorry," he said.

"It's okay. Is everything all right?"

After a long breath, he muttered, "No."

I lifted my hand to the side of his face, using my thumb

to rub a black smudge on his cheek. He gave me the weight of his head and closed his eyes.

"Want to talk about it?" I asked.

"How about I take a shower and then fill you in?"

"Okay." I nodded.

His hand stroked my knee one last time before he left.

I got out of the chair and went to the kitchen to turn on the coffeepot. I'd need a lot of caffeine to make it through the day. When I heard the shower turn on, I walked upstairs to see if Roe was still sleeping. She was zonked so I decided to jump in the shower with Jess. Stripping off my pajamas, I crept silently into the bathroom and opened the shower door.

Jess was standing underneath the spray, his head bent down, letting the water run down the back of his head and neck. His arms were above his head, resting against the shower wall, and his eyes were closed.

Fitting myself to his back, I wrapped my arms around his waist and did my best to ease my man's troubled mind while I cleaned the fire from his body, replacing the nasty smell with clean and fresh green apple.

By the time we made it out of the shower, I needed to hustle to get to work on time. I roused Rowen out of bed and we hurried through our morning routine.

Jess left as soon as he was dressed so I didn't get the scoop from him after all. But he knew I was anxious to hear what had happened, so he stopped by the hospital shortly after ten, bringing a triple Irish cream latte with him. Sitting together in the waiting room, he told me about the fire.

"A house on Second Street was burned down last night. Guy that lived there lost everything except what was in his garage."

I gasped. "Oh my god. Is he okay?"

"Yeah. Just totally fucked. When I say he lost everything, I mean everything. If you've got any extras from moving here, let me know and I'll take stuff to him."

"Absolutely. I think I've got some kitchen extras in the attic. How did the fire start?"

Shaking his head, he said, "Someone threw a gas can through his living room window, followed by a burning torch."

"What?" I whispered, my eyes bugging out. "Why would someone burn down his house? He could have gotten hurt. Or worse, killed!"

"I don't know. It's completely fucked up. Talked to him for a while but he was in shock. Couldn't hardly speak. I gotta head to the fire station after I leave here and see if Nick learned anything new. Then I'm gonna try and talk to the guy again. See if he has any enemies that would do this."

"Does he need somewhere to stay?" I asked.

I wasn't really keen on having a stranger in my house but the poor man had lost all of his possessions in one night. I could put up with a guest for a few days, especially now that I had the guest bedroom all set up.

"He's a stranger, Georgia," Jess scolded.

"I know that. But he needs help. Besides, you know everyone. You know him, right? Is he a bad guy?"

"No. He's not a bad guy. Nice enough. Don't know him very well. Works as a janitor at the school. But he's still not staying at the farmhouse."

"Where's he going to stay then?" I asked.

"He's just got to find a place to stay while he's waiting on insurance. I'm sure he'll get a payout. Probably within the week. Until then, he's staying with Everett Carlson."

"Everett?"

I hadn't seen Everett yet today but I was definitely going to track him down after Jess left.

"Yeah. He lives next door. Was out there all night."

"Really?" I said. "That's nice of Everett to take him in."

"Ha. I bet Maze doesn't think so. Actually surprised you haven't gotten the scoop from her yet. She was with him last night. Came outside wearing his shirt and sweats."

"You're kidding!" I jumped up from my seat to kneel in the chair.

"Nope."

"Wow. She said they'd gone out a couple of times but that he hadn't seemed too interested in being more than friends. I guess that changed."

Jess checked his watch and stood up to leave. We'd just made it to the front doors and he'd given me a quick kiss good-bye when "Gigi!" sounded behind me. Jess rolled his eyes and pulled on his sunglasses, heading out, while I turned to greet a very excited Maisy.

CHAPTER THIRTEEN

GIGI

"So? What do you think?" he asked.

We were exploring my new garage after work. Ryan and his crew had just finished this morning.

"It's, ah, big."

And it was. Huge. Way bigger than anything I needed.

"I'm not quite sure why I need all of this extra space. I could fit two extra vehicles in here plus all of the boxes I have stored in the attic with room to spare."

He smirked at me like he knew something I didn't.

"It's nice though," I said. "I like that the outside matches the house. And the little windows all along the sides and the front were a nice touch. Makes it seems less garagey."

"Garagey?"

"Garagey. You know, not pretty. Usually garages are so boxy and practical. Big white doors that don't coordinate with the rest of a house."

"So you like that I had him make it 'pretty.'"

"Yes. I like that it's pretty." I stuck my tongue out at him.

He could tease all he wanted. I didn't feel one ounce of shame that the aesthetics of the garage were my favorite part.

"I had them put in a thermal water heating system so it will stay cool in the summer and warm in the winter. Won't skyrocket your heating bill. Does that rank above pretty?"

"Nope."

"That bench is custom built over there for tool storage. The cart and drawers, specially brought in. Does that rank above pretty?"

"Tools? No. Definitely not." I laughed.

He took a deep breath and sighed. "So you're saying you would have been fine with anything I decided to have them build as long as you got those fancy little windows, the wooden doors out front, the barn-style hardware and the expensive lights that match the front porch."

"You're learning, Sheriff," I said, patting his arm.

I was glad the garage debacle was over. Jess followed me inside and I toed off my shoes.

"Football game starts soon. We've got to get moving," he said.

"Huh? Football?" I asked. I had planned to have a nice relaxing night at the farmhouse. An unplanned trip to town wasn't at the top of my list of Friday night fun activities.

"Yeah. There's a home game tonight at the high school," he said.

"Let's just stay here. In case you haven't noticed, honey, the Ellars girls are not really the sporting event type."

"Think of it as a social event then. We need to leave in forty-five. We'll just get hot dogs at the game for dinner."

"How is a football game a social event?"

"Whole town comes out to watch and gossip. Lots of

folks have seen us around town but lots haven't. You and Roe will be the center of attention. She'll love it," he said.

"Ah . . . I thought you were trying to sell me on going. I'm not too keen on being tonight's gossip topic. That isn't helping your argument."

"I have to go. People expect the sheriff to participate in town events. Also expect the sheriff's girls to be with him."

I opened my mouth but he cut me off.

"And I'm not selling you on going. I'm telling you you're going."

"Now you're making me mad, Jess," I said, fisting my hands on my hips. "You don't get to order me around."

I was sick to death of Jess telling me what to do. It was like the garage situation all over again. Well, kind of. Sure, this was just a football game and nothing to get worked up about. It was the principle of the matter that had me angry.

He didn't listen. Instead, he started unbuttoning his shirt. "Get changed. Dress warm."

"Hold it. I don't want to sit outside in the cold, watching a game I don't understand. We're not going."

He huffed. "Fuck, you can be difficult."

"I'm not being difficult!"

Jess ignored me and tilted his head toward the stairs, bellowing, "Rowen!"

"Yeah?" she yelled back.

"Want to go to a football game?" he asked as her little feet pounded down the stairs.

"Yeah!" she screeched.

"Good. Me too. Your mom doesn't. Guess it's just me and you," he said.

I inhaled a deep breath and closed my eyes, trying to slow my racing heartbeat. I was not happy that he was ordering me around. And then using Rowen to guilt me into going? I wasn't getting any happier here.

"Why don't you want to go, Mommy? I want to go with Jess," Roe said.

Traitor.

I inhaled and reminded myself not to snap at her just because I was angry with Jess.

"Well, baby girl, I'm tired. It's been a long week and we haven't gotten to spend much time with Jess since he's been working so much. I thought it might be nice to stay home, just the three of us."

"If you come to the football game with me and Jess, then it will be the three of us, right?" she asked.

A smug grin spread across Jess's face.

"Fine," I muttered.

Once again, I had let Jess walk all over me and get his way.

"BABY," Jess said.

I didn't respond. My eyes stayed glued to the windshield.

I was mad at myself for letting him push me into this. I should have stood my ground and stayed home.

"Freckles," Jess called again.

My silence continued.

When we were together, I never drove my car. He always went to the driver's side and I let him. And since I was new to Prescott, if he drove, then he didn't need to narrate directions. But I also knew it was part of his manly man ways. Jess drove. The end. When I didn't answer, he pulled over to the side of the road.

Maybe I needed to rethink letting him always be the driver.

"What's wrong?" he asked.

"Nothing. I'm fine," I lied.

"You're not."

"I am."

"You need to talk to me," he said.

"I'll be fine," I said, trying to sound sincere. "Let's just get to the game. I'm hungry."

"Georgia, tell me. Please."

I turned to look at him, shifting my whole body in the seat.

"Jess, you've been working around the clock. There's nothing wrong with me wanting to stay at home and spend some time together, you know. You didn't even hear me out. We have to decide things together."

"I should have listened. But tonight will be fun. You'll like it."

"It's football," I said, the word tasting sour.

"Give it a try?" he asked.

"Fine."

He leaned across the console for a quick kiss before driving us to town.

We parked in a huge gravel lot, already packed full, and walked toward the stadium. Roe was in the middle, holding onto our hands as she skipped along in her suede boots.

The football stadium was much bigger than I would have imagined for a town the size of Prescott. After passing a long concession stand, we climbed a set of stairs leading to the bleachers above us. I took in the nearly full stands and then double-checked my watch.

The game wasn't supposed to start until seven and it was

only six-thirty. I figured we were early, but from the looks of the full crowd, I was wrong. The only empty seats left were located in the undesirable spots, up high and on the edges. Apparently, to be on time for a Prescott High football game, you had to arrive shortly after lunch.

Jess bent to pick up Rowen, who wrapped her legs around his waist with practiced ease. Then he grabbed my hand and pulled me behind him to the middle of the bleachers. About five rows up, he stopped by a row already quite full of people.

And of course it would be, the seats were perfect. Right in the middle. High up enough to see the whole field without the railing in your way.

"Ah, Jess, shouldn't we keep going up to an empty row?" I asked.

"This is where I sit," he said. "They'll make room."

Of course he'd have a reserved spot in the best available location. My guess was that the people of Prescott would make room for him no matter where he wanted to sit.

A lot of faces were aimed my way, giving me a thorough inspection. I was happy to spot a few I recognized and focused on them instead of the strangers staring me down. In our row was Silas Grant. Behind him and off to the side was Maisy.

"Brick, come on in. There's plenty of room," a man sitting three seats in called before people started squeezing together to make an opening.

Jess nodded and shuffled sideways down the row, still carrying Rowen, until we reached the open space next to Silas.

"Gigi," he said.

"Hi, Silas."

"First game?" he asked.

Jess started chuckling, so I elbowed him in the ribs.

He let out a "humph" while I told Silas, "Yes, first game."

"It's a good year to become a fan. Mustangs are a great team this year. Favored to win the state championship," he said.

"Which one are the Mustangs?" Roe asked.

"Green team. That's who we're cheering for. Right down in front of us," Jess said.

"Who are the red guys?" she asked.

"Sheridan Pioneers. We want the green team to get the football past the red team and into the end zone down there," he said, pointing out all of the different spots on the field.

"Oh." Her chin fell and her eyes filled with tears.

"What's wrong, Roe?" I asked.

She didn't answer.

"Little bit?" Jess whispered. "What is it?"

Roe finally looked up and the tears fell onto her cheeks. "The bad guys are red and my sweater is red. Does that mean I can't be a Mustang?"

"Of course not, sweetie," I said, holding back a laugh. "You can cheer for them. It doesn't matter that you're wearing red."

"It does matter! I'm not dressed right!" my mini-diva cried again.

We were starting to draw a bit of an audience. "Do you want to wear your coat?" It was a deep purple and would blend better with the sea of green we were sitting in.

"Okay." She sniffled.

"Want a hot dog, little bit?" he asked.

"Yeah," she said, nodding enthusiastically, all smiles

again now that her wardrobe better supported the home team.

"Georgia?" he asked.

"Sure," I said. "And a Coke. Juice box for Roe."

"Okay. Be back."

As soon as he vacated his seat, Maisy climbed down from behind us and took his place.

"Hey!" she said. "I didn't know you guys were coming tonight. Awesome!"

"Hey, yourself!" I said while Roe jumped up to give her a big squeeze.

"Meet my family."

Behind us was an older couple I assumed were Maisy's parents and two men, one on either side of her parents.

"This is my mom, Marissa, and my dad, Brock Holt," she said. I shook both of their hands and introduced myself.

"These are my brothers," Maisy continued, "Beau and Michael."

Maisy looked exactly like her mom except for her eyes, which were her dad's. Brock had wide shoulders and a huge frame. Jess was a big guy but even seated, Maisy's dad and brothers were obviously bigger.

Michael was younger and hadn't quite filled out his frame yet. But Beau was built. Mountainous. Everything about him was square and angular, his shoulders, jaw, hands. He was a younger version of his father except for the dark brown beard covering his jaw and the lack of a protruding beer belly.

"Brick's woman," Beau said.

"Um . . . yeah." I liked that Jess called me his girl and not his woman. I didn't like "woman," it made me feel old.

"How are you liking the hospital?" Marissa asked.

"Oh . . . it's been great," I said, smiling. "I love working with Maisy."

"Well, we sure have heard a lot about you, Gigi," she said. "We're glad you two have become such fast friends."

"Me too."

We chatted a bit more about general Prescott things until I saw Jess heading back down our row. I took a quick inventory of the stash in his arms.

Six hot dogs, two sodas, one juice box, Skittles, popcorn, peanut butter M&Ms and something green tucked under his arm.

"Did you leave anything left at the concessions stand for the other patrons?" I asked.

He grinned, setting the food down on the bench and then did his round of greetings to Maisy and her family.

"You find those missing hikers?" Jess asked Beau.

"Yep. Found them about a mile up from the trailhead," Beau said.

"Figure it wouldn't take you long." Jess chuckled, then told me, "Beau is head of Search and Rescue in Jamison County. We take the dispatch calls at the station and then coordinate with his team."

"Gotcha." I nodded.

"I work at the Forest Service office too. Fits well since most of our rescues are people lost in the woods," Beau added.

Jess and Beau chatted a bit more before we turned to eat our food. After inhaling four hot dogs, Jess pulled out the green bundle he'd stowed under the bench.

"Here, little bit. Give this a try," he said, unfolding a small Mustangs sweatshirt.

"Yay!" She immediately started stripping off her coat.

"Jess, you shouldn't spoil her," I whispered.

He shrugged. "She's gonna get one eventually. Might as well be tonight."

"Yeah, but I don't want her to think that if she throws around some drama and tears she can get whatever she wants."

He shrugged again. Other than that, he made no acknowledgement that he'd heard me, let alone agreed with me whatsoever, meaning he was totally going to spoil her.

Another example of him not listening to me.

"Thank you!" Rowen told Jess before throwing herself into his chest.

"Anything for my girls," he said, kissing the top of her hair.

Then he hoisted her up so he could begin the unsuccessful attempt of trying to teach the Ellars girls about football.

———

"SO WHAT'S new with you and Everett?" I asked Maisy.

The first half of the game was almost over and she had come with Rowen and me to the stadium restrooms.

Before the night of the fire, Maisy and Everett had gone out a few times but each date had been completely platonic. She had started to think Everett was just in need of a friend and wasn't that interested in a relationship. Then the night of the fire had happened.

"Oh, he's dreamy," she swooned. "We've spent every night together since the fire. He's actually kind of shy. Which is weird, right? He's a hot doctor. Who would have thought he'd be shy? I have to practically drag stuff out of him. We're just spending as much time together as possible. Mostly in bed, where he is definitely not shy. I was hoping we could all go out together. Like a double date."

I hadn't gone out to either of the bars in Prescott but was looking for an excuse to check one out. Not that I was a big bar goer. It wasn't for the drinking. I just wanted to see what a small-town Montana bar was like.

"Sounds like fun. Let me talk to Jess."

"Sweet!" She nudged my shoulder as we walked out of the bathroom with Rowen. "So how's it feel to be the talk of the town?"

"Huh?"

"Uh, you didn't notice the whole place checking you out?" she said.

"They were? Why?"

"Gigi, you walking into the football stadium on Jess's arm is news. Big news. He's never brought anyone here before. People have been speculating about how serious you two are getting. Him bringing you to the game in front of the whole town? Means he's making a statement. Claiming you and Rowen officially."

"Ah . . . Maisy, it's just a football game. I don't think Jess meant it to be some sort of 'claiming' ritual."

"Let me educate you a bit about Prescott High sports. Everyone comes to see what everyone else is doing. Sure, we all cheer for the kids and hope they win, but that's just the sideshow. We really come to see what people are up to, what they look like, if they've gained weight and who they're with. It's the second biggest gossip spot in town behind the Coffee Club."

"Seriously?" I asked, suddenly feeling very exposed.

"Yeah, seriously."

"So, ah, what are they saying about me?" I wasn't sure if I really wanted the answer.

"That you're perfect for Jess. That he seems happier around you than he's ever been. Like, ever," she said.

"That's not too bad, I guess." My heart swelled at the compliment.

"No, it's amazing! They love you. Well . . . almost everyone. Some of the local single girls who have been trying to snag Jess for years are being total bitches."

"What? Why?"

"They're just jealous. Talking about how you waltzed into town, took over the farmhouse and that Jess is with you because he's always wanted to live there. That if it wasn't for the house, he'd still be with Andrea Merkuso. They were having a long-term fling before you showed up."

I didn't know what to say so I just kept walking. All of the joy I had felt a few seconds ago vanished. I'd been happily ignorant of Jess's previous relationships. But having Maisy put a name to his past made my chest ache. Some of it was jealousy. Some of it was insecurity on my part, especially feeling like I was under a microscope for the whole town.

"Don't worry, Gigi. It's really just Andrea talking trash. She's a skank and has skanky friends too. Who cares what they think? Just because she used to hook up with Jess doesn't give her the right to be catty, you know? I'll point her out if I see her tonight."

"Ah . . . okay," I muttered.

People were pouring out of the stadium at halftime and we were weaving in and out of the crowd. My hand tightened around Rowen's to ensure I was pulling her right behind me.

We had almost reached the stairs when a hand clasped my upper arm. I gasped and spun around, about to cuss out the person who had so rudely grabbed me when I looked up into Jess's face.

"Oh, hi," I said, relaxing.

"Hey. I was calling you. Didn't you hear me?"

"No, sorry," I said, still a little dazed.

"You okay?" he asked.

"Yeah, great," I lied.

"Georgia."

"Later, Jess, okay?"

He stared at me for a few seconds and then nodded.

Roe had been taking in the wonder of the crowd but when she finally realized we'd met up with Jess, she jumped up into his arms to get a better view.

Jess led me to a group of men huddled next to the bleachers. Silas was there talking to Beau and another man I'd never met.

"Nick. Meet Gigi and her daughter, Rowen," Jess said.

"Pleasure." Nick shook my hand.

"Nice to meet you, Nick."

"Nick runs the fire department, Freckles."

"Ah. Busy week for you then."

"You could say that. We haven't had a fire in town in years. I forgot how much paperwork I have to do. Usually, I just help Beau and the Forest Service with forest fires. They can't seem to handle them without me," he teased.

This must have been the hot guy hangout spot because Nick was equally as handsome as Beau and Silas. Jess outshone them all but their circle was entirely good-looking. Which explained the group of girls lurking close, trying to hide their stares and giggling.

Nick appeared to be much more jovial than any of the other men in the group. He had a mischievous smile and a short brown beard that matched the color of his shaggy hair.

The men started talking about the football team and I got lost in thought.

I couldn't help but look around the moving crowd. I wondered if any of the people looking at us thought I was reaching beyond my league, trying to be with Jess. Had he been with any of the women milling around, staring at us?

When I closed my eyes, I heard Nate Fletcher calling me an ugly whore. I remembered the hateful email he sent me after I'd sent him an ultrasound picture of baby Rowen. He'd accused me of being desperate to trap him because that was the only way I could get a rich, handsome man like him. How many people in the Prescott crowd were wondering what a beautiful man like Jess was doing with me?

Jess's hand jerked and I snapped out of my head. I followed his glare into the crowd until I saw its target.

Wes.

Striding toward us with a leggy blond on his arm.

All of the men in our huddle had their eyes trained on Wes as he made his approach. Tension clouded the air.

Jess was pissed, his frame strung tight, but Silas was dangerous. Silas looked at Wes like he wanted to commit murder. Now I knew why Maisy thought he was terrifying.

Wes stopped in front of the group and turned his eyes on me, the blond on his arm looking straight at Jess.

Wes's eyes were glassy again and rimmed with dark circles. The skin on his face was splotchy.

"Gigi. I see you haven't decided to leave Prescott's Good Prince yet," Wes smirked. "And aren't you cute," he said to Rowen. "What's your name, princess?"

Roe burrowed into Jess's chest without an answer.

"Back off, Wes," Jess warned.

At this juncture, the blond piped up. "Hey, Brick. I tried calling you a few times. Did you get my messages?" She threw me a fake smile.

Bitch.

It was blatantly obvious I was with Jess, standing here holding his hand and leaning into his side while my daughter rested on his hip.

"Yeah, Andrea, I got them," Jess said. "Me not calling you back should have been your first clue to leave me alone. This can be your second. Lose. My. Number."

Andrea. Jess's ex.

My heart plummeted into my belly.

Of course she was beautiful. A little fake, but very pretty. Her hair was long and straight, shiny under the stadium lights. Her makeup was thick but applied perfectly. And she was thin. I bet she didn't have an ounce of extra fat on her, certainly not an extra ten pounds.

"Now, Sheriff, is that any way to treat one of your constituents?" Wes asked.

"Not the place, Drummond," Nick said.

"Ah . . . Nick Slater. Did you find any evidence as to who started that fire? I bet it was someone much, much smarter than you. Someone who knows exactly how to create a burner bottle and leave no trace," Wes said.

Had Wes just admitted to starting that fire? If it wasn't him, he knew who had.

"Enough," Silas growled.

Silas's face was granite and his hands were clenched at his sides. If he lost his control, Wes didn't stand a chance.

I studied Wes, hoping he wouldn't run his mouth and

push Silas over the edge. I did not want my daughter witnessing a fight. Luckily, Wes's confidence faltered and he stopped pushing the men's buttons. With one last sneer aimed at Jess, he grabbed the blond's arm and started backing away.

Jess had been wrong about Mustang football. It wasn't a sporting event and it wasn't a social event either.

It was a damn soap opera.

———

I WAS LYING on my stomach in bed, the sheet covering the lower half of my naked body. My arms were crossed underneath my face and I was turned away from Jess. He was propped on his side, tracing invisible patterns on my bare skin.

My body felt like a limp noodle but my mind was stressed.

We had watched the second half of the game, mostly in silence. Silas never had returned, and even though we'd had an empty space beside us, Rowen had stayed on Jess's lap. After a Mustang victory, we'd said our good-byes, driven home and gotten Roe into bed.

The second her bedroom door had clicked shut, Jess had picked me up and carried me to bed. The orgasm he'd given me had drained my energy reserves, and rather than go to the bathroom like usual, I'd turned onto my stomach and reverted into my head, attempting to wrap it around everything that had happened.

Wes Drummond was a menace. He was battling with Jess and I was in the middle. I did not like that he had tried to talk to my child. At all. And I had a feeling he had brought Andrea over to us tonight just to rile me and Jess up.

Besides Wes, my mind whirled around Jess and Andrea. Even though I desperately wanted to stop, I kept picturing them together. Each time, my stomach rolled. The mental images were playing on repeat. Him touching her pretty face. Her long, shiny hair draped across his body. Him kissing her. Her skinny body underneath his.

I just kept seeing them together and it was making me crazy.

"What's going on in your head?" Jess asked.

"Weird night."

"Yeah," he agreed. "What happened when you took Roe to the bathroom?"

I thought about dismissing him for a minute, just saying I was tired and it was no big deal. But I didn't want to lie to Jess.

Besides, he'd sniff out a lie and badger me until I gave in.

"Maisy told me that people around town have been talking about me. About us," I said.

"Figures. Small town. But it's nothing to get worked up about. You already know people in this town talk. And it won't be the last time. Gotta try and let it roll off."

"I know that," I whispered. "It isn't that. I mean, it is, but it isn't."

"Then what?"

"She said that woman from tonight. Andrea? That she was saying nasty stuff about me. That you were only with me for the farmhouse. Otherwise, you'd be with her."

His hand stopped moving on my back. In one swift move, he grabbed me by the hips and twisted me onto my back. His chest pinned me down as his eyes blazed into mine.

"We covered this already and I'm not doing it again. You've got nothing to be worried about with this house," he said.

"I know." I sighed. "But that doesn't mean I like to hear it as gossip."

"I'll give you that. What else did Maisy say?"

"She told me about you and Andrea. That you were together. And I know . . ." I raised my hands up in surrender. "I know it is just petty jealousy. That you were with her before me. But still, I don't like it. I don't like having the image of you and her together in my head. And I can't seem to get it out. She's so pretty."

He stared down at me for a few seconds and then threw his head back, laughing. His chest shook so hard that the bed started to rock.

"Jess!" I slapped my hands to his chest. "It's not funny. I'm being serious. This is really bothering me."

"Freckles, you just made my night."

"What? Me being upset just made your night? That's twisted, Jess. And not very nice."

"Baby, I fucking love that you're jealous."

"Huh?"

"I've been doing my best to keep my mouth shut when we walk around town and other men are checking you out. And I've been patient, not asking about Roe's father. Because the thought of you with someone else? Having a baby with someone else? I don't like it."

I didn't like the idea of him with another woman. Not at all, especially Andrea. But the fact that he was jealous too lessened the sting. Though I'm sure the men around town were not staring at me for the reasons he thought. I'm sure they were just curious.

"It wasn't much fun learning about her from someone else," I said. "I'm not saying I need a roster of the women you've had in bed, but in the future, if we're out and about and you know someone you used to sleep with is going to be there, a head's up would be nice."

"Can do," he said. "But, baby, Andrea is about the only one you need to worry about. Don't really like talking about it but we probably need to."

"Talking about what?" I asked.

"The past. I'd prefer we just move forward, but this town's too small for you not to hear rumors. I'd rather it came from me so you know the truth."

"Okay, you're starting to freak me out again."

"Don't get freaked," he said. "Just listen. I haven't dated anyone serious my entire life. Always casual, no commitments. Not once in thirty-four years. Not until you. Andrea and I were just casual. On and off hookups for about a year. Besides her and a girl I hooked up with in high school, I've never been with the same woman more than once. Always one-night stands with women passing through town so there was no risk I'd ever see them again."

I didn't like hearing it, but at least now I knew.

"Okay." I sighed. "Hop off me. I need to get cleaned up and dressed for bed. I'm wiped out."

Jess didn't budge.

"What?" I asked.

"Not tonight, baby. But soon, I need to know about Roe's dad."

I nodded, whispering, "Soon, but not tonight."

He shifted off me so I could trudge to the bathroom,

dreading when "soon" became "now" and I'd have to share about Rowen's father, a man I had vowed never to lay eyes on again.

A man whose voice told me in the back of my head that I wasn't good enough for Jess.

CHAPTER FOURTEEN

GIGI

"I don't care what you are seeing on that thing. It's wrong," my patient yelled. He was pointing at my iPad and before I could respond, he muttered, "Idiot."

"I'm sorry, Mr. Johnson," I said. "I wasn't here when you got your medications but from what your chart says, I can't give you any more right now. It could be dangerous to your liver if you take too many pain medications in such a short period of time."

His chart indicated he had already received more than enough oxycodone for his back pain. I didn't know why it hadn't kicked in yet but giving him more wasn't an option until I talked to a doctor.

"Find someone else. You're too dumb to figure it out. Where's Ida? Bring her back."

I inhaled a long breath and tried to keep my cool. I wasn't a big fan of someone calling me an idiot or dumb.

"Let me check with Dr. Carlson about your medications, okay?"

Mr. Johnson had come into the ER this afternoon complaining of back pain so fierce it was making him nauseous. He'd come in while I was on my lunch break so Ida had admitted him and given him the oxy per Everett's order.

"Fine. Get your ass outta here and check with the doctor, bitch. I don't care what you see on that damn thing. Nothing you people have given me is helping."

I was done. I was going to let the other affronts go, but this last insult was one too many.

"Stop. I'm sorry you're in pain, Mr. Johnson. But being rude to me isn't going to help. You will treat me with some respect. Enough name calling and yelling," I said, using my mom voice.

He huffed but didn't say anything in response.

"Now if you'll excuse me, I'll go and find Dr. Carlson."

I stomped immediately to the nurses' desk, where I closed my eyes and tried to relax my hands, which were balled into tight fists.

"Gigi? Are you okay?"

"Great," I deadpanned, turning to see Everett. "I was actually coming to find you but I needed a minute."

"Is everything okay?"

"Yeah." I let out a loud breath and sagged my shoulders. "Mr. Johnson is in ER room three. He's spent the last ten minutes yelling at me because he is still in pain and I wouldn't give him more oxycodone. His chart said he'd gotten the max dose about an hour ago. So I told him I'd come talk to you and see if there was something else we could do."

"Strange. The dose should be kicking in by now," he said. "But let me go in and talk with him. See what kind of symptoms he's having."

"Sounds good. Let's go."

"Oh, I can handle it if you'd like, Gigi. If he's been rude or inappropriate, you don't need to deal with him again."

"That's nice of you to offer, Everett. But I want to be in there so that if there is a follow-up order, I can take care of it. And I don't want him to think he can intimidate me. I'll be fine."

After another thorough check of Mr. Johnson, Everett decided to give him a small dose of morphine through an IV drip. I stayed at the back of the room, observing, until Everett gave me the order. I thought that morphine combined with the oxy was an awful lot of medication, but I wasn't a doctor and decided to trust that Everett knew what he was doing.

And it seemed to work.

Fifteen minutes later, Asshole Mr. Johnson turned into Nice Guy Mr. Johnson and he apologized for his behavior.

"Thanks, Everett. He seems much better now," I said after walking up to the ER counter.

"You don't have to thank me, Gigi. It's my job. I'm glad to have helped."

"Why do you think the oxy didn't work?" I asked.

"I was actually a bit puzzled by that myself. I checked his chart and the amount Ida gave him should have been more than enough. But I've seen some patients who have a high tolerance," he said.

"Then wouldn't it have taken longer for the morphine to work? He seemed to instantly feel better once I started the drip."

"Morphine and oxy are fundamentally different

compounds. And it could be that the morphine worked better because we gave it to him intravenously. But I agree, it does seem odd that he reacted to one so quickly and allegedly not the other at all," he said.

"Allegedly?"

He inched closer so he could talk in a low voice. "I've seen patients like him before, Gigi, when I worked in bigger hospitals. I'm sure you ran across them during your time in Spokane too. They come in complaining of an ache or pain. Something almost impossible for a doctor to diagnose. Back pain. Knee ache. Sprained joints. Other than giving them medication and telling them to rest, there isn't much else we can do for treatment. They know that. So they come in with the same pain, over and over, and leave with a brand new prescription."

"Oh," I mumbled. "You think he's a pain pill addict? That he was faking it?"

"I don't know. The only other option is that Ida made a mistake and didn't give him enough oxy," he said.

"I doubt it." Ida was the senior nurse at the hospital and the epitome of thorough.

He nodded. "Me too. She isn't likely to have made a mistake like that."

Mr. Johnson had shown me two very different versions of himself in the last hour. But a painkiller addict? He didn't seem the type.

"An addict?" I asked.

"Maybe. I'm just speculating. The addicts I've seen in the past came into the hospital on a fairly regular basis. But that was in much bigger hospitals. It was easier for them to blend in. They could avoid seeing the same doctor over and over. Here, it would be much more difficult."

"His chart said he's been in a couple of times but that was spread out over five years."

"True. He might be traveling out of town to other hospitals. I just don't know. It could legitimately be that his body just didn't respond to the oxycodone," Everett said.

Jess was still trying to find out who was selling prescription drugs in Prescott. If I didn't know there was a dealer on the loose, my mind would have never suspected Mr. Johnson of drug abuse. But now I couldn't rule it out.

———

WE WERE SITTING across from each other in Jess's booth at the café. The Mustangs had an away game and Rowen was finally having a sleepover with Bryant's daughter. So, much like our first date, Jess and I were alone for dinner.

"I've known Gus Johnson for years. He's no drug addict," Jess said.

Nurses weren't supposed to share patient information with people outside of the hospital staff, patient confidentiality and all. So if I needed to share something about my day with Jess, I always used general terms to describe the situation. And I never used a patient's name.

I was surprised when he knew exactly who I had been talking about.

Correction. I was shocked.

"How did you know who I was talking about?" I asked.

"I was at Silas's place today when Gus came in and said he tweaked his back."

"Oh. Well. Still, you don't know he isn't an addict. He could be an expert at hiding it," I said.

"Freckles, believe me when I tell you he's no drug addict."

"But don't you think it's all a little too suspicious? I mean . . . he works at Silas's ranch. He could have picked up hidden pills there and known exactly where to look. Maybe he was the one that hit and killed that baby calf. Plus he had to have been faking it when he said he was still in pain today. No person can get that much oxy and not be feeling *good* an hour later."

He chuckled.

"What? What's funny?"

"Gus works on the ranch. He'd be the last person to hit a calf with his truck. He'd know exactly where they were and he'd stay away."

"Oh," I grumbled. "I guess that makes sense."

The waitress came over and took our orders while Jess told me about his day. We were so wrapped up in our conversation that we jerked in surprise when Wes Drummond slipped into our booth. He slid right next to me, pushing me further toward the wall and trapping me in.

Before Jess or I could say anything, he held up both hands and said, "No trouble, Brick. I swear."

"What do you want, Wes?" Jess asked through a clenched jaw.

Wes scrubbed both hands over his face and then ran them through his hair, making it stand up in all directions. "Nothing. Shit, I don't know."

Wes wasn't clouded with his usual air of confidence and defiance. His eyes were clear. Bloodshot, but not glassy like I'd seen before.

"Wes, we're not talking with Georgia here," Jess said.

Wes ran his hands through his hair again before saying, "I called Lissy."

Jess's face turned hard as stone. I wasn't sure who Lissy was but the fact that Wes had called her was clearly not something Jess liked.

"Stay the fuck away from her. Don't fucking call her. She's gone. A memory for you. Don't pile your shit on her."

"I miss her. Fuck. I just needed to hear her voice. Get some perspective. Shit is coming down fast."

Wes's rambling made no sense and I hoped Jess understood.

"Wes, we gotta talk about this somewhere else. You gotta come clean before that shit crashes down on your head," Jess said.

"Can't. He's closing in, Brick. Crazy as fuck. Not just about money. Wants the town. Power. He's obsessed. Fuckin' smart." Wes talked without looking directly at Jess. His body squirmed and he bounced in the seat.

"Who? Who is, Wes?"

Wes flinched at Jess's question. It was like a light switched on and he realized where he was. As quickly as he'd come into the booth, he slid out, mumbling, "Sorry." A few long strides, and he was out the door.

I didn't know what to say so I just sat there. I wanted to ask who Lissy was and who she was to Wes but didn't dare break the silence. Jess was pissed and needed a minute to calm down.

His hands were fisted on the table and he was staring down at the space between them. He stayed silent until the waitress brought us our food.

"Fuck," Jess muttered.

I reached out my left hand and covered his right fist.

He forced a smile. Only one side of his mouth tilted upward.

I started to take my hand away but he grabbed hold before I could. Neither of us had anything else to say after that. We just ate our dinners with one free hand. Him using his left, me using my right.

Walking out of the café, I asked Jess to take me to his place. I was curious and had been looking for an excuse to visit. Without Rowen, tonight was perfect. He always spent the night at the farmhouse and it seemed strange that we'd been dating for this long and I hadn't been there yet.

"It's not much, Freckles," he said.

"I don't care. I just want to see where it is. What it's like."

We drove away from the café and headed toward the side of town closest to the river.

Four blocks from Main Street, we turned into a cul-de-sac. The homes all matched, every one with a similar layout but all in different colors. A couple of them had large garages at the back. One had a big swing set in its fenced yard.

Of course Jess's house would have a big garage. It wasn't as huge as mine but it certainly wasn't small. His was a typical garage with a big white door. Garagey.

The house was a single story plus a basement. The yard was well kept, but there were no accents. No flowerbeds or planters.

Jess unlocked the door and pushed it open, letting me walk in first.

"Go ahead, Freckles. Explore away."

The only way to describe Jess's place was "bachelor pad." All the walls were white. The carpet was a plain, shag tan. He didn't have any extras. No knickknacks. No area rugs to add color. No painted walls. No framed pictures. No toss pillows or comfy blankets on the couch.

Just the manly man essentials. Reclining chair. Fridge for beer. Big TV.

"I like your bachelor pad."

"Thanks, baby," he said, thumbing through a stack of mail.

What Jess's place lacked in décor, it made up for in cleanliness.

"Did you come here and clean today? It's spotless. If you can clean like this, I'm putting you on the chore wheel with Rowen."

He chuckled. "Neighbor comes over once a week and cleans for me. She owns the cleaning service here in town. Cleans the station too."

"Gotcha. Well, she's talented. I don't see a speck of dust anywhere. I might have to pick her brain for what she uses."

"Want me to see if she can clean the farmhouse?" he asked.

"Uh . . . not right now. It isn't hard to clean. I just try and do a little every night. Plus it gives me chores for Roe to do. Haven't you noticed?"

"Yeah. I noticed. Just thought it might be nice to have that extra time. She's reasonable, Freckles. Wouldn't cost too much."

I shrugged. "We'll see."

If things got busier, I'd consider it. But right now, I liked cleaning the farmhouse. It was a good stress reliever and the more I cleaned, the more familiar I became with each room, making the farmhouse feel like it was mine.

"You ready to go?" he asked.

"We just got here, Jess. What's the hurry? Don't you

want to stick around for a while? Actually be in your own house for once?" I asked.

"No."

"Uh . . . why?" I reached out to touch his bicep. "You know, we could stay here tonight. Switch it up. We were going to stay here a couple weeks ago but that never happened. Now we could."

"No."

"You're going to need to give me more than just 'no.' "

He turned, placing one hand on my hip as the other slid down and palmed my ass.

"I've been waiting to take you all over the farmhouse. Now's finally our chance. We're gonna take advantage," he said.

Sex someplace other than my bed at the farmhouse? Hot.

"Time to go," I blurted and walked straight to the door. Jess and his chuckle followed close behind.

Jess was all over me the instant the front door closed. He attacked my mouth, his tongue plundering relentlessly. I matched his intensity and we frantically stripped off each other's clothes, leaving them in a pile in the entryway. Once we were both naked, he pushed me into the house toward the living room.

"Turn around, baby," he said, breaking our kiss.

I spun around and saw that I was right behind the couch. Jess's hands wrapped around me from behind and started kneading my breasts, his thumb and middle finger pinching my nipples, making them rock hard.

He moved his mouth to my neck and started peppering kisses from behind my ear down to my shoulder, then working his way back up, the entire time tweaking my nipples. His erection prodded my ass. I pushed my hips back, grinding against his hard cock. I moaned as I started to build, thankful that we could be as loud as we wanted tonight.

He stopped kissing me. His hands grabbed my hips.

"Bend over."

I bent at the waist and leaned into the couch, my forearms keeping me from toppling over the back. He lined himself up with my entrance, and with one smooth stroke, he was buried deep. It took a minute for me to adjust but soon my wetness began to make us both slick and I relaxed to the feel of him inside me.

"Gonna make you scream tonight, Georgia," he said.

"Oh, god," was all I could say. I wanted that. Badly. To be brought so high that when I burst, nothing could stop my screams of ecstasy.

He started pounding into me. Hard and fast. Each stroke slapping our skin together, the sound echoing through the living room.

"Harder, Jess."

He took my plea as his permission to let go and release all of the restraint in his strong body. He slammed into me relentlessly, each hit taking me higher and higher, his hands pulling my hips back onto his cock as he thrust forward with his powerful hips.

I rose up on my toes and the change in angle sent me over the edge. I screamed his name before I buried my face into the couch and exploded around him, coming harder than I ever had before.

He kept pounding through my orgasm as my inner walls clenched and pulsed. I was starting to come down when he groaned with his own release. When he had emptied himself inside of me, he planted his cock deep and bent down so his stomach was resting on my back.

"Fuck, baby," he moaned.

"Hmm." I sighed, totally relaxed and sated.

We stayed there in the living room for a few minutes, naked with Jess inside me. Having finally been able to let go and enjoy each other's bodies without the fear of my daughter barging in on us.

"More sleepovers," I whispered.

Jess chuckled and slowly pulled himself out.

I stood back up and turned to wrap my arms around his waist and kiss his chest.

"I like seeing my come drip down your leg, Freckles," he said.

"Then you get to clean up your mess, honey," I teased.

"You let me fuck your mouth in the shower, it's a deal."

Jess had endurance. I had a feeling tonight he was going to show me just how much.

I tipped my head back to look at his face. Then I lifted my eyebrows and grinned. He grinned back before hauling me upstairs in a fireman's hold.

Straight into the shower.

After that, we came downstairs and went at it on the dining room table. Then the kitchen.

We were absolutely scheduling more sleepovers.

CHAPTER FIFTEEN

GIGI

"If you two want to make it to town while there's still candy left, we gotta go. Now!" Jess bellowed from downstairs.

"Coming! One more minute," I shouted back. "Okay, baby girl. What do you think? Is it okay?" I asked Roe.

"I love it, Mommy!" she squealed.

She was standing in front of my full-length mirror, assessing the final touches I had just placed on her purple princess costume.

Jess had warned me that the forecast was calling for snow, so I'd had to make a few modifications to her Halloween costume so she could trick-or-treat without catching pneumonia.

Weeks ago, Jess had shattered my Halloween plans by telling me that the farmhouse was too far from town to get any trick-or-treaters. I loved handing out candy and I had been disappointed, but then he had offered his house as a replacement and I'd gotten to work, planning.

But before we went to his place, we were participating in Main Street's annual trick-or-treating event.

I put on my hat and Rowen and I hurried downstairs.

"Ready!" I said with a smile, ignoring his disapproval of my outfit.

I never wore a full costume but I liked to add Halloween touches to my normal clothes. Tonight, I had on orange and black socks, black heels and a floppy witch's hat.

"Roe, you've got your bucket," I said, seeing her swinging it wildly at her side. "Okay, let's roll."

We stepped onto the front porch, now decorated in country Halloween chic, and navigated our way down the front steps piled with eleven pumpkins. Smiling at the Halloween splendor I had created, I rushed to the car in my not-so-practical shoes, giddy with excitement.

Fifteen minutes later, we had picked up Jess's mom and were pulling into his driveway.

"Oh my," Noelle mumbled.

Earlier in the week, I had asked Jess if we could invite his mom to come trick-or-treating with us. I thought it might be nice to get to know her better, and with a flurry of Halloween activity, it would be easy to avoid any awkward silences if she got spacey.

"Yeah, Ma. It's not over the top at all," Jess drawled.

"Hey!" I said, backhanding him on the arm.

Jess thought I had gone too far with the decorations. There were a lot, but I didn't think it was too much. Just some spiders, webs, bats, ghosts and spooky lights. I'd also put up a couple of clever tombstones ("RIP Anita Shovel" being my favorite) because they were hilarious. And there were a couple of skeletons scaling the house too.

"I don't know why you're hitting *me*, Georgia. I told you to stop two days ago. Did you listen?"

Instead of answering, I scrunched up my nose.

Guilty.

I had been planning to stop. Really. But I kept finding new decoration ideas on Pinterest.

Every night, Rowen and I would sneak over and augment the spooky décor and then race to the farmhouse before Jess could get there for dinner.

"No. You didn't. I see I've got some new additions since I was here Tuesday," he said.

"You know, I'm not sure why you're so worked up about this. Roe and I did all of the decorating and I already promised you we'd come take it all down. And besides, look at how amazing it is! I just don't see how this is really even affecting you. Really. You get to just sit back and enjoy."

"It's not affecting me, huh? Was it you who had to threaten David down at the paper with a night in a cell if he put a picture of my house in the newspaper next week?"

Okay, maybe it was borderline excessive.

"This shit's getting me noticed. Something I do not want, Freckles. And here you are, hitting me."

"Well . . . sorry. But it's too late now. Besides, it's Thursday. You only have to endure it for one more day and then we'll clean it up over the weekend. It's not like you're here much anyway."

He grumbled something under his breath I didn't catch, but I was pretty sure it included the f-word.

I wasn't going to let his annoyance wreck the night. He'd just have to get over it. The Ellars girls loved all things

Halloween. Decorations. Costumes. Candy. All of it. The end.

Roe hauled in a load of candy on Main Street. Everyone commented on how cute she was in her costume. She beamed under the praise, spinning and twirling her dress.

The whole town of Prescott seemed to be out on Main Street. Jess introduced me to more people in that hour than I had met collectively in my entire life. By the end of the trip, I started warning people that I might mix up names.

Jess and Roe left to walk through his neighborhood while Noelle and I manned the house, doling out handfuls of candy to all the monsters, superheroes, princesses and fairies that visited. The one little girl who was dressed as a police officer got two handfuls.

I closed the door and turned to sit back down next to Noelle on the couch. Jess didn't have wine in his house but I'd thought ahead and brought provisions. I was on glass number two while Noelle was still nursing her first.

I took in a long breath, relaxing into the couch. Though it wasn't much to look at, Jess's couch was comfortable.

"You're a good mother," Noelle said.

"Uh . . . thanks."

Her comment took me off guard. I appreciated the compliment but I wasn't sure what had brought it on.

"You know, Ben Coppersmith used to call me every week," she said. "On Tuesdays. He never missed a Tuesday. Not in nineteen years. I knew he'd passed when he didn't call."

"He died on a Saturday night," I said. "In his sleep."

"He was always there for Jess. Even after he moved. Practically gave him that house. Except of course when he actually gave it to you. That house has been the pride and joy of my son's life. Good of Ben to give him that. Good of him to keep in touch too. Checking in with me to make sure Jess was doing okay."

The doorbell rang again and I jumped up to answer it, glad to have a reprieve from the strange conversation.

"I never remembered Halloween," Noelle said when I sat back down. "I don't think the kids ever had costumes until they were old enough to get them on their own."

I didn't know what to say to that so I kept quiet.

"I wasn't much of a mother to my kids. I tried, but . . ."

My heart ached for her. She clearly loved her children, but she just wasn't mentally equipped to care for them properly. It made me sad for Jess and his sister. But it made me sad for Noelle too.

Being Rowen's mother was the greatest gift in my life. Going all out at Halloween, cooking her favorite dinners, painting her room just the right color. All those things brought me immeasurable joy. Noelle had missed out on that.

I leaned forward and gently patted her knee.

"I don't know your daughter, but I've spent the better part of three months getting to know your son. And he's a wonderful man. I'd give yourself a little more credit," I said.

She gave me a small, reluctant smile. "Thanks, Gigi."

WE HAD JUST DROPPED off Noelle and were making our way to the farmhouse. Roe was wired. Beyond wired. She was bouncing up and down and kicking her legs frantically back and forth in her car seat.

Not only had Jess taken her through his neighborhood to

collect more candy, but he'd also let her eat it along the way. A four-year-old stuffing her face with candy. For over an hour.

We were almost to my gravel drive when Jess's phone rang. He listened for a minute before veering to the side of the road, shutting off the car lights and shoving it in park.

"Jess, what's going on?"

"One sec," he mouthed, holding up a finger.

Roe was babbling in the back and I turned around to tell her to shush. When I turned back to Jess, he was off the call.

"Dispatch says there's a gang of punk kids going around vandalizing country houses. They're taking advantage of people being in town. Spinning donuts in the yards, smashing pumpkins, spray-painting doors."

"What?" I gasped. "Oh no. Did they get the farmhouse?"

"I don't know yet. You two stay here. I'm gonna walk down and check it out. Got your phone?"

I nodded.

"Keep it close. I'll call if you can come down. You see anything other than me coming down the drive, call 9-1-1 immediately and drive back to my house. Got it?"

I nodded again. "Be careful."

I was totally freaked out that he was leaving me in a dark car with my daughter while he wandered out into the black night alone.

He reached over and pulled his badge and a set of hand-cuffs out of the glove compartment. After he tucked them into his pocket, he patted my hand quickly and climbed out the door.

He had his gun on him already. If we were heading into town, he almost always brought it. It was on his belt when he was in uniform. If he was in plain clothes, it was tucked away, hidden under his clothes. Tonight, it was holstered under his arm at his side, beneath his sweater and coat.

"Where's Jess going?" Roe asked.

"He's just checking out a couple of things, baby girl. We're going to hang out here. Okay?"

"Can I go with him? Please," she begged.

"No, sweetie. How about you tell me what kind of costumes you saw when you were walking around with Jess?"

My ploy worked and she yammered on and on about the different costumes she had seen tonight while I sat in the front, clutching my phone, barely listening to her. With every minute that ticked by, I got more and more anxious.

I was squirming in my seat ten minutes later, about to call Jess, when flashing lights came up behind us. Two cruisers flew by, speeding to the farmhouse.

When the lights disappeared from my view, I slid over into the driver's seat, ready to turn on the car and get the hell out of there. I was reaching for the keys when my phone vibrated in my hand. I jumped about six inches out of the seat and fumbled it in my lap before seeing it was Jess.

"Hello?"

"Come on down. Prepare Roe. The fuckers here when I came down. Caught the three of them. They're sitting cuffed on your front lawn. Smashed all the pumpkins but that's it."

"Oh my god," I whispered. "Are you okay?"

"Just fucking pissed," he said.

"Okay. Be there in a sec."

I twisted to the back, not at all sure how I was going to explain the concept of vandalism to a four-year-old girl and warn her about seeing handcuffed criminals on our front lawn.

———

ROWEN WAS inside watching a movie on the couch as I stepped outside, taking in the scene on my lawn.

Jess was talking to his two deputies, Milo and a younger man I'd never met. The three vandals, dressed entirely in black, were sitting with their butts on the grass and hands cuffed behind their backs.

Jess had met us at the car and immediately taken Roe from her seat and carried her inside, shielding her eyes from the trio of juvenile assholes and the broken remains of eleven pumpkins scattered on the grass. He had instructed me to get her settled and then come back out to make my official statement.

The mood in Jess's huddle was tense. Too tense, so I tried to lighten the air. Was I annoyed that these kids had made a mess? Sure. But it was just smashed pumpkins. We weren't dealing with murderers here.

"Well, good thing we had so many pumpkins, honey. It must have taken them quite a while to destroy them all. Saved me from having to clean up spray paint off my front door."

Jess's jaw clenched tight. Milo and the other deputy coughed to cover their laughs, making him even angrier.

Mental note. No joking when Jess was pissed.

"Georgia, need you to give Milo a quick recap on the record," Jess said.

My summary was brief, having missed most of the action while I was sitting in the car. Milo asked a few questions and took a couple notes on his small spiral notepad. Then he and the other deputy said good night and started loading the vandals into cruisers.

Two of the kids never once acknowledged me as they were escorted to the back of the police cars. Their gazes were firmly fixed on their shoes, their heads hanging down and their shoulders shamefully slumped.

But as he was walking to the back of the police car, the third turned to me with a glare as cold as ice. One side of his mouth turned up in an evil snarl, causing my spine to shudder.

This kid was absolutely the ringleader. I'd have bet my life on it. He looked at me like I was the one in the wrong. Like he was entitled and had every right to vandalize my property. Like I was to blame for his arrest and it was my fault that he'd gotten caught breaking the law.

As he trudged toward the police car, he held my gaze. Right before he could be pushed inside, he bent and spat on my lawn.

"You'll be sorry. Watch your back, bitch, because I'm going to make you pay for this. Shouldn't have made a statement."

That pushed Jess over the edge. He stormed from my side and got right into the kid's space, leaning down so far that the kid had to bend backward at his waist.

"Don't push me, kid. I'll bury you. Think you can come to *my* house, trash it, then threaten *my* girl? If you ever so much as think about her or this place again, I'll fucking end you."

The kid lost his attitude and had the good sense to look terrified, knowing full well that Jess would make good on his promise. Without giving him a chance to respond, Jess grabbed him by the back of the head and forced him into the car.

My heart thundered and I stopped breathing, not starting again until the cruiser's taillights had disappeared.

Standing on my lawn, stunned, I barely registered Jess pulling me tightly into his side. My arms were crossed on my stomach and I was cold. The temperature had dropped and even with his body heat to keep me warm, I was shivering.

It had started snowing while we were outside. Round, fat flakes floated down from the black sky above, resting lightly and peacefully where they landed. Any other night, I would have thought they were the loveliest snowflakes I'd ever seen.

But not tonight.

Not when I was surrounded by an ocean of broken pumpkins. Not when my daughter was locked inside my house to keep her safe. And not with that asshole kid's threatening glare burned into my brain.

I shivered again. And it had nothing to do with the snow.

———

HALLOWEEN WAS TOUGH. After a fitful night's sleep, I had gotten up early to start picking up pumpkin rinds. Thankfully, it hadn't snowed much and the broken bits hadn't been frozen into the grass.

I dropped off an exhausted Roe at Quail Hollow and went to work, glad to have a distraction from the drama. I let the patients and their issues consume my morning. I let them distract me from the worries swirling in my head.

All I wanted was a peaceful and quiet life. Since moving to Prescott, I'd had more confrontation in a three-month period than I could have imagined possible.

That was saying something, considering how much Nate, his parents and their attorneys had put me through.

The seventh and eighth months of my pregnancy had been spent emailing lawyers and reading legal agreements. The Fletchers had been certain that I'd gotten pregnant on purpose to steal their fortune. Every night I had gone to bed stressed and anxious.

But at the worst of it, I had always known it would eventually pass. That things would settle down. And it had. Once the paternity test results had been delivered, the legal attacks had stopped and Nate had signed his way out of Rowen's life.

But this was different.

I didn't see an end.

Would our evening conversations always be spent discussing drug dealers? Would our lunch breaks be spent talking through an arson case?

I was the sheriff's girlfriend and would always be a target. People like Wes and these punk kids would always come at me or Rowen to toy with Jess.

And he would always be a cop. It was who he was and I was proud to be by his side.

But until last night, I hadn't realized exactly how that would affect my life and Rowen's.

And I didn't know if I was strong enough for it.

He needed a woman who could stand by his side and prop him up on the bad days. I'd been doing my best but I wasn't sure if it was enough. If I was strong enough for him.

I couldn't help but think that he could find someone better.

By the end of the day, my head was pounding and my heart was troubled. But, somehow, I mustered the strength to set my worries aside and let Jess give me an update on the vandalism.

The kids had vandalized six different homes, including the farmhouse. The worst one, a couple miles away from mine, had gotten the entire front of their house spray-painted with obscenities.

"That's horrible," I said. "I feel so bad for those poor people that have to repaint their entire house. What kind of trouble will the kids get into?"

"They're all under eighteen so they'll face misdemeanor charges as juveniles. Probably end up with a fine and some community service hours. Two of them confessed. Their parents will punish them far worse than the law ever could at that age. They'll learn their lesson," he said.

"What about the third kid, he didn't confess?"

"Third was the little shit that threatened you. I don't know him or his parents. They're new in town. Built a monstrosity of a house up in the foothills. Haven't seen them around town much. Usually when they're here, they act like they're too good for Prescott. The kid stayed quiet until his parents got to the station and demanded a lawyer. They just couldn't believe their precious angel would do such a thing."

My eyes widened and my mouth fell open. "Is he going to get away with it?"

"No. He'll get punished. But with lawyers adding red tape, it'll just take a while. There's no way he gets away with it. Not after I caught him in the act."

"Well, I'm glad it's over. Having the pumpkins gone will be good motivation for me to tear down Halloween decorations and put out the Thanksgiving stuff."

"Seriously?"

"Seriously, what?" I asked, confused.

"Thanksgiving decorations?"

"Well, yeah. I decorate for every holiday."

"What are we talking about here? Does Thanksgiving have more or less than Halloween?"

"Thanksgiving, less. Christmas, you don't want to know."

He stood to take his dishes to the kitchen sink, grumbling something under his breath I didn't catch. But this time I was able to clearly make out the f-word.

———

WE FOLLOWED the normal bedtime routine and once Roe was asleep, I went downstairs to find Jess on the couch, watching TV. I had wanted to talk to him about my conversation with his mother and her phone calls with Ben, but with all the drama, I had forgotten last night.

"Honey?" I said, taking a sideways seat on the couch.

"Yeah?"

"So, last night, your mom said a few things to me that were, well, random."

"That's her. What'd she say?"

"Well . . . first she told me I was a good mom, which was sweet of her to say," I said.

"You are. A *great* mom."

"Thanks." I blushed a little and couldn't help but smile. I knew I was a good mom but Jess saying it with such confidence and conviction made my heart swell with pride.

"Anyway, she started telling me about Ben. How he gave you this house. That it's your pride and joy and—"

Jess jumped from the couch, and using all of the strength he had in one arm, threw the remote at one of the big chairs.

If not for the thick cushions, the remote would have shattered. He tipped his head down to me with angry eyes.

"Fucking not this again."

"Wh—"

"What do I have to do, Georgia? Huh? What do I have to do to convince you that I don't want this fucking house?" he yelled.

"Jess—"

"Sell it."

"What?" I asked, breathless.

"Sell it. Call the realtor tomorrow. You and Roe will move in with me this weekend."

"Sell the farmhouse?"

"As far as I can tell, selling this place is gonna be the only thing I can do to show you that I want you. Not this," he said, throwing a hand up in the air.

I stood from the couch and approached him with gentle hands. "Honey—" I started but was stopped when he interrupted me. Again.

"I mean it, Georgia. I'm done fighting with you about this. And if selling this place is what it takes, then we're doing it. Jesus. It's just a fucking house!"

Jackass Jess was making an appearance. Not only was he letting his temper get the best of him, but he wasn't listening to me. And I'd had enough. I was sick of him talking over me. Always getting his way.

Not this time.

"Stop." I shoved my palm in his face.

He didn't like that much. His eyes got bigger and his face turned red.

But before he could open his mouth, I said, "I wasn't talking about the house, Jess. Something you would have known if you hadn't effing interrupted me a hundred times. I *know* you're not with me for the house. I get it. What I was going to tell you was that your mom was telling me about Ben. And that Ben had been calling her for years. I wanted to know if you knew that. Okay? That's what I was going to tell you."

His anger evaporated and he raised his arms to touch my shoulders but I shrugged them off.

"Georg—"

"No," I said. "You don't get to sweet talk your way out of this. You messed up, Jess. Don't. Yell. At. Me. Watch that temper and quit ordering me around. I get that you're in charge most of the time, but you don't get to fly off the handle here. I won't be yelled at. I won't be told what to do. I've had enough of that from other men and I won't take it from you."

And with that, I stormed upstairs.

I immediately went into the bathroom where I started ranting to myself.

"That man makes me so effing mad! I just wanted to talk to him about his mother. *His* mother. But no. He jumps to conclusions and yells at me. That's how it always goes. And then I get so mad I am forced to yell back. I don't like the yelling. I'm tired of the yelling! I'm tired of being pushed around!"

Jess had just lost our argument and I wondered how he would react. Our last shouting match, the one after he'd yelled at Rowen, had left us not speaking for almost a week. What was I in store for tonight?

I heard the bedroom door close and seven seconds later, the bathroom door opened.

Pressing against my back, Jess wrapped me up and

puffed out a loud breath.

"Sorry," he said.

That was unexpected. I'd been ready for him to be all nice and sweet. To kiss me so that I'd give in and he'd get his way. Instead, he'd owned his mistake. I was impressed.

"I don't want to fight, Georgia," he said, bending to whisper in my ear.

"I didn't start it, Jess."

"Sorry. Shouldn't have jumped to conclusions. And I'm sorry I yelled."

I relaxed my weight into him.

"I feel like I can't talk about the farmhouse or my history here without you getting freaked. I don't know what to do other than move you out to get you to understand what we have is not about the house," he said.

"It took me a while, but I get it. You're with us for us. For me," I said. "I want you to be able to share. This place means a lot to you. To both of us. Don't hold back because you think it will freak me out. It won't."

"Okay." He held my eyes in the mirror.

"You can't talk over me. I can't stand it," I said. It reminded me of Nate and the last thing I wanted was to see any similarities between him and Jess.

"You're right. I'm sorry."

"I hate fighting."

"Me too," he said. "Are we done?"

I nodded.

"Good," he said right before spinning me around and lowering his mouth to mine.

He kissed me until I could barely stand on my own, my legs weak and wobbling. Then he held me up and kissed me some more until I was so turned on, I begged him to take me to bed.

———

"TIME'S UP, FRECKLES," Jess whispered.

Like most nights, I was tucked into Jess's side and we were talking quietly before we fell asleep. Him speaking to the top of my head, me talking into his chest.

"Time's up for what?" I asked.

"I feel like we're getting you there. To a spot where you know I won't hurt you. Where you know you can trust me. But something's still out there. I know you've still got doubts. I need to know what you're guarding yourself from. Guessing it has to do with Roe's dad, but you gotta tell me."

I took in a slow breath, completely filling my lungs and holding it until it burned. Then I blew it out and sagged into Jess's side. This wasn't going to be a fun conversation but he was right, he needed to know.

"I got drunk at a friend's wedding. Had a one-night stand with a groomsman. Got pregnant."

"I'm assuming he didn't take it well," Jess said.

"That would be an understatement. Had I known what an asshole he was, I never would have slept with him. But I don't regret it because I got Roe."

"What'd he do?"

"His family had money. They thought I was after it. Or that I was trying to trap him into marriage. I don't know. But they just attacked me. Said Roe wasn't his. Called me a gold digger and a whore. When I emailed Nate to tell him we were having a girl, they filed harassment charges against me.

It was crazy and went on for months and months. Finally when she was born we could do a paternity test."

"Then what?" Jess asked.

"They offered me money to go away."

"Fuck," he muttered.

"Yeah. Nice people," I deadpanned. "I told them they could keep it as long as Nate signed away his rights and promised never to contact me or Rowen."

Jess stayed quiet for a while, letting my story sink in. "What's his last name?" he finally asked.

"Fletcher. Why?"

"Just want to make sure that if I ever meet him, I shake his hand. The dumb fuck brought the most beautiful woman in the world into my life. Owe him my gratitude," Jess said.

I squeezed him a little tighter.

"That's sweet, honey. But if you ever meet him, I'd much prefer several punches to the face in lieu of a handshake. Okay?"

He chuckled. "Anything for my girl."

CHAPTER SIXTEEN

GIGI

"Hi, Sheriff," I called, walking into Jess's office.

"Freckles," he rumbled, standing from his black leather desk chair to greet me.

"I think that desk gets messier every time I come and visit."

He grunted before leaning down to deliver a quick kiss to my cheek.

One thing I liked about our relationship was that neither Jess nor I felt the need to go at each other in public. It's not that I had a problem with couples who liked mauling one another in front of strangers. If they needed that for their relationship to work, more power to them. To each their own. Jess and I just didn't need it.

We were more of a hand-holding, kiss on the cheek, arms around each other type of couple. And I liked it. Not that I didn't like it when Jess attacked my mouth or hauled me around in the bedroom. I did. A lot.

But there was something special and sweet about his gentle touches when we were in public. I would feel his kiss on my cheek for hours, the tingles lingering from where he brushed his soft lips to my skin.

I was visiting the station to try and convince Jess that we should go out tonight with Maisy and Everett. Ever since the first Mustangs game, Maisy had been asking repeatedly when we could have a double date. I had been putting her off, not because I didn't want to go but because there was a lot of stuff going on. Jess working extra shifts when he didn't have a dispatcher. Nights spent at my dining room table crafting Halloween decorations. Cleaning up the mess caused by the demolition of eleven pumpkins.

But Maisy had asked me again this week and I didn't want to put her off again. There were only two obstacles standing in the way of a night out: finding a babysitter and convincing Jess. If I could hurdle them both, I told her we'd be up for it.

Finding the babysitter, which I'd thought would be the more difficult of my two tasks, turned out to be a snap. One of Rowen's teachers at Quail Hollow had volunteered.

Now all I needed to do was get Jess on board with an evening at the Silver Dollar Saloon. We'd have a few drinks, share some laughs and check out the Prescott bar scene.

So here I was, standing in Jess's office with a box of donuts in my hand.

"Whatcha got there?" he asked.

"Donuts. Cops like donuts."

He eyed me suspiciously. "You brought donuts? Why?"

"Can't one of Prescott's newest citizens bring the local law enforcement crew a box of donuts to show her gratitude for their service?"

"Georgia," he grumbled.

"Okay. It's bribery. Maisy really wants us to meet up with her and Everett tonight for a couple of drinks. Can we? Please?" I shoved the box of donuts in his face, hoping that the amazing smell of freshly baked maple bars would make him say yes.

"What about Roe?" he asked.

"Covered. The babysitter is coming over at seven-thirty," I said.

"Already got a sitter, huh?"

Damn. "Ah . . . yes?"

He drew in a long breath but on the exhale said, "Fine."

"Yay!" I shouted. I stood on my tiptoes, reaching for a kiss, and just before our lips touched, I saw his small grin.

Jess grabbed the box of donuts and went back to his chair. Popping the lid off the box, he inhaled a maple bar in five huge bites.

"How's the day off?" he asked, wiping crumbs from his mouth.

"Excellent."

Since the move, I hadn't taken a single day off work and I needed to start using my vacation time. So today, I was having a Gigi Friday. Roe was at preschool and I had the day to myself.

It was only ten in the morning and I had already cleaned the farmhouse, gotten groceries, including a stop at the bakery for donuts, and gassed up the Explorer. I didn't have any chores left to do but maybe a load of laundry. So after lunch I was planning to bake cookies, paint my toenails and curl up in front of the fireplace with a book.

Bliss.

"Want to go to lunch with me today?" I asked.

"Probably should have asked me before I ate that bar," he said.

"Hmm . . . well, I needed you to have the donut so you'd agree to take me out tonight. If that means I have to forgo a lunch date, so be it."

He chuckled. "Pick me up in a couple hours. I'm just working on paperwork today to get caught up. I'll be going crazy by noon."

"You got it, Sheriff," I said, giving him a two-finger salute.

"Okay, honey. From the looks of the disaster that is your desk, you've got a lot going on. I'll drop these off at dispatch on my way out."

Standing up out of his rather uncomfortable guest chair, I leaned over to grab the box of donuts.

His hand slapped down so fast on top of the box it made me jump back.

"Don't even think about it," he said.

Holding my hands up in surrender, I backed out of the room. Then I blew him a kiss and left the station.

On a whim, I popped downtown to the salon. Miraculously, they were able to get me in for a pedicure with no appointment. Sitting in a massage chair, I let the hot water soaking my feet work its magic and relax my mind.

Gigi Fridays were the absolute best.

———

"I *LOVE* THIS PLACE!" I told Maisy, sitting down at our table. Jess and I had just arrived at the Silver Dollar Saloon.

The bar was a huge horseshoe taking up the middle of the square room. The walls behind it were covered in mirrors and liquor bottles. There were old, rickety stools everywhere and not a matching pair to be seen. But the coolest part was the bar top itself. The whole thing was covered in shiny copper.

The bar was dark and musty and the cement floors were stained and slightly sticky. If I had to use the bathroom, I would absolutely be hovering my ass over the toilet. There was no way my bare bum was ever going to touch a surface in this place. And even though it was now a non-smoking bar, the decades of smoke from years past had seeped into the walls. When we left, I'd smell like an old ashtray.

It was awesome!

"I'm so glad you guys are here!" Maisy said, doing a fast assessment of my outfit. "Nice jacket."

I was in a pair of black skinny jeans, a cream blouse and nude heels. Over my top I had pulled on my favorite tan leather jacket.

"What do you want?" Jess asked.

"A vodka cranberry with a lime, of course."

"Of course," he mocked, heading off to the bar.

We sat and visited with Maisy and Everett for a while. Mostly Maisy and I talked while Jess and Everett sat and listened. Everett was so quiet, after an hour, I didn't think he had said more than four words despite Maisy's and my unsuccessful attempts to draw him into the conversation. I'd never seen him act so shy.

While Jess only had two beers, he made sure that my drink glass was never empty.

After an hour, Maisy and Everett called it quits. Maisy seemed disappointed (and a little miffed at Everett) to be leaving so soon. But Everett had been acting so strange it had become awkward.

"Wanna play pool?" Jess asked after I hugged Maisy good-bye.

"Yeah!"

My bottomless drink glass was starting to get to me so there was a good chance I was shouting rather than talking in a normal decibel range. But I didn't care. The jukebox in the corner had been going all night, playing classic country as loud as they could get it without driving people away. At least I wasn't louder than the music.

As I followed Jess, I grabbed a fistful of his white thermal Henley, then shoved my other hand in his back jeans pocket. I was buzzed and happy. Doing a little groping of Jess's hot ass seemed totally appropriate.

We didn't stay at the bar late.

After sending the babysitter home, I pulled Jess upstairs and undressed him as quickly as I could. He let me take control and ride him until I came. Then he flipped me over and took over until he came. We were still primed so we went at it again in the shower.

Buzzed sex with Jess was off-the-charts hot.

Crawling into bed, I assumed my standard sleeping position at Jess's side.

"Where'd you learn to play pool?" he asked.

"Ben taught me."

He huffed before his chest started shaking.

"What's funny?"

"Guess Ben refined his teaching technique between the time he taught me and the time he taught you. You're good, baby. Never lost a game to anyone before. Except Ben," he said.

My smile stretched across my face. "I think Ben used to let me win, just so I would keep playing."

"Maybe." Jess grinned.

I crossed my hands on his chest, resting my chin on my knuckles so I could maintain my view of Jess's amazing blue eyes while we talked. "You know what I've been wondering? Ben said in his letter that he loved it here. In Prescott, and in the house. And he had you. Why would he move to Spokane?"

Jess cupped the back of my head and wrapped his other arm around my shoulders.

Oh no. That wasn't a good sign.

"Ben was married."

I sucked in a short breath. I'd had no idea the man who had been like a grandfather to me had ever been married.

"His wife, Claire, was great. Sweet. Kind. Loving. Spent time at church making meals for the shut-ins. Made quilts for folks stuck in the hospital. Always made dinner for me if I was over, enough for me to take plenty home when I left. Always taking care of people." He gave me a squeeze. "Kind of like you."

I tipped my chin to give him a light kiss on his chest.

"I asked Ben once why they didn't have kids. I guess Claire couldn't. Always figured that was part of the reason he took me under his wing," Jess said.

"Hmm . . . maybe," I whispered but I knew it wasn't true. Ben could have had a hundred kids and still would have looked out for Jess. That's just the type of man he was.

"Anyway. Claire was having some problems with one of her legs. Can't remember what. But they took her in for surgery. I remember coming over after she was home and bringing her flowers. She looked happy, rested. Just fine. Then two days later, a blood clot worked itself loose and traveled to her brain. Had a massive stroke and died."

232

Tears started running down my face, falling onto his chest.

"Ben loved Claire. With everything he had. She was his world. I don't think he could take being here without her. So about a month after she died, he found a job in Spokane and moved. Didn't hardly take a thing with him. Donated most everything to Claire's church. Asked me to take over care of the farmhouse."

I was heartbroken for Ben. I wish I had known but I understood why he hadn't told me. Even after twenty years, the loss of his wife had still been too painful to discuss.

"It makes sense why he kept this place," I whispered, drying my eyes.

"Yeah. Claire's buried over by the big grove of trees. The one on the north corner of the property."

"Oh my god. She is?" I whispered.

"Yeah."

I dropped my forehead to Jess's chest. "In Ben's will, he asked to be cremated and his remains given to me. His will said to keep them until I knew where to put them. I didn't know what he meant. So I packed them up and now they're up in the attic. Now we can put them where they belong."

The ache in my chest got stronger and I gave in to a new batch of tears. Tears of loss for Ben. For me. Tears of elation that Ben could finally rest with his beloved Claire.

Jess stroked my damp hair and kissed the top of my head. He whispered reassurances that everything would be all right. And he held me in his strong arms until my crying subsided and turned into small hiccups.

"Will you take me there tomorrow?" I asked.

"Yeah."

"Thanks, honey."

"Anything for my girl."

———

JESS

"This is a beautiful place," Georgia said.

We stood by Claire's white tombstone, surrounded by a tall grove of trees with swaying prairie grasses at our feet, the snowcapped mountains as a backdrop.

"It sure is," I agreed.

I often thought of Ben and what he'd taught me when I was young. All of the things a father would teach a son. The most important lesson Ben had ever taught me was the one he'd done without words. It was how he loved his wife.

Ben didn't need anything in the world as long as he had his Claire. When he was around her, he'd light up.

There had never been a woman that sparked a light in my soul. Not until Georgia.

It started the first night I came to the farmhouse and she was standing on the porch, giving me shit. Her mass of hair piled in a mess. Wearing the ugliest fucking sweater I'd ever seen in my life. One I'd seen her pull on countless times since.

She was the light I'd been looking for.

Now I just needed to make sure she knew it. That I undid all of the damage that asshole had done. And then I could work to make her as happy as Ben had made Claire.

———

"WHAT THE HELL, JESS!" Georgia shouted. "You're just telling me this now? That was weeks ago. You should have told me then. How could you keep this from me?"

She was in the kitchen, banging and clashing pots and pans around as she made dinner.

I'd just told Georgia about Wes's visit to the station on the Sunday that I had snapped at Rowen.

Wes had just been messing with me, so I'd planned on keeping it a secret. I didn't want her freaked out and worried.

But, thanks to Milo, she'd found out tonight.

Just because I didn't expect Wes to make a move didn't mean I hadn't taken precautions. Someone from the station would watch over Quail Hollow each afternoon until Georgia collected Rowen.

Usually, I made a point to drive down myself. I'd park a few blocks down and watch until they were both safely driving home. But if I couldn't do it, I asked Sam or Bryant to take my place. But today we'd all been busy so I'd asked Milo.

I'd given him a quick briefing and asked him to be discreet, which to him meant standing outside the Quail Hollow door and escorting Georgia to her car. Of course when she had asked him what was going on, he'd spilled.

Fucking Milo.

If I didn't like him so much, I'd kick his ass.

"Sorry I didn't tell you sooner. I just didn't want you to worry," I said.

"You don't get to decide that on your own. You can't keep making decisions for me, Jess! Especially with something like this. When it involves my safety or Rowen's, you don't get to walk all over me."

Fuck.

My shoulders fell. She was right.

"I'm used to making the decisions without input. At work. With my mom. I wasn't trying to walk all over you."

"Then stop doing it," she said. "You have to talk to me or this is never going to work."

"I will," I promised.

I'd been going about things all wrong with Georgia. She wasn't like my mother. She didn't want to have things done for her or to be left in the dark. If I was going to keep her in my life, make her happy, I had to start including her in making decisions.

She stopped pacing and planted her hands on the island, dropping her head toward the floor.

"I can't do this," she whispered.

"What?" I said. "What do you mean?"

Was she going to try and break up with me just because of this? She was fucking wrong if she thought I'd let her. She was mine and I wasn't letting her push me away.

"I'm not strong enough for you," she said. "You need to be with a woman who can live with the threats. The stories about drug dealers and . . . whatever else comes along. Someone who won't freak out."

My hands fisted on the island. I wanted to grab her shoulders and shake some sense into her. What the fuck did she mean she wasn't strong enough? She was the strongest woman I'd ever met.

But I took a deep breath and calmed my temper, reminding myself to be patient. She was just scared and this was just another thing she could use to push me away. She just needed time, time to see that I wasn't going to hurt her.

To see that she was the only woman for me.

"Georgia, look at me," I ordered from across the island.

236

"You are strong enough. When I need you, you're there. Not once have you let me down."

"Yes, but—"

"No," I said. "You are. You might not see it now, but you will. And besides, this will all settle. Things right now are . . . crazy. It's not like this normally."

"But Jess—"

"Stop," I said, rounding the island.

Taking her face in my hands, I pressed my forehead to hers.

"Please just give it time. Please? You'll see," I whispered.

Her breath whooshed out in a long sigh. Her shoulders relaxed and she leaned her head into my hands.

"Okay," she whispered.

I bent lower, brushing my lips against hers.

Time. We needed time. And I needed to take back control of Prescott. Then she'd see that her fears were for nothing.

We'd get back to the boring times. To the days when we'd be lucky to have two traffic stops in a week. I never thought I'd miss those days but fuck did I ever.

Georgia wouldn't have anything to worry about as soon I put an end to all of this shit with the pill dealer and with Wes. And I would. Now more than ever, I was determined to pin Wes down. He wasn't going to get away with wrecking my town and scaring my girls.

CHAPTER SEVENTEEN

GIGI

The days of November went by in a happy blur.
I was giving Jess the time he'd asked for, trying not
to worry and trusting that he would keep Rowen and I safe.

Jess had spent the majority of his working days in the
mountains, searching for signs of traffic to Wes's meth house.
He'd put in grueling days, hiking trails and searching for
signs in the snowy hills. Unfortunately, he hadn't found a
trace. Yet.

Thanksgiving was the only day he'd taken off, so I'd put
together a huge feast. We'd had Noelle over to spend the day
with us. I'd been happy to have her there to visit with
because apparently, Thanksgiving also meant watching football. Though I had come to enjoy the social aspect of the
Mustang games, watching football on TV was excruciating.

So while Jess had lazed on the living room couch, us girls
had planned where to put my Christmas decorations. Today,
for the first time ever, I was skipping my honored Black

Friday morning shopping tradition. That's how excited I was to decorate my farmhouse.

"It's bullshit. You know that? Complete effing BS. These big box stores keep trying to shove it down our throats earlier and earlier every year. Christmas displays up before Halloween. They can't even leave Halloween alone! I mean, at least wait until November. And then take them down in January. These people that leave multicolored lights up in their windows and on their gutters until Valentine's Day are nuts. I mean, it's just pure effing greedy that stores put Christmas stuff up too early and pure effing lazy when people can't get their stuff down when the holidays are over."

I was talking to myself about the appropriate timing of Christmas decoration and un-decoration.

While I was blabbing to no one, I was standing on a very tall ladder, holding a huge, heavy evergreen garland that I was stringing up on the overhang of the front porch. The garland matched the big wreath I'd already put on the front door.

Since I was talking to myself and carrying a heavy garland and a hammer all while standing on a very tall ladder, I wasn't paying much attention to my footing.

And because I wasn't paying much attention to my footing, I soon found myself no longer standing on the very tall ladder. Instead, I was on my ass, on the ground, in the snow. The bottom of the ladder right in front of my face.

My wrist throbbed because I had used it to break my fall. The heavy garland and hammer were no longer in my hands but in the snow, along with my ass.

———

"AREN'T you women supposed to be shopping on Black Friday, Gigi? Not falling off ladders?" Dr. Peterson had just finished wrapping my sprained wrist in the ER.

"To hell with Black Friday. I take my Christmas decorating very seriously, Dr. Peterson. Shopping must wait." I smiled.

He grunted a laugh. "I guess so."

I had learned my lesson from the rattlesnake incident and called Jess as soon as I could drag my ass off the ground. He'd had Roe with him at the sporting goods store downtown. They had left shortly before I started decorating to pick out a sled for Rowen.

So I'd waited on the front porch, clutching my wrist until they'd gotten home.

When Jess helped me pull the Christmas decorations out of the attic last night, I absolutely should have listened when he'd said he would hang the tall stuff.

"I've called in a painkiller prescription for you to the pharmacy. But you know the drill. Ice if it gets swollen. Hot compress if it's achy. Try not to use it for a few days," Dr. Peterson said.

"Will do." I hopped down from the ER bed. "Thanks, Dr. Peterson."

Jess and Roe were sitting in the lobby waiting for me. I aimed my feet in that direction and headed to meet an angry-at-Georgia-because-she-didn't-listen-to-me Jess and a mad-at-her-mother-because-she-hurt-herself-and-now-we-couldn't-go-sledding Rowen.

Jess didn't speak to me on the way back to the farmhouse. Neither did Roe.

Roe's silence ended when we got home and she asked to

play with the cats. Jess had created an area in the garage for Mrs. Fieldman, Rose, Peony and Captain Lewis. He'd even put in a cat door so they could go in and out at their leisure. Roe thought it was amazing because she could fit through it too.

While Rowen's anger was short-lived, Jess's lasted much longer. He had disappeared somewhere after we'd gotten home and come back in right before lunch. He'd eaten in complete silence, not even talking to Roe.

"I'm sorry, honey. I should have waited for you," I said as Jess brought his lunch dishes into the kitchen.

"Yeah, you should have."

"I didn't mean for it to happen. It was an accident."

He pulled in an angry breath and let loose what he'd clearly been keeping inside these last few hours.

"You know, I've been taking care of people my whole life. My mother. My sister. This town. Because if not me, then who? So why is it that the one person who I actually *want* to take care of won't let me?"

I didn't get to answer before he started yelling.

"Fuck! I'm so *fucking* mad at you, Georgia! You could have broken your neck! And then what? What would have happened to Rowen? To me?"

I hadn't thought about it that way. Tears flooded my eyes as the realization dawned. I could have left my daughter today with no one in the world to care for her.

"I see it's sinking in," he snapped before walking away.

I'd taken on so much these past few years. Not that I'd had much choice. I guess much like Jess, if not me, then who? The only other people I'd had to depend on were my mom and Ben. Now both were gone. And even when they had still been with us, Mom had been sick and Ben's aging body couldn't have done everything his mind thought it could have. So that meant everything had fallen to me.

Cooking. Cleaning. Laundry. Grocery shopping. Yard work. Holiday decorating.

Everything.

What else was I supposed to do?

But Jess was right. I couldn't afford to be reckless with my safety or my life. I was all Rowen had. I couldn't risk abandoning her just to hang up a Christmas ornament.

And I had Jess. Why hadn't I let him help?

Because I was stupid. Extremely stupid. And stubborn.

My stomach rolled. Anytime Jess and I were fighting, I got sick. And, along with my throbbing wrist, I was getting a headache. It was time for a pain pill and a nap.

I set Rowen up with a movie and changed into some comfy lounge pants and a sweatshirt. My pill kicked in shortly after *Tangled* started playing and I fell into a deep sleep on the couch.

I woke up a little fuzzy, my eyes dry and foggy, and saw the clock on the mantel. I had slept for five hours. No wonder the movie was over and Roe was no longer on the couch.

My girl's sweet voice echoed from the kitchen.

"Jess, can you give me my bath and read me my stories tonight?"

"Uh, Roe, I don't know what the rules are with little girls and bath time," he said.

"There aren't any rules, silly." She giggled. "You just have fun! Except Mommy doesn't let me splash water outside the bathtub."

"Roe, that's not what . . . I, uh, tell you what. Go put on

your swimming suit. You can wear that in your bath tonight," he said.

"Yay!" she yelled, jumping up and down.

I laughed from the doorway and both of them turned to see me standing there. Roe came bouncing over and hugged me as she screeched, "Jess is giving me my bath!"

"Great," I smiled, bending to kiss the top of her hair. When I stood back up, Jess was grinning, my signal that he was ready to forgive me. I squeezed Roe before she scooted out of the room. Then I walked straight to Jess, wrapping my arms around his waist.

"I'm sorry. You were right. I was stupid and reckless. I've gotten used to doing things myself. It's a hard habit to break."

"Me, Georgia. You depend on me. Okay?" He pulled me tighter into his chest.

I relaxed into his body and nodded. I was glad he had accepted my apology and we could stop fighting. The knot in my stomach started to loosen.

"You know, I want to take care of you too. If you'll let me," I said.

He let out a long, frustrated sigh. "You do, Georgia. Every day. Creating a warm place for me to come to every night. Letting me unload after work. Pushing back when I'm an asshole. Arguing with me. Calling me 'honey.' Being my girl. All those things are what I need and how you take care of me. And if you'd get outta your head, stop doubting me, you'd see that I've been letting you take care of me all along."

Damn.

He was right. Again.

"Well . . . I guess I'll just keep doing that then," I muttered.

He chuckled while we held each other. I looked up and

locked my eyes with his. I'd never tire of that bright blue color.

Roe came bounding back into the kitchen, wearing her pink ruffled swimming suit and her orange goggles.

"Are you going to kiss Mommy?" Roe asked Jess.

"I was thinking about it. That okay with you?"

"Yep! I like it when you kiss her. It's just like when the prince kisses the princess. Are you a princess, Mommy?" she rambled.

Jess and I both laughed at my wonderful girl. Then Jess leaned down and pressed his lips to mine. His tongue darted out and the tip touched my lower lip.

"You know, Jess, she's only four. You can give her a bath without the suit," I whispered.

He smiled and whispered back, "Nah. She's excited. Maybe next time."

Jess walked out of the kitchen, hand in hand with my daughter. It was on the tip of my tongue to tell them both, "I love you." Because I did. I loved them. I loved him.

I had never been in love with a man. Maybe if I'd had more experience, I would have realized it sooner. It felt strange that we hadn't said the words to each other yet, but looking back, it had been there for a while.

With every touch, every kiss, it was simply unspoken. Unspoken, but never missing.

———

MAISY and I were sitting at my dining room table, embellishing sweaters with Christmas flair. It was a couple of weeks before Christmas and these sweaters were going to be our attire for the Christmas party I was hosting at the farmhouse in two days.

Technically, it was Jess's party, not mine. Each year he threw a holiday party at the station for his deputies and their families. Party planning was not his forte, him being a manly man and all, so when he'd asked for my help I'd immediately taken charge.

I'd recruited Maisy to help me in exchange for an invitation to the party on Saturday night. She, like me, was all over it.

"Is Everett excited for the party?" I asked.

"I guess," she mumbled, attaching a string of lights with a battery pack to the waistband of her sweater.

"Is he not a Christmas party fan? Or is it the sweater? Jess is annoyed about the ugly sweater theme."

She set down her lights and moped. "Things haven't been going great these last few weeks. Ever since that night we all went out for drinks, he's been distant. Always making an excuse at the last minute to cancel our plans. Doesn't come find me at work to talk like he used to. He's just been brushing me off. Granted, he makes sure I am there at night. We have sex, which is still great, but then after, he still doesn't talk to me. Just rolls over and falls asleep."

"Sorry, sweetie," I said.

"It's okay. I mean, it's not like he talked much before, you know? Maybe he is just really busy. And this is part of us getting past the new phase."

"Maybe."

Jess and I had been together longer than Maisy and Everett and we were still hot and heavy, enjoying the time spent getting to know each other. Though the more we were together, the more I wondered if we'd ever cool off.

"We'll see. It's not like I'm going to dump him or anything. I just don't know how to talk to him about it without him getting mad at me or shutting down even more." Her shoulders sagged. "What would you do, Gigi?"

I reached out and patted her hand. "I guess . . . try and talk to him. Be honest about how I was feeling. Ask him if there was something I had done."

"Yeah," she muttered.

"Be yourself, Maisy. If that doesn't work for him, then maybe he isn't the guy for you. Okay?"

She nodded.

We went back to work on our sweaters in silence.

I hoped that Maisy and Everett would work through their issues. They made a cute couple and she wanted so badly for things to work out. If he didn't want to see her anymore, I hoped he would find the nerve to tell her and that this distant behavior wasn't his way of breaking it off. Maisy was a catch. And if he couldn't see that, she was better off without him.

———

JESS and I were having drunk after-party sex. My face was in the pillow, my arms under it and braced on the headboard. I was up on my knees, my ass tipped in the air.

He was pounding into me from behind, pulling my hips into him with each thrust so he could fuck me hard. Really hard. Amazingly hard and I was loving it.

I had already come twice and he was building me up a third time. The first one had come from his mouth when he'd gone down on me the minute we'd gotten to the bedroom.

He hadn't even bothered to get me to bed. He'd just pushed me up against the door and fallen to his knees.

After I came, he'd picked me up and thrown me on the bed. He'd undressed in a hurry, tossing clothes all over the place, and then yanked my ugly sweater over my head, sending it flying in the direction of the garbage can. No sooner had it hit the floor before he was inside me. My second orgasm had ripped through me while I was on my back, Jess's mouth attached to my nipples and his cock setting a fast and deep rhythm.

And now I was pressed forward, thoroughly enjoying having Jess behind me.

"Oh god, Jess, keep going. Harder," I said, turning my head sideways on the pillow.

"Yeah, baby," he said, obeying my command.

As he picked up his pace, he reached around my hips to find my clit with his middle finger. A couple hard flicks and I was done. My eyes screwed shut and I planted my face into the pillow so I could moan through my release, my sex clenching around his cock as he kept going harder and harder.

"Fuck, Georgia," he groaned as my orgasm triggered his. He bent forward, still thrusting, and let me take his weight as he shot himself inside of me.

We stayed like that for a minute until I couldn't take his weight anymore and shifted underneath him. He let me go and fell onto the bed, lying on his side, facing me. I turned to my back so I could take a few deep breaths and get some oxygen flowing back into my veins.

"We are totally having drunk sex more often. Even if that means you have to get loaded here on a random

Wednesday night, I don't care," I declared, still trying to catch my breath.

"Keep the Crown stocked and you got yourself a deal."

We both burst out laughing before cleaning up and sliding into bed for our post-sex, pre-sleep cuddling.

"Thanks for the party, Freckles."

"You're welcome, honey. It was fun. Did you like it?"

"Yep. It was a good night."

"Next year, no eggnog," I said. "No one drank it and I felt guilty throwing it all out. But there was no way I was going to keep it. Gross."

He chuckled and pulled me tighter to his side. "What's up with Everett and Maze?"

"Ah, she said he's been kind of distant. Why?" I was surprised that he'd care about my friend's love life.

"Seeing him with her, getting a bad vibe. First at the bar. Then tonight."

"Yeah. He's been a little weird when we've been around them lately. He's just shy, I guess, which is a lot different than he is at work. Maybe he just puts on a good show for patients, I don't know. But she's, well . . . Maisy. The complete opposite of shy. They're a lot different."

"Hmm," Jess muttered.

We were quiet for a few more minutes until I recalled my conversation with Sam earlier at the party. He had told me how much he liked the farmhouse now that it had been updated. He hadn't been over since Ben lived in it. And the way he talked, it sounded like a lot had been changed over the years.

"What kind of updates did you do to the house after Ben moved away?" I asked.

"A lot. Why?"

"Sam said it looked great. He made it sound like the place was completely different. I was just curious if there was anything still left that was Ben and Claire's."

"Like I told you, I spent a lot of time here keeping it up. When I was still a kid, I did the stuff that didn't cost much but my time. Then after I got back from the academy and had a paycheck, started doing more. Put up new siding and shutters outside. Tiled the laundry room and entryway. New bathrooms. New kitchen. I didn't change the layout but other than that, everything is different from when Ben was here."

"Why?" I asked.

"Wanted it to be different if he ever came back. I thought he wouldn't want the same house that was his and Claire's," he said.

I was glad he'd done that for Ben because I think he would have been right.

"You did an amazing job, honey. I love this place."

I was glad he didn't have to give it up after all. That we could both enjoy the house and our time here spent together. I wondered if that is what Ben had been going for all along.

CHAPTER EIGHTEEN

GIGI

It was the week following the Christmas party and I was at work, sitting at the nurses' station on the second floor. With Christmas just a little over a week away, we'd had a heavy flow of visitors, people coming in to see family members who were stuck in the hospital during the holidays.

I had never seen so many poinsettias before, outside of a grocery store. Not a single room in the unit was without at least two. One older lady had five and she gave me a beautiful pink one to take home tonight after work.

My last set of rounds were finished and I was double-checking I had everything done when my phone rang.

"Hi, honey," I answered, seeing it was Jess on the screen.

"Georgia."

My heart rate instantly skyrocketed and I started panicking. His voice was filled with pain.

"What? What is it? Is it Roe? Is it your mom?" I asked.

"They're both fine," he said. "It's Wes."

I let out a deep breath, my panic immediately subsiding, knowing my daughter was okay and nothing had happened to his mother.

"What's happened with Wes?" I asked.

"Need you to come to the station," he said. "Now."

"Okay. Should I pick up Rowen first? Or will we be done in time for me to get her?"

"Leave her at school."

"Okay, I'm just leaving. Tell me, though, are you all right?" I asked.

"No."

I drove nervously from the hospital to the station. My stomach was in tight knots. Walking in, I headed straight to Jess's office. I gave out quick waves to everyone but I didn't bother to stop.

Every other time I'd come to the station, the blinds to Jess's office had been open. Now they were closed shut. When I got to the doorway, Jess was behind his desk, his head in his hands, propped up by both of his elbows.

"Hi," I said, closing the door behind me.

The look on Jess's face was devastating. His eyes were red, like he'd been rubbing them all day. His hair was a mess, sticking up in all directions from running his hands through it over and over. The only time his hair looked like that was when we were in bed together and the person running her hands through his hair was me. That look was sexy as hell. This was absolutely not.

I walked around the edge of his desk and straight into his space.

He turned his chair to face me with his legs spread wide. Once I was close enough, his arms came around my waist and he pulled me into the space between his legs. The top of his head went straight into my belly and his hands spread out on the small of my back.

I wrapped my arms around him, my fingers diving into his hair. Then I bent down to kiss the back of his head. I didn't say anything, just held onto him as he held onto me. He'd tell me when he was ready.

"Wes was found murdered this morning," he said.

I gasped and my muscles tensed.

Murder in Prescott? Things like that weren't supposed to happen here.

And it wasn't a nameless, faceless person. It was Wes. I knew him. Not that I was his friend. But still, I knew him.

As I was trying to process Jess's words, he leaned away but kept his hands at my back.

"What happened?" I asked.

He propped me up on the edge of his desk so we could face each other. Sadness poured out of his blue eyes.

"Silas called me this morning. He was driving on an old county road out by his place and saw a body in the creek off to the side of the road. Went to check it out, saw it was Wes," he said.

I squeezed my eyes shut for a second and took in a breath. I needed to be strong for Jess. This was my chance to prove to him, and myself, that I had what it took to be a cop's girlfriend. Jess trusted me to be that person. I didn't want to let him down.

Jess was going to be holding up the whole town. Everyone would count on him to make Prescott safe and put the killer behind bars. He'd take on the weight of all of Jamison County to make that happen.

I buried my fears deep and steeled my spine.

"Went up there, saw Wes in the creek. From the looks of

it, he'd been there all night. Blood everywhere. Three different stabs to his gut," he said.

"Stab wounds?"

He nodded.

"Do you have any idea who did it?"

He nodded again. "Coroner had just pulled up when Milo called, sitting here at the station. Said some kid had just walked in to report a murder."

"The killer walked into the station?"

"No, it was a witness. Christ, Georgia. He was just a kid. Nineteen, twenty maybe. He was fucking flipped out and spilled the whole story."

"What happened?"

"He was over at a friend's house. Smoking meth. Getting loaded. When it got late, the place cleared out except for this woman and an older guy he'd never seen before. This woman starts bragging about how she knows Wes and can score them more drugs."

At the mention of Wes's name, he dropped his head and took a minute to collect himself.

I couldn't imagine how he was feeling. He had known Wes a long time, even if they were enemies.

"I guess up until that point, the older guy had kept fairly quiet. But as soon as Wes's name entered the mix, he started to get real mad. He told this kid and the woman that Wes owed him four hundred dollars. Then he pulled out a gun and forced the woman to arrange a meeting with Wes. That's why they were all where Silas found Wes's body."

"So this older guy killed Wes over four hundred dollars?"

Jess nodded.

Four hundred dollars? It didn't seem real. "If this guy had a gun, why would he stab Wes?" I asked.

"I'm not sure. When they pulled up to the meeting place, the woman tore off the second the gun wasn't pointed at her face, and the kid ran to hide in the trees. He couldn't hear what happened but one minute this older guy was talking to Wes and the next he'd pulled out a knife and was stabbing him."

Bile creeped up the back of my throat but I swallowed it down.

"Why did it take so long for the kid to get down here?" I asked. "If Wes had been stabbed, maybe he could have been saved."

"He didn't have a ride. The murderer drove off in Wes's truck. The kid had to hike out through the woods, nearly froze to death."

"Oh my god," I whispered.

Jess nodded and we stayed quiet for a few moments.

"Did I ever tell you Wes and I used to be best friends when we were kids?"

My eyes widened in shock. Two seconds ago, if someone had asked me if I could be more stunned, my answer would have been absolutely not. Not after Jess had described the details of a hateful and senseless murder. But here I was, speechless. I couldn't get my mouth to work so I just shook my head.

"Yeah. We grew up together. Me, Wes and Silas were always tight," he said.

"I'm so sorry, Jess."

"Stab wounds to the stomach won't kill you instantly." His eyes stared blankly at my knees. "Means Wes bled to death. Lying there alone in the cold. What do you think he was thinking about?"

The corners of my mouth turned down as my chin

started to quiver. My heart was breaking for Jess. He had spent the morning looking at the dead body of his childhood friend. And then the afternoon learning about how his former friend had been murdered.

"I don't know, honey," I said, reaching out to stroke his hair. "But I hope it was good things. Memories of times when he was happy."

He pulled me into his lap and squeezed me so tightly, I struggled to breathe. But I didn't say a word. I just sat there and did my best to remain strong.

I left the station about an hour after I'd arrived, needing to pick up Rowen. Jess had a long night ahead of him and doubted he'd make it to the farmhouse before midnight.

Sam had tracked down the woman from the party and taken her statement, which matched the kid's. Bryant had wrapped up the crime scene and gotten an APB out for Wes's murderer. With any luck, the killer was dumb enough to still be driving around in Wes's truck.

So while his deputies were working on the murder case and I was driving home, Jess was driving to the Drummond farm to tell Jack and his wife, Annie, that their son had been killed.

I prayed the whole way home, still shocked this was happening.

I prayed that Jess would make it through this horrible night and that he'd find Wes's killer quickly. That he'd be able to get closure for Wes's family, himself and the town.

I prayed that he would find the strength to tell his friend's parents that they would never again see their child.

And I prayed that Rowen would grow up healthy and happy. And that I would never be on the receiving end of that kind of message.

———

TWO DAYS LATER, Wes's killer had not been found.

Jess was being flooded with questions from concerned citizens. People stopped by the station all day long to see what he was doing to find the murderer. Reporters were sucking as much information from him as they could.

The Prescott newspaper had run a special edition this morning. I'd been curious about how much the public was being told, but after reading the newspaper, I knew it wasn't much.

The paper was three pages and entirely dedicated to covering the murder. Considering how little information Jess had released to the press, the newspaper was ten percent speculation about the murder details and ninety percent a report on Wes Drummond's life.

I thought the whole thing was entirely unnecessary. About an hour after the Coffee Club met yesterday morning, everyone in the county knew that Wes had been murdered.

Tomorrow, Wes's murder would be making the bigger Sunday papers in Montana. Reporters from Bozeman, Billings and Missoula had called Jess yesterday to get the official press release.

Rowen and I hadn't ventured far from the farmhouse this weekend. Other than an overdue trip to the grocery store, we were lying low. I didn't want people approaching me while I was with my daughter and asking what I knew about Wes's murder. So we stayed at home and waited each night for Jess to come back.

Jess had arrived late on Thursday from the Drummonds' house. Rowen had been long since asleep when he pulled in but I had gotten ready for bed and waited up for

Jess, reading on the living room couch. As soon as I'd heard his truck coming down the drive, I'd hurried to the front door and met him in the entryway. After he'd shrugged off his coat, we'd wrapped our arms around each other and held tight, standing just inside the door, unmoving.

Last night had been a repeat of the same.

Tonight, I'd swapped the living room couch for my office chair. Earlier, I'd lit a fire so it was warm, but I was still cuddled up underneath a cozy blanket. I must have drifted off because one minute I was reading and the next minute I was in Jess's arms and he was carrying me upstairs to bed.

"Sorry, I fell asleep."

"It's okay."

"Do you want to put me down so I can walk?" I asked.

"No."

I wound my arms around his shoulders and buried my head in the crook of his neck, content to let him carry me upstairs in his big, strong arms.

When we got to the bedroom, Jess set me down on my feet but didn't let me go. He just held me close to his chest with one arm banded around my shoulders, his gaze so intense my cheeks flushed.

"Jess?" I asked.

He didn't respond. He just kept his eyes on mine for what felt like an eternity until, finally, he broke the silence.

"Had a horrible few days. Don't know how I would have made it through if I hadn't had you to come back to every night. I love you, Georgia."

I stood there motionless, holding his ice-blue gaze while his words rang in my ears. I wasn't scared or unsure of what to say, I just didn't want to break the silence. Because the sound of Jess saying he loved me in his deep voice was something I wanted to remember for the rest of my life.

When I had committed his words permanently to memory, I smiled.

"I love you too."

A huge smile spread across his handsome face. I took it in, committing it to memory too, before his smiling mouth dropped intently toward mine.

The next morning, I cooked us all a big Sunday morning breakfast. While Jess and Rowen were in the living room watching TV, I made scrambled eggs, sausage patties, breakfast potatoes and French toast.

When we'd woken up, Jess had told me he wasn't going to the station. It wasn't because he didn't have a mountain of work to do, but because he needed a day off. One day to take a step back and collect himself before another brutal week as the county's sheriff.

After Jess had announced his plans, I'd declared it a pajama day. We weren't leaving the house and we weren't getting dressed. The only exception being for Roe. She could wander outside to the garage and play with the cats if she wanted, but other than that, we were staying in and we were lounging in the living room wearing sweatpants.

And if that meant I had to watch football morning, afternoon and night, so be it.

"Thanks, baby. That was great," Jess said after demolishing a huge plate of nachos, his choice for a game-time snack.

Games, actually. I learned that Sunday Night Football started at eleven in the morning with multiple games going before the one officially dubbed the night game.

I was turned sideways in the couch, my legs extended so

my feet were resting on top of Jess's thighs. Rowen was sitting on the floor at the coffee table, glitter pens and markers scattered everywhere so she could color in one of twelve Disney princess coloring books she had out. She had just finished coloring a page, rather beautifully I was proud to see.

"This is for your office." She shoved the picture in his face. "It's messy and needs some pictures."

I burst out laughing. "Leave it to a four-year-old to tell you how it really is."

Jess grumbled but the corners of his mouth turned up.

I was glad to see him smiling and relaxed. I'd wanted to ask him more about his relationship with Wes but not until we were together and comfortable. When he was here with us in a safe place and there would be no interruptions to our conversation.

"You said the other day that you and Wes were friends," I said.

"Yep. As far back as I can remember. Must have started when I was little. Think my dad and Jack used to get together. Brought us boys along to play. Why?"

"I was just wondering what happened. You turned out, well . . . you," I said, throwing a hand out to indicate all of the goodness that was my Jess. "And Wes, well, he took a dark path."

"Honestly? I don't know. Thought about it a lot, especially as he kept getting deeper and deeper. He was a different person growing up. All through high school, we stayed tight. Worst we did was drink. I left for the academy. Came back two years later and he was different. I tried to pull him out. Get him back. But . . . it was like he didn't care. About anything. Family. Friends. Nothing. I asked Lissy about it a hundred times but she never would tell me what happened."

"Lissy?" I recalled Wes mentioning her name at the café a couple of months ago but I never had remembered to ask Jess who she was.

"Felicity. My sister."

Right. His sister. He rarely talked about her and I wanted to know more, but I didn't want to stop him while he was talking about Wes.

"How would she know what happened with Wes? Just because she was living here?" I asked.

"No. Wes and Felicity dated for years. Hooked up when she was a freshman in high school. Were together until the day she left. I came home the week before her graduation. Figured he'd be proposing to her. She'd be moving to the Drummond farm, gearing up to raise her and Wes's babies. Shocked the hell out of me when I came home and he was a wreck. Couldn't believe it when she left him behind the day after she graduated."

"Huh," I muttered.

"Yeah. Been fourteen years and she still won't tell me what happened. Silas won't either."

"You lost me again. Silas?"

"Silas stayed around after we graduated. Started working on his family's ranch. He knows what happened while I was gone but he's as tight-lipped as Lissy. And right after she left, he up and joined the army. Did ten years. Came home right as I was running for sheriff."

"I don't understand why he won't tell you what happened. Especially if it had something to do with your sister," I said.

"Yeah. Me too. I asked him so many times I lost track.

Finally stopped when he got so pissed at me one night he punched me. Not many men could get the jump on me, except Silas and maybe Beau. Broke my nose."

"What?" I gasped. "He hit you?"

"Who hit you? It's not nice to hit," Rowen chimed in from the floor, my outburst taking her attention away from coloring.

"Oh. Ah, no one, sweetie. We were just, ah, talking about football," I stuttered.

"There's lots of hitting in football, Mommy," Rowen said, totally buying my bold-faced lie. "But Jess said it was okay because they're grown-ups and because it's part of the game. He said that they get paid good money to take the hard hits. If the pussies can't take it, they should be kicked out of the league."

My jaw dropped wide open. My four-year-old daughter had just said "pussies."

"Ah . . . Roe. I thought we talked about keeping our talks in the garage a secret. Just between me and you. Remember?" Jess said.

"Secrets aren't nice, Jess," she scolded.

"Shit," he muttered.

I closed my eyes and shut my mouth, counting to ten. Then I had to count backward because when I hit ten, I was still really, really, *really* mad.

"Now, Freckles—" Jess started, but I stopped him by shoving my palm in his face.

"I'm going to let this go," I said. "With a reminder that she is a sponge. She'll suck up anything you say, even when you don't think she's paying attention. Now in order for me to let this go, I am going upstairs to take a long, hot bath. By the time I'm done, I'll be over it and no longer mad at you.

But I promise you this, Sheriff. The day that any teacher calls to discuss Rowen's language, I'm going to give them your number. *You* get to deal with it."

He grinned, clearly amused at my declaration.

He knew full well that I'd have a talk with Rowen later about using bad words and that if her teacher ever did call me, upset by her language, I'd apologize profusely and promise it would never happen again.

"Love you," Jess said as I stood to go and take my bath.

"Yeah, yeah, yeah. Love you too. Whatever," I muttered.

CHAPTER NINETEEN

GIGI

C hristmas was in four days and Jess was driving us to Wes Drummond's funeral. I wanted to be baking cookies. Or wrapping presents. I did not want to be going to a drug dealer's funeral.

But it was important to Jess, so Rowen and I were going.

Noelle was with us too. She'd known Wes quite well since he had been her son's best friend and her daughter's boyfriend, and his murder was taking its toll on her already fragile mind.

The whole town would likely be at the funeral, so it was being held in the school's auditorium. There weren't any churches large enough to hold the large audience.

I'd never been in the auditorium before, and much like with the football stadium, I was impressed by its size. There were two columns of seats in the middle of the room, another off to the left of the stage and a fourth to the right.

The casket sat center stage. It was a simple design, made

of gleaming wood. Large framed pictures of Wes bracketed it on either side, some of him as a child with his family, some from his teenaged years. None resembled the man in his thirties I had known.

The service started promptly at two o'clock but before the pastor walked up to the podium, he escorted an older couple to seats in the front row. The woman's face was red and puffy. The man's face was blank and his skin was pale.

"Poor Jack and Annie," Noelle whispered.

Jack and Annie. Wes's parents.

My heart instantly hurt for them, and the ache continued to get worse as the service went on. Mostly the pastor talked about the good things in Wes's life but I appreciated his acknowledgement that Wes hadn't been a perfect man and had lost his way.

The funeral concluded and everyone started shuffling toward the cafeteria for the reception. The bottleneck at the doors gave me a chance to people watch.

Small groups of three to four people huddled together in the aisles, and a larger group stood around Wes's parents up front.

One woman stood up front alone, looking at one of the picture collages. She was in profile but she was stunning. Her honey-blond hair was pulled back into a swirling bun at the nape of her neck. Her figure was perfectly silhouetted in a black pencil skirt and silk blouse. And even though we were inside, she was wearing a pair of huge framed sunglasses.

There was something familiar about her, like I'd seen her around town before but I couldn't quite place her.

I was just opening my mouth to ask Jess who she was

when a blond flash came out of nowhere and crashed into his body.

Andrea Merkuso.

Correction. Andrea Merkuso with her arms wrapped around Jess's waist and her blond head burrowed into his chest.

I blinked a couple of times and clamped my teeth together to keep my jaw from dropping open.

Did this woman seriously have the gall to plaster her body into his while I was standing right there?

Yes. Yes, she did.

I guess she was clueless after all.

Jess's arms immediately flew up to the sides, like he was scared to touch her. But after the shock subsided, he unlocked her arms from his waist and picked her up, forcefully setting her down a foot away. She stumbled a little before she regained her balance.

"What the fuck?" he rumbled.

She seemed surprised. What had she been expecting? Jess to pull her into his arms and express his undying love?

"I just thought you might need me," she cried. "We both knew Wes for a long time."

Never in my life had I been the jealous or possessive type before. But when it came to Jess, I couldn't help myself. I was the one who got to touch him. I was the one who got to wrap arms around him.

Me.

I pulled in another breath and closed my eyes, reminding myself that the last thing I needed was to become gossip fodder for starting a catfight at a funeral.

When I opened my eyes again, Jess was close to losing

his cool too. He was leaning down into Andrea's space with a look that was beyond frightening.

"Andrea, get this through your head. We are done. Stay away from me. I am with Georgia. The woman standing right there."

I gave her a bitchy smirk and a little finger wave.

Her face screwed up in a scowl.

I rolled my eyes and turned away from Skankasaurus to look at Jess. "You ready, honey?"

He closed his eyes and his chest expanded with a long breath. Either he was still mad or he was trying to hold back laughter because he found the combination of my eye roll, finger wave and smirk amusing.

It was probably a little bit of both.

"Yeah. Let's go," he said.

And we all walked to the cafeteria, leaving a red-faced and fuming Andrea Merkuso behind.

———

"DO you want anything else to eat, sweetie?" I asked Rowen.

"No, I'm done."

We were sitting at one of the long tables in the cafeteria and had just finished a quick snack from the plethora of reception food trays. Rowen and I were waiting for Jess and Noelle, who were paying their respects to Wes's parents.

For two hours we'd been here, mostly standing around while Jess was approached time after time by various Prescott residents. Each one asking how he was coming along with his investigation. I figured there were only a handful of people in the building who hadn't talked to him yet, meaning that with any luck, we'd be free to leave soon.

Rowen had been her usual self, a trooper. When she got tired of standing, either Jess or I would pick her up for a bit. But after hours, she was getting bored and fidgety. There was only so much staying still a four-year-old could take.

"You're doing great, baby girl. Thanks for being my good girl. I know this isn't much fun," I said.

"Can we go?" she begged.

"Not quite yet, Roe. But soon."

"Okay," she pouted.

Deciding we needed to change the subject, I started talking to her about Christmas. Every third day she would change her mind about what she wanted Santa to bring her. Thankfully, she listed off three things that were already wrapped and hidden in my closet.

"Your kid is wrecking my coat," a female voice behind me snapped.

Standing right behind my chair was the blond woman from the auditorium, both of her hands planted firmly on her hips.

Now that she was closer and no longer in profile, I realized she was not just stunning. She was *gorgeous*. She had high cheekbones, a perfectly straight nose and full lips. I couldn't see her eyes because she was still wearing sunglasses, likely to cover them if she'd been crying.

"I'm sorry, your coat?" I asked.

"It's under the kid's seat," she said, jerking her chin in Rowen's direction as her lip curled.

I frowned. There were many other ways she could have announced there was a problem with her coat. Many better and nicer ways.

Bending to peer under Rowen's chair, I saw there was a

black wool coat under her feet but I wouldn't say that Rowen was wrecking it. She wasn't even touching it.

And it wasn't like the floors were wet or covered in dirt. The whole place was spotless. The janitorial staff had likely cleaned less than three hours ago, when the last group of children had left after their lunch hour.

Pulling the coat from underneath the table, I gave it a quick inspection. There was nothing wrong with it and it wasn't dirty. But before I could hand it to the woman, she snatched it away.

"She's destroyed it."

"Uh . . . no, she hasn't. And she didn't knock it on the floor. It wasn't on either of our chairs when we sat down and I didn't notice it under the table. Otherwise, I would have picked it up."

I stood from my chair. Having her tower over me wasn't going to work. I wanted a more equal footing, though even standing, she was a couple of inches taller than me.

Rowen stood too and hid behind one of my legs. I reached back and put my hand on her shoulder, pulling her tight against me.

"You obviously have no clue how much this coat is worth. If you did, you and your kid wouldn't be treating it like trash."

Bitch.

I was going to tell her that we didn't give a damn about her coat and as far as I was concerned, she could shove it up her ass. But I didn't get that chance because right as I was opening my mouth, my eyes caught movement over her shoulder.

Silas walked right into the middle of our conversation.

"Gigi," he said.

"Hi, Silas."

Here I was again: at a funeral dealing with a bitchy blond and trying to calm myself down.

The woman huffed and turned to Silas, her mouth screwed up tight, and even though I couldn't see her eyes, I imagined they were shooting lasers at him.

"Is she yours?" the woman asked him.

Silas's glare was fierce. The only time I'd seen him look scarier was when he'd faced off against Wes during the football game. This time wasn't quite as scary, but it was a close second.

"She's mine." Jess's body heat was at my back.

"Felicity?" Noelle gasped.

No way. Had I almost gotten into a verbal smackdown with Jess's sister?

"Hi, Mom," Felicity said.

Shit.

Noelle let out a strangled noise and embraced her daughter. For the first time, Felicity's bitch face softened and she seemed genuinely glad to hug her mother.

They held each other for a minute until Noelle stepped away, wiping tears from both eyes, the smile on her face stretched wide.

I was happy for Noelle. After waiting years, she was finally able to hug her daughter.

I reached back and gave Rowen a little squeeze with my hand.

Silas didn't say another word. He just spun around and walked away. Obviously he was not a fan of Jess's sister. But I had a feeling there was a story there. Something had happened between those two and I suspected that whatever it was, it involved Wes.

"There a reason why you didn't tell us you were coming today? Why we haven't seen you in *fourteen fucking years* and you don't let us know you're in town? Then when we do see you, you're being a bitch to my girls?" Jess asked.

He must have heard way more than I'd initially thought because he was not happy.

"Well, hello to you too, big brother."

"Lissy," Jess warned in his menacing tone.

If he had spoken to me with that voice, I would have told him anything he wanted to know. But not Felicity. She just stood there, her face blank as his warning rolled by, leaving her completely unaffected. Maybe she wasn't scared because she had grown up with him. Maybe I'd get used to that tone too and one day I'd be immune.

Felicity turned back to Noelle, taking her mother's hands in her own, again softening her features before speaking.

"I'll be here through New Year's, Mom. I flew in last minute this morning but I arranged for a couple of weeks off work," she said.

"Are you going to stay at home with me?" Noelle asked hopefully.

"The motel had a room. I'll get checked in and stay there. It's not that I don't want to see you. I just didn't want to intrude on you over the holidays and cause extra work for you to have a guest. But I'm planning to be over every day. Okay?"

"Oh . . . okay," Noelle said. She dropped her head and stared at the floor for a few moments, still holding Felicity's hands. Then she looked up to me with worried eyes. "Oh, ah, Gigi, about Christmas . . ." Noelle started but trailed off.

We were having a big Christmas dinner at the farmhouse

in three days. Much like Thanksgiving, it was going to be me, Jess, Rowen and Noelle.

"You're both welcome to come over for the day," I said. "I've already done the shopping and we'll have enough food for an army."

I stepped away from Jess, moving toward Noelle and Felicity. Sticking out my hand, I introduced myself to Jess's sister.

"Hi, I'm Gigi. I think we got off on the wrong foot. Maybe we should start over?" I hoped that she would be pleasant, if not for me or Jess, at least for her mother.

She tipped her head down toward my hand with a small grimace on her lips. I thought for a second she was going to dismiss my peace offering, but then her perfectly manicured fingers touched mine for a light shake.

"Felicity. Pleasure." It wasn't said nicely but it was certainly an improvement.

"This is my daughter, Rowen," I said, introducing Roe, who was now attached to Jess's leg.

"Hmm," Felicity said, tipping her head in Rowen's direction.

"Lissy," Jess said. "Fuck. Can you take off those fucking glasses? In case you hadn't noticed, we're inside."

"Jess! Watch it with the language," I said.

"Relax, Georgia. Roe knows that there are words she can't say. 'Fuck' being one of them. Right, little bit?" he asked her.

"Right," she confirmed with a single nod.

I threw my hands in the air, muttering, "Whatever".

"Lissy—" Jess started but she interrupted him by shaking her head and tipping her chin to the floor.

"Not today, Jess. Please," she pleaded quietly.

She lifted her head back up and slid her sunglasses off her face and into her hair.

I'd been right, the sunglasses were to hide her eyes. They were bright red and ringed with deep purple circles underneath. Felicity hadn't shed a few tears for Wes, she had cried him a river.

Jess tensed and backed off from grilling his sister.

"Okay. Not today. But we'll expect you for Christmas. You want to get together before then, give me a call," he said.

She slid her glasses back onto her face. "Okay. I was going to do some shopping tomorrow. Walk around downtown and see what's new. Maybe we could meet for lunch?"

"Noon. Meet you at the café."

"Fine. Now if you'll excuse me, I need to go and pay my respects to Jack and Annie."

She hugged Noelle one last time and walked out of our huddle, directly toward Wes's parents.

As Felicity approached, Annie burst into tears and rushed to embrace her. Felicity stood there stiffly while Annie sobbed into her black silk shirt. Jack approached the women and threw his arms around them both. His affection seemed to relax Felicity a bit and she wrapped a hand around his waist and leaned her head into his shoulder.

A lump formed at the back of my throat. Watching them together was heartbreaking.

Jess watched them for a minute and then reached down to hoist Rowen up on his hip. Grabbing my hand, he said, "Time to get my girls home," and guided us out.

"Let's do something fun," I suggested on the drive home after we'd dropped off Noelle.

"Today?" Jess asked.

"Yep. Today. After Mom's funeral, I took Rowen to a

carousel and we rode it for hours. And after Ben died, we drove to an amusement park and spent the day on roller coasters."

"Okay. Like what?" Jess asked.

"How about sledding?"

"Sledding!" Rowen shrieked.

I started laughing. Sledding it was.

An hour later, we were bundled up and having a blast, the sadness from earlier all but gone.

"Can you go with me this time, Mommy?" Rowen asked.

"Yeah!" I said.

We were sledding in the foothills of the mountains behind the farmhouse.

The hill Jess had found us wasn't too big, but for Roe and her purple plastic sled, it was just right. She was bundled up into so many layers she could barely waddle her way up this hill as it was. So far, Jess had carried her sled up the hill and ridden down with her while I'd stood at the bottom and taken pictures.

Now it was my turn.

Roe and I trudged up the hill, hand in hand. At the top, she promptly settled her little bum in the sled as I maneuvered behind her and stretched my legs around her sides.

"Ready?" I asked.

"Yay! Let's go!" She cheered and started rocking her body, trying to inch the sled over the edge.

I planted my gloved hand in the snow and gave us a heave.

We flew down the hill. The fluffy snow flew up and blasted us in our faces. Roe bounced in the air whenever we hit a bump. As we sped past Jess at the bottom, I put out my feet and slowed us down. Then I grabbed Roe and toppled us sideways, laughing and tickling her as we rolled around in the snow.

Breathless, I lay on my back and looked up into the blue, sunny sky.

Winter in Montana was wondrous. Cold, but majestic. Everything sparkled like the whole world was covered in glitter. And it was bright, almost blinding.

I'd worried that winters would be cold and depressing, that for the better half of the year, we'd be stuck inside wearing wool socks and huddling under blankets. Not that it wasn't cold. It was. But the sunshine made it seem warmer than it was, and as long as it wasn't a blizzard, Rowen and I could spend plenty of time outside this winter enjoying the crisp air.

"You alive?" Jess asked, standing over me to shade my face.

"Yep. How are you?"

"I'm good." He smiled.

I smiled back before turning to Roe on the ground beside me. "Let's go again."

CHAPTER TWENTY

GIGI

When my alarm went off at six o'clock, Jess rolled away from me and buried his face in the pillows.

"Wake up," I ordered, kissing the space between his shoulder blades.

"Georgia, you don't need my help getting the prime rib in the oven." He yawned.

"It doesn't need to go in for another hour. But we need to get up so we can wake Roe and open presents."

"What? No. She can come wake us up," he said into the pillow.

"Jess, this is our tradition."

"New tradition. We sleep in on Christmas."

"Until my mom passed, I can't remember a single Christmas, even when I was in college, that she didn't wake me up early and drag me out of bed to start opening presents. And I loved that. I loved it so much that I have always done the same for Rowen," I said.

He waited about ten seconds before throwing his legs over the side of the bed to roll out. Then he grabbed me under my armpits, hauling me up so I was kneeling in the bed.

"You wake her up, I'll start coffee." He kissed my forehead and moved into the bathroom.

Hours later, coffee cup in hand, I was surrounded by a mountain of crumpled wrapping paper and opened boxes. Jess and I were sitting on the office floor and had just watched my little girl open her Christmas presents. She had shouted with delight each time she discovered what was under the paper. Then she'd take her gift, hug it tight and welcome it to her house.

She was hilarious. My cheeks hurt from smiling.

No matter what would happen the rest of the day, I knew this Christmas in the farmhouse would rank as my all-time second best Christmas—the first being the last Christmas with my mom, which had also been my first with Rowen.

Jess had completely spoiled Roe with a bunch of smaller gifts and his big-ticket item, a new iPad. She'd been so happy when she opened it that she'd thrown herself into Jess's arms and kissed him at least twenty times on the cheek. He'd started tickling her and they'd both ended up laughing together, collapsed on the floor in the middle of the paper mountain.

I'd snapped a quick picture and unless it was blurry, it was going up in the living room next to the photo of Mom and Rowen on their Christmas morning.

"Time to start putting your presents away and then we need to get dressed, baby girl," I told Roe.

"Okay," she chimed.

"I'm gonna hit the shower, then head over to the house and pick up a few things," Jess said.

"No!" Rowen shouted and clung to one of Jess's legs. "Don't leave."

"Relax, I'm coming back, little bit. I've got a couple more presents stashed at home that I need to bring over."

She jumped up and down with excitement at the mention of more presents.

But I was *not* excited. I was nauseous. My skin felt cold and my hands were getting clammy. The feeling came over me suddenly and it started when Jess had said the word "home."

I hated that he called that house in town his home. He was wrong. His home was here at the farmhouse. With us.

"Rowen, can you please start taking your presents upstairs?" I mumbled but my voice sounded weak and crackly.

She agreed and piled her little arms full of new stuff, waddling her way toward the door and up the stairs.

"What's wrong?" Jess asked.

"This is your home," I said in my weird voice.

"What?" he asked.

I inhaled a deep breath and found my regular voice. "*This* is your home."

He stared back at me for a few moments, unmoving, either confused by my declaration or not yet ready to make that big of a step in our relationship. I hoped it was the former because I was one hundred percent ready for Jess to live with us. He practically was already.

But I didn't want to freak him out, not on Christmas, so I started backpedaling.

"I mean . . . I want you to think of it like your home. And

if someday you wanted to move in officially, well . . . that would be great. But if you're not ready for that, if it's too soon, I completely understand. We can just—"

Jess stopped my rambling by slamming his lips down on mine and immediately taking advantage of my open mouth. His hands framed my face and the sickness vanished from my body. I was feeling *just* fine.

I was feeling effing awesome.

He wanted to live here with us and make this his home. I was so overjoyed and relieved that I latched onto his shoulders with my hands and pulled myself into his big body, slanting my head so we could melt into each other.

He thoroughly kissed me with passion and love, telling me without words how much my asking for this house to be his home meant to him. I poured as much feeling and emotion into our kiss as I could. My body started tingling all over and I forgot to breathe.

Jess pulled away from my mouth when Rowen marched into the room and asked, "Are you guys kissing? Again?"

"Yep," we said simultaneously, our faces pressed together, smiling.

"You guys sure kiss a lot. Why do grown-ups kiss on the lips? Do you like kissing? How do you breathe? Did Jess get his spit on you, Mommy?"

As she blathered, she collected more presents to take upstairs.

I sucked in a few deep breaths between my giggles but kept the huge smile on my face.

"I take it you're going to move in?"

"Yeah," Jess said.

"Good."

"I'm gonna take my shower and head into town. Maybe

grab the rest of my clothes while I'm there. Tomorrow, we can clear out the garage. Not much else over there I want. That okay with you?" he asked.

"No."

He tilted his head and his eyebrows came together.

"I want your washer and dryer," I said.

He grinned. "Anything else?"

"My Christmas present." I held out my hand, palm up. "Fork it over, Sheriff."

"Bedroom. Drawer in my end table," he said.

"Yours is—"

"In the top of your spice cabinet."

"What are you doing in my spice . . . never mind. Since you know where yours are at, you can go get them yourself. It will save me from getting out the stepladder."

I raced upstairs as he padded to the kitchen. Sitting on the edge of the bed, I opened the drawer.

Inside was a beautifully wrapped, long, skinny box. The gold foil paper was tied with an intricate bow made of silver, gold and white threads.

I carefully pulled off the threads and paper. When I peered inside the box, my eyes blurred with tears.

"Do you like them?" Jess asked from behind me.

I whirled around and saw him in the doorway.

"Shit." At the sight of my tears, he rushed to my side.

"They're beautiful, Jess. I love them. Thank you."

Inside the box was a necklace and earrings I would wear all the time. The necklace was on a thin, white-gold chain. Dead center was a single solitaire diamond, the jewel at least a carat. Not too big and ostentatious but certainly not a chip. When I put it on, the diamond would sit perfectly at the base of my throat.

It was exactly the type of necklace I would have picked out for myself. I could wear it to work and not worry about it hanging too low and getting in the way.

The earrings were two diamond solitaire studs. The stones were slightly smaller than the necklace's diamond and unless the occasion called for a larger pair of earrings, I would wear these almost every day too. Even on pajama days.

"Jess, these are too much," I said.

"Not too much at all."

"These were not cheap. Plus everything you bought for Roe . . ." I trailed off, mentally tallying up the sum he had spent on us for Christmas.

"I've been waiting thirty-four years to find the right woman. Finally did. Now I get to spoil her, so just get used to it."

"Why?" I whispered.

"Why, what?"

"Why me? Why'd you pick me as your girl? I mean, I'm just me and you're . . . well . . . you. Perfect."

He took in a deep breath and closed his eyes for a few moments. When he opened them, his eyes had changed. They were no longer soft and gentle. They were firm and determined.

"I'm not sure where you got it in that head of yours that I'm too good for you. Because the way I see it, it's the other way around. And it stops today. No more."

Jess's hands framed my face, his thumbs stroking my jaw gently.

"Baby, you've got the biggest heart of any person I've ever met. I've never known a soul who would have taken on an old man just so he wouldn't be alone. Someone needs help, the first thing you think about is how you can do it. Christ, you offered to move a stranger in with you so he'd have a place to live after his house burned down. And you've raised the most precious little girl on the planet. When you look at her, you see beauty, don't you?"

"Well . . . of course. She's my daughter."

He shook his head a couple of times. "She's you," he said. "In every way, she's you. When you look at her and get that feeling of pride in your chest? When you look at her face and into her eyes and it makes your heart hurt she's so beautiful? Georgia, that's how I feel when I look at you."

His words, describing exactly how I felt about my daughter, moved me so deeply that I started crying again, completely unable to stop the emotion.

Swiping the tears as they fell, he whispered, "I love you. Everything. How you don't back down during an argument. How you take care of Rowen. Take care of me. That you don't mind including my mother. How you invite my sister over for Christmas minutes after she treats you badly. So let me buy you whatever the fuck I feel like for Christmas, birthdays or just whenever. Okay?"

I nodded and sniffled.

"Okay."

Jess's words penetrated deep into my heart.

We'd been together for months and I had always doubted us. But we made sense. I thought he was perfect. He was. But what his words finally made me realize was that he thought I was perfect too. We were perfect together.

Perfect sense.

I sniffled one last time and twisted my head out of his hands to get my necklace. After I put it on, I screwed on my earrings.

He lifted a finger to the jewel at my throat and muttered, "True beauty."

My throat tightened again and if I didn't change the subject, I'd start blubbering like a baby again. And I didn't want to cry anymore. Not on Christmas.

"I didn't know we were going big for Christmas, honey. I didn't get you much," I said.

Compared to the jewelry, what I'd gotten him was peanuts. I'd bought him just a pair of nice leather gloves, a new plaid flannel shirt and a framed picture of him and Rowen for work. Just little things.

He chuckled for a second but then it grew and grew until he was full-on belly laughing. His big, thunderous sound filled the bedroom.

"What? What's funny?"

He shook his head and reached out a finger to touch the tip of my nose. "You gave me a house today. I'd say I'm the one who has some catching up to do."

"Oh," I muttered.

"Yeah, 'oh.'"

I hadn't thought about the farmhouse as a gift but I could see how he would. "I love you too, you know?" I whispered.

"Yeah. I know," he whispered back.

———

JESS

"Thanks for taking Ma home," I told my sister as we stood together on the farmhouse porch.

We were waiting outside while Ma collected her things and said good-bye to Georgia and Rowen.

Georgia had cooked us an amazing Christmas dinner, the first homemade Christmas I'd ever had since Ma and I normally went to a local steakhouse. After our meal, we'd sat and visited. We'd given Ma her gifts and Georgia had even found the time to get something for Lissy too.

I was glad that Lissy had dropped her bitchy attitude and been so nice to Georgia and Rowen tonight. My sister came across badly at times, but she had a good heart. I wasn't sure why she put up such a front. Maybe it was because of Dad. Or Wes. She'd never talked to me about it, so I had no clue.

"No problem. Thank you for having us over. It was nice. Really nice," Felicity said.

"Best Christmas I've ever had."

"You love her?" she asked.

"With all my heart."

"I'm happy for you, Jess. I like her. And the kid."

"You still working from home?" I asked, changing the subject.

"Uh . . . yes. Why?"

"You could work from Prescott. Got a house in town that's yours if you want it," I said.

The only thing that could make my day better would be to convince Lissy to move home. I hadn't realized just how much I missed her these last fourteen years. But having her back, especially now that I'd found Georgia and Rowen, it would be like having all the pieces of my heart close by. My family.

"It's been strange, being back here. I guess . . . well, I guess I thought that it would be different. Unfamiliar. That things would have changed so much it wouldn't feel like home. And there are some new things but for the most part . . . I don't know. It still feels like it used to," she said.

"Think about it?" I asked.

"I will. But if I do decide to move back, I won't take your house. Thanks though."

"It's not like I'm living there, Lissy."

"When did you move in here?" she asked.

"Today. I'm getting the last of my stuff tomorrow."

"Huh," she replied and then started laughing.

"What?"

"I bet old Ben Coppersmith took one look at her and knew she'd be perfect for you," Felicity said, still laughing and looking at Georgia through the windows.

Fuck. Me.

I hadn't thought about it like that, but she was probably right. Christ, I even remembered Ben asking me from time to time if I'd met anyone yet.

"Sell your house, Jess. Put the money away for the kid's college fund. There's a lot I would have to decide on to move back. A lot of history to overcome. So we'll see. But don't get your hopes up. Okay? I have a life in Seattle. I like it there."

"Okay. I'm happy as long as you'll consider it."

"I promise."

Our conversation ended when Ma made her way through the front door. Everyone said their good-byes and I helped carry presents and a huge box of leftover food to Felicity's rental car.

Walking back up the steps, I pulled Georgia tight to my side while Rowen rested high on my hip. Together, the three of us waved good-bye to my mother and sister.

Then we went inside to enjoy some time together. Just the three of us.

My family in my house.

Without a doubt, it was the best Christmas I'd ever had.

GIGI

"Hello," I said into the phone.

"Gigi?"

"Hi!" I said to Maisy. "How are you? Did you have a nice Christmas?"

I was excited that she had called. I hadn't talked to Maisy since before Wes's funeral. I was missing her bright and sunny smile that I'd come to look forward to seeing each day.

"Uh . . . no. Not really. Do you think I could come over?" she asked.

Maisy's voice was flat, without its usual exuberance.

"Sure. We're not doing much today so come on over whenever. Jess and Rowen left a little bit ago to go to his house in town. He's officially moving in so he went over to grab a load of stuff."

"Oh, that's, ah, great. I guess if it's okay, I'll come over now?" she said.

I'd expected her to be screaming into the phone. She had been pulling for Jess and me from the beginning. The fact he was moving into the farmhouse should have sent her into joyful hysterics.

Something was definitely not right in the world of Maisy Holt.

Maisy arrived five minutes after her call and so far had yet to look me in the eyes. She dodged my attempt to give her a hug and kept speaking to her feet.

"Would you like some coffee?" I asked as she sat down in an oversized living room chair.

"Yes, please," she said. "No. Wait. No coffee. I don't want coffee."

"Ah, okay. Would you like some water?" I asked.

"No. I'm okay," she said. Still no eye contact.

Sitting down on the loveseat opposite her, I curled my feet underneath me and took a long sip of my coffee. "How was your Christmas? You seem a little . . . off. Is everything okay with your family?"

"Yeah. They're okay," she muttered.

I quietly drank my coffee. I figured when she was ready, she'd tell me what was going on. But after five minutes of fairly uncomfortable silence, the air around us started to get heavy. I couldn't take it anymore so I broke the silence.

"Maisy? What's wrong?"

She finally looked up and her big doe eyes filled with tears.

"No. I'm not okay. Oh god, Gigi. This has just been the worst Christmas of my life!" she cried.

The dam holding back her words broke and her explanation came flooding out.

"So you know how Everett was super distant before the ugly sweater party but then was great that night?"

"Yeah. It looked like you two were back to normal," I said.

"We were. Until the next day. He kicked me out of his house the next morning. He actually woke me up and said I had to leave. So I left, thinking I was done. Who needs a boyfriend that kicks you out? Jess would never do that to you. Right?"

"Right," I said.

I had assumed things were going well with Everett. Apparently not.

And Maisy was right. Jess would never kick me out of his bed and she did not need a boyfriend who thought that was acceptable.

"Yeah. So I decided to break up with him. I just couldn't take all of the drama, you know? It was draining me. I was exhausted and tired and totally over feeling sick because of stupid Everett Carlson.

"So I went back that night to dump his ass. But then he was apologetic. Said he'd just had a lot on his mind. We went back to normal and I was super happy. I even invited him to my family's house for Christmas."

"Well that's good," I said.

"I thought so too. But he ruined it!"

Maisy started sobbing again. I knew where this was going. "Sorry." She sniffled and wiped away some tears.

"It's okay, sweetie. You take as much time as you need and cry all you want."

"So Everett decided to drive us to my parents' house. He said he wanted his car in case the hospital called. Fine. No big deal. If he got called in, I could just get one of my brothers to bring me home. So he picks me up and the entire trip in the car, he doesn't say a word. Not one word. Not hello. Not even Merry Christmas."

"What? That's weird."

"I know, right?! When we got to Mom and Dad's, I asked him if he was okay and he didn't even answer. He just got out of the car and walked inside. Not a single word! So I'm, like, freaking out."

"Was he like that the whole time?" I asked.

"Ha," she huffed. "Nope. Because three minutes after we got there, he dumped me. In front of my family!"

"No way," I said as my eyes bugged out.

Everett Carlson was now at the top of my asshole list. Well, not the top, but close. After all this time, the nice doctor who I had come to like and respect had turned out to be a jerk. A huge jerk.

"Yes, way." Her tears had all dried up and she was moving onto the post-breakup angry stage.

"He tells me that we just don't work. I'm too young and he's too busy trying to establish his career here in Prescott. And he said I had too much growing up to do. That he wasn't interested in putting in the time while I matured. Oh, and my favorite part. That I say 'like' too much."

Damn.

Yes, Maisy was young but he'd known that when he started dating her. Saying that she needed to grow up was way over the line. Everett should have kept that to himself.

"Can you believe it? He was too much of a pansy to break up before the holidays but he finds the nerve on Christmas? Who does that?" she asked me rhetorically.

"I'm so sorry," I said.

She had been sitting up straighter as she got angrier and angrier. But now that her story was over, her shoulders slumped and she slunk back into the seat.

"He left right after that. Which was probably good because I think Beau was about ready to hit him. I just . . . I don't know, it was so humiliating."

"I don't think you need to feel embarrassed, Maisy. That was *all* Everett."

"I mean, all this time he's been distant. Why couldn't he have just come out and told me he didn't want to date?"

"I don't know," I said. "But in the long run, it's good that it's over. You don't want to be with someone who would treat you like that."

Maisy sat quietly for a second before bursting into more tears, dropping her face into her hands.

I got up from the loveseat and sat on the edge of the coffee table, leaning forward to stroke her shoulder.

"It's okay. You'll get over him. You just need to give it some time."

"I'm pregnant," she whispered between sobs.

Well, that was unexpected.

Now her reaction was making more sense. The sobbing and how she wouldn't meet my eyes when she had arrived. This wasn't just about the breakup. She was dealing with some major problems.

"You're positive?" I asked.

"Yeah," she said. "What am I going to do? How am I going to tell him? I'm on birth control. I get the shot religiously every three months. I didn't plan on this. What if he accuses me of doing this on purpose?"

"He's a doctor, Maisy. He'll know that birth control doesn't always work," I said.

"What about my family? They're going to be so disappointed in me. I'm only twenty-four. They had plans for me. I had plans for me. Now they're ruined."

I pulled her hands into mine and looked into her sad eyes. Not too long ago, I had been in her place, so I offered her the best advice I could.

"One day at a time. That's all you can do. You might be right and your family might be disappointed, but it won't last forever. They'll come around and be there to support you. And your plans will change but they don't have to end. You just have to make a few adjustments," I said.

"Thanks, Gigi."

"Anytime, sweetie."

"I don't know how to tell Everett," she said.

"The sooner the better. But if I could make one recommendation, do it in private. Telling Rowen's father at a restaurant didn't work out so hot for me."

"Okay," she said.

And she would be okay. One day she would realize this wasn't the end of her life. It was just the start of a different one.

CHAPTER TWENTY-ONE

GIGI

"That machine's going in the garbage," Jess said as he stomped into the kitchen.

It was Friday and New Year's Eve. We were hosting a special farmhouse sleepover for Bryant's daughter and three of Rowen's friends from Quail Hollow. At the moment, five little girls, all six years old or younger, were upstairs in Rowen's room singing Disney princess anthems on her karaoke machine.

As I had promised while in the hospital after the barn incident, I'd bought Roe the singing machine. It came as no surprise that she was thrilled to have it. She had used it a few times but then stowed it away in her closet. I guess it wasn't much fun to sing karaoke by yourself. And since it had been put away, Jess hadn't heard it yet.

Tonight, the girls had been using it continuously for the last two and a half hours and he'd heard enough.

I was in the kitchen, making the girls hot chocolate with

marshmallows and some snacks. It was well past their normal bedtimes but what good were sleepovers if you had to go to bed on time?

After cocoa and munchies, the girls were going to play beauty parlor in the dining room. I'd set out a pile of eye shadows and glitter strings for their hair.

"If you throw the karaoke machine away, Rowen might insist you move into the garage," I told Jess.

"Not a problem. There isn't fucking karaoke out there."

"Just let me get these snacks done and I'll bring them down here, okay? No more singing," I said.

"Fine." He went to the fridge and pulled out a beer.

My eyes bugged out as his throat swallowed the whole bottle in four enormous gulps. When that bottle was emptied, he tossed it in the trash and grabbed another. This time it only took three swallows to drain it dry.

"Uh . . . are you okay?" I asked.

He let out a huge belch. It was loud and long. I'd never heard him do that before so my eyes got even bigger and my jaw fell open.

"Better," he said.

His phone rang before I could say anything.

"Lissy," he answered, looking more and more irritated the longer he listened to his sister. "Fine," he said before hanging up.

"Lissy and Ma are coming over. Lissy wanted to say good-bye before she leaves Sunday and thought you girls could drink some champagne," Jess said, not at all sounding happy that his family was coming over.

"Uh . . . did you tell her that there are five little girls here? She doesn't seem to really . . . like kids much."

"Then I guess they won't stay long."

"Jess! That's not nice."

He grumbled something under his breath and walked out of the kitchen.

Fifteen minutes later, Felicity and Noelle joined us. Felicity took one look at the dining room table filled with little girls and immediately went to open the champagne. Much like her brother, she downed her first two glasses without hesitation. Noelle just smiled her sweet smile and watched the kids play.

Jess was nowhere in sight. He had disappeared right after saying hello to his mother and sister.

I was sipping champagne glass number two when my phone rang. It was Maisy.

She must have told Everett she was pregnant and was calling to give me a report.

"I need to take this, sorry," I told Felicity and Noelle, moving to the office.

"Hi," I answered.

"Gigi?" she said, crying.

"Uh-oh. I'm guessing that you talked to Everett?" I asked.

"Yep. And it was awful!" she sobbed.

"Do you want to come over here and talk about it?"

"Are you sure?" she asked.

"Of course. Come on over. But I'll warn you that we're having a sleepover with four of Rowen's friends. And Noelle and Felicity are over too," I said.

"Oh . . . well, I'm not sure—"

"Come over. We can talk in the kitchen. And maybe some girl time will make you feel better."

I ended our call and walked out of the office, colliding

with Jess's chest. I wasn't sure where he was going but I noticed another beer in his hand.

"Oh . . . hi, honey. Maisy is coming over," I said.

"Fine," he muttered and then walked around me to disappear again, the bottle tipped to his lips.

———

"HE WAS JUST SO CLINICAL. Like I was a patient. He acted like it wasn't even his baby we were talking about. That he had no part in its creation. He just sat there and calmly told me to think about having an abortion. I was looking at him and I didn't even know him," she said, standing at the kitchen island.

"I'm sorry, Maisy." Though it was far better than the way Nate Fletcher had reacted, it still wasn't great.

"Did you ever?" she asked quietly.

"Did I ever, what?"

She turned her head in all directions to make sure we were alone. "Think about having an abortion?"

I was making her a cup of cocoa but I stopped at her question.

"No," I said. "Even though I was scared and nervous, I knew I wanted a baby. I picked out names early on. Rowen for a girl, Coby for a boy. And after that, the baby was real. It was my baby with a name. So no, I never thought of an abortion. It just wasn't an option for me."

She pondered what I had said for a few moments, then she smiled. "Coby, I like that. Would you care if I used that name if the baby is a boy?"

I smiled too.

Her life would never be the same. It would be better after she jumped over a few hurdles.

"Not at all," I said. "Coby Holt. I love it!"

"Me too," she said, her eyes twinkling. "How do you think it's going to work? With Everett? If he doesn't want anything to do with me or the baby, what will happen? It's not like he can avoid us. We live in Prescott."

"That's the million dollar question. He'll have to come to terms with it. Or else, I guess he won't. Rowen's father signed over all of his parental rights. Maybe Everett will do the same. We'll just have to wait and see," I said.

"Yeah," she muttered.

"But don't fret too much about it now. This is a lot of news for him. Don't give up yet. You two didn't work as a couple but you never know. Given some time and thought, he might come around. Turn out to be a better dad than a boyfriend."

"Yeah," she muttered again.

"And you have a strong support system. Don't forget that. You've got a great family all living close. And friends. Me. I'll do whatever I can to help you navigate through this. I've been there. It's not easy but it is so worth it," I said.

"Yeah," she said again, this time sounding more confident.

"When will you tell your family?"

She took in a deep breath. "Tomorrow, I guess."

"Good idea," I said. "Better now than later."

"Did you tell Jess?" she asked.

"No. And I won't. Not until you're okay with people knowing."

"You can tell him. After tomorrow, everyone that I need to tell in person will know."

I resumed mixing her cocoa so we could go back to the living room with Felicity and Noelle.

"Gigi? Do you like the name Mabel for a girl?"

I gave her a huge, wide smile. "Love it."

———

JESS and I were finally in bed.

The girls had worn themselves out and crashed around midnight. They were all sleeping on the floor of the living room in a "tent." I'd made a huge canopy over the living room furniture out of some bed sheets and blankets. Then on the floor, we'd piled all of the extra blankets and pillows I could find.

They'd giggled and laughed in their makeshift beds while I sat in the office reading, waiting until I heard the last of their chatter and could come upstairs to Jess.

He had finally emerged from wherever it was he'd been hiding about twenty minutes before his sister and mother took off. Then he'd come upstairs to escape the girl gaggle.

I climbed into bed next to him as he shut off his light.

"Happy New Year's." I slid tight into his side and threw my leg over his.

"You too, baby," he said, leaning down to kiss my forehead.

"Where'd you disappear to tonight?" I asked.

"Huh. I'm not telling."

I laughed into his bare chest.

"We need to make a deal, Freckles. No more winter sleepovers. Have them when there isn't snow on the ground so I can take off and go camping. Avoid the torture."

My laughter continued. "I can do that."

"And we're putting a maximum female capacity in place. No more than a four to one ratio, women to men," he said. "Includes kids."

"So, I've got some baby news," I said when my laughing subsided. "I hope you're excited. I am."

His body tightened, causing me to jerk my arm off his torso and hold it in mid-air.

"You're pregnant?" he asked.

"Huh?" I said. "Oh, no. Not me. Maisy. Maisy's pregnant. And Everett dumped her on Christmas. Then he asked her to have an abortion. Can you believe it?!"

He didn't answer. He just stared at the ceiling with a clenched jaw.

I knew he wasn't an Everett fan but I didn't think he'd get this upset. I put both hands on his pecs and shook his chest. "Jess? What?"

"I thought your baby news was you telling me you were pregnant," he said.

"Ah . . . no." I replayed the last minute in my head.

He'd thought I was telling him that I was pregnant and his whole body had tensed. Every muscle. Did he not want kids? I already had Rowen but that didn't mean I hadn't thought about having more kids one day.

He was great with Rowen and would be great with a child of his own. I wouldn't push him into having kids if he didn't want to but I would be disappointed. I had been an only child and I didn't want that for Roe.

"Do you not want kids?" I asked.

"What? Where the fuck did you get that?"

"Well, you got all tense. And you just said you thought it was because I was telling you I was pregnant. So . . . there," I said, waving my hand in the air.

He sighed and relaxed. "I tensed because I was holding back from rolling you over and celebrating. If you were having my baby, I'd do some serious work to show you how happy that would make me. But we can't have sex tonight because there's a hoard of girls downstairs. So I tensed. And then you said it wasn't you."

"So you want to have kids?" I asked.

He brought his fingers up to my face and ran them across my jaw. Then his hand traveled over my hair and to the back of my neck.

"Baby, the way we're going, I've got a kid. She's downstairs. And yeah. Adding a couple more to our family is something I sure as hell want to do someday."

My heart swelled so big I was sure it was going to burst. Jess had said a lot of wonderful things to me before. Saying I had true beauty. Saying he loved me. But saying that Rowen was his kid topped them all.

It was everything.

"I love you, Jess," was all I could say as a huge smile spread on my face.

"I take it you're good with having a couple more babies?" he asked, grinning.

"I love you, Jess," I repeated.

I was definitely okay with having a couple of Jess's babies.

"Stop saying that, Georgia. I just told you I can't fuck you. Stop making me want to."

I lifted my hand and gave him a two-finger salute.

"You got it, Sheriff."

"Christ, she never listens. Why couldn't I have a girl that listens?" he asked the ceiling.

I collapsed into his chest and started laughing again.

"Love you too, Freckles," he said to the top of my head.

And just like the little girls camped out in the living room, I fell asleep giggling and smiling.

————

"GEORGIA?" Jess called.

"Laundry room!"

I was moving a load of clothes from the washer to the dryer, a load that took the normal amount of time to wash now that Jess had replaced my older washer-dryer set with the nicer one from his house. I was looking forward to coming back in forty-five minutes to a dry load of clothes rather than to a damp bunch that needed another cycle.

Bliss.

He rounded the corner from the kitchen.

"I just got a call from my realtor. Got an offer on the house," he said.

"What? Already? That's amazing! It's only been a week."

"Yep. You know the guy whose house was torched? It's him. He's the buyer," Jess said. "Realtor said he got his insurance claim. Doesn't want the hassle of building a place so he's just going to buy. Offered cash for the house, five thousand less than my asking price, but he could close this month. Wants it furnished too so I wouldn't have to sell all my shit or find storage. He'd take it all."

"Well? What do you think?"

"I think I'd be stupid to turn it down," he said.

"And you're not a stupid man."

"It would give us some extra cash. I was thinking we could put an addition off the side of the farmhouse. Expand off the office. Add a room or two. Maybe another bathroom."

"No, Jess, that's your money. You should save it. Buy something you want. A new boat or, I don't know, a nicer truck to haul around the boat you already have," I said.

He narrowed his eyes and frowned. "Sometimes I feel like spanking your ass."

My spine jerked straight. A spanking? Now I was pissed. "What the effing hell does that mean?"

"Means you didn't hear me last week at Christmas. Or last night in bed," he said.

"Oh right. I didn't hear you. That's funny since I fully recall each of our conversations, Jess. But please, explain it to me again. Because I can tell you right now if you so much as raise your pinky finger in the direction of my ass, I'll make sure—well, I'll make sure . . ." I stuttered, having trouble finding a threat that would convey just how serious I was.

"Yeah? You'll make sure what?"

"I'll . . . I'll make sure you have to eat your own rotten, disgusting, horrible cooking for the next twelve months. One whole year of nasty macaroni and weird salami sandwiches. Except for holidays. No one should have to eat that on holidays. But every other day, you eat your own cooking."

He had only ever cooked for us once, but that had been enough. I shuddered and gagged just thinking about it.

He roared with laughter.

"I mean it, Jess!" I yelled.

But he just kept on laughing.

I stormed out of the laundry room, thinking I needed cookies, but he followed me.

"Now listen up, Freckles," he said, picking me up and planting my butt on the kitchen counter.

I opened my mouth to tell him to screw off but before I could get the words out, he clamped one of his big hands on top of my mouth.

I couldn't believe that Jess had just put his hand on my mouth to keep me from talking. My eyes got so big I worried they were going to pop out.

"I told you at Christmas to get used to me spoiling my girls. That was the same day you told me this was my home. So putting on an addition with money from my previous home is spending it on something I want. I'm spending it on *my house*," he said. "So like I said in the laundry room, you didn't hear me. Are you with me now?"

I couldn't respond because his big mitt was still covering my mouth. So I narrowed my eyes and gave him my strongest glare.

"I'll take that as a yes," he said. "Now about this cooking thing."

"Hey! What are you guys doing? Why do you have your hand on Mommy's mouth, Jess?" Rowen interrupted us.

"Well, little bit, I needed to make a point to your mother. Thought I'd have a better chance if she wasn't talking back. But putting your hand on another person's mouth is something you can only do if you're a police officer. So don't do it at school or I'll have to arrest you," he lied.

I rolled my eyes.

"Oh. Okay, Jess. I won't do it."

"Now I got a question for you," he said to her. "What did you think of that dinner I cooked for you and your mom a while back?"

"Blech. It was gross. Really yucky. But Mommy bought me that new Tinker Bell movie because I ate three bites of everything."

Traitor.

"Huh. I see."

At this point I was over having his hand covering my mouth, so I did the only thing I could think of that might make him remove it. I stuck my tongue out and licked his palm.

He jerked his hand back quickly, surprised by my tactic.

"Ha!" I shouted victoriously, raising both arms in the air.

He wiped his palm while his shoulders started to shake.

He'd made his point, though the method in which he'd gone about making it wasn't the best. But this was our house now. So if he wanted to build an addition for potential new family members, so be it.

"I give up, Sheriff. My only request is that if you have to cut the office down to make a hallway, leave enough room for my chair in front of the fireplace," I said.

"Glad we got that sorted," he said, grinning.

"Me too. Now if you'll let me down, I'll go back to the laundry. Since I'm no longer mad at you, I don't need to bake five dozen cookies."

"How about you let me piss you off again but just enough you feel the need to make one dozen? Chocolate chip?" he asked.

I gave him one last eye roll, and then I pushed him away so I could hop off the counter.

And then I made him a batch of chocolate chip cookies.

I WAS STANDING at the kitchen sink, cleaning up the dinner dishes, when I saw a flash of light outside beyond the backyard and into the trees.

For a minute, I thought the light must have been a reflection in the kitchen window. But then I saw it again.

Just a quick flash way back in the woods, like someone was walking along out there with a flashlight to guide their way.

But that was crazy. Who would be walking in the forest at night in the dead of winter? It was only twenty degrees outside. I must have imagined it. So I stood there at the window for five minutes and waited for the light to flash again.

It didn't. There was nothing out there. No lights. No people in my trees. Nothing.

I was paranoid.

I shrugged it off and finished my chores so I could go see what Rowen and Jess were doing.

It was a mistake to ignore it. I should have said something to Jess. But by the time I realized it was a mistake, it was too late. Way too late.

CHAPTER TWENTY-TWO

JESS

"Georgia," I rumbled into my phone.

"Hi, Sheriff," she said. "Have you thrown anyone in the slammer yet today?"

I chuckled. She always found some new joke or way to tease me about being a cop. I loved it. I loved that she was smart and had a quick wit. That she kept me on my toes.

"Not yet," I said. "But it's looking like it's gonna be a good day."

"Oh, yeah? What's happening?"

"Got a tip. Couple of guys were up snowmobiling in the mountains and ran across an old shack. Had a real strong chemical smell so they didn't get too close but thought it was worth reporting. I'm thinking they stumbled onto Wes's cookhouse."

"Seriously?" she asked.

"Yep. Driving up now. Milo and Beau are behind me."

"That's so great, honey. I hope you find it. But why is

Beau going with you? It doesn't seem like a real Searchy and Rescuey thing to do," she said.

I chuckled again. "Searchy and Rescuey." Not as funny as "garagey" but it still made me laugh.

"Beau is Forest Service, Freckles. Snowmobilers reported the shack was on national park land."

"Gotcha," she said. "Aren't meth houses extremely dangerous? Should you be going near it?"

"We're just checking it out. If it is the cookhouse, we'll call in the state authorities. Then we'll have a specialized team come in for cleanup."

"Okay. Be careful," she said.

"I won't be able to meet for lunch today."

This morning, I'd fucked her in the shower before Rowen had woken up. Then I'd watched her get ready for work, something I tried to do every day. I loved watching her bend over the sink as she put on her makeup, her ass sticking up as she leaned in toward the mirror. But my favorite part was watching her fix her hair. She'd blow it dry and when she was done, it would be full and soft. Within the hour, it would settle and take on its normal volume. But right then in our bathroom, with her long hair all big and her body wrapped in a towel, she stopped my heart.

And gave me a hard-on. It usually took me the entire drive to work to get it back under control.

This morning while I'd been watching her, we'd made plans to eat lunch together at the deli downtown. Now that I was heading up into the mountains, I'd be lucky if I made it back home before dinner.

But missing lunch was worth it if I found the cookhouse. I needed this break. I needed to make some progress on all of these fucking open cases. The unanswered questions were plaguing my mind and I was starting to have trouble sleeping.

It had been over two weeks since Wes's murder, and both the killer and Wes's truck had vanished off the face of the earth.

On top of having a murderer at large, I had made no progress in finding the prescription pain pill dealer. I'd had deputies in plain clothes walking all around town for a month. They'd wander around, searching for suspicious packages stashed in strange places and watching for people hanging around odd areas of town. But nothing had come up.

And then there was Silas's trespassing case. I had marked it unsolved but it was still bothering me. I hated unsolved cases, especially ones involving a friend. We'd probably never find who killed Silas's calf. No witnesses had come forward and unless they did, it would be impossible to make any arrests.

So finding Wes's cookhouse, even after Wes was dead, would be a good day. A really fucking good day. I wouldn't have to worry about someone stepping up and taking over Wes's production location.

"I think destroying the source for an unknown but likely large quantity of illegal crystal meth trumps a lunch date with your roommate," Georgia said.

"Roommate?" I asked.

"Just trying it out."

"Try something else."

"Will do, Sheriff."

"Okay. See you tonight."

"Love you. Bye," she said and hung up the phone.

She ended the call before I could tell her that I loved her too. But I figured I could tell her tonight when I got home.

Wrong.

———

FUCK, it smelled bad.

Not even the clean mountain air combined with the scent of pine from the trees could overpower the stench of chemicals burning my nostrils.

We'd come up on the mountain shack about forty-five minutes after driving through barely there trails and winding between trees. It was no wonder that weeks and weeks of searching for the cookhouse hadn't turned anything up. Wes had built that fucker so far off the traveled trails it was a miracle we'd found it today. A couple of times on the drive up, I'd had to stop and get out to make sure I was following the snowmobiler's tracks.

But after one last sharp turn, there it was, sitting in a small clearing of pine and fir trees. It was an old, shitty one-room trailer house. The exterior walls were an off-white color with brown water spots in a couple of places. The door and all the windows were boarded up with plywood sheets.

Tucked away back in the trees, about two hundred feet off the house, was a propane tank. Wes must have been using gas to run the meth cook stove and heat the trailer.

"That fucking stinks," Milo said at my side, covering his nose.

"No shit."

"I think I've got a couple extra bandanas in the truck. I'll go get them," Beau said and jogged away.

As I got closer, I felt it. Something was off. A knot was forming in my gut.

I slowed my progress and walked with more caution, looking around the house to see if I could spot what was making me nervous.

I knew this feeling.

When we'd been kids, Silas, Wes and I had played capture the flag on the Drummond farm. We'd each hide a flag and then set off to find where the other boys had hidden theirs. The winner was the first boy to return to our starting point with one of their opponent's flags. Silas and I had usually hidden our flags in dark building corners or behind large trees. Our strategy had been similar. Find a good hiding spot and then search as fast as you could to find an opponent's flag before someone found yours.

But not Wes.

Wes had always put his flag in a fairly open area. He'd forgo the time spent locating the perfect hiding place to set up traps. One time, he'd set a snare and caught Silas by the ankle. I'd found Wes laughing as he watched Silas swinging upside down from a tree.

Walking up to the cookhouse felt like walking up to one of Wes's flags.

I veered off of my original path to the door and instead went toward a window. Before I opened that door, I wanted a better look around. Maybe I could pry off the board to a window and peek inside the shack.

But Milo didn't notice my change of direction. He just kept on walking straight up to the front door and reached out to twist the knob.

And that's when I saw it. A trigger on the door.

"Milo, stop!" I shouted.

But it was too late. Milo turned to look at me, confusion mixed with fear written on his face. He took a step back but the damage had been done. I'd heard the click.

And then the propane tank in the trees exploded.

———

GIGI

"What did he say?" I whispered to Maisy.

We were sitting behind the ER counter where I was on rotation for the week. Everett had been avoiding Maisy since she'd called him on New Year's Day to tell him that she was keeping the baby, but they'd finally run into each other today.

"He was, like, normal. It was weird. He acted like he had this summer before we'd even started dating. He was all business, but pleasant at least. He just asked me how work was going in the clinic and if we'd had any interesting patients this week. Weird, huh?" she asked.

"Yeah. Well, I guess it's better than being uncomfortable and awkward around each other. Or him being a jerk. Whenever Rowen's father saw me, he'd call me a slut and a cow—exactly what a pregnant woman wants to hear. If I were you, I would take the all-business Dr. Carlson," I said.

"You totally need to tell me about Rowen's father. I've gotten bits and pieces from you this last week but I think I need the whole thing."

"Okay," I giggled. "Though there isn't too much to it. He's a supreme asshole. I never plan to see his face again. The end. Have you heard from your parents at all this week since you told them you were pregnant?"

"Yeah. Mom's called me every day since, asking how I was feeling and if I needed anything. She's been great. You were right. After the shock subsided, I think she started to get excited about being a grandma," Maisy said, smiling.

"Good. I'm glad."

"I've got to get back to the clinic. Want to have lunch later this week?" she asked.

"Yes, just let me know which day," I said.

She hadn't made it three feet from the desk when we heard screeching tires at the ER doors. In the middle of the ambulance entrance was a large, forest-green truck. On the driver's side door was a shield with the words "US Forest Service."

I lost sight of the shield when the driver's side door flew open and Beau Holt jumped out of the truck.

Beau, who was supposed to be with Jess and Milo in the mountains looking for Wes's meth cookhouse.

Beau, who was sprinting to the other side of the truck.

Beau, who saw Maisy and screamed at her to bring a couple of stretchers out.

I stood frozen behind the ER counter as Beau pulled two people out of his truck. Both unconscious. Both unmoving. Both covered in blood.

My eyes stayed locked on Beau as those two people were taken by Maisy and the other nurses to two different ER bays. I could hear Dr. Peterson and Everett starting emergency triage procedures in both ER rooms.

Beau walked to me, still standing frozen at the ER counter, with pain and sorrow on his face. His hands were covered in blood that was not his own.

I kept my focus completely on Beau. Because if I let myself look anywhere else, I knew that I'd see Milo in ER room one with Everett. And Jess in ER room two with Dr. Peterson, who was using EKG paddles on Jess's bare chest to try and restart his lifeless heart.

So I kept looking at Beau until I couldn't see him anymore. Until I couldn't see anything anymore but the backs of my eyelids. Because I had screwed my eyes so tightly shut that all I saw was black.

Get it together.

Get it together.

Get it together.

About a minute after I had squeezed my eyes shut, I started chanting. And about a minute after I started chanting, I got it together.

Somehow I managed to detach my heart from my brain so I could get to work. The last thing Jess and Milo needed was to be in a hospital where one of the few nurses available was stuck frozen at the desk.

So I let years of practice and experience take over and I walked into Jess's room completely on autopilot.

It was the hardest thing I'd ever done.

I stayed on autopilot until I was alone hours later, on one of the three worst days of my life.

———

"WHAT HAPPENED?" I whispered to Beau.

We were sitting with our backs against a wall on the second floor of the hospital. My knees were bent and I had my arms wrapped around my shins. Beau was sitting next to me, his arms draped over the tops of his bent knees.

"I don't know. We were all walking up to the shack together. All three of us. The smell was so strong my throat was burning. So I told Milo and Jess that I'd grab us some bandanas from my truck. I was bent digging in the back seat and I heard Jess yell, "Stop." I stood up, then all I saw was the explosion. A big propane tank by the shack just blew. Shot straight up into the air, flames were everywhere. Next thing I knew, I was on my back. Just like that," he said, snapping his fingers.

"It was like a heat wave pushed out from the fire and tossed me in the air. Knocked me straight onto my back. All of those trees by the tank, the trunks, they just broke. Like snapping a toothpick in half. When I got up and looked around, I saw Milo first."

Beau stopped for a minute to close his eyes and tip his head back against the wall. I didn't prompt him or ask him to keep going. At this point, I wished he would stop. Just leave the next part unsaid. Because I knew what he was going to tell me and I didn't want to hear it.

But he continued, oblivious to my silent wishing. "Jess was coming to. He was on his back, looking up and over at me. He got thrown right into a fallen tree. Landed with such force that one of the old limbs was sticking out right through his side. We packed it with some snow and I helped Jess in the truck. I put as much snow as I could on Milo. I don't know if it was enough . . ."

I forced a breath and closed my eyes.

"Drove as fast as I could. Panicked the whole time. Milo was still out in the back. Jess was cussing. He said that if Wes were still alive, he'd kill him for this. I was so focused on driving, Gigi, I didn't notice when he stopped talking. But then right before we pulled up to the hospital, he said, 'Love Georgia. She's my light.' Then that was it. He closed his eyes and fell against the door."

My eyes were leaking a steady stream of tears but I wasn't crying out or sobbing. I didn't have any of that left. The day had drained me completely. Emotionally and physically. All I had left were silent tears.

"I should have gone to Jess first," Beau said.

"No," I heard from above us.

Everett was standing against the wall opposite us.

"Milo was the right one to go to first. Packing snow on his burns was smart. If you hadn't done that to take some of the heat out, they would have been ten times worse. You saved his life," Everett said.

Beau didn't respond. He just lifted his head off the wall and turned to me. "Do you need a ride home?" he asked.

"No," I whispered. "It's only eight. Rowen will still be awake and I can't . . . I can't explain all of this to her tonight."

How was I going to tell her about Jess? I couldn't think about it. It was too much. Telling her would make this day all too real.

"Right," Beau said and stood up. He started walking down the hall but not before he stopped and stared down Everett. At least Everett had the intelligence to look at his feet and not stare back. With all Beau had been through today, a challenge from his sister's ex-boyfriend would have pushed him over the edge. Not that Everett was the challenging type.

"Let me know if you need anything, Gigi," Everett said, pushing off the wall to leave.

"Everett? Thank you. You saved their lives today. And I'll always be grateful for what you and Dr. Peterson did for Jess. That he's alive in there because of you," I said, tipping my head toward Jess's recovery room.

"It's my job, Gigi," Everett said.

"Thank you for doing your job," I whispered, my voice cracking.

"You're welcome. Good night."

I needed a bit of alone time, some space to replay the day and get it sorted in my head. Tomorrow, I would need to tell Rowen about Jess's injury. Noelle too.

When Beau had brought in Milo and Jess, they had been in bad shape. Minutes away from death. I shuddered to think what would have happened if Beau hadn't been able to get to the hospital so fast. If he had hit just one roadblock or delay, today would have ended much, much worse. And that was saying something because as it was, it was really effing bad.

Milo had been treated for burns and a concussion. The burns were so severe that Dr. Peterson and Everett had sedated him so he wouldn't wake up. Then they'd called Mercy Flight to airlift Milo to Spokane's burn unit.

It was likely he'd be there for months and even when he was healed, it was doubtful he'd ever look the same again. His arms and torso had sustained the worst burns. He could cover those up with clothing. But there were still burns on his face that would scar.

Jess had lost a lot of blood. The puncture wound from the tree had gone through his body, leaving a hole about the size of a golf ball from front to back. Because he'd lost so much blood, his heart had stopped beating just before Beau had arrived at the hospital. Dr. Peterson suspected he'd gone only a minute without oxygen to his brain and they'd been able to revive him before taking him into surgery.

Six hours. Jess had been in surgery for six hours, getting a tear to his liver repaired and the other internal bleeding stopped. When the doctors came out of the operating room, they told me Jess had been extraordinarily lucky. If that branch had been an inch closer to the center of his body, it would have severed his spinal cord, leaving him paralyzed. As it was, he was now stabilized and would eventually make a full recovery. All he'd have to deal with were some scars.

He was off of the sedation drugs but hadn't woken up yet. Since I wanted to be here when he did, I'd asked Maisy if she could pick up Rowen and take her home. She'd been more than happy to help and had offered to spend the night at the farmhouse so I could stay with Jess.

Beau had stayed by my side all day, waiting to hear that his friends were going to live and giving me silent support. I didn't know him well, but after today, I would be eternally grateful. The Holts were good people. The best. And I was glad I was here in Prescott where they could be a part of my life.

I wasn't alone anymore.

Standing up from the floor, I walked into Jess's room.

He was in a white hospital gown underneath a dull blue blanket. He looked smaller, lying in the hospital bed. His large body still took up most of the space and his feet were hanging off the end, but still, he looked smaller. Smaller than my Jess, who towered over me and picked me up like I weighed no more than a feather.

It hurt to look at him. The ache in my chest was crippling.

I scooted a chair up to his bed and took one of his hands in both of mine. "I'm here, Jess. Whenever you wake up. I'm here. Just wake up, honey. Please, wake up soon. I don't want to lose you. I can't lose you. Rowen can't lose you. We need you. So come back to us. Come back to me," I whispered.

I laid my head next to his thigh but kept his hand clutched tightly in both of mine. No matter how long it took,

I was going to be the first thing Jess saw when he woke up from today's nightmare.

———

JESS'S EYES fluttered open and searched the room. He turned his head and brilliant ice blue met my gaze.

"Hi, honey," I whispered.

Finally, he was finally awake. It felt like I had waited a year to see those beautiful eyes open.

It was five o'clock in the morning the day after the explosion. I'd stayed awake all night long, sitting next to Jess's side, holding his hand and thinking about all of the reasons why he was so special to me. How I would work every day for the rest of my life to make sure he knew it.

"Hey, baby," he whispered back.

His voice was rough and scratchy. It sounded nothing like his normal deep rumble.

But it was perfect.

CHAPTER TWENTY-THREE

GIGI

"**G**eorgia," Jess called from the bedroom door.
"Closet!" I was hanging up his shirts and putting away a basket of laundry.

It had been almost a month since the explosion. Jess had spent a grumpy week in the hospital followed by a grumpy week at home. But once he could start moving around again, his spirits had lifted and he'd spent the next two weeks designing our addition.

Today, he had gone back to work, antsy to get up to speed, though I wasn't sure why he'd felt out of the loop. His deputies had been over constantly.

He hit the closet door and snapped, "What the fuck is this?"

"What the eff is what?" I turned.

He held out a postcard and I leaned in to read it.

"Well, you're the cop, but this looks like a birthday post-card from my dentist, Sheriff," I said.

"Want to tell me why it says your birthday was last Wednesday?"

"Ah . . . because it was."

"There a reason why you didn't tell me?" he asked.

"I didn't want a birthday this year."

"You didn't want a birthday."

"Yes. I didn't want a birthday," I said.

"That's not really your choice."

"I disagree, since it was my birthday. All I wanted was for it to pass just like any other day," I said.

"Fine. No birthday. How about instead you tell me why you've been acting strange since the explosion?"

"What? I haven't been acting strange," I lied.

I had been acting strange. I knew it. He knew it.

I just couldn't help it.

Every day I struggled to push back the fears swirling in my head, fears that had been haunting me for the last month.

Every time I looked at Jess, all I could see was his body covered in blood. When he talked to me, I heard the flatline beeping of the heart-rate monitor.

"You have been acting strange since the explosion. Don't fucking lie to me. I live here. I see it. So what's going on?"

"Nothing. I'm fine," I lied again.

"Georgia."

I didn't answer. I just went back to the laundry because I wasn't going to tell him. He could badger me all he wanted, but I wasn't ready to talk about it yet.

"Fine," he clipped.

I bent to pick up a stack of his T-shirts but right as my fingers brushed the cotton, I was pulled backward and sent flying through the air, Jess's arms wrapped around my belly, my hands and legs flailing.

"Jess! Be careful! You'll hurt yourself!" I yelled.

He ignored me and kept moving. When we reached the bed, he tossed me down onto my back.

"What are you doing?" I sat up on my elbows.

He grabbed the hem of his black T-shirt with both hands and yanked it up and over his head. Then he unbuttoned his jeans and stripped them off along with his briefs.

We hadn't had sex since the morning of the explosion and my body instantly heated at the sight of a naked Jess standing over me. Even though he'd missed a month of work-outs, his muscles were still bulging. His cock was starting to get hard as my eyes traveled up and down his body.

I missed sex.

He grabbed my ankles and pulled me to the edge of the bed, his fingers going straight to the button on my jeans. In a flash they were gone, along with my panties. Next was my top and bra.

Jess came down on me hard, his mouth attaching to mine as his fingers frantically moved over my entire body. He started at the top, feeling his way from my shoulders to my breasts. He gave my nipples each a hard tug and kept going down.

His hands spanned my ribs and then glided over my stomach to rest on my hips. They slid down my thighs until they reached the backs of my knees, where he bent them up and around his waist. My ankles latched together on his back.

His mouth never left mine as his hands rubbed and pressed into my body. It was rough and hard, his touch almost bruising as he worked his hands and fingers over my skin.

"Jess," I gasped, aching for him.

"Gonna fuck you hard, baby. Hard and deep. So rough you'll feel me all day tomorrow. Then you're gonna tell me what the fuck is going on in your head. Why the fuck you're shutting me out."

I couldn't respond. All I could do was moan. I loved it when he said stuff like that to me, when he told me how he was going to fuck me before he did just that. I loved it so much my whole body shivered.

"Jess, please," I begged.

He lined his cock up with my entrance and pushed in an inch.

"Jess, now."

"You're gonna tell me what I want to know, baby. Say it," he ordered.

I shook my head. I wasn't going to tell him.

He pushed in another painful inch, his cock teasing me. It wasn't enough to help ease the ache. I needed all of him.

"Say it, Georgia."

"Okay," I breathed.

The second the word left my lips, he drove his hips forward hard and buried his cock to the hilt.

I moaned into his neck as my head jerked up and collided with his shoulder. I kept moaning as he fucked me just like he said he would: hard and deep. His hands moved roughly over my body as his cock thrust in and out with no restraint.

My legs started to tremble behind his back and a rush of heat poured over me as I came hard and fast.

"Fuck. So fuckin' tight. Missed your pussy, baby," Jess said into my ear.

He picked up his pace, pounding into me, over and over again.

"Jess, it's too much," I whispered.

"Take it, Georgia. Just let go," he ordered, not slowing down.

I blanked my mind and let go, coming again so powerfully my body split in two.

"Fuck," Jess groaned into my hair as he let go too. I felt his release hot inside me. He planted his cock deep to keep our connection after he finished coming.

With his weight on top of mine, I let my hands wander across his muscled back. I had missed him so much this last month, missed feeling his heavy weight on top of me, like he was keeping me anchored to him. Anchored to us.

And I'd missed feeling his body linked with mine. Even though what we'd just had was fucking, pure and simple, it was also him making love to me. Showing me with his hands, his mouth and his cock that I was his love.

My hands wandered up and down his back and then down his sides. My fingers froze when they hit his scar. I couldn't see it but I didn't need to. I knew exactly what it looked like. It was rough and jagged. The skin was still raised and hot pink.

I traced the line where his stitches had been just three days ago, lightly going back and forth over the mark on his beautiful back. A mark he would have forever. A reminder that he'd almost lost his life and that I had almost lost him in mine.

My chin quivered. Time was up. There was no keeping my breakdown at bay any longer. Jess wouldn't need to coax it out of me because it was already pouring out through the tears in my eyes.

"Let it go, baby." He rolled onto his back, pulling me on top of him.

"I almost lost you," I sobbed into his neck. "All I can see is the blood, Jess. I can't stop seeing it. Seeing you on that stretcher with blood dripping to the floor. Seeing Dr. Peterson restart your heart, your body jolting off the stretcher when he shocked you. I can't stop seeing it."

He didn't say anything. He just wrapped his arms around my back and held me tight.

"What if that happens again? What would we do if it were worse? I don't know if I can survive it. Losing you. I don't want to be like Ben. Wandering around, living a life without a life. I am so scared it's paralyzing me. If I don't keep myself distracted and exhausted, it comes back. I just can't stop seeing it and wondering when it will happen again."

"Baby, you can't think like that," Jess whispered.

"You weren't there, Jess. You didn't see it. See how bad it was."

"I wish it hadn't happened, that you hadn't been there. But it did and you were. We have to move past it. Get back to where we were. You gotta reengage with us. Stop pulling away from me."

"I don't know how," I whispered.

"Yes you do," he said, giving me a little shake. "All you gotta do is let me in there. Let me show you the way out so we don't live a life in fear, scared that with every move it'll be over. It could happen again, Georgia. You know that. None of us know when it's our time."

I nodded.

He was absolutely right. And it wasn't like I hadn't known it before. Lives could be cut short, but that didn't mean it still wasn't terrifying.

"I don't want to lose you. All my life I've been losing

people. My dad before I even got to know him. My mom way before it was time. Ben. And I survived all of those. Somehow I made it through. And each time, I knew I was strong enough to make it. But I don't know if I could survive if I lost you, Jess. I don't think I'm strong enough," I said quietly.

"You're stronger than any person, man or woman, I've ever known, Georgia. I don't want you to have to survive me but if you have to, you'll do it. Because you'll have to for Rowen. And I want you to be happy, even if I'm not here to share that with you."

His words brought on a whole new batch of tears. I hated to think of life without him. I wouldn't be happy, I couldn't be, if he wasn't here.

"But it's not gonna happen," he said. "I'm okay. Gonna be okay. We're gonna live it good while we can. And my living it good is with you. With Roe. We finally get to be happy. So I need you to be with me, not letting your fears drive you away."

"Okay," I breathed. It was a deep breath, my shoulders sagging forward, releasing all of the tension I'd been holding in them for the past month.

"Roll off me. I need to see your face," he ordered. "We need to talk about this birthday thing," he said once I was on my back.

"It's not a big deal, honey. I haven't really celebrated my birthday since my mom died."

"Big deal to me, Georgia. Birthdays. Holidays. My chance to make it special for you. Tough for me to do that when I don't even know when it's your birthday."

"Well . . . now you know and you can do something next year. January twenty-sixth. Rowen's is March fifth."

I already knew his birthday was April thirteenth. I'd asked Noelle at Thanksgiving so I'd be sure not to miss it.

"First year together. I wanted to do something special."

"That's sweet," I said, lifting my hand to stroke his cheek. "But just do it next year. I can wait."

"I can't. So guess we'll just do it now," he said.

"Do what now?" I asked.

"Put my ring on your finger."

"What?" I breathed.

"Got a ring in the gun safe out in the garage. You feel like wearing it for the rest of your life?"

I blinked a couple of times and replayed his words in my head to make sure I had heard them right. Then my face split into a wide smile as my heart swelled with overwhelming happiness. Nodding, I whispered, "Yes."

Jess's proposal wasn't a big show of flowers and diamonds. He didn't try and wow me with a huge affair or a fancy surprise. But it was pure Jess. He felt like doing it right there, so he did it.

And it was perfect.

His wide, white smile matched my own. His ice-blue eyes were shining bright. He leaned down to kiss me but I couldn't bring my lips together. My smile was permanent.

"Love you, baby," he said into my teeth.

"Love you too."

"You want me to go out to the garage and get your ring?"

"Later," I said.

I forced my lips together so I could kiss him.

After he made love to me again, he pulled on some clothes and went to get my ring.

In one night, Jess had helped erase my fears. Because

when I looked at him now, I didn't see the hole in his side or all the blood. I didn't hear his heartbeat flatline.

I heard him asking if I wanted to wear his ring for the rest of my life. And I saw the light dancing in his eyes after I'd said yes, gladly, knowing that ring wouldn't leave my finger until the end of my days.

He was right. Anything could happen to us but while we had the chance, we were going to live it good. Together. With Jess as my husband and me as his wife. With Rowen as our daughter and, one day, her siblings that we made together.

We were absolutely going to live it good. The best.

———

ROWEN and I were at the dining room table the next morning, eating our breakfast.

Since I had a few minutes with her before preschool, I could talk to her about Jess and me getting married. I wanted her to be the first to know.

And I wanted to tell her by myself.

Not that I didn't think Jess would be great with her, but it had been just the two of us for so long, I wanted to make sure she knew that I loved her and that Jess and I getting married would never change that.

"Roe?" I called as she finished a bite of Froot Loops.

"Yeah, Mommy?"

"I wanted to talk to you about something, baby girl. Something about me and Jess."

"What is it?"

"Well, Jess asked me if I would marry him last night. In a wedding. That means he would become a part of our family forever. I want to marry him but I also want you to be okay with that."

"Isn't he a part of our family already?" she asked.

I let out a small chuckle. "Yes, sweetie. I guess he is already a part of our family."

"If you have a wedding to Jess, does that mean I get to wear a pretty dress?"

"Of course. Any dress you want," I promised.

"Yay! Can it be purple?"

"You bet. Whatever you want."

I smiled as she went back to her cereal. Not much fazed my Rowen. Or maybe she didn't get what I was telling her. But it didn't matter. She'd understand it eventually. All she needed to know right now was that we were her family and we loved her.

While she finished eating, I gave my gleaming ring another thorough inspection.

A round-cut diamond, about a carat and a half, sat in a solid white-gold band. The edges of the diamond were encased in white gold so that the stone wouldn't snag on anything. The band itself had smaller diamonds all the way around, inset into the metal.

"Mommy?" Rowen called, taking my attention away from my ring.

"Yeah?"

"Does that mean Jess can be my daddy?" she asked quietly. Her fingers were drumming on the table and she wasn't looking up from her cereal.

"Do you want him to be your daddy, Roe?"

"Yeah. If he wants to," she said.

"I think he'd really like that, sweetie. Maybe tonight when he gets home you can ask him."

A huge smile broke across her face. "Okay."

I smiled too, letting a warm wave of happy course right through my body and settle straight in my heart.

———

"HELP! I need help! My son, he's in trouble!" I heard shouted from the ER doors.

A tall, lean man rushed in with a teenager at his side. The kid was barely moving. His father had ahold of him underneath one of his arms, the other braced behind the kid's back. The kid's head was hanging down and his feet were dragging on the ground.

I shot up from behind the desk and ran to the wall to grab a wheelchair, pushing it over as fast as I could so the father could drop his son into the seat.

"Come this way," I ordered, immediately wheeling the kid to an ER room. The second I cleared the doorway, I pushed the call button for Everett.

When we got into the room, the father helped me get the kid into the bed. Once he was lying back against the pillow, I got a look at the kid's face.

Him?

It was the face of the asshole punk kid who had come to my house on Halloween and broken all my pumpkins. The same asshole punk kid who had threatened me on my lawn before Jess had shoved him into the back of a police car.

I turned to his father.

"Can you tell me what's wrong with him, sir?" I asked.

His father ran his hands through his short brown hair. "Scottie. His name is Scottie. And I don't know what's wrong. He was supposed to be in school. It's a Friday. Why wasn't he in school? I just don't know what he was doing at home. He left for school this morning and I was meeting my wife in Bozeman. I was driving over to pick her up at the airport. But I forgot my wallet so I had to turn around. I came home and saw his car in the garage. Then I found him passed out on the living room couch."

Pausing to dig in the front pocket of his khaki corduroy pants, he pulled out a handful of red and yellow pills.

"Here," he said, handing them to me. "These were on the coffee table. One of them was open and there was powder everywhere."

I took the pills and set them on a tray at the same time Everett came rushing into the room.

"You paged?" he asked.

"Yes. This is Mr. . . ."

"Pierce. Scott Pierce."

"Mr. Pierce. He found his son passed out at home not long ago. These pills were next to him," I told Everett.

Everett started asking Mr. Pierce a series of questions after ordering me to get an IV started in Scottie's arm.

"Are you going to pump his stomach?" Mr. Pierce asked Everett.

"No, I don't think we'll need to. Those look like oxycodone pills. If he took them or was inhaling their contents, then we can get rid of the opioids in his body by using an antidote. Do you have any idea how much he's taken?" Everett asked.

"I don't know. Why is he taking pills? He's a good kid. Why is he doing drugs?" he asked the room.

"Mr. Pierce, I'm sorry to ask. But did you find a note with these pills? Any indication this was an attempted suicide?" Everett asked.

"What?! No. Scottie wouldn't do that. Never. He's a good kid."

I had a feeling that Mr. Pierce didn't know as much about Scottie as he liked to think. After all, not three months ago, he'd been vandalizing other people's homes, including mine, with no regard to the homeowners' feelings or the consequences of his actions.

"Okay. We'll get the antidote started. It will take a while to work through Scottie's system. Would you like us to call anyone for you?" Everett asked.

"Ah . . . no. I'll step out and call my wife," he said and left the room.

"Gigi, let's give him the max dose of the antidote," Everett ordered. "If he doesn't wake up in an hour, give me a call. I'll swing by before then if I can but I've got a couple other patients upstairs to see to. It might take me a while to finish up with them. Just call if anything comes up."

I worked for the next fifteen minutes to get Scottie situated with the IV drip and to admit him into the hospital's system. His father hadn't returned to his room yet. He was pacing back and forth in the waiting room with his phone attached to his ear.

Where had Scottie gotten the pills? Had he gotten them from his parents' medicine cabinet? Or were these from the same dealer that Jess was looking for?

Unless he confessed to buying them illegally and agreed to discuss it with the police, I didn't think there was anything Jess could do. And this kid didn't seem like the type to confess to anything. He hadn't confessed to vandalizing the country houses on Halloween, why would he confess to participating in illegal drug trafficking? But maybe an overdose and a trip to the emergency room would scare some sense into him, or at least some sense into his parents.

Scottie groaned when I came into his room.

"Scottie? Can you hear me?" I asked.

He slowly shook his head and opened his eyes, groaning again.

I stayed by his side for a few minutes until he finally started to come to.

"Where am I?" he asked groggily.

"You're in the hospital, Scottie. Your dad found you at home. Did you take some pills?" I asked.

"Who are you?" he asked. "Wait. I know you. You're that bitch who got me arrested. Fuck you. Where's my dad?"

Okay, so a trip to the emergency room *hadn't* scared any sense into him. He was still an asshole punk.

"Nice," I mumbled. "Your father's in the waiting room. I'll get him."

But right as I was about to leave his room, he said, "You tell that cop boyfriend of yours about this, cunt, I'll fuckin' gut you. Your kid too."

I froze in the doorway, my back to Scottie. I was glad he couldn't see the effect his words had on my face, that he couldn't see the terror he'd caused.

I couldn't make my mouth work to respond and I didn't try to find the courage to try. I just forced one foot in front of the other and kept moving forward. With every step, my heart beat so loudly it blocked out all other sounds.

Everett was heading my way. He must have seen the panic on my face because he stopped dead in his tracks and stared at me.

But I didn't stop to talk to him. I just kept walking straight to my manager's office where I told her I needed to be done for the day. She knew something was wrong but she didn't ask questions. She just let me go.

Then I went straight to Quail Hollow and collected my daughter. It was an overreaction, but I needed her with me, close at my side so I could be sure nothing would happen to her. That I could protect her.

Patient confidentiality be damned. The second Jess got home tonight, he was going to learn all about Scottie Pierce and his threats against me and Rowen. Because if I couldn't protect her, I knew that Jess could.

CHAPTER TWENTY-FOUR

GIGI

It was a little after five and I was expecting Jess home in an hour. I didn't want to have our normal Friday night meal at the café. Scottie Pierce's threat was still too fresh. I needed to stay inside in my home where I felt safe.

I also didn't want to discuss Scottie's threat with Jess in public. I didn't know exactly how he was going to react but it wouldn't be good. Likely, he'd blow a gasket and shout obscenities for ten minutes. That, or he'd go all silent and scary and get that menacing look in his eyes.

Scottie's words had been looping in my ears, and every time I heard them, a shudder would run down my back. I'd been queasy since leaving the hospital.

I wouldn't feel one ounce of sympathy for Scottie, no matter how badly Jess retaliated. The punk couldn't talk to people like that. If his parents weren't teaching him that lesson, Jess would.

Since we wouldn't be eating out tonight, I was in the

kitchen working on dinner while Rowen watched her iPad in her room.

I was standing at the kitchen sink, washing my hands, when a flicker of light caught my eye from the window. The sun set not long after five o'clock during these winter days so the light was easy to see in the darkness.

It was just like the light I had seen last month. But this time, it wasn't going away and there wasn't just one light, but two, both of which were moving toward the farmhouse, growing bigger and bigger as they came my way.

My heart thundered as the lights came closer. My nervousness turned to full-blown panic as bodies emerged, attached to both lights. I couldn't make out any features but I knew they were men. Men walking out of the woods, holding flashlights and walking to my house through the snow.

It wasn't right, I could feel it. This situation was wrong. People didn't hide out in the woods and walk up to a house in the dark. Worry and fear took control of my mind and I stood at the sink, panicking, watching them get closer.

What the hell was I doing? Men were coming to my house and I was just standing here, watching?

I snapped out of my trance. The men hadn't crossed the backyard yet so I had a minute, maybe two, before they were at my door.

One minute wasn't enough for me to get Rowen and drive the hell out of there but it was enough for me to get my daughter out of the house.

Sprinting upstairs, my heart beating out of my chest, I grabbed her off her little bed. She started to protest when I took the iPad out of her hands but then she looked at my face and knew things weren't right.

I needed her to hide but it couldn't be in the house.

What if they came in and searched for her? On the spur of the moment, I decided to send her to the garage. It was locked and she could get in by crawling through the cat door.

"Roe, I need you to do exactly what I say," I said as I carried her down the stairs. "No questions, baby girl. Just do it. There are some men walking up to the house and it's scaring Mommy because I don't know who they are. I need you to run to the garage, sweetie. Crawl in through the kitty door. Hide out with Mrs. Fieldman and the kitties until Jess gets home or until I get here. Do not come out for anyone else. Just me or Jess. No one else. Even if you know them. Got it?"

I felt Rowen's panicked breaths against my cheek but I didn't stop moving.

"Got it, Roe?" I repeated.

She nodded.

"Good. That's my good girl. I love you. You can do it."

I pushed her out the front door, glad she hadn't taken off her boots when we'd gotten home.

"Run. Rowen, run." I hoped that whoever was approaching hadn't made it to the house quite yet.

Her eyes filled with tears but she turned on her heels and ran to the garage.

I shut the door and crept to the living room, crouching by the window as I watched her cross the front lawn.

I had just sent my baby girl outside alone and in the dark. Panic morphed to horror. Had I made the right choice? Would she be safe?

When her little bum disappeared through the cat door, I breathed a sigh of mild relief. I would never take that garage for granted again, or the fact that Jess had gotten it built so quickly.

She was safe. Until I knew what was happening, she was safe.

I slipped away from the window and curled into the living room corner. Then I waited. Waited for the something bad I knew was coming my way.

The ticking clock on the mantel was booming, much like my heart.

Why hadn't I grabbed my phone? I should have grabbed my phone. Stupid!

I'd been so worried about Rowen that I'd left it on the kitchen counter.

Stupid. Stupid. Stupid!

Before I could make a dash to the kitchen, boots thudded as the men made their way over the porch. Every step was like a tremor, exponentially increasing my fear with each shake.

The doorbell rang.

What? I didn't know what I had expected, maybe for them to kick in the door or break through the glass window, but a ringing doorbell wasn't it.

Was I being paranoid? Had Scottie Pierce's threat pushed me over the edge of sanity?

I forced myself to stand and walk to the door.

Until I knew exactly what was going on, I didn't want these strangers poking around the house. I especially didn't want them going anywhere near the garage. I needed them to stay focused on me and away from where my little girl was hiding.

I squinted through the marbled glass window, hoping to see who was here. One man's back was to the door, but my panic subsided a bit at the other's familiar face.

"Everett?" I asked, inching the door open.

"Hi, Gigi."

"What are you doing here? And why did you come through the woods?"

But before he could answer, the man he was with turned around.

John Doe.

The man who had been beaten to a pulp my first day working at Jamison Valley Hospital. What the hell was going on here? Why was Everett with John Doe? And what was his real name?

My mind raced through its memory banks. Benson. Alex Benson. That was his name.

"We need to go, Carlson. The cop usually gets home around five-thirty or six. You want me to grab the kid?" Benson asked Everett.

"No!" I screamed. Pure terror ran through my veins.

"Leave her. She's nothing and there isn't time," Everett said.

My panic lessened marginally now that I knew he wasn't interested in Rowen.

An evil gleam was shining from Everett's brown eyes. "Time to go, Gigi."

His hand flashed before two prongs jabbed into my ribs a split second before the whole world went black.

———

JESS

Something wasn't right.

I could feel it in my gut. Clicking the button on the visor, I started easing the truck into the garage but slammed on the brakes when Rowen's little body came darting around the hood.

Opening the door, I frowned down at her.

"Rowen, you can't run around a truck like—"

What the fuck?

Her skin was white and covered in big red splotches. Tears streamed down her face as her whole body shook.

"What's wrong?" I asked, kneeling in front of her.

"Mommy," she sobbed and fell into my chest.

"Mommy what, Roe?" I pressed, gently shaking her little shoulders.

"Mommy came to my room and said I had to come out here and hide. She made me crawl through the kitty's door and hide with them because there were scary men coming to the house. But she didn't come to get me. Where is she? I want Mommy!" she wailed.

What the fuck was going on? Who came to the house and where was Georgia?

I picked up Rowen and ran with her clutched to my neck toward the house.

The front door was open a crack. Whoever had come here hadn't shut it completely when they'd left. I toed it open with my boot and started walking carefully through the entryway.

"Shh, Roe," I whispered in her ear. "Can you sit here for a minute while I look around the house?"

She nodded and I set her down right inside the door.

I should have left her in the garage while I checked the house but she wouldn't have let me. She was freaked, so the entryway was the best I was going to get.

I slid my gun from its holster, creeping silently into the house. I cleared the living room first, then made my way past the office toward the kitchen. The stove was on and whatever Georgia had been cooking was boiling. Her phone was sitting on the counter by the sink.

The knot in my gut was tightening. There was no way she would have left her phone if she hadn't been panicked. She would have taken it with her and shut off the stove. Unless whatever she saw had freaked her so much that all she did was focus on getting Rowen to the garage.

Fuck.

I crept quickly and quietly through the rest of the house but there wasn't a sign of her. Nothing. And nothing was out of place.

I stowed my gun and went back to Rowen. Kneeling in front of her, I asked her question after question about what had happened.

She didn't know much. Once she'd made it to the garage, she'd done as her mother had asked and hidden in the cat's alcove. From in there, she hadn't seen or heard a thing happening at the house.

I got her situated in the living room under Georgia's favorite fleece blanket, hoping its warmth and the lingering scent of her mother's vanilla shampoo would help her stop shaking.

Then I went into the kitchen and took a better look around.

She must have been here when she'd gotten spooked. My eyes darted to the clock. Five-thirty. Georgia couldn't have been gone for long because the pot on the stove would have been burning, not just boiling. And she usually didn't get home until just a little after five.

Georgia had told Rowen that men were walking up to the house. But who?

I shut off the stove and grabbed the flashlight from the cabinet on top of the fridge before running outside.

I got to the lawn and saw two sets of tracks, one leading to the door and the other leading away. Both going along the same path, past the side of the house and through the backyard.

Pulling out my phone, I called dispatch. I needed help. I needed my deputies to help me find my fiancée.

An hour after I'd made the call to dispatch, the farmhouse was crawling with people.

All of my deputies had come, each abandoning their Friday evening plans to come to my aid. Sam was going through the house, looking for anything I might have missed on my quick walk-through. Bryant was with Rowen, talking to her again to see what else she could remember. And the rest of my deputies were making calls around town, asking if anyone had seen Georgia.

Nick had showed up early on, having heard the call come through dispatch at the fire station. On his way, he'd called Beau and Silas, who'd arrived not long after he had.

The four of us set out to follow the tracks in the snow, hoping it would lead us to a clue as to where Georgia had been taken or who had taken her.

As we hunted for clues, I let Beau take the lead. He was the best tracker in this part of the state and was often called out of Prescott to assist other Search and Rescue teams when they were having trouble finding a lost hiker or climber.

We followed the tracks through the snow-covered lawn and into the grove of trees beyond the backyard. We'd just hit the tree line when Silas called out. Nick and I bolted to his side while Beau kept tracking.

"You find something?" I asked, running to his side.

"No. But look at this area. Someone's been back here for a while, not just today. This whole area's been walked on multiple times. The patch over there is iced over. A guy probably sat there a couple days ago during the melt. It froze back over when the temp dropped yesterday."

Beau ran toward us after he finished his search.

"Tracks go past the trees to a clearing. There's tire tracks all over. Someone drove back in there a lot and parked behind that rise so you wouldn't see the vehicle from the house," he said.

"Then they must have walked over here and hid out," Nick said. "Watched the house from this distance. With any decent set of specs, they could see in through all the back windows. They probably watched her at the kitchen sink."

"Fuck me," I muttered. "Who would stake out the house? And why take Georgia?" The only person I could think who would do that had died before Christmas. And even Wes wouldn't have crossed that line. "Fuck. Fuck. Fuck!"

I was losing it. My stomach was so tight I almost doubled over.

Beau's phone rang and he stepped away from our circle.

"Anyone made any threats to you lately?" Nick asked.

I racked my brain. "Wes. The only other one that comes to mind was that kid who smashed the pumpkins on the porch at Halloween. Said a few things to Georgia. But he was just a punk kid. Rich little fucker who's been spoiled rotten."

"Better check him out. What's his name? I'll run back, have Sam go talk to him," Silas said.

"Scott Pierce, Jr.," I said. "Lives up the canyon in that

new development area. Biggest house on the hill. He's an entitled prick but he couldn't have done this himself."

"Got it," Silas said and turned to leave.

"Silas?" I called. "Go with Sam. Those parents give you any grief, tell them you're a deputy. Press them hard. They'll want to bring in their fucking lawyer but don't let them. Get to that kid. If he knows something, make him talk. I'll cover your back if it goes south."

If the Pierce kid knew anything, Silas would get it out of him. Sam was a good interrogator but Silas would scare the living piss out of that kid until he coughed up whatever it was he had.

"Maisy's been taken too," Beau called to Nick and me.

"What the fuck?" Nick said at the same time I cursed.

"Mom went by to see her," Beau said, "find out if she was feeling okay. Her place was trashed. Looks like she tried to fight them off. Shit was all over the floor. The front door was wide open. Mom called me right after she hung up with dispatch."

I couldn't believe this was happening. Who the fuck would take Georgia *and* Maisy? I could see someone taking Georgia if they were trying to get to me. But Maisy? It didn't add up.

"I need to get back to Roe," I said. "Beau, you and Nick take Bryant to Maisy's place. See what you can find. It's gotta be the same people. There's no way two nurses get taken from their homes in the same night by different people."

"You got it, Brick," Nick said.

And they all ran back to the farmhouse.

An hour later, I was no closer to finding Georgia than I had been when I'd gotten home. And I hadn't heard back from Beau, Nick or Silas.

I desperately wanted to be out there looking for her. Pacing through the house was killing me. But the second I'd walked through the door from the backyard search, Rowen had latched onto my side and hadn't let go.

And I didn't want to leave her. I couldn't leave her, not alone in this house without me or her mother.

I hated to think of what was happening to Georgia. While I was pacing, was she being beaten? Or worse? Was she alive?

I let those thoughts cross my mind for a second until I pushed them out. I wouldn't let myself think the worst. I needed to focus on finding her and taking care of Rowen. Georgia would want that. For me to take care of Roe first, before anything else. So that's what I did.

I held her tight as I paced, checking in with deputies and making phone calls. Not once did I put her down and not once did she let go of the firm grip she had on my neck.

"Jess?" Rowen whispered.

"Yeah?"

"If Mommy doesn't come home, can I still live with you?" she asked.

"Mommy's coming home Roe. Okay? I promise. We'll get her back."

"What if she doesn't?" Tears were rolling over her cheeks, landing on my shirt.

"You'll always be with me. No matter what. You're my girl," I said.

"Then you'll be my daddy?" she asked.

"I already am, little bit."

She buried her face in my neck and I kissed the top of her hair.

Talking about the possibility of not finding Georgia was making me sick. I had to sit down. The panic was crippling.

Was this how Georgia had felt when she saw me in the emergency room? Because if it was, I had been too hard on her. I had dismissed her fears and told her it was going to be fine.

I'd had no fucking idea.

This couldn't be it. I needed her back. I needed my light.

I swallowed the lump in my throat.

If I lost it, Rowen would too. And by some miracle she was holding it together. The strength of this girl never ceased to amaze me.

Jostling Rowen, I pulled out my phone as it rang.

"Silas."

"Pierce's parents were home. The kid OD'd today. Dad found him passed out this afternoon and rushed him to the hospital. It looks like he's been snorting pain pills. Gigi was his nurse in the ER today. Carlson was his doctor. The kid's still there, been at the hospital all night per Carlson's orders."

"What? How did we not hear any of this?" I asked.

"I don't know," Silas muttered.

"Carlson should have called it over. Physicians are required to notify the local authorities when minors are admitted for drug abuse," I said.

Think, Jess. Think.

"It's got to be something to do with this kid. My gut's telling me he's the link. I'm going to the hospital to talk to him myself. Meet me there with Sam," I ordered.

Once I got a reluctant Rowen situated with my team, I got in my truck and flew into town. Scottie Pierce was going to tell me what the fuck was going on, even if I had to beat it out of him.

CHAPTER TWENTY-FIVE

GIGI

I woke up alone on a cold cement floor, lying on my side with my hands bound behind my back.

Everett and Benson had taken me to a basement, judging by the small rectangular windows topping the concrete-block walls. Tall metal shelves lined the room, stacked with extra medical supplies. In the corner, a bed was wrapped up in plastic.

We were at the hospital.

I had never been in the hospital's basement before. During my initial tour, my boss had pointed to the basement door but hadn't brought me down here. The basement door was right by the staircase that led upstairs to the second floor. I'd walked by that door countless times but never through it.

My body was shivering violently, both from the cold and my fear. When Everett took me from the farmhouse, I hadn't been wearing a coat and my feet were bare. It was freezing cold lying here on the cement floor in only a pair of torn jeans and a long-sleeved olive thermal.

How long had I been here? I'd taken off my watch to cook dinner. No light came from the basement windows, but it was dark so early these days that didn't tell me much. It could be six o'clock in the evening or three o'clock in the morning.

I hoped that Rowen was okay and Jess had found her in the garage. That Everett hadn't changed his mind and gone after her once I'd blacked out.

How was Jess ever going to find me? My phone was on the kitchen counter. My car was parked in the driveway. And unless Everett left a trail of breadcrumbs for Jess to follow, which I highly doubted, he wouldn't know the first place to start looking.

I laid my head back down on the floor and curled my legs tightly into my chest, trying to keep as warm as possible. My head jerked up to the doorway as a loud metal door slammed shut. The thud of boots echoed off the cement walls, louder and louder, as footsteps came my way.

Everett strode into the storage room, followed by Benson. He was carrying a woman in his arms. But it wasn't just a woman.

It was Maisy.

Her blond head was tipped back, a gash on her temple. Her arms and legs were dangling by her sides.

Oh my god! Please let her be alive.

"Well, well. Look who's finally awake," Everett said with a snide grin.

"What's going on?" I asked.

He watched me struggle to sit up. His glare was filled with hatred. I was looking at a stranger.

He wasn't the Everett I knew, the nice, handsome doctor I'd worked with for over six months. He wasn't the quiet or shy man Maisy had dated this fall. There wasn't a trace of the compassion or kindness I had seen in him before.

It was all gone.

Replaced by anger and arrogance. His eyes were cunning and evil. This was absolutely not the Everett I knew.

"Gigi, always so curious," he said. "You'd have been better off to be like our dear Maisy here. Stupid. Benson, put her down over there," he ordered, pointing to the hospital bed.

Benson dumped Maisy on the bed. She drooped down, not moving a muscle, but her chest expanded with a breath. Unconscious, but alive. I hoped that whatever they had done wasn't hurting her baby.

"Please, Everett. Don't hurt us. I don't know what's going on but please just let us go," I pleaded.

"Scottie told you about me, didn't he? I knew it when I saw you walk out of his room. You were putting it together."

"Putting what together?" I asked.

"Don't play stupid, Gigi. It doesn't suit you. You know full well that I'm the one supplying the junkies in town with prescription pills, not to mention half of the high school students. Scottie just couldn't keep his mouth shut, could he? Well, we'll be taking care of him tonight too." The snarl on his face was pure evil.

"What? He didn't tell me anything! I swear, Everett! I don't know what's going on. Please. Please just let me and Maisy go," I begged.

"Don't lie, Gigi."

"I'm not. I swear! I don't know anything. Please, Everett,

please don't hurt us. Maisy is pregnant. I have a little girl that needs me. Just let us go," I begged again, my eyes filling with tears.

"No. That whore is not having a child. I won't allow it. She had her chance. She could have had an abortion and then none of this would be happening to her. But she didn't. So now she will pay the price for her disobedience."

He was crazy. Certifiably crazy.

I couldn't reason with him. Begging wasn't working. What was I going to do? I needed to think. I needed to get the hell out of here. But I wasn't leaving Maisy here alone.

My mind raced, forming, then dismissing different escape plans. Nothing I thought of would work. I searched the room frantically but nothing would cut the zip ties at my wrists.

"Benson," Everett said, "go pay Scottie a visit. He's on the second floor. Find out what he said to Gigi. Then shove enough oxy down his throat so he'll never wake up again."

This wasn't happening. I hadn't just heard Everett order a man to go kill a teenaged kid.

"Everett, no!" I shouted. "He didn't tell me anything about you. He just said that if I told Jess he was taking pills that he would hurt me and my daughter. I swear. Please. You don't need to kill him. He's just a kid! Let him be!"

"Too late, Gigi," Everett said. "Scottie thought he could step up and join my crew. This was his test. He failed and now he's out." He pointed to the door. "Benson, go."

This was a nightmare. Any minute I would wake up, safe at home in the farmhouse with Jess. This couldn't be happening.

"Why?" I asked Everett. "Why are you doing this?"

"I want money and selling pills is quick cash. Especially

with no competition. I'm tired of solving other people's problems so I'll exploit them instead, feed on the weaknesses of the poor and stupid. Soon I'll leave, maybe move to the Maldives and never look back."

Competition? He had to mean Wes. He was the only other drug dealer in Prescott. At least I hoped. With Wes out of the way, anyone wanting drugs would have to go through Everett.

"You killed Wes?" I gasped.

"I'm an extremely intelligent man, Gigi. Of course I didn't kill Wes. Mr. Benson killed Wes. Besides, he had his own debt to settle after that beating Drummond gave him this summer."

"Wes beat him up? Why?" I asked.

"I was moving in on what Wes considered his territory. His beating was intended to be a message. A threat. And I don't respond well to threats. Something the late Mr. Drummond learned all too well."

"But why me? Why Maisy? What are you going to do to us?"

"I'm afraid you have become too well informed. I've had Benson at your house keeping an eye on you and your beloved sheriff," he said.

I thought I'd been imagining those lights the first night I saw them. I should have mentioned something to Jess. Stupid.

"Jess will find me. He's out there looking now. I know it. You won't get away with this."

"Now, Gigi. I've told you that I don't respond well to threats. The sheriff is nowhere near here. He has been so focused on Wes that I've gone completely unnoticed. And

I've made sure to act like a timid and shy mouse whenever he's around," he said arrogantly.

"He knows there is someone in town selling pills," I snapped.

"Yes. He does. But he's so far away from my trail it will take him years to put it all together."

Months ago, that day with Gus Johnson, I'd made the wrong assumption. He'd known it because he *was* the dealer. And damn it, I hadn't told Jess about that either. He might have seen it from a different angle.

A heavy weight settled in my heart. If I didn't escape, I was dead. Everett was a psychopath intent on killing me. I would never again feel my daughter's arms wrapped around my neck or hear her tell me she loved me. I would never again feel Jess's kiss on my head as I slept tucked into his side.

I closed my eyes and tried to calm my racing heart.

Think. Think. Think.

You can do this.

Find a way out.

I could do it. I just needed to keep it together and wait for my opening. Everett was so arrogant, surely he would make a mistake. Right?

Please let him make a mistake. Please. Please. Please.

From my position against the far back wall, I could see through the storage room's door and into the hallway. If I could just make it out and up the stairs, I'd be free. There were people working upstairs. I just had to get to them.

If it was the evening shift, someone would be in the ER. If it was the night shift, the nurses would be on the second floor. But even if I didn't see any of the staff, if I could just make it upstairs to a phone, I'd be safe.

I focused on finding my opening, desperately trying to block out the fear in my mind. I was going to make a run for it. He hadn't tied my legs, so even if I couldn't get my arms free, I could still run. I might have to come back for Maisy.

The sound of the stair door opening again snapped my eyes to the doorway. I was expecting Alex Benson to stroll through with another life on his hands. But it wasn't Benson. It was Ida.

"Ida!" I screamed. "Help us! Run, please get help!" Hopefully, my warning would give her a few extra seconds and she'd have a head start on Everett.

My shouting stopped when she grinned at me. She wasn't running. She was down here on purpose.

"Scottie's done," she told Everett. "Benson left to prep the site for these two. Here's another dozen pills." She handed him a little baggie full of oxycodone.

"Good," Everett said. "Stash them over in the corner with the others and then go back upstairs. Wait for me to call. I need to do a few things here before we'll be ready to leave."

My heart plummeted into my stomach with crushing disappointment. All hope was lost.

Not Ida. Please not her too. I had respected her. I had liked her. I had trusted her. Now that was dead. She was an evil stranger who'd betrayed me and betrayed Maisy.

This nightmare just kept getting worse.

With her task complete, she looked at me and snarled, "Bye, Gigi."

Her whisper sent chills through my spine. The weight in my chest was getting heavier and heavier. Every passing minute things were getting worse and the fear just kept building.

How long had she had been helping Everett steal pills from patients? She'd been smuggling them right out from under all of us. No wonder Mr. Johnson hadn't responded to the oxy. He hadn't gotten any.

To think of all the patients these two had seen over the last year, all of the pain that they'd endured because they'd been given fake pills. It was sick and cruel.

My head whirled to Maisy as she stirred on the bed, the plastic crumpling and squeaking as she shifted around.

"Oh, good. Now that she's awake, we can move this along," Everett announced.

Maisy looked to Everett and then over to me on the floor. Her eyes filled with panic when she saw the plastic ties around my wrists.

"Maisy, love," Everett said, walking to the bed. "I want you to understand that your actions have brought this upon you. You should have terminated this pregnancy. I told you I had no interest in fathering a child. But no matter. The fetus will not be alive much longer."

He reached into his pocket and pulled out a prescription bottle.

"You're going to take these," he said. The pills rattling as he shook the bottle. "You might survive them. That fetus won't."

"No!" she screamed but stopped when he whipped out a hand and slapped her.

"You will. Or I'll slit Gigi's throat right in front of you."

She shook her head frantically and pushed herself as far away as she could.

This wasn't a nightmare. This was hell. Maisy and I had been kidnapped and taken straight into hell.

He leaned his body over hers, pinning her to the bed, and started prying open her mouth.

"Stop!" he bellowed.

She was kicking and clawing at his hands, twisting her head out of his grip.

The sound of her screams filled my ears. I had to get us out of here. I had to stop this madness. I wouldn't let him force those pills into her mouth and take us to the "site" that Benson was preparing.

With Maisy fighting, Everett wasn't paying attention to me.

Maybe together we could stop Everett long enough to make a run for it. We just had to get to a phone. That's all we needed. One phone call, and Jess would save us.

Silently, I leaned against the wall and used it to stand myself up. My plan was crazy but it was all I could think of. I backed up a few steps and squared my shoulders. Then, bending my knees, I prepared for my attack. All I had was my body. It wasn't much but with enough force, maybe I could ram into Everett and throw him off Maisy.

Jess had spent months teaching me about football, the strategy, the rules . . . and how the players landed those body-slamming tackles. How a smaller player could take out a larger opponent.

So, I took a deep breath and then I went for it.

I sprinted the short distance between me and Everett. Ducking my head into one shoulder, I slammed into his waist with the other.

The impact sent us both spiraling to the floor. I landed with a hard thud, Everett just inches away. It took him a second to realize what had happened but by then I was frantically scrambling to get back onto my feet.

"Gigi!" Maisy screamed.

"Run, Maisy! Run!" I yelled.

She jumped off the table as Everett regained his balance. He turned to me, now on my feet, and raised his fist. A split second later, my face erupted, his fist moving too fast to see.

Blinding pain radiated through my cheek and eye. My knees collapsed and cracked against the cement floor.

Everett was seething, his body looming over me while I stayed on my knees, trying to clear the white spots from my vision. "You stupid bitch. I'll fucking rip your heart out for that."

From the corner of my good eye, I saw Maisy frantically searching the shelves by the bed. Everett's back was to her as he shouted in my face. Something in a box must have caught her attention because she immediately went for it.

"Fuck you! Fuck you, Everett! You'll pay for this," I shouted to give Maisy a few more seconds for whatever she was doing.

Everett's lip curled. He raised his fist again and my eyes darted to Maisy behind him. In her hand was a scalpel still in its sterile wrapping. She was clutching it in her fist so hard her knuckles were white.

Everett noticed my eyes wander and he started to turn. But just as he did, Maisy jammed the scalpel into Everett's throat.

Blood sprayed from his neck as he screamed, frantically clutching the scalpel that was choking him. I didn't know where she had hit him but if it wasn't deep enough or if he managed to pull out the scalpel, he could come after us.

Maisy was standing frozen behind Everett, her eyes wide. Her face and hand were splattered with his blood.

"Maisy!" I yelled, standing. "Maisy, let's go!"

She took a big step back, still watching Everett, but then her wide eyes found mine.

"Run!" I shouted again.

She shook off the shock and we both took off through the storage room, running as fast as we could. My arms tied behind my back were slowing me down but I just kept moving. Maisy tried her best to keep me from falling to the floor as we ran. Down the long hallway. Up the stairs. Through the door.

With every step, I prayed Everett Carlson wasn't just a step behind.

———

JESS

I met Silas and Sam at the ER entrance and marched right past them, straight through the glass doors to the stairs to find Scottie Pierce. I rounded the railing but before my foot could hit the first step, a door by the staircase burst open.

Georgia came flying out, Maisy hot on her heels.

"Georgia!" I lunged forward to catch her as she tripped.

She collapsed into my arms, her hands tied behind her back. One side of her face was fucked up. A puffy red welt covered her cheek and her eye was nearly swollen shut.

Maisy hit me next. She clung to my shirt, trying not to fall to her knees. Her face was covered in blood.

Fuck.

I lifted Georgia with one arm while bracing Maisy with the other. I almost dropped them both until Silas grabbed Maisy, picking her up and pulling her tight to his chest.

I hoisted Georgia to her feet, then reached for my pocketknife.

"Everett!" Georgia yelled. "Jess, he's downstairs. He was going to kill us but Maisy stabbed him so we could get away and he's been selling the pills in town and Alex Benson killed Wes and he left us to drug Scottie too and Ida's in on it—"

She was talking so fast I could barely understand her.

"Breathe, baby," I said, trying to calm her down. The veins in her neck were visibly throbbing from her racing pulse.

She sucked in a breath and started shaking. While she pulled it together, I prioritized, quickly processing all of the shit she'd just told me.

"Where's Carlson?" I asked her calmly.

"Downstairs in the storage room."

"Sam, head upstairs. Find a nurse, anyone other than Ida. Help Scottie. Get Peterson or Seavers here, now."

"On it," Sam said.

"Silas, you stay here with Maisy. Call Bryant. Get him down here to lock down Ida. Then have him put an APB out for Benson," I ordered.

Silas didn't answer, he just pulled out his phone and started dialing.

"Georgia, you stay here with Silas. If Peterson or Seavers gets here before I'm back, get them upstairs," I said.

"Okay," she nodded.

I gave her a quick kiss on the forehead and finished cutting her loose.

"Is Rowen okay?" she asked.

"She will be now," I said. Her eyes closed in relief.

One last hug and I left her. Slowly, with my gun in hand,

I crept through the basement, being cautious in case Carlson had any surprises waiting.

But there were none.

Everett was lying in a pool of his own blood. Dead.

I knelt down next to Everett to get a closer look at the stab wound in his throat. It was deep. Maisy had shoved that fucking scalpel in far, and it must have hit a major artery. He'd choked on his own blood.

Good riddance.

———

GIGI

Prescott buzzed for weeks following the events at the hospital.

Everyone in town was talking about Everett Carlson and Alex Benson. Since they were outsiders, their actions hadn't been nearly as upsetting as Ida's, a lifelong Prescott resident. The good citizens of Prescott were outraged that one of their own had been involved in such a betrayal.

Bryant had arrived at the hospital shortly after Jess had gone into the basement. He'd arrested Ida and she'd immediately confessed to assisting Everett in smuggling drugs from the hospital. She'd also spilled that Everett's operation had gone beyond Jamison Valley into neighboring counties with small hospitals. Four other nurses were currently under arrest for their involvement.

As part of her confession, Ida had given up Alex Benson's whereabouts. Bryant had found him at a remote spot in the mountains where Benson had been digging two shallow graves.

Ida was currently awaiting sentencing but Benson had been immediately transferred to the state penitentiary where he was serving the first of two life sentences for the murder of Wes Drummond and the attempted murder of Scottie Pierce.

Sam had gotten to Dr. Peterson in time to save Scottie's life. They'd pumped his stomach and administered an antidote for the narcotics that Benson had forced down his throat. Not long after his release, Scottie and his parents had left Prescott. Their mansion in the foothills was listed for sale the day after they left.

Dr. Seavers had also come in that night and checked on Maisy. An ultrasound showed that no harm had come to Maisy's baby from Everett's kidnapping, but Maisy was an emotional wreck. Her ex-boyfriend and the father of her unborn child had intended to murder her baby and likely her.

It hurt my heart to think of what she was going through. I'd tried calling her every day, but her mother, who had moved in with her until she was feeling better, would always answer and tell me that Maisy didn't want to talk yet. I didn't press too hard. I knew she'd come around in time, and right now she just needed some space. I could give her that.

For a little while.

Jess had done his best to spend as much time with me after the incident as possible. But it was a busy time for the sheriff. Not only had he closed Wes's murder but the arson case as well.

During Benson's confession, he'd spilled that Wes had been the one to start the fire at the janitor's house. Wes had intended to go after Everett but had been given the wrong address. He'd needlessly destroyed a man's possessions because he hadn't bothered to confirm the house number.

While Jess worked, I stayed close to the farmhouse.

For the first week after that horrible Friday night, I didn't leave the house. My face needed time to heal, and I wanted to keep Rowen close to my side. She didn't feel the need to stray far away from her mother either, so we had spent a lot of time cuddling together on the couch, having a Disney princess movie marathon.

But after a week, I knew I couldn't hide out any longer. I had to get back into town and out of the house. Eventually, I would need to go back to the hospital and face my fears.

But not just yet.

My first trip into town was going to be for dinner at the café.

———

"HI, DADDY!" Rowen yelled through Jess's office door.

"Hey, little bit," he said, standing from his chair and picking her up.

For the last week, Rowen had only called Jess "Daddy." I wasn't sure if they had talked about it or what, but I didn't care. I was effing loving it. Every time she said it, I smiled and looked to Jess, who was always smiling back.

"We were thinking of eating at the café tonight. Is that okay with you, Sheriff?" I asked.

"Anything for my girls," he said, shifting Rowen to one side and leaning in to give me a light kiss.

"Can you get away now or should we go kill some time?"

"Let's go," he said and grabbed my hand, pulling me behind him and out the station's front door.

He put Rowen in her seat and then opened my door for me. But before I could step in, he put a hand at my belly and pushed me back, sliding in front of me.

And then he kissed me.

A kiss so long and deep, I forgot all about the bad stuff in life and just remembered the good. Because we had a lot. And we were going to live it good together.

"Stop kissing! You're always kissing. I'm sick of it. Let's go! I'm hungry for french fries!" Rowen shouted.

Jess pulled his lips away but didn't make another move. He just stood there, holding my eyes with his, ice blue shining down at me with more love than I had ever expected to find in my life.

"You okay, baby?"

"I am now," I said. Because I absolutely was. As long as he was with me, I would always be okay.

"Love you, Georgia."

"Love you, Jess."

EPILOGUE

O*ne year and eight months later . . .*
"Gigi?" Maisy called.

"Dining room!"

I was sitting at the table, filling little jack-o-lantern baggies full of homemade Chex mix for Rowen's first-grade Halloween party tomorrow.

"Hey!" she said.

"Hi!" Standing from the table, I reached out for Coby. She handed him over and I proceeded to tickle and kiss him until he squirmed and protested so much I had to set him down. Maisy and I followed him into the living room as he waddled his way over to the stack of toddler toys in the corner, plopping down on his bum to play.

"Where's Benny?" Maisy asked me as she sagged into the couch.

"He's out with Jess and Roe in the garage. He was

making a huge Chex mix mess so I took him out there and told Jess he had to watch him for at least an hour. But I'll run out and grab him so he can play with Coby," I said, darting outside to get my son.

Benjamin Coppersmith Cleary had been born exactly nine months after Jess and I had gotten married.

I'd stopped my birth control a week before our wedding since Jess and I had decided we didn't want to wait too long to have a baby. Neither of us wanted Rowen to be too much older than her future siblings. When I quit taking my pills, I figured we had at least six months until it worked its way out of my system. But by my calculation, it had only taken six days.

"Jess?" I called into the garage.

"Up here!" he yelled.

Jess had gotten antsy this summer without any sort of construction project. Our addition had been finished right before Ben was born, and after six months of nothing for him to work on, he'd declared he was building himself an office space above the garage. The staircase against the back wall was done and now he was finishing the room that extended off the end of the building so that the garage was still pretty, per my only design request.

Walking up the stairs, I heard Rowen bossing Ben.

"No, Benny! That's Daddy's socket wrench. You can't have it. Here, you can have this one from your own toolbox," she said.

"Maisy's here, honey, so I'm going to take Benny into the house so he can play with Coby."

"Okay, I want to finish hanging this sheet of drywall, then I'll come in," he said.

Bending down to pick up baby Ben, I hefted him up on my hip. He was the perfect mix of me and Jess. He had my hair, which was currently streaked with drywall dust, and my freckles. But he had gotten his dad's ice-blue eyes and he was going to be big like Jess. Not quite one year old, and he already weighed enough that I couldn't carry him around for too long.

"Rowen, do you want to come in?" I asked.

"Can I stay with Daddy?" Not only did she have drywall dust in her hair but it was also covering her arms and face.

"Sure, baby girl," I said and blew her a kiss.

Rowen had become a daddy's girl. Wherever Jess went, Rowen was not far behind. And shortly after we'd gotten married, he had legally adopted her. For weeks, she had insisted on us calling her by her full name, Rowen Grace Cleary.

Walking back to the house, I took advantage of my minute alone with Ben and relentlessly kissed his chubby cheeks. Once we got inside, he would immediately lose interest in his mother in favor of toys and his little friend.

Maisy and Coby were over for dinner, something we tried to do at least one Sunday every month. It gave the boys, who were only four months apart, a chance to play together and Maisy and me a chance to gossip.

Maisy had had a rough time those first few months after the hospital incident, but her parents had urged her to start seeing a therapist and that seemed to help her deal with not only Everett's kidnapping, but also the fact that she had killed him.

One night, right before Jess and I were married, she had come to the farmhouse to talk. It was the first time we'd been face-to-face since the night at the hospital.

She had asked me if I thought there was anything else she could have done, some other way to incapacitate Everett, a way to change the outcome. I had answered her honestly. Everett was crazy. He never would have stopped until he had succeeded in killing us. I was sure of it.

Our friendship had grown since that night, and though I had made a lot of new friends in the short time we had been living in Prescott, Maisy was my closest. My best friend and confidant. She was also the maid of honor at my wedding.

Jess and I had gotten married shortly after the incident at the hospital. We had a simple ceremony at church and then catered a dinner for family and friends at the farmhouse.

Felicity had come back to Prescott for the wedding, and with both of her children close, Noelle was the happiest I had ever seen her. Silas had been Jess's best man, both wearing simple black suits. Rowen and Maisy had stood next to me in lavender chiffon dresses.

My gown had been simple white with a bit of a Grecian flair. I'd worn Jess's diamonds and my hair had been pulled back in a bunch of intricate knots and twists.

Our wedding was simple, but perfect. Rowen and I walked hand in hand down the aisle to Jess where we said our vows.

My favorite picture of our wedding day was framed and hanging on the wall between the living room and dining room. Rowen was in profile, kissing Jess's cheek. I was looking up at them and laughing. And Jess, with one arm around my shoulders, was looking at the camera with a huge smile on his face. Whenever I looked at that picture, which was a lot, a warm wave of happy washed through me.

I situated Ben with Coby so they could play with blocks and sank into the couch next to Maisy.

"So in case you didn't know, your sister-in-law is a bitch," Maisy said.

I laughed. "I've seen her in action, remember? What happened?"

"Silas came over to the motel today because he was helping me fix a broken sink. When he finished, we were visiting at the reception desk. She pulls up in her fancy car and gets out, heading to her room. But then she glances over and stops dead in her tracks when she sees Silas with me. I swear, Gigi, if she could have turned green, she would have. She must think there's something going on with me and Silas. She gave me the bitchiest look I have ever seen on any woman's face. Ever. Well . . . except for Andrea Merkuso. She's a bigger bitch. But Felicity ranks not too far behind."

"There's something between those two, Silas and Felicity. I'm sure of it," I said.

"Ha! Well then you'll love this next part. He doesn't know I saw him, but last night, Silas went into her room around eleven and came out after midnight. Coby wasn't sleeping so I was doing some paperwork in the office."

"No way!" I yelled, bouncing up on the couch. "I knew it!"

"Yep." Maisy grinned.

"I love that you own the motel. You have the best gossip."

After the attack, Maisy never did come back to the hospital. Not once. Not even to have Coby. When she'd started going into labor, Beau had driven her over to a hospital in Bozeman. And anytime Coby needed a checkup or was sick, she'd either drive him to Bozeman or ask Dr. Seavers to make a house call.

Maisy had overcome a lot when it came to Everett. Her

strength and resilience were inspiring. Coby was the spitting image of his father, but it never shook her. Every day, she ignored the resemblance and only saw her beautiful baby boy. So if giving up her nursing career was something that she needed to do to live a happier life with her son, I was all for it. Though I did miss working with her.

Her position at the hospital had been filled by a nurse from the burn unit in Spokane that had treated Milo after the explosion. Her name was Sara and she was a kind and shy young girl. Perfect for Milo. They had fallen in love while he was there and the day he had come back to Prescott, she had come with him.

After she'd quit her job at the hospital, Maisy had taken over management of the Fan Mountain Inn, Prescott's one and only motel. The owners had been on the cusp of retiring and looking to spend more time traveling. Four months ago, they'd made her a hell of a deal to purchase the motel.

"So what else is happening at the motel? Any hot photographers come by?" I asked, giving her a smirk and raising my eyebrows.

She giggled and we gossiped while our boys played together on the floor.

I loved these Sundays with my family and my friends at the farmhouse. Even though it had a rough start, this new life that Rowen and I had risked living in Prescott was a dream come true.

I would never get the chance to tell Ben how much his farmhouse changed my life. But I hoped that when I went to visit him, buried next to his Claire, that he could hear me from above.

———

JESS and I were lying upstairs in bed. The kids were both asleep downstairs.

He had just made me come twice, once with his mouth and then again with his cock, and I was on my back, trying to catch my breath.

My husband was hot. So effing hot and I couldn't get enough of him. He knew my body inside and out and he used that knowledge as often as possible to make me moan his name. Something that he thought was effing hot.

"Fuck, baby. That was intense."

"Hmm . . . it's all those hormones," I said, grinning.

He rolled over on his side and propped himself up on an elbow.

"Hormones?" he asked.

My grin turned into a smile. "If it's a girl, can we name her after my mom?"

The light danced in his eyes. Ice blue. I loved his eyes. I couldn't get enough of them either.

In usual Jess style, he didn't answer my question. Instead, he slammed his mouth down onto mine. It took me all of two point five seconds to get way turned on, beyond turned on, and we started at it again.

I was taking his kiss as a yes to my earlier question.

Bliss.

Like I had done every night of our married life, I fell asleep tucked into Jess's side but not before I whispered, "Love you, honey," into his chest.

And just like he had done every night of our married life, he whispered back, "Love you, Freckles."

Eight months later, Adeline Claire Cleary was born.

———

THE JAMISON VALLEY series continues with *The Clover Chapel.*

ACKNOWLEDGMENTS

Thank you, Bill, for believing in me, for always supporting my ever-changing dreams and making sure I never lost faith in myself. To my beta-readers and amazing friends Chandra and Kaitlyn. To Sarah Hansen for your creative genius. To Julie Deaton for your polish. And a million thanks to my unbelievable editor, Elizabeth Nover. Your advice and guidance were priceless.

ABOUT THE AUTHOR

Devney is a *USA Today* bestselling author who lives in Washington with her husband and two sons. Born and raised in Montana, she loves writing books set in her treasured home state. After working in the technology industry for nearly a decade, she abandoned conference calls and project schedules to enjoy a slower pace at home with her family. Writing one book, let alone many, was not something she ever expected to do. But now that she's discovered her true passion for writing romance, she has no plans to ever stop.

Don't miss out on Devney's latest book news.
Subscribe to her newsletter!
www.devneyperry.com